Eisenhower Public Library
4613 N. Oketo Avenue
Harwood Heights, Il. 60706
708-867-7828

DEMCO

STETTIN STATION

Also by the Author
in the John Russell Series

Zoo Station

Silesian Station

STETTIN STATION

DAVID DOWNING

SOHO

Copyright © 2009 by David Downing

All rights reserved.

First published in the UK in 2009 by Old Street Publishing

Published in the United States in 2010 by

Soho Press, Inc.
853 Broadway
New York, NY 10003

Library of Congress Cataloging-in-Publication Data

Downing, David, 1946–
Stettin station / David Downing.
p. cm.
ISBN 978-1-56947-634-5 (hardcover)
1. Americans—Germany—Berlin—Fiction. 2. Journalists—Germany—Berlin—Fiction.
3. Secret service—Germany—Berlin—Fiction. 4. Germany—History—1933–1945—Fiction.
I. Title.
PR6054.O868S73 2010
823'.914—dc22
2009049935

10 9 8 7 6 5 4 3 2 1

This novel is set in Germany and German-occupied Europe in the final months of 1941. It opens on November 17th 1941, the day that the Japanese First Air Fleet sailed from Japan's Inland Sea on the first leg of its long voyage to Pearl Harbour. None of the novel's characters, fictional or otherwise, knew that such a voyage was underway until December 7th, when the First Air Fleet reached its destination and brought America into the war.

STETTIN STATION

Ways of leaving Berlin

There was no doubt about it – two years into the war, the Third Reich was beginning to smell.

The U-Bahn was unusually ripe that morning, John Russell thought, though it was only the sheer severity of the pong which gave rise to any surprise. Berliners seemed increasingly reluctant to use the hyper-abrasive standardised soap, which removed both dirt and skin, and there was no alternative to the chemical-rich standardised food, which had created a city-wide epidemic of flatulence. Some laid particular blame on the grey, clayey bread, others on the miracle ingredient which turned the ersatz butter yellow. But whatever the cause, the U-Bahn was the place to experience the consequences, and several of his fellow passengers were travelling with their noses buried deep in scarves and handkerchiefs.

At the far end of the violently rocking car – adequate suspension was a casualty of the rubber shortage – two middle-aged men in leather coats were looming over an attractive woman and her young child. They were all smiles, but her rapidly changing facial expressions bore all the unease of a potential victim, and her relief at reaching her stop was obvious to all but her unwitting tormentors.

The Gestapo seemed to be all over the capital these days, their numbers rising steadily since the onset of the Russian campaign and the economic downturn which had soon accompanied it. Over the last month, since the announcement of victory in early October and the subsequent collapse in morale when that had proved a mirage, the swelling numbers of leather-coated myrmidons had been ever more noticeable, and the fact that these two were pestering women on the U-Bahn offered clear proof that the bastards' numbers had outstripped the availability of their beloved black Mercedes.

The impression of political screws tightening was the main reason why Russell had finally decided it was time to get out. There was, however, no point in applying for an exit permit – with his history, the Germans wouldn't let him go until the United States formally entered the war, and maybe not even then. Even if they did prove unexpectedly willing to abide by international conventions in his particular case, Russell foresaw months of internment, trapped in a camp somewhere, waiting and wondering whether any of the freshly arrested were coughing up his name along with the blood and the broken teeth. It was not a pleasant prospect.

Nor were there any circumstances in which the Nazis would let his girlfriend Effi go. She might not be Marlene Dietrich, but her name and face were recognisable to a lot of Germans, and Joey Goebbels would never allow such a public defection. And if the authorities did, for reasons best known to themselves, let Russell go, they could always use her as a hostage for his good behaviour. All the stories he had not been allowed to file, the stories he hoped to tell once he escaped the cage, would have to remain untold. His exit – their exit – would have to be an illegal one.

The Americans wouldn't offer any real help, despite his years of admittedly half-hearted time in their employ. Russell's main contact at the Consulate had said that they would try to get him out, but that there was nothing they could do for Effi; the two of them were not married, and even if they were, well, surely Russell could see the problem. He could. These last few weeks, with the undeclared war escalating in the Atlantic, the German security agencies were no longer respecting the diplomatic rules, and had even invaded the Consulate on one occasion. If he and Effi sought sanctuary there, it seemed more than likely that Heydrich's goons would simply stride in and drag them back out.

Only the comrades remained, and the emergency telephone number he'd been given more than two years ago. This belonged to a photographic studio in Neukölln which he had used for work in his freelance days, and the burly Silesian named Miroslav Zembski who owned and ran it. Russell had used the number once in September 1939, and had thereafter deemed it prudent to avoid all contact with Zembski and his studio. Until the previous Friday, that is, when he'd called the number from a public telephone on the Ku'damm.

Someone had answered, at least in the sense of picking up the phone. A slight intake of breath was all Russell heard at the other end, and he had probably imagined the whiff of malevolence seeping down the wire. He had put the phone back after a few seconds, and concluded that a personal visit to the studio would be unwise. But three more days of ominous news from Washington – Japan and the US really did seem to be sliding into war – had reignited his sense of urgency, and put him on this train to Neukölln. He knew he was being reckless: if Zembski wasn't there, then at best he had disappeared, at worst he was under arrest, and Russell would gain nothing from finding out which it was. Yet here he was, needing to know. Like a moth to a very real flame.

He told himself that Zembski would probably be there, that his own telephone call could have been picked up by a child or an idiot while the fat Silesian was busy taking pictures, that he was, in any case, an innocent customer with a film in his pocket to prove it, a highly appropriate set of shots of his son Paul at a *Jungvolk* passing-out parade. The risk was negligible, he told himself, the potential prize enormous.

He emerged from the U-Bahn entrance on the western side of Berlinerstrasse, and walked under the S-Bahn bridge in the direction of the studio. The last time he had visited it, the street had been full of traffic, the air full of savoury smells, the buildings awash with neon and full of things to sell. Now it reminded him of a German colleague's words, that these days the capital had all the colour of a corpse. The lights were out, the odours dubious, the shop windows at least half empty. The sky seemed to be clearing, a state of affairs which Russell and his fellow-Berliners had once anticipated with some relief, assuming – fools that they were – that such conditions would make it easier for the RAF to see and hit their industrial and transport targets. But no, the British pilots seemed incapable of hitting anything relevant to the war effort. Their bombing campaign was like an Italian lottery in reverse – your chances of losing were extremely remote, but no more remote than anyone else's. Some dear old grandmother in her suburban apartment was as likely to catch it as IG Farben – in fact probably more so, because the pilots were presumably targeting the chemical giant.

Russell stopped outside the restaurant which sat across the road from Zembski's. The photographer's name was still above the door, but the drawn blackout curtains precluded any view of the interior. Was there anyone in? There was only one way to find out.

Crossing the empty road, Russell pushed open the door with what he hoped was the brashness of innocence. There was nobody behind Zembski's counter, on which lay a tripod, still attached to a clearly broken camera. A middle-aged man in a dark grey suit was sitting on one of the chairs which the photographer had used for family portraits, his leather coat draped across another, his hands cradled in his lap. His younger partner was sitting almost behind the door, arms folded across the front of his coat. A gun lay on the cabinet beside him.

'How can I help you?' the older man asked with a heavy Bavarian accent. He was about forty, with sharpish features that ill-suited his general bulk, rather in the manner of an over-inflated Goebbels.

'Is the studio closed?' Russell asked. 'Where is Herr Zembski?' he added, realising a few seconds later that acknowledging an acquaintance with the studio's owner might prove unwise.

'He is no longer here,' said the younger man. He was a Berliner, dark and thin, with the sort of face that would always need shaving.

'He has gone out of business,' the first man said. 'Please sit down,' he told Russell, indicating a chair and taking a notebook and pencil from the inside pocket of his jacket. 'We have some questions.'

'What about?' Russell asked, staying on his feet. 'And who are you?' he added, hoping to play the outraged innocent.

'Gestapo,' the older man said shortly, as if it hardly needed saying.

It didn't, and Russell decided that asking to see the man's identification might be pushing his luck. He sat down.

'Your papers?'

Russell handed them over, and noted the flicker of interest in the Gestapo man's eyes.

'John Russell,' he read aloud. 'American,' he added, with a glance at his partner. 'Your German is excellent,' he told Russell.

'I've lived here for almost twenty years.'

'Ah. You live on Carmer Strasse. That's near Savigny Platz, is it not?'

'Yes.'

The man turned to his accreditation from Promi, as the Ministry of Propaganda was almost universally called. 'You are a journalist. Working for the *San Francisco Tribune*.'

'Yes.'

His interrogator was now scribbling in the notebook, copying down relevant details from Russell's identity and press documents. 'You have been to this studio before?' he asked without raising his eyes.

'Not for a long time. Before the war I used it whenever I needed photographic work.'

The eyes looked up. 'A long way from Savigny Platz. Are there no studios closer to home?'

'Zembski is cheap.'

'Ah. So why did you stop coming here?'

'I changed jobs. The paper I work for now uses the big agencies for photographs.'

'So why are you here today?'

'A personal job.' Russell took the envelope of snapshots from his inside pocket, silently blessing his own forethought, and handed them over. 'I wanted one of these enlarged, and I've lost the negatives. I remembered

Zembski doing something similar for me years ago, and doing it well. They're of my son,' he added in explanation.

The older Gestapo man was looking through the pictures, his younger partner peering over his shoulder. 'He's a good-looking boy. His mother is German?'

'Yes, she is.'

Russell felt a sudden, almost violent aversion to the way the two men were staring at the pictures of Paul, but managed not to show it.

The photographs were handed back to him.

'So Zembski won't be back?' he asked.

'No,' the older man said with the hint of a smile. 'I believe he returned to Silesia.'

'Then I will have to find another studio. Is that all?'

'For the moment.'

Russell nodded, a tacit recognition that a conditional release was all that anyone could hope for in such difficult days, and the younger Gestapo man even opened the door for him. Once outside he play-acted a period of hesitation, ostentatiously checked that his ration stamps were in his pocket, then headed across the street to the café opposite, where he made a further show of inspecting the meagre menu on display before venturing into the steamy interior. Twice in the distant past handwritten notes on the studio door had pointed Russell in this direction, and on both occasions he had found Zembski amiably chatting with the proprietor, an old man with thick Hohenzollern sideburns. The latter was still there, propping up his counter and eyeing Russell with more than a trace of suspicion. The only other customer was reading a paper by the window.

'Remember me?' Russell asked. 'Zembski used to do a lot of work for me before the war. I came in here to collect him more than once.'

A non-committal grunt was all the reply he got.

Russell took a deep breath. 'And now there's a couple of Heydrich's finest camped out in his studio,' he went on more quietly, hoping that he hadn't misjudged his audience. 'Do you know what happened to him?'

The proprietor gave him a long stare. 'Nothing good,' he murmured eventually. 'It's not much of a secret, not around here anyway. The authorities came to call, soon after midnight on Thursday. There were two cars – I saw them from upstairs – I was just getting ready for bed. They just knocked the door down, woke up half the street. I think there were four of them went in – it's hard to see across the street in the blackout, but there was a moon that night. Anyway, there were shots, two of them really close together, and a few minutes later one man came out again and drove off. A van arrived after about half an hour and two bodies were carried out. It was too dark to see who they were, but I'm guessing one of them was Miroslav. He hasn't been seen, and two of the… two men have been arriving each morning and leaving each night ever since. What are they doing in there?'

Russell shrugged. 'Nothing much that I could see. Asking questions, but I've no idea why. Was Zembski mixed up in anything? Politics, maybe?'

It was a question too far. 'How should I know?' the proprietor said, straightening up to indicate the interview was over. 'He just came in here for coffee, in the days when we used to have some. That and a talk about football.'

All of which left a lot to be desired, Russell thought, walking back up Berlinerstrasse towards the U-Bahn station. Particularly for Zembski, who presumably was dead. But also for himself. His only hope of an illegal escape was apparently gone, and worse: in the unlikely but still conceivable event that Zembski was alive, his own name might be one of those being mentioned in the interrogation. Russell counted the days – more than four had passed, if the café owner's memory was accurate. In the old KPD it had always been assumed that most prisoners, if denied the chance to kill themselves, would eventually break, and the only obligation placed on Party members was to hold out for twenty-four hours, thus giving their comrades a good head start on the inevitable pursuit.

Zembski must be dead, Russell thought, as he descended the stairs to the U-Bahn platform. The Silesian would have given up his grandmother by now, let alone a casual fellow-traveller like himself.

Some certainty wouldn't go amiss, though. Zembski had falsified a passport for him once, and a few months later had helped him get a woman comrade out of the country. She had killed an SS Colonel, but Zembski had not known that. He had known that Russell was in touch with Moscow, but not that the German authorities were aware of those contacts. The potential for confusion was enormous, and Russell earnestly hoped that the Gestapo were suitably confused. They usually liked some semblance of clarity before turning their dogs on a prominent foreigner.

As the U-Bahn train rumbled north he remembered that even the Gestapo were legally obliged to inform a family of a relative's death. Zembski's cousin Hunder, who owned the garage across the river where Russell's car was waiting out the war, might have some definite information.

Russell changed onto the Stadtbahn at Friedrichstrasse, travelled the single stop to Lehrter Station, and made his way through the tangle of streets which lay to the east of the rail yards. The garage office seemed deserted, which was hardly surprising given the virtual cessation of private motoring that had accompanied the Wehrmacht's long, petrol-hungry drive into Russia. The gate hadn't been locked though, and Russell finally found an old mechanic with his head under the bonnet of a Horch in the farthest corner of the yard.

Hunder Zembski had been called up two months ago, the man told him, grimacing as he straightened his body. The Army needed all the mechanics it could get, and being almost fifty hadn't saved his boss. 'You have to be almost ready for burial to get an exemption,' the man said. 'Like me,' he added proudly.

After paying his car a sentimental visit, Russell retraced his steps to Lehrter Station and took the S-Bahn home. Darkness had almost fallen by the time he emerged from Zoo Station, and as he walked the short distance to Effi's apartment on Carmer Strasse a host of invisible hands were pulling and fixing blackout curtains into place on either side of the street.

Their own were already in place – in recent weeks, with both of them working long days, natural light was a weekend luxury. Russell treated himself to a glass of their precious wine, the penultimate bottle of a case which some lust-crazed producer out at Babelsberg had optimistically bestowed on Effi. It tasted slightly sour, a clear sign that they weren't drinking it fast enough.

There was food in the flat – his double rations as a foreign journalist and her variable perks as a reasonably prominent actress meant they never ran short – but the only real temptation were the two eggs. Effi had boiled an extra meal of potatoes yesterday for such an eventuality, and Russell put half of them in the frying pan with as little of the bilious butter as he could manage, eventually adding one of the eggs. He took his plate through to the living room and turned on the radio, half hoping that Effi didn't get in until after the next news bulletin. As a foreign journalist he was allowed to listen to foreign broadcasts, but Germans were not. Many Berliners he knew ignored the prohibition, keeping the volume down low enough to foil any spying ears, but he and Effi had agreed that in their case the risk was unnecessary. There were enough times he could listen on his own, either here in the apartment or at one of the two foreign press clubs, and nothing to stop him telling her what he had heard.

The BBC news, when it came, was only mildly encouraging. On the Moscow front, the Germans had suffered a setback outside Tula, but the failure to mention any other sectors probably implied that the Wehrmacht was still advancing. The RAF had bombed several north German ports with unstated results, and the British army facing Rommel in North Africa was henceforth to be known as Eighth Army. What, Russell wondered, had happened to the other seven? The one piece of unalloyed good news came from Yugoslavia, where a German column had been wiped out by Serb partisans, and the German High Command had promised a retaliatory reign of terror. Some people never learned.

He switched the radio to a German station playing classical music and settled down with a book, eventually dozing off. The telephone woke him with a start. He picked up expecting to hear Effi, and an explanation of what had held her up. Had the air raid sirens gone off while he was asleep?

It wasn't her. 'Klaus, there's a game tonight,' a familiar voice told him. 'At number 26, ten o'clock.'

'There's no Klaus here,' Russell said. 'You must have got the wrong number.'

'My apologies.' The phone clicked off.

Russell pulled his much-creased map from his jacket pocket and counted out the stations on the Ringbahn, starting at Wedding and going round in a clockwise direction. As he had thought, Number 26 was Puttlitz Strasse.

It was gone half-past eight, which didn't leave him much time. After checking his street atlas he decided it was walkable, just. He wrote a hurried note to Effi, put on his thickest coat, and headed out.

The moon was rising, cream-coloured and slightly short of full, above the double-headed flak tower in the distant Tiergarten. He walked north at a crisp pace, hoping that there wouldn't be an air raid, and that if there was, he could escape the attentions of some officious warden insistent on his taking shelter. As the moon rose, the white-painted kerbstones grew easier to follow, and his pace increased. There were quite a few people out, most of them wearing one or more of the phosphorescent buttons which sprinkled the blackout with faint blue lights. Vehicles were much thinner on the ground, one lorry with slitted headlights passing Russell as he crossed the moon-speckled Landwehrkanal.

It was ten to ten when he reached the Puttlitz Strasse Station entrance, which lay on a long bridge across multiple tracks. Gerhard Ströhm was waiting for him, chatting to the booking clerk in the still open S-Bahn ticket office. He was a tall, saturnine man with darting black eyes and a rough moustache. His hair was longer than the current fashion, and he was forever pushing back the locks that flopped across his forehead. Physically, and only physically, he reminded Russell of the young Stalin.

'Come,' Ströhm told Russell, and led him back out across the road and down a flight of dangerously unlit steps to the yard below. As they reached the foot an electric S-Bahn train loomed noisily out of the dark, slowing as it neared the station.

'This way,' said Ströhm, leading Russell into the dark canyon which lay between two lines of stabled carriages. His accent was pure Berliner, and anyone unaware of his background would have had a hard job believing that he'd been born in California of first-generation German immigrants. Both parents had been lost in a road accident when he was twelve, and young Gerhard had been sent back to his mother's parents in Berlin. Bright enough for university in 1929, his strengthening political convictions had quickly disqualified him from any professional career in Hitler's Germany. Arrested in 1933 for a minor offence, he had served a short sentence and effectively gone underground on his release. For the last seven years he had earned a living as a dispatcher in the Stettin Station goods yards.

Russell assumed Ströhm was a communist, although the latter had never claimed as much. He often sounded like one, and he had got Russell's name from a comrade, the young Jewish communist Wilhelm Isendahl, whose life had intersected with Russell's for a few nerve-shredding days in the summer of 1939. Ströhm himself was obviously not a Jew, but it was the fate of Berlin's Jewish community which had caused him to seek out Russell. Some six weeks earlier he had slid onto an adjoining stool in the Zoo Station buffet and introduced himself, in a quiet compelling voice, as a fellow American, fellow anti-Nazi, and fellow friend of the Jews. He hoped Russell was as interested as he was in finding the answer to one particular question – where were the Jews being taken?

They had gone for a long walk in the Tiergarten, and Russell had been impressed. Ströhm exuded a confidence which didn't feel misplaced; he was clearly intelligent, and there was a watchfulness about him, a sense of self-containment more serene than arrogant. Had it ever occurred to Russell, Ströhm asked, that those best placed to trace the Jews were the men of the Reichsbahn, those who timetabled, dispatched and drove the trains who carried them away? And if the men of the Reichsbahn provided him with chapter and verse, would Russell be able to put it in print?

Not now, Russell had told him – the authorities would never allow him to file such a story from Berlin. But once America had entered the war, and he and his colleagues had been repatriated, the story could and would be told. And the more details he carried back home the more convincing that story would be.

In a week or so's time, Ströhm had informed him, a trainload of Berlin's Jews would be leaving for the East. Did Russell want to see it leave?

He did. But why, Russell had wanted to know, was Ströhm taking such a personal interest in the Jews? He expected a standard Party answer, that oppression was oppression, race irrelevant. 'I was in love once,' Ströhm told him. 'With a Jewish girl. Storm troopers threw her out of a fourth floor window at *Columbiahaus*.'

Which seemed reason enough.

Ströhm had suggested the simple Ringbahn code, and six days later Russell's phone had rung. Later that night he had watched from a distance as around a thousand elderly Jews were loaded aboard a train of ancient carriages in the yard outside Grunewald Station, not a kilometre away from the house where his ex-wife and son lived. A few days later they had watched a similar scene unfold a few hundred metres south of Anhalter Station. The previous train, Ströhm told him, had terminated at Litzmannstadt, the Polish Lodz.

This was the fourth such night. Russell wasn't sure why he kept coming – the process would be identical, like watching the same sad film over and over, almost a form of masochism. But each train was different, he told himself, and when a week or so later Ströhm told him where each shipment of Jews had ended up, he wanted to remember their departure, to have it imprinted on his retina. Just knowing they were gone was not enough.

The two men had reached the end of their canyon, and a tall switch tower loomed above them, a blue light burning within. As they climbed the stairs Russell could hear engines turning over somewhere close by, and the clanking of carriages being shunted. Up in the cabin there were two signalmen on duty, one close to retiring age, the other younger with a pronounced limp. Both men shook hands with Ströhm, the first with real warmth; both acknowledged Russell with a nod of the head, as if less certain of his right to be there.

It was an excellent vantage point. Across the Ringbahn tracks, beyond another three lines of carriages, the familiar scene presented itself with greater clarity than usual, courtesy of the risen moon. Three canvas-covered furniture trucks were parked in a line, having transported the guards and those few Jews deemed incapable of walking the two kilometres from the synagogue on the corner of Levetzowstrasse and Jagowstrasse. Taking out his telescopic spyglass – a guilty purchase from a Jewish auction two years earlier – Russell found two stretchers lying on the ground beside the front van, each bearing an unmoving, and presumably unwilling, traveller.

The remaining 998 Jews – according to Ströhm, the SS had decided that a round thousand was the optimal number for such transports – were crowded in the space beyond the line of carriages, and making, in the circumstances, remarkably little noise. Their mental journey into exile, as Russell knew from friends in the Jewish community, would have begun about a week ago, when notification arrived from the Gestapo of their imminent removal from Berlin. Eight pages of instructions filled in the details: what they could and could not bring, the maximum weight of their single suitcase, what to do with the keys of their confiscated homes. Yesterday evening, or in some cases early this morning, they had been collected by the Gestapo and their Jewish auxiliaries, taken to the synagogue, and searched for any remaining passports, medals, pens or jewellery. Then all had been issued with matching numbers for their suitcases and themselves, the latter worn around the neck.

'The Reichsbahn is charging the SS four pfennigs per passenger per kilometre,' Ströhm murmured. 'Children go free.'

Russell couldn't see any children, although his spyglass had picked out a baby carriage lying on its side, as if violently discarded. As usual, the Jews were mostly old, with more women than men. Many of the latter were struggling under the weight of the sewing machines deemed advisable for a new life in the East. Others, worried at the prospects of colder winters, were carrying small heating stoves.

The loading had obviously begin, the crowd inching forward and out of his line of vision. At the rear, a line of Jewish auxiliaries with blue armbands were advancing sheepdog-style, exhaling small clouds of breath into the cold air, as their Gestapo handlers watched and smoked in the comfort of their vehicles.

There were seven carriages in the train, each with around sixty seats for a hundred and fifty people.

One man walked back to one of the auxiliaries and obviously asked him a question. A shake of the head was all the response he got. There was a sudden shout from somewhere further down the train, and it took Russell a moment to find the source – a woman was weeping, a man laid out on the ground, a guard busy slitting open a large white pillow. There was a glint of falling coins, a sudden upward fluttering of feathers, white turning blue in the halo of the yard lamp.

There was no more dissent. Twenty minutes more and the yard was clear, the furniture vans and cars heading back toward the centre of the city, leaving only a line of armed police standing sentry over the stationary, eerily silent train. Feathers still hung in the air, as if reluctant to leave.

A few minutes later a locomotive backed under the bridge and onto the carriages, flickers of human movement silhouetted against the glowing firebox. A swift coupling, and the train was in motion, moonlit smoke pouring up into the starry sky, wheels clattering over the points outside Puttlitz Strasse Station. Even in the spyglass, the passengers' faces seemed pale and featureless, like deep sea fish pressed up against the wall of a moving aquarium.

'Do we know where it's going?' Russell asked, as the last coach passed under the bridge.

'That crew are only booked through to Posen,' Ströhm said, 'but they'll find out where the next crew are taking it. It could be Litzmannstadt, could be Riga like the last one. We'll know by the end of the week.'

Russell nodded, but wondered what difference it would make. Not for the first time, he doubted the value of what they were doing. Wherever the trains were going, there was no way of bringing them back.

He and Ströhm descended the stairs, retraced their path between the lines of carriages to the distant bridge. After climbing the steps to the street they separated, Russell walking wearily south, his imagination working overtime. What were those thousand Jews thinking as their train worked its way around the Ringbahn, before turning off to the East? What were they expecting? The worst? Some of them certainly were, hence the rising number of suicides. Some would be brimming with wishful thinking, others with hope that things weren't as bad as they feared. And maybe they weren't. Two families that Russell knew had received letters from friends deported to Litzmannstadt, friends who asked for food packages but claimed they were well. They were obviously going hungry, but if that was the worst of it Russell would be pleasantly surprised.

He reached home soon after midnight. Effi was already in bed, the innocence of her sleeping face captured in the grey light that spilt in from the living room. Staring at her, Russell felt tears forming in his eyes. It really was time to leave. But how was he going to get them both out?

Propagandists

Shortly before five the following morning, Effi Koenen let herself out of the apartment and walked down to the stygian street. The limousine was ticking over, its slitted headlights casting a pale wash over a few yards of tarmac. The only evidence of the driver was the bright orange glow of a cigarette hanging in mid air. It seemed absurd that the studio still had petrol to burn when the military was apparently running so short, but Goebbels had obviously convinced himself that his movie stars were as vital to the war effort as Goering's planes or the army's tanks, and on a cold November morning Effi found it hard to disagree with him.

'Good morning, Fraulein Koenen,' the driver said, expunging his cigarette in a shower of sparks. She recognised the voice. Helmut Beckman had first driven her to work almost ten years earlier, and she still felt grateful for the trouble he'd taken to calm her beginner's nerves.

Effi took the seat beside him, as she did with most of the drivers. As she'd once told a disbelieving co-star, she felt a fraud sitting in the back – she was happy to play royalty on stage or on screen, but not on the journey to work. The view and the conversation were also better, although these days the former usually amounted to a black tunnel stretching into an uncertain distance.

'I took my wife to see *Homecoming* at the weekend,' Beckmann said once they had turned the first corner, heading for the Ku'damm. 'You were very good.'

'Thank you,' Effi said. 'And the film?'

There was a short silence, as the driver arranged his thoughts. 'It was well done,' he said eventually. 'I can see why it won that prize at the Venice Film Festival. The story was...well, there wasn't much of a story, was there? Just a succession of terrible things happening one after the other. It was a bit...I suppose *transparent* is the word. The writer had his point to make, and everything was lined up so he could. But I guess when you work in the business you notice things like that. And it was certainly better than most. My wife loved it, though she was really upset that you were killed.'

'So was I,' Effi said lightly, although in fact she'd been rather glad. Her character, a German schoolteacher in the territories acquired by Poland in 1918, had succumbed to a stray Polish bullet only minutes before salvation arrived for her fellow Germans in the form of the invading Wehrmacht. She had hoped that her overblown martyrdom would further undermine the credibility, and propaganda value, of the film, but from what she could gather, Frau Beckmann was far more typical than her husband. According to John, acts of violence against Polish POW workers had risen markedly since the film's release a few weeks earlier.

'But she didn't think much of the lawyer,' Beckmann added. 'And when I told her Joachim Gottschalk had turned down the part she got all weepy. She still hasn't got over what happened to him.'

'Few of us have,' Effi admitted. 'Joschi' Gottschalk had committed suicide a couple of weeks earlier. He had been one of Germany's favourite leading men, particularly among female cinema-goers, and the Propaganda Ministry had been more than happy to bank his bulging box office receipts so long as he kept quiet about his Jewish wife and half-Jewish son. But Gottschalk had chosen to parade his wife before a social gathering of high-level Nazis, and Goebbels had blown his diminutive top. The actor had been ordered to get a divorce. When he refused, he was told that the family would be separated by force; his wife and child would be sent to the new concentration camp at Theresienstadt in the Sudetenland, he to the Eastern Front. Arriving at the film star's home to enforce this order, the Gestapo had found three dead bodies. Gottschalk had taken what seemed the only way out.

News of his fate had not been officially released, but as far as Effi could tell, every man, woman and child in Berlin knew what had happened, and many of the women were still in mourning. There had even been talk of a studio strike by his fellow professionals, but nothing had come of it. Effi hadn't particularly liked Gottschalk, but he'd been a wonderful actor, and his family's fate had offered a chilling reminder – if one was really needed – of the perils of saying no to the Nazi authorities.

'What are you shooting today?' Beckmann asked, interrupting her reverie. They were driving through the Grunewald now, following the red lights of another limousine down the long avenue of barely visible trees. A procession of stars, Effi thought dryly.

'We're re-shooting the interiors with Hans Roeder's replacement,' she said. 'There aren't many, and they decided it was easier to shoot them again with Heinz Hartmann than write the character out of those scenes which haven't been shot.' Hans Roeder had been one of the few Berliners killed in a British air raid that year, and only then by falling shrapnel from anti-aircraft fire. Unlike Gottschalk he had been unpopular, essentially talentless, and a ferocious Nazi. A Goebbels favourite.

How much longer, she asked herself. She had always loved acting, and over the years she'd gotten pretty damn good at it. Over the last ten years she'd done her share of propagandist films and stage shows – one of her and John's favourite pastimes had been ridiculing the stories the writers came up with – but she had also done work that she was proud of, in films and shows which weren't designed to canonize the Führer or demonize the Jews, which did what she thought they were supposed to do, hold up a mirror to humanity, loving if possible, instructive if not.

But now there was only the propaganda, and today she would be back in the costume of a seventeenth-century Prussian countess, bravely resisting a Russian assault on Berlin. The moral of the film was clear enough: the writers had not burdened the story with any conflicting ideals. As far as she could tell, the main crime of the Russians – apart, of course, from their initial insolence in invading Germany – lay in their physiognomy. The casting director had scoured the acting profession for men with a Slavic turn of ugliness, and come up with more than enough to fill the screen.

All of which pleased her no end. Even Frau Beckmann would struggle to find this film convincing.

When his number 30 tram eventually hove into view, Russell noticed with some dismay that it was one of the older vehicles. More and more of these were being brought back from the breakers' yards to replace modern relatives now gathering rust in the depot for want of spare parts or a mechanic to fit them. They were certainly more beautiful – this one had exquisite porcelain lamps attached to its inner sides – but that was all that could be said for them. They were almost as slow as walking, and their lack of springs ensured that every bump in the track was experienced to the full. This particular one was packed, and despite the cold weather smelt as rank as yesterday's U-Bahn.

The passengers thinned out a bit on Tauenzien Strasse, and quite a lot more on Potsdamer Strasse, but there were still a lot standing when an obviously pregnant woman got on at Potsdamer Platz, the yellow star conspicuously sewn across the left breast of her rather threadbare coat. Russell watched the expressions of his fellow passengers, wishing he had a seat to give up. Many simply turned their heads, and most of those that didn't looked angry, as if they'd been insulted or threatened in some way. But not all. Much to Russell's surprise, a young German in an army uniform abruptly got to his feet and offered the Jewish woman his seat.

She tried to refuse, but he was having none of it, and, with a quick smile of gratitude, the woman sat herself down. The soldier then looked round at his fellow passengers, daring any of them to raise a protest. None did, at least verbally, leaving Russell to wonder what would happen if the woman's champion got off before she did. In that event, he decided, he would pick up the torch. He hadn't hit anyone in several years, but there was something about living in Hitler's Germany which cried out for that sort of release on a fairly regular basis.

In the event, his services were not required; both he and the woman got off at the Brandenburg Gate, she heading in the direction of the Reichstag, he down Unter den Linden, past the barely-functioning American Consulate and Goebbels' 'fumigated' Soviet Embassy, towards Kranzler's and what passed these days for a morning coffee. He bought a *Völkischer Beobachter* from the kiosk outside, took a window seat in the sparsely populated restaurant, and got out the appropriate pink, yellow and white ration sheets for his ersatz coffee, watered-down milk and real sugar. One of the ancient waiters eventually noticed him, lumbered over, and laboriously cut off the requisite stamps with the small pair of scissors which hung like a fob watch from the front of his waistcoat.

War speeded up the process of dying, Russell thought, but tended to slow down everything else.

He examined the front page of the *Beobachter*, and the black-rimmed photograph of Generaloberst Ernst Udet that filled most of it. Udet, the head of the Reich Air Ministry's development wing, had been killed the previous day while test-piloting a new German fighter.

Russell had seen the Great War ace's flying show back in the 1920s, and Udet had never struck him as a real Nazi, just one of those people who are supremely gifted in one narrow sphere, and never apply much thought to anything else. The job of creating a new Luftwaffe would have appealed to him, but he wouldn't have worried too much about how or why it might be used. According to German friends, Udet had been more responsible than anyone for the highly successful Stuka dive bomber, and Russell hardly felt inclined to mourn his passing. Paul would though, and Russell could see why. Only the U-boat aces could compare with the fighter pilots when it came to the sort of lone wolf heroics that young boys of all ages loved to celebrate.

A state funeral was planned for the coming Saturday. And unless he was very much mistaken, Paul would want to go.

Russell went through the rest of the paper, secure in the knowledge that all the other papers would be carrying the same stories. Some, like the *Frankfurter Zeitung*, would be better written, others, like the *Deutsche Allegemeine Zeitung*, would be tailored to a particular class sensibility, but the political and military facts would not vary. What one paper said, they all said, and all were equally disbelieved. The German people had finally woken up to the fact that the claimed tally of Russian prisoners now exceeded the stated number of Russians in uniform, all of which chimed rather badly with the sense that those same Russians were fighting the German army to a virtual standstill. Each week another pincer movement was given the honour of being the most gigantic of all time, until it seemed as if the whole wide East was barely large enough to accommodate another battle. But still the enemy fought on.

And yet, despite themselves, the German newspapers did offer their readers a mirror to the real situation. It was merely a matter of learning to read between the lines. Over recent weeks, for example, there had been many articles stressing the inherent difficulties of the war in the East: the inhuman strength of the primitive Russian soldier, the extremes of climate and conditions. Prepare yourself for possible setbacks, the subtext read, we may have bitten off more than we can chew.

Russell devoutly hoped so. He drank the last of his coffee with a suitable grimace, and got up to leave. He had twenty minutes to reach the Foreign Ministry, which hosted the first of the two daily press conferences, beginning at noon. The second, which was held at the Propaganda Ministry, began five hours later.

Outside the sun was still shining, but the chill easterly wind was funnelling down the Unter den Linden with some force. He turned into it, thinking to check out the window of the closed American Express office on Charlottenstrasse, which someone had told Effi about. The reported poster was still in pride of place, inviting passers-by to 'Visit Medieval

Germany.' Either the authorities had missed the joke, or they were too busy trying to catch people listening to the BBC.

Russell laughed, and received an admonitory glance from a passing soldier. Further down the street he encountered two women dressed in black, with five sombre-looking children in tow. Their soldiers wouldn't be coming back.

At the Foreign Office on Wilhelmstrasse he climbed the two flights of bare steps to the Bismarck Room, took one of the remaining seats at the long conference table and nodded greetings to several of his colleagues. As ever, a pristine writing pad sat waiting on the green felt, a sight which never ceased to please Russell, knowing as he did where the pads actually came from. They were manufactured at the Schade printing works in Treptow, a business owned and run by his friend and former brother-in-law Thomas, and mostly staffed by Jews.

The Berlin Congress had been held in this room in 1878, and the furnishings seemed suitably Bismarckian, with dark green curtains, wood-panelled walls and more Prussian eagles than Goering had paintings. An enormous and very up-to-date globe sat on one side of the room; a large map of the western Soviet Union was pinned to a display stand on the other. The arrows seemed perilously close to Moscow, but that had been the case for several weeks now.

At noon precisely, Braun von Stumm strode in through the far doors and took the presiding seat at the centre of the table. A diplomat of the old pre-Nazi school, he was much the more boring of the two principal spokesmen. His superior Dr Paul Schmidt – young, fat, rude and surprisingly sharp for a Nazi – was more entertaining but even less popular. He tended to save himself for the good news.

The first question of the day was the usual plant, dreamt up by the Germans and asked by one of their allies, in this case a Finn. Would the German Government like to comment on the American plan to ship large numbers of long-range heavy bombers to the Philippines, from which they could reach Japan? The German Government, it became clear, would like to comment at length, on this and every other aggressive move which the warmonger Roosevelt was making these days. The American journalists doodled on their pads, and Russell noticed a particularly fine caricature of von Stumm taking shape under the scurrying pencil of the *Chicago Times* correspondent.

As usual the spokesman sounded as if he was speaking by rote, and his languid diatribe eventually petered out, allowing a Hungarian correspondent to ask an equally spurious question about British brutality in Iraq. This elicited another long answer, moving the doodlers onto the second or third page of their pads, and twenty minutes had passed before a neutral correspondent got a word in.

Would Herr von Stumm like to comment on foreign reports of Wehrmacht difficulties around Tula and Tikhvin? one of the Swedes asked.

The rings around both Moscow and Leningrad were tightening daily, von Stumm announced, then promptly shifted the discussion a few hundred kilometres to the south. The battle for the Crimean capital of Sevastopol was entering its final phase, he said, with the German 11th Army now launching ceaseless attacks on the Russian defences that surrounded the beleaguered city.

More dutiful questions followed from the Italian and Croatian correspondents, and time was almost up when von Stumm finally allowed an American question. Bradley Emmering of the *Los Angeles Chronicle* was the lucky man. Would the spokesman like to comment on the BBC's claim that a German freighter flying an American flag had been seized in mid-Atlantic by the US Navy?

No, von Stumm said, he would not. The BBC, after all, was hardly a reliable source. 'And that, gentleman,' he said, getting to his feet, 'will be all.'

It wasn't. 'Would the spokesman like to comment on the widespread rumour that *Generaloberst* Udet committed suicide?' the *Washington Times's* Ralph Morrison asked in his piercing nasal drawl.

Von Stumm seemed struck dumb by the impudence of the question, but one of his aides swiftly leapt into the breach. 'Such a question shows a deplorable lack of respect,' he snapped. Von Stumm paused, as if about to add something, but clearly thought better of the idea and stumped out.

The Americans grinned at each other, as if they'd just won a major victory.

Russell found Morrison on the pavement outside, lighting one of his trademark Pall Malls. 'How did he do it?' Russell asked.

Morrison looked around to make sure that no one was listening – the 'Berlin glance' as it was called these days. 'My source in the Air Ministry says he shot himself.'

'Why?'

'Not so clear. My source says it was over a woman, but he's also been telling me for months that Goering and Milch have been using Udet as a scapegoat for all the Luftwaffe's problems.'

'Sounds right.'

Morrison shrugged. 'If I find out anything for certain, I'll pass the story on to Simonsen. He should be able to place it on his next trip back to Stockholm. There's no way they'd let any of us get away with as much as a hint, not with a full state funeral on the way.'

'True.' Russell checked his watch. He was due to meet Dallin in an hour, which left him time to eat a bowl of soup at the Adlon before walking to their usual meeting place in the Tiergarten. The soup proved better than he expected – the Adlon still managed to produce a decent meal, especially for its old habitués – and the sun had emerged once more as he ventured across Pariser Platz, though the Brandenburg Gate and onto the camouflaged Chaussée, or the East-West Axis as it was now called. Huge nets interlaced with lumps of foliage were suspended above the arrow-straight boulevard, which would otherwise have offered the perfect direction-finder for anyone seeking to bomb the government district.

Russell headed out across the still-frosty grass in the general direction of the Rose Garden. No one seemed to be following him, but it wouldn't matter if they were – the Germans were already aware of his meetings with the intelligence man from the American Consulate. Indeed, they were probably under the impression that they had set the whole business up.

In the summer of 1939, Reinhard Heydrich's foreign intelligence organisation, the *Sicherheitsdienst* or SD, had seized on Russell's known contacts with the Soviet NKVD and blackmailed him, or so they believed, into working for them. But when war broke out his Anglo-American parentage made him more relevant to the Abwehr, the Wehrmacht intelligence service that was run by Admiral Wilhelm Canaris, and the SD had graciously handed him over. It had taken the Abwehr several months to claim the gift – as Russell later found out, Canaris had been knocked for six by the depravity of German behaviour in Poland – and when they did finally pull him on board, his duties proved much lighter than expected. Russell had considered refusing, if only to test the continuing potency of the original SD threats to Effi and his family; but if all the Abwehr wanted was help translating English and American newspaper articles, it didn't seem worth the risk. And there was always the chance that working for Canaris might provide him with some protection against Heydrich.

This happy arrangement had continued through the first winter of the war, and the calamitous spring and early summer of 1940.

Throughout that period Russell had also been paying off another debt. Although his mother was American, he had grown up in England and felt essentially English. He was a British national, with a passport to prove it. As Hitler's aggressive intentions became clearer, and the possibility of an Anglo-German war grew ever more likely, he had faced the certainty of deportation and years of separation from Paul, Effi and everyone else he cared for. In March 1939 the Americans had offered him a deal – an American passport, which would allow him to remain in Germany, in exchange for a little low-level intelligence work, contacting possible opponents of the Nazis in the fast-expanding Reich. He had accepted their offer, and safely managed a few such contacts before the war broke out. Over the next year, much to Russell's relief, the Americans had disappeared into their shells, and made no demands that he couldn't ignore or endlessly defer. But in the autumn of 1940, with France *kaput* and England on the ropes, they had started pressing him again. Rather than seek out the contacts they prescribed, any of whom might turn him in to the Gestapo, Russell had come up with a suggestion of his own – could he not act as a safe, neutral and deniable channel between the Americans and the Admiral's Abwehr, passing on information which each had an interest in the other knowing? Russell knew that the Abwehr had created such links with the British through Switzerland – why not operate a similar arrangement with the American Consulate here in Berlin.

He secured a meeting with the Canaris's deputy General Oster, and finally a meeting with Canaris himself. The Admiral had liked the idea, and so had the Americans. Since November 1940, Russell had been carrying messages between them, and feeling very pleased with himself. The work was safe in itself, and more to the point, gave the Abwehr and the Americans respectively good reason to keep him out of Heydrich's clutches and spare him any riskier assignments.

It seemed too good to be true, but his luck continued to hold. After Hitler's invasion of Russia, Russell had braced himself for new approaches from the SD and the Soviets, but neither had yet made contact. The latter, he assumed, would find it difficult to reach him, and the former had apparently lost track of his existence. He only hoped that yesterday's visit to Zembski's studio hadn't started bells ringing in Heydrich's belfry on Wilhelmstrasse.

He had almost reached the Rose Garden, with more than ten minutes to spare. He walked on around it, in the vague direction of the huge concrete flak tower which loomed over the distant zoo. Despite the sunshine the Tiergarten was virtually empty; there were two women pushing prams and several men in uniform enjoying a kick-about, along with the usual army of darting squirrels. Scott Dallin was nowhere to be seen, which probably meant that he was already sequestered in the Rose Garden.

The American was sitting on one of the benches, hands in pockets and overcoat collar turned up, a hat concealing most of his golden-brown hair. 'Hi,' he said. 'Jesus, it's cold.' Russell sat down beside him.

Dallin was another tall Californian, but any resemblance to Gerhard Ströhm ended there. If the latter looked like a refugee from *The Ragged Trousered Philanthropists*, the former might have stepped out of a Scott Fitzgerald novel. He always looked well turned-out, even when most of his Consulate colleagues had been reduced to scarecrows by the clothing shortage – though he did have a tendency to wear the sort of colours that suited sunny California rather better than corpse-grey Berlin.

Money was the obvious reason. Dallin had grown up in Santa Barbara the son of a water tycoon, so one of Russell's friends at the Consulate had told him. He had attended an Ivy League college in the East, and encountered no apparent problems in securing a plum post in the diplomatic service. When he had arrived in Berlin a year or so ago it had been his first trip out of America, and it had showed. Dallin wasn't stupid, but he knew very little and didn't seem sufficiently aware of that fact. His obvious doubts about Russell probably stemmed from reading the official file and discovering his communist past. A man like Dallin would have no idea how anyone good or intelligent could become a communist, and would therefore assume that the man in question was either a knave or a fool. And since Russell was obviously not a fool, the odds on his being a knave of some sort had to be high.

'Imagine how cold it's getting outside Moscow,' Russell said.

'I guess that's something,' Dallin agreed. 'But let's get this over with. What's the word from the Admiral?'

'He has some figures for you,' Russell said, pulling a folded sheet of paper from his inside pocket and passing it over. 'Oil and manpower. Oil and manpower *shortages*, to be precise.'

Dallin studied the figures, and let out a low whistle. 'These don't look so good for Adolf.'

'If they're true, they're not.'

'You think they're faked? An under-estimate, I suppose.'

Russell shrugged. 'I've no way of knowing, but my guess is not.'

'So why pass them on? It's an admission of weakness.'

'Ah. The second half of the message is that Stalin is considering a separate peace. Provided Moscow doesn't fall, that is – Uncle Joe will only negotiate from a position of strength.'

Dallin thought for a moment. 'I don't get it,' he said eventually. 'Is there a connection?'

'Canaris doesn't mind you – us – supporting the British, in fact he wants that to continue, because one thing he dreads is a German victory in the West. But he doesn't want us joining up with the Russians, because the other thing he dreads is a German defeat in the East. So his main aim is to prevent that happening, to keep the two wars separate. The statistics are supposed to convince us that the Soviets will avoid defeat whether we help them or not, and the separate peace rumour – which is almost certainly a fiction – suggests that helping them would be against our own interests, and that any tanks we send them might eventually be used against us.'

Dallin looked suitably confused. 'Does the Admiral know which side he's on?'

'Good question. He hates communists as much as he hates Nazis, and he probably hates democrats too. But now that the Kaiser's gone there's not much else on offer. I think the only thing you can say for certain about Canaris is that he *is* a German patriot. He wants Germany – his Germany, not Hitler's – to survive the war, and that will only happen if the Russians and their German communist allies are kept at arm's length, and if Hitler and the Nazis are deposed, allowing Canaris and a few like-minded generals to strike a deal with the West. None of which is impossible, but as a sequence of events you'd have to say it was pretty unlikely.'

'Oh, I don't know,' Dallin said, rubbing his hands together. 'Look how eager you Brits were to push Hitler east, until someone in London had the bright idea of guaranteeing Poland.'

'True, but Churchill wouldn't do a deal last year, and I'd say Britain's position is stronger now than it was then.'

'Unless Moscow really does fall.'

'It won't.'

'You have some private intelligence?'

'Nope. Just a hunch.' Or just wishful thinking, he thought to himself. 'What have you got for the Admiral?' he asked.

'Only one thing really. We want the Admiral to understand that if the Japs attack us in Asia, we won't just meet them head on, we'll also declare war on Germany. Tell him that we'll have no choice, because our strategic plan calls for fighting and winning a European war before we deal with the Nips.'

'Is that true?'

'Who knows? But if the Germans believe it, it might encourage them to restrain the Japanese for a few months more. And if the Japs don't take any notice and attack us, Hitler might reckon we're going to attack him anyway, and be fool enough to get his declaration in first. Which would save Roosevelt the job of persuading Congress that the two wars were one and the same.'

'Nice,' Russell said. 'How are things going in Washington? With the Japanese, I mean?'

'Time is definitely running out, which brings me to another matter. You remember Franz Knieriem?'

It was not a name that Russell had been hoping to hear. 'Vaguely,' he lied.

'He was one of the men on that list you were given in New York, back in '39. An official at the Air Ministry. You decided against contacting him.'

'I remember.'

'Why?'

Russell thought back. He had engineered an innocent meeting with the man, and had decided to take it no further. The credentials had been perfect – an ex-Social Democrat with a brother who had died in Dachau, an effusive character reference from an old colleague now living in America – and the possibility of gaining access to restricted Air Ministry files had certainly appealed to Washington; but Russell had formed an instinctive distrust of the man. Franz Knieriem, he had decided, might well be the death of him.

But how to explain that to Dallin? 'I just didn't trust him,' he said, knowing how inadequate it sounded.

'Nothing stronger than that?' Dallin predictably asked. 'Because we need you to try again. We'll probably be out of here in a few weeks, and the chance will be gone. Look, I'll tell you what we need to know and why. Last June, when Hitler was in Florence, he told Mussolini that he would have a trans-Atlantic bomber ready for service by the end of this year. One that could make it to New York and back from the Azores. Now we haven't found a trace of this bomber, and it may just be a figment of Hitler's imagination, but, something like this, we have to be sure. New Yorkers don't want to be settling down to a Yankee game next season and suddenly find there are German bombers overhead.'

'It doesn't sound very plausible, does it?'

'No, but we can't afford to ignore the possibility.'

And I can't afford to take the risk, Russell thought.

'If the guy calls the Gestapo, you can just make a run for the Consulate,' Dallin suggested, as if this was something people did every day.

'They'd come in and get me.'

'Why? The cat would be out of the bag, and creating a diplomatic incident wouldn't put it back in again.'

'And my girlfriend? You've already told me that there's nothing you could do for her.'

'There isn't. At least, I don't think so. Let me have another try, see what I can do. In the meantime, will you at least think about it? If we get into the war, you'll be separated from your girlfriend anyway.'

'I'll give it some thought,' Russell said, seeing no point in a blank refusal.

But he had no desire to contact Knieriem again. The way things were going, Dallin and Company would soon be gone, and he was confident he could string the matter out until they were.

It was getting dark when the studio limousine dropped Effi off at the main entrance of the Elisabeth Hospital. She had been visiting the wounded once a week for a couple of months now, a willing participant in Goebbels' latest campaign to raise morale among the troops. There were supposed to be three of them there tonight, but the other two had cried off, one actress claiming a headache, the other a queasy stomach. The experience was generally depressing, but it *was* only a couple of hours, and Effi had felt like flaying them.

An orderly insisted on escorting her through the maze of corridors, happily chatting as they walked – he seemed to remember her films better than she did. Reaching the first of the military wards, she announced her arrival to the staff nurse, Annaliese Huiskes, whom she knew from previous visits.

'Anyone you particularly want me to see?' Effi asked.

'No. Just as many as you can manage. They'll all be delighted.'

A bit of an exaggeration, Effi thought, as she headed for the visitor-less bed. There were always quite a few who were happy to see her, but some had visitors of their own, and others simply turned their heads in mute refusal. Those that welcomed her would often ask about her work, and which other stars she had met. Some would flirt, but more wanted to talk about their girlfriends and wives. The hardest were those who had lost limbs or suffered other disfigurement, and were fearful that they would no longer be wanted.

Her first man – boy, really – was initially almost too star-struck to talk. She slowly won him round, asking the usual questions about family and friends and how he was mending, trying to satisfy his curiosity about life in Babelsberg and the glamorous world of movies. Eventually she was passed, like a prize that had to be shared, from patient to patient and on into the next ward, down a queue of stunned or frightened faces that formed a knot in her throat and brought her perilously close to tears.

Most of the men refused to talk about the war, but those who were willing could talk of little else. 'You can't imagine what's it's like,' they would say, some resentfully, others almost in wonderment, as if they themselves were already finding it hard to credit their memories.

'So tell me,' Effi would reply.

'You're better off not knowing,' the soldiers would say, almost proudly.

'It's always better to know,' Effi would say, though some of the stories gave her reason to doubt it. The boy of eighteen showered with the flesh of his best friend, suddenly headless trunks collapsing in almost comic slow motion, the constant fear of losing one's genitals and no longer being a man.

And then there was the guilt. They had all done it – arriving in a Russian village, stealing the food and the shelter, pushing women and children out into the dark and the cold. 'It was them or us – what else could we do?'

'And what if they resist?'

'Then we shoot them. The children too. Once you've shot the mother you have to shoot the children. How would they survive on their own?'

Her last patient, a young man in his mid-twenties with neat blond hair and the sort of rugged outdoor face which the Propaganda Ministry liked on its posters, had needed shrapnel removing from his neck, but seemed set for a quick recovery. His mind, though, was in such turmoil that he could hardly lie still, twisting his head this way and that, convincing Effi that he would rip out the stitches that criss-crossed his throat. 'The Russians will fight on,' he told Effi, as if he was resuming an interrupted conversation. 'They can't retreat and they can't surrender, so what else can they do? If they retreat then their people shoot them, if they surrender then either we shoot them or they starve. There's no food for prisoners. That's just the way it is. But you can't fight an enemy that won't retreat or surrender. You just have to keep killing and killing and hope that he'll run out of soldiers before we do. But he won't, will he?' the soldier almost shouted. 'The Führer must know this, so why does he keep telling us to attack?'

'Sssshhh,' Effi said, afraid the man would talk himself into trouble. 'We can't know what the Führer knows. He may be getting false reports from his generals.'

The man's eyes lit up. 'That must be it. Someone should tell him. You should tell him. You're famous.'

'I will,' Effi promised.

'All my friends are dead,' he said.

'You're not,' Effi said. 'And you have to get better, and get back to your wife and children. They need you.'

The soldier gave her a questioning look, as if to check her sincerity. 'You're right,' he said without conviction. 'I must get better.'

As she leaned over to kiss him on the forehead she saw tears glistening in his eyes.

Visiting time was over, and she made her way back down the wards, smiling at the men she had spoken to. Annaliese Huiskes was sitting back in her chair, a glass of pinkish liquid in her hand, looking as tired as Effi felt. She was almost thirty, Effi knew, and prettier than she looked tonight.

'Come in,' Huiskes said, reaching inside a desk drawer for a bottle and a second glass. 'Have a drink.'

'Of what?' Effi asked.

'Hospital schnapps. We have the raw alcohol, and one of the doctors is good at giving it different flavours. This one's not bad.'

A drink did seem like a good idea, and it tasted no worse than some of the cocktails that the better hotels were now serving up.

'How did it go?' Huiskes asked.

Effi sighed. 'I hope I help. Some of them anyway. The last man I saw – Becker was the name above the bed – seemed very disturbed.'

'I'll leave a note for the night shift. But he's one of the luckier ones.' She drained her glass, looked at the bottle, and abruptly returned it to the desk drawer. 'It's hard to keep track,' she said. 'There're so many coming and going – more than ever these last few weeks. I hope that just means that we're getting a larger share than before, but who knows? I have a friend in the SS Hospital, and that sounds even worse. One night one of her patients started screaming, 'I can't do it anymore!' and most of the others joined in, until half the ward was screaming and the other half weeping.'

'Do what, I wonder,' Effi murmured.

'Killing people, of course. In their hundreds, thousands even. Jews mostly, but Russians too. They force them to dig huge graves, line them up on the side, and then shoot them. Row after row. Her patients can't stop talking about it, she says.'

'Why?' Effi wanted to know. 'Why are they shooting so many?'

Annaliese shrugged. 'Who knows? I haven't heard from my Gerd for weeks,' she added, as if he might have the answer.

'Where is he?'

'Somewhere in the south. He's with 60th Motorised. I worry about him not coming back, and I worry about who he'll be if he does come back.'

After the meeting with Dallin, Russell had walked the short distance south to the Abwehr headquarters, a five-storey building on Tirpitz Ufer overlooking the Landwehrkanal. The Section 1 offices seemed busy, but section chief Colonel Hans Piekenbrock only made him wait a few moments. After listening to Russell's report of what Dallin had said, the Colonel made a face. 'Is that all?'

'Yes.'

'Very well.'

'But there is one other thing.'

'Yes?'

'When I started working for the Abwehr in this way I made it clear to the Admiral that I could not continue doing so if Germany became involved in a war with my own country.'

'I believe that was the understanding,' Piekenbrock agreed.

'So I will be permitted to leave with all the other journalists?'

'That is my understanding,' the Colonel confirmed.

'That's all I wanted to know,' Russell said, getting up. He only wished he could believe it.

It had grown visibly darker during his brief visit, and the chances of his reaching the second daily press conference on time were remote. But why bother? He wasn't going to learn anything significant, and if one of Goebbels' minions inadvertently let something slip, he wouldn't be allowed to file it. His job was a joke, whichever way he looked at it.

He turned west along the canal towpath, thinking Effi might be home early for once, only to remember as he reached the Cornelius Bridge that this was her hospital night. A drink, he thought, and after skirting round the Zoo he made tracks for the bar on the Ku'damm where he'd last encountered some real whisky. Crossing Hardenbergstrasse he suddenly remembered that Effi's last film was showing just up the road at the Ufa-Palast.

She had, unusually for her, refused to see the film with him when it first came out, and he had never gotten around to seeing it on his own. He walked on up to the giant cinema, which had been the largest in Europe until Hamburg built a bigger one. The early evening showing was beginning in less than fifteen minutes.

There was a long queue at the box office, and the cinema itself was more crowded than he expected, with over three-quarters of the seats filled. Russell settled into an aisle seat near the front, just as the recorded orchestra struck up a rousing theme over shots of the German countryside. The film was dedicated to those Germans whose forefathers had emigrated to the East and faced the ensuing hardships, chief among which, it soon transpired, was proximity to Poles.

Effi soon appeared on screen, sporting a Brunhilde hairstyle and dressed like Babelsberg's idea of a humble schoolteacher. Watching her, Russell always felt an absurd pride, as if he had anything to do with how good she was. She dismissed her loving class of bright young Germans and walked home through the town, accompanied by looks from the local Poles which mingled disgust and lechery in equal measure. Her father, the local German doctor, was waiting with news that the German hospital was being closed down.

So far, so predictable, Russell thought; but as the film unfolded he was left with a grudging respect for its makers. It could have been so much worse – such films usually were. This one occasionally teetered on the edge of unintentional farce – the scenes with the Jews were risible as ever – but in general the temptation to over-egg the pudding was manfully resisted. For once in Babelsberg's Nazi life, actions were allowed to speak louder than the cartoon villains, and it worked. Once Effi's father had been beaten to death, his lawyer friend shot and blinded and another young girl treated to a stoning, the audience were ready for Effi's reluctant declaration of war on the local Poles. In her final stirring speech, delivered to her fellow Germans after they'd all been imprisoned for listening to a Führer broadcast, she painted an idealistic picture of the future, and the Reich of which they'd soon be a part, where 'all around the birds are singing and everything is German.' In a bad film it would have sounded ludicrous, but in this one it somehow worked – by this time even Russell found himself rooting for the poor beleaguered minority, and very upset by the final shooting of Effi's character. When the Wehrmacht arrived to put things right, he felt like shaking a fist though, unlike many in the audience, refrained from actually doing so.

Making his way out of the cinema, he understood why Effi had not wanted him to see it. It was a powerful film. All those German families – and there were millions of them now – whose sons were away in Russia or Yugoslavia or Africa would feel better about their being there. And if the dreaded letter should arrive, they would have some consolation in knowing that their sons had died for such an irrefutably noble cause. Effi had been that convincing.

Arriving home to the empty apartment, Russell realised he had not bought any food. There were plenty of potatoes though, one rather sad looking onion, and an egg, which he decided to save. He sliced both as thinly as he could, and placed them in a frying pan with salt and a little ersatz butter over a low heat. They were browning nicely when Effi arrived.

She threw her bag down, burrowed into his arms and squeezed him as tightly as she could. They kissed.

'Hello,' she said.

'You've been drinking,' he said, tasting the schnapps on her breath. She looked exhausted.

'I certainly have, and I feel like more. Is there any wine left?'

Russell poured her a glass. 'I saved you an egg.'

'I've eaten.' Hours ago, but she didn't feel hungry. 'Put the egg in the potatoes, and I'll have a taste.'

Russell did as he was told. 'Another early start in the morning?'

'Oh yes. All this week, but that should do it.'

'How was the hospital?'

'The same as ever. Terrible. Heartbreaking. Infuriating. It's impossible not to feel sorry for most of them, but some of the things they admit to… it's hard not to feel that they deserve everything that's happened to them. I know they're just following orders, so it's not really their fault, but it is their fingers on the triggers. But… I don't know. What would any of us do in the same situation?'

Russell stirred in the egg. 'The one thing I do know is how hard it is to break ranks. The pressure to conform, to go along with the consensus, is enormous. You need virtually everyone on board to start a mutiny.'

Like everyone screaming 'I can't do it anymore', Effi thought. She told him what Huiskes had told her about the SS hospital. 'It was Annaliese who gave me the drink,' she added. 'She has a bottle hidden in her drawer in the ward office. I expect they all do.'

'More than likely.'

'And there's no end in sight is there? It's all gone downhill in a few months. Victory after victory for two years and suddenly we're holding our breath. I was looking down the ward this evening and thinking that these are the casualties of success – what on earth is failure going to look like?'

'We'll know in the next few weeks. Whether or not he's failed, I mean. It's impossible to tell at the moment. We don't know how much the Soviets have left, or how quickly the winter will set in. One interesting thing I heard today – the weather's already turned in Siberia, so the Soviets are safe from the Japs until spring. That's a lot of men they can bring west.'

'Hmmm. How was your day?'

Russell took the loaded plate across to the table, placed it between them, and handed her a fork. 'The usual rubbish.' He told her about the press conference, and offered an edited version of his meeting with Dallin – despite precautions, they were never completely sure that the Gestapo hadn't managed to plant a microphone. 'Then I went to see *Homecoming*,' he admitted.

'Oh, did you?'

'You were really good.'

'I know.'

'And that makes you feel bad.'

She gave him a wry smile. 'Of course. It makes me feel part of it. Just like the boys I talk to, gunning down Jews. I'm sure they're good at their job too.'

'It's not the same,' Russell said, and it wasn't. Not completely.

'Isn't it? It feels like it is. I'm not doing another film like that, John. I'd rather quit.'

'Would they let you?'

'I think so,' she said, for the first time considering the possibility that they wouldn't.

'What would you do?' Russell asked.

'I've no idea,' Effi said getting up. She walked through into the living room, and a few seconds later the Tommy Dorsey Orchestra were easing into 'I'll never smile again'.

She reappeared in the archway. 'Come dance with me.'

Betrayals on offer

'Lunch at the Adlon?' Ralph Morrison asked, as he and Russell reached the pavement outside the Foreign Ministry. It was a miserable day, a thin mist of rain hanging in the air.

'Why not?' These days most Americans were *persona non grata* in most of Berlin, but the Adlon Hotel remained a welcome exception.

'Another hour I'll never get back,' Morrison complained, as they walked up Wilhelmstrasse. 'I even found myself missing that bastard Schmidt this morning. At least he lies with some panache. That idiot Stumm, well, what can you say?'

'If they really have taken Kerch, that's bad news,' Russell said. 'Puts them too damn close to the Caucasus oilfields.'

'I know.'

'Did you get any more on Udet? None of my contacts would tell me anything.'

'Oh yes. He shot himself all right. And left a note blaming Goering – "Oh Iron Man, why have you deserted me?" or some such rubbish. Why do fighter aces never grow up?'

They reached the Adlon entrance and walked through to the restaurant. Gestapo technicians had invaded the hotel a few months earlier and planted hidden microphones everywhere, but over the intervening weeks most had been discovered by the staff, and the guests discreetly warned. Morrison and Russell headed for an area of the large room that was generally considered safe. There was no chandelier directly above their table, and the latter's underside was clear.

Russell had got to know Morrison quite well since his arrival some six months before, as Jack Slaney's replacement. A burly Mid-Westerner in his mid-thirties, Morrison had arrived knowing little about Germany, but he had inherited most of Slaney's excellent sources, and proved a quick learner. If he sometimes appeared even more cynical than his predecessor, that was probably because reporting from Berlin no longer bore any relation to traditional journalism.

The ritual with scissors and ration tickets completed, the two men sipped at what passed for beers in Hitler's triumphant capital. 'I did pick up another story in my trawling,' Russell admitted. 'I was talking to a German friend this morning, a journalist. Apparently the editors of all the big city dailies were called in to Promi yesterday, and told to lay off the winter clothing story. The official line is that it's all waiting at the railheads for distribution, but the trains are in chaos so who knows when they'll get there, and they're worried that the troops will write home and tell their families that nothing's arrived and they're all freezing to death. So no one's supposed to mention the subject, and there's a complete ban on pictures of soldiers in their summer uniforms.' Russell laughed. 'Photographers have been sending back too many pictures of Red Army men in thick coats guarded by shivering Germans in denim.'

Morrison shook his head in amazement. 'Have they really been that incompetent?'

'You bet. The astonishing thing is that they're still advancing. Stalin must be matching them balls-up for balls-up.'

Their lunch arrived, boiled cabbage and potatoes with a few suspicious-looking pieces of sausage. If this was what the Adlon was serving, God help the rest of the Reich.

'The thing about the Nazis,' Russell went on, 'is that everything's short term. They gabble on about thousand-year Reichs but they don't do any real planning. There's a fascinating article in the *Frankfurter Zeitung* this morning about the importance of infantry in the Russian campaign. Well, it's not fascinating in itself, but the fact of it is. An article like that would have been inconceivable a couple of months ago – all anyone wanted to talk about were the panzers and the Luftwaffe. Short-term weapons, weapons that win quickly, *blitzkrieg*. And I think that whoever wrote that article has realised that *blitzkrieg* has failed in Russia, that only the infantry can win it for them now.'

'Do they have the infantry?'

Russell shrugged. 'My guess would be not, but that may be wishful thinking.'

As he ate, another likely consequence of the German emphasis on tanks and tank-supportive planes occurred to him. If German production had all been geared to *blitzkrieg* over the last few years, there was no chance of Hitler having a fleet of long-range bombers up his sleeve. Russell could understand why Dallin and his Washington bosses were worried: their country was accustomed to immunity from such threats, and the appearance of German bombers in the skies above Manhattan would certainly wreak havoc in the American psyche. But there was no substance to this particular piece of paranoia, and nothing to be gained from his seeking out Franz Knieriem.

Nothing for the Americans, that was. He might earn himself a few points by showing willing. He could at least find out whether the man was still living at the same address – there was no risk in that. And there was always the chance that Knieriem had moved, which would give him grounds for further procrastination. If his luck was really in, the address was now a bomb site.

The slivers of sausage actually tasted quite good, unlike the cabbage and potatoes which tasted of salt and little else.

A waiter materialised at his elbow. 'A call for you, sir,' he said. 'In reception.'

It was his ex-wife Ilse. 'You always told me I could reach you there,' she said, 'but I never quite believed it.'

'Now you know.'

'It's Paul,' she told him. 'He's said something he shouldn't have at school, and…'

'What did he say?'

'I don't know. I'll find out when he gets home. But they want to see his parents, and Matthias is in Hannover.' Paul's stepfather, a thoroughly respectable German businessman, usually acted *in loco parentis* where the authorities were concerned. 'I'd rather not go alone,' Ilse added.

'What time?' Russell asked.

'Six o'clock. Say half past five here.'

'I'll be there.'

'Thanks.'

Russell replaced the earpiece. Another missed press conference performance at Promi, he thought. Another silver lining. But what about the cloud – what had Paul been saying?

Russell left plenty of time for the endless ride out to Grunewald, but one tram broke down and the driver of the next seemed unwilling to risk a speed of more than ten kilometres an hour. Getting round the city grew more frustrating by the day, except for those with the right connections. Arriving ten minutes late at the Gehrts' house, he found Matthias's Horch staring out of an open garage door, its numberplate adorned with the priceless red square which allowed its owner the luxury of continuing use. Russell felt like unscrewing the numberplate there and then, but a written permit was also required.

Ilse opened the door before he had time to ring the bell. She looked worried.

'Well?' Russell asked. 'What's it all about?'

'Two jokes, and one was about Hitler. Paul should know better.'

'Where is he?'

'In his room.'

Russell climbed the stairs, wondering what sort of reception he was going to get. Over the last few months his fourteen-year-old son had seemed increasingly exasperated with him, as if Russell just didn't get it – whatever *it* was. Ilse thought it age-related, but the boy didn't seem to behave the same way with her or his stepfather, and Russell knew that his being English, and the complications which that had necessarily caused in Paul's German life, had more than a little to do with their recent difficulties. But there was nothing Russell could do about that. 'It's like your snoring,' Effi had told him when they talked about it. 'I want to murder you, and knowing you can't help it makes it even worse. I can't even blame you.'

He crossed the large landing, and put his head around Paul's half-open door. His son was doing his homework, tracing one of the maps in his Stieler's Atlas. 'Another fine mess you've got yourself into,' Russell observed. Paul loved Laurel and Hardy.

'What are *you* doing here?' Paul exclaimed. 'If you go to the school, it'll makes things worse.'

Russell sat down on the bed. 'They know you have an English father, Paul. It won't be news.'

'Yes, but…'

'What were the jokes?'

'They were just jokes.'

'Jokes are sometimes important.'

'Well I can't see that these two were. All right, I'll tell you. Describe the perfect German.' Russell had heard this one, but let Paul supply the punchline – 'Someone blond as Hitler, slim as Goering and tall as Goebbels.'

Russell smiled. 'You forgot clever as Ley and sane as Hess. What was the other?'

'One man says: "When the war's over I'm going to do a bicycle tour of the Reich." His friend replies: "So what will you do after lunch?"'

Russell laughed. 'That's a good one.'

'Yes, but it's just a silly joke. I don't really think we'll lose the war. It's just a joke.'

'They'll call it defeatism. And the first joke – these people take their racial stereotypes seriously. And they don't like being mocked.'

'But everyone tells jokes like those.'

'I know.'

'John, we have to go,' Ilse called from downstairs.

'Coming,' he shouted back. As he got up he noticed the picture of Udet on the wall, alongside Mölders and the U-boat ace Gunther Prien. 'It was sad what happened to Udet,' he said.

Paul looked at him disbelievingly. 'You didn't like him.'

Russell had no memory of saying so to his son, but he probably had. 'He was a wonderful pilot,' he said weakly.

'I want to see the funeral march on Saturday,' Paul insisted.

'Fine,' Russell agreed. 'I'll check the route.'

He kissed his son's head, and went back down to Ilse. 'We just nod our heads and look humble,' she told him as they started down the street towards the school. 'No arguments, no smart replies. And no jokes.'

'You'll be saying he gets it from me next.'

'Well he does, doesn't he? But I'm not blaming you. I like it that he doesn't believe most of what they tell him.'

'What does Matthias think?'

'He's angry. But then these days he's angry about anything that reminds him of the government we've got. He'd rather just wake up when it's all over.'

It was the first time Russell had ever heard his ex-wife criticise her current husband, and he felt rather ashamed of enjoying the moment.

They walked through the school doors and down the corridor to Paul's classroom, where his teacher, a grey-haired man in his fifties or sixties, was marking a pile of exercise books. A large map of the western Soviet Union adorned one wall, complete with arrows depicting German advances. Russell wondered if the teacher knew that he and Ilse had met in Moscow, two young and eager communists out to change the world. No jokes, he reminded himself.

The teacher's name was Weber. He proved stern and apparently humourless, but also surprisingly reasonable. It turned out that one boy had repeated Paul's jokes to his own parents, and the father had turned up at the school in a rage that morning. The boy had not named Paul as the source, but once the matter had been discussed in class, Paul had privately informed Herr Weber of his guilt. The teacher had no intention of divulging Paul's name to the complaining parent, a man, he implied, who was somewhat over-zealous in ideological matters. Paul had an excellent record in the *Jungvolk*, Herr Weber went on, and had started out well in the *Hitlerjugend*, but, like many spirited boys of his age, he clearly felt the urge to test the boundaries of what was permissible. Which was all perfectly normal. But in days like these, such testing could have disproportionate consequences, and it was highly advisable for both teachers and parents to clarify those boundaries wherever they could.

Ilse and Russell agreed that it was.

Herr Weber gave them one wintry smile, and thanked them for coming in.

It was gone seven when Russell reached the Halensee Ringbahn station, and dense layers of cloud hid the moon and stars, promising one of the deeper blackouts. Accidents were common on the S-Bahn in such conditions, with passengers opening doors and stepping out onto what they mistakenly hoped was a platform.

Russell got off to change at Westkreuz, and stood on the Stadtbahn platform in the near complete darkness for what seemed like ages, listening to the murmur of invisible people and watching the patchwork of glows as passengers on the opposite platform dragged on their cigarettes. He would be arriving late at the Blumenthals, not that it mattered Jews were not allowed out after 8pm, which certainly simplified the task of finding them at home. Especially now that their telephones had all been disconnected.

The Blumenthals were one of several Jewish families that he – and often Effi as well – visited on a fairly regular basis. At first this had been work-inspired, part of Russell's attempt to keep track of what was happening to Berlin's Jewish community as the war went on. It quickly became clear that they could also help in many ways, some small, others increasingly significant. Ration tickets could be passed on, and news of the outside world did something to lessen the sense of helplessness and isolation which many Jews now felt. There was also the sense, for him and for Effi, that they were keeping the doors of their own world open, refusing to be trapped in what a German colleague had once called 'the majority ghetto'. And some of the Jews had become friends, insofar as true friendship was possible in such artificially skewed relationships.

A train finally rattled in behind its thin blue light, and Russell had no trouble finding a seat in a barely-lit carriage. Several Jews were standing together at one end of the carriage, presumably on their way home from a ten-hour shift at Siemens. They were not talking to each other, and he could almost feel their determination not to be noticed.

Leaving Börse Station, he picked a path up the wide Oranienburgerstrasse with the help of the whitened kerbs and an occasional tram. The Blumenthals – Martin, Leonore and their daughter Ali – had a small two-room apartment in one of the narrow streets behind the burnt-out ruins of the New Synagogue. This was reasonably spacious by current standards, but something of a come-down for the family, who had once owned a large house in Grunewald and several shops selling musical scores and instruments. Martin now worked in a factory out near the Central Stockyards, cutting and treating railway sleepers. He was the same age as the century, a year younger than Russell, but he looked considerably older. Hook-nosed and with protuberant lips, he looked like a caricature *Der Stürmer* Jew; by contrast, his wife Leonore was simply dark-haired and petite, while his seventeen year-old daughter Ali, with her fair hair and green eyes, could have passed an audition for Tristan's Isolde.

Leonore answered the door, apprehension shifting to relief when she saw who it was. Martin leapt up to offer his right hand, his left clutching the copy of *Faust* he seemed to be forever reading. 'Come in, come in,' he urged. 'It's good to see you. I'm fed up with talking to other Jews – their only topic of conversation is themselves, and how terrible everything is.'

'Everything *is* terrible,' Russell said, refusing Leonore's armchair and sitting himself down at the table. As if to prove his point, she picked up the coat she'd obviously been working on and continued with her task of re-attaching a yellow star.

'Yes, but it serves no purpose to talk of nothing else. Everything passes, even these… gentlemen. America will enter the war, and that will be that. It's strange – the last war they entered, I was a boy shooting at them. This time I shall invite every last one of them around for dinner.'

Russell laughed. 'I think Leonore might have something to say about that.'

'Chance would be a fine thing,' Leonore said. She was upset about something, Russell thought.

'It will happen,' Martin insisted. 'Tell me, what's the news? Since they took our radios away we have no idea what's actually happening.'

Russell gave him the edited version, as seen from London and Washington – the Russian war in the balance, the looming breakdown in Japanese-American relations.

'Surely the Japanese won't attack America?' Martin mused. 'How could they hope to win such a war?'

'Most people think they'll attack the British and the Dutch, and hope that the Americans stay out,' Russell told him.

They went over the Japanese options until even Martin's curiosity was exhausted. 'Where's Ali?' Russell asked Leonore, seizing his chance. It was Ali who had introduced him to her parents, after Thomas had taken her on as a bookkeeper at his Treptow factory.

'At the cinema,' Leonore admitted.

'Without her star,' Martin added proudly.

'Without her star,' Leonore echoed. 'My Aunt Trudi was taken,' she went on. 'I think you met her once. She lived in Wedding on her own, insisted on it, and her health's been good for a woman over seventy. She got the notification last week, and she left the day before yesterday as far as we know. I wanted to see her off, but she refused; she said she didn't want a big fuss, but I think she was afraid they'd take me too.'

'A train did leave the night before last,' Russell said, but thought better of admitting that he'd watched it go.

'Then she's gone.'

'Many things are terrible,' Martin said, 'but not everything. Frau Thadden, the woman upstairs, is a real friend to us – she doesn't think any less of us because we are Jews. And a few nights ago a policeman banged on our door. We feared the worst, but he wanted to tell us to pull our blackout curtain tighter – some light was showing. If some of his colleagues saw it, he said, then we'd be in trouble, and he didn't want that. You see,' he said, turning to his wife, 'there are many good Germans.'

'I know there are,' she said. 'But Aunt Trudi is still gone.'

Seeing his stricken expression, she relented, and gave him a wonderful smile. After all, Russell realised, the heart that clutched at straws was the heart she'd fallen in love with.

'Have any of your friends heard any more from those who've been sent East?' he asked.

'Yes,' Leonore said. 'Two of them. I wrote it down as you asked,' she added, taking down a recipe book. 'It seemed a good hiding place,' she explained, leafing through the pages. 'Here we are. Two letters from Lodz. One from someone's uncle who left on October 17th, the other from an old friend who left on the 25th. Both said they were fine, and not to worry about them.'

'And they were in the right handwriting?'

'Yes, I asked.'

'Well, that's good news,' Russell thought aloud.

'Better than it might be,' Leonore agreed absent-mindedly. 'This sounds like Ali,' she said, relief in her voice, and a few seconds later the seventeen year-old let herself into the flat. She was pleased to see Russell, but clearly disappointed that he hadn't brought Effi. 'She's just finishing a film,' Russell started to say, only to be interrupted by the rising whine of the air raid sirens.

Martin looked at his watch. 'They're early tonight,' he complained. 'Let's ignore it for once,' he added, without conviction. Leonore was already reaching for her overcoat, and Ali was pulling her jacket with the star out of her bag. Martin picked up the suitcase that was already packed for such eventualities, and they all tramped down the stairs. Outside, a barely visible procession was heading down the street towards the shelter. Looking up at an impenetrable sky Russell reckoned the RAF needed better weather forecasters – the chances of hitting anything relevant on a night like this had to be zero.

The Jews had been allocated their own segregated area at one end of the basement shelter, about a sixth of the space for almost half of those present. Russell ignored the local block warden's direction and joined them, almost hoping for a row. The warden restricted himself to a nasty look, and went back to ticking off arrivals on a long list.

The shelter itself reflected the poverty of the neighbourhood. Old wooden benches lined the sandbagged walls, along with a few double-decker cots for the children. The ceiling had been recently reinforced with new beams, but the provision of fire extinguishers and pick-axes showed a lack of confidence in the cellar's ability to survive a building collapse. A couple of tables, several kerosene lanterns and a single pail of water completed the inventory.

All around Russell, families were settling in, mothers putting their youngest to bed and entreating their older siblings to entertain themselves as quietly as possible with whatever toys had been brought. Those adults spared the responsibilities of childcare were taking out books, shuffling cards or, in several cases, staring forlornly into space. His list apparently complete, the block warden was working the lever on the air suction pump, and staring malevolently at Russell. Look at me, his expression seemed to say, expelling the stench of the Jews and sucking in good German air.

Russell gave him a big smile, and went back to people he cared about. Ali was giving two young Jewish girls a lesson in how to play skat, while her mother just sat with her back to the wall, eyes closed. Martin, as usual, was eager to talk about how the war was going, and how soon it might end. After about ten minutes the flak opened up, first the loud cracks of those on roofs in the nearby government districts, then the deep boom of those in the huge flak towers. There were two of the latter – the old one in the Tiergarten and the recently completed monstrosity in Friedrichshain Park – and by Russell's reckoning their current shelter was halfway between them. As safe as it got, at least when the sky was clear; on a night like this it probably didn't matter – both gunners below and bombers above would be aiming blind.

The guns fell silent after forty-five minutes, and the all-clear sounded fifteen minutes after that. Children were woken or carried home sleeping, card games abandoned and bags re-packed. Russell said goodnight to the Blumenthals and walked briskly down to Oranienburger Strasse. Searchlights were still nervously scanning the clouds, casting a dull yellow glow across the city, and for once he could see where he was going.

The last ones went out as he reached Börse Station, returning Berlin to its customary gloom. From the elevated Stadtbahn platform only one fire was visible, a kilometre or more to the north-west, somewhere close to Stettin Station. It seemed pathetic change for so much expenditure of effort and fuel, not to mention the sundry lives that had inevitably been lost – one or two plane crews perhaps, a handful of Berliners killed by bombs or falling shrapnel, the rising number of rape-murders committed under cover of the blackout.

It was almost midnight when he reached home, and Effi, as expected, was asleep. Less predictably, she had left a note asking him to wake her. And when he saw the communication which lay underneath it, he understood why. The Gestapo wanted to see him. At their Prinz-Albrecht-Strasse headquarters. In just over ten hours time.

He walked into the bedroom, sat down on the bed and shook her gently by the shoulder. 'You wanted me to wake you.'

'Yes,' she said sleepily. 'The note. Do you know what it's about?'

'Probably my visit to Zembski's studio. I don't think there's anything to worry about. If it was anything serious they would have waited for me.'

'That's what I hoped. Give me a kiss.'

He did so.

'And come to bed.'

He got undressed and climbed in, expecting that she'd gone back to sleep. But she hadn't.

The sky was still leaden on the following morning. Russell spent twenty minutes vainly searching for a particular jacket, then ate a desultory breakfast at the Zoo Station buffet. After a five-minute journey on the U-Bahn had brought him to Bismarckstrasse, he walked through several backstreets to Knieriem's old house. There was no sign of life within, but one of the neighbours eventually emerged. Yes, she replied in response to his question, Herr Knieriem did still live there, but he always left very early for work.

Russell walked back to the U-Bahn at Bismarckstrasse, and caught an eastbound train to Potsdamer Platz. Reaching street level he walked along the back of the Fürstenhof Hotel with the intention of turning into Prinz-Albrecht-Strasse. This route was cordoned off, and a group of Russian POWs were waiting under guard at the end of a side street. An unexploded bomb, Russell assumed. Someone had told him that POWs were used to defuse them.

He retraced his steps and almost ran the longer route around the Air Ministry – it didn't pay to be late for a Gestapo summons. The grey five-storey megalith loomed into view, and as he approached the double doors rain began to fall. It seemed a poor omen.

The reception area was little changed since his last summons in 1939, the usual mishmash of Greek columns, heavy Victorian curtains and

Prussian bronzed eagles. The giant swastika had disappeared, replaced by a huge bulletin board bearing the Party's quotation of the week. The current incumbent was more long-winded than usual: 'Just as our ancestors did not receive the soil on which we stand today as a gift from heaven, but rather through hard work, so also today as well as in the future, our soil and with it our lives depend not on the grace of some other people, but only on the power of a successful sword.' The bracketed 'Words of our Führer' was somewhat redundant.

A Rottenführer in Gestapo dress uniform sat alone behind the huge reception desk. Russell showed him the summons, and was asked politely enough to take one of the seats beneath a portrait of the uniformed Adolf. He did so, and told himself for the twentieth time that morning that there was nothing to worry about. None of his current activities were illegal. The Gestapo might frown on his attempts to find out what was happening to Berlin's Jews, but the Nazis were making no real secret of their persecutions and deportations, and gathering – as opposed to publishing such information could hardly be considered a crime. His links with American Intelligence were sanctioned by the Abwehr, a veritable pillar of the military establishment. As far as he could tell, he had done nothing illegal since 1939, and the Gestapo must have better things to do than investigate crimes that might or might not have been committed more than two years ago.

So why did he feel like vacating his bowels? Because he had seen the corridor of grey cells that lay beneath this marble floor, and had actually visited Effi in one of them. Because he had been treated, for just a few minutes, to a world of screams and whimpers and even more ominous silence. Because he knew what the bastards were capable of. Because Zembski might be down there right now.

Another five minutes passed before a second Rottenführer arrived to lead him, via lift and several short corridors, to a door on the top floor. His escort knocked, received an invitation to enter, and gestured Russell to do so. There were two men inside, one seated in uniform, one standing in what seemed an expensively tailored suit. In most other respects they looked remarkably similar. Both were in their thirties, with greased blond hair swept back from their foreheads; they could have passed for contestants in a Heydrich look-alike contest, in the unlikely event that one was ever held. Neither would have won, however, since both lacked Nazi Germany's great unmentionable, Heydrich's classically Jewish nose.

'I am Hauptsturmführer Leitmaritz,' said the seated man, indicating the seat that he expected Russell to occupy. 'Of the *Geheime Staatspolizei*,' he added formally.

'Obersturmbannführer Giminich,' the other man said in response to Russell's questioning look. 'Of the *Sicherheitsdienst*,' he added, with what might have been interpreted as a malicious smile.

Happy days are here again, Russell thought to himself. 'So how can I help you?' he asked pleasantly.

'By answering a few questions,' the Hauptsturmführer said shortly. He was peering short-sightedly at the document in front of him, and Russell would have bet money there were spectacles in his desk drawer. Over the man's shoulder he could see a veil of smoke over Anhalter Station half-masking the distant Kreuzberg. The rain must have stopped.

'You told a Gestapo officer at the Zembski photographic studio that you had not been there since the beginning of the war.'

'That is correct,' Russell replied.

'And your reason for going there this week was to have a photograph of your son enlarged?'

'Yes.' Obersturmbannführer Giminich was now pacing to and fro behind Russell's chair. A tried and tested tactic of intimidation, Russell thought. It worked.

'Did you ever meet with Herr Zembski socially? A drink, perhaps.'

'No, it was a purely professional relationship.'

'"Was"?' Giminich asked. 'Have you any reason to think that Zembski is dead?'

'None at all. The Gestapo officer at the studio told me he had gone out of business and returned to Silesia. So our professional relationship is presumably over.'

'The officer was mistaken,' Leitmaritz continued. 'Zembski has been arrested.'

'For what?'

'For activities detrimental to the state.'

'That could mean a lot of things. What sort of activities?'

'That will be revealed in due course.'

'At his trial?'

'Perhaps.'

'Do you have a date for that?'

'Not as yet.' The Hauptsturmführer was showing signs of getting flustered, but not Giminich. 'You did have at least one other thing in common with Herr Zembski,' he said from somewhere behind Russell's head. 'You were both communists.'

Russell tried to look surprised. 'I had no idea Zembski was a communist. Is that what all this is about? As I'm sure you know, I left the Communist Party in 1927.' He was surer than ever that Zembski was dead, and increasingly convinced that something had turned up in their search of the studio that made them suspicious of himself. But what? The only thing he could think of was Tyler McKinley's passport photograph, which Zembski should have destroyed after replacing it with Russell's. But even if that had turned up, it wouldn't prove anything. The doctored passport had long since disintegrated in the Landwehrkanal, and Tyler might have visited Zembski himself. The men interrogating him had a lot of suspicious connections, Russell realised, but nothing to tie them together. And they were hoping that he might inadvertently provide one. This was a fishing expedition, pure and simple.

The sense of relief lasted only a few seconds. 'We also wish to talk to you about your work for the Abwehr,' Giminich said.

Russell had the feeling he'd been ambushed. 'I would need official authorisation to discuss that,' was all he could think to say.

He needn't have bothered. 'You have to admit it's a rather strange situation – an Englishman with an American passport working for German military intelligence,' Giminich said. Leitmaritz was now just sitting back in his chair watching.

'I suppose it is,' Russell agreed. 'But it was your organisation which – I suppose "persuaded" is the most appropriate word among friends – which persuaded me to do some intelligence work for the Reich, and which then passed me over to the Abwehr. With, I might add, many thanks for my services.'

'True, but your work for the *Sicherheitsdienst* involved operations against the Soviet Union, which I presume – despite your youthful involvement in the communist movement – you now consider our common enemy. Your work for the Abwehr must involve you in business relating to England and America, enemies of the Reich but not, presumably, enemies of yours. A conflict of interest, no?'

'My work for the Abwehr does not require me to take sides.'

'How can that be?'

'I translate newspaper articles. Hopefully the clearer the idea each side has of the other's intentions and needs, the sooner we can bring this war to an end.'

Giminich snorted. 'You consider that *not* taking sides? You think that peace is what Germans are hungering for? In the end perhaps, but only after victory. A premature peace could only help our enemies.'

'I cannot see how governments misunderstanding each other helps anyone.'

'That is the Abwehr view?'

'That is my view,' Russell said, with a sudden realisation of where all this was heading.

'And these are your only duties?'

Russell paused, wondering whether fuller disclosure or clamming up might prove the wiser option. Given the effect clamming up had on such people's blood pressure, and the probability that they already knew about his meetings with Dallin, he opted for a qualified version of the former. 'I sometimes act as a courier for Admiral Canaris.'

'Ah,' Giminich said, as if they were finally getting somewhere. 'Between the Admiral and who else?'

Russell shook his head sadly. 'I'm afraid you'll have to ask him that. I'm not at liberty to share such knowledge.'

'We *are* all on the same side,' Giminich insisted.

'Even so. I would need the Admiral's permission to share such information with you.'

There was a prolonged silence behind him, as Giminich weighed up the pros and cons of applying other, more painful, forms of pressure. Or so Russell feared. The pros were obvious, the cons hard to calculate for anyone not versed in the intricacies of Heydrich's long duel with Canaris for overall control of German intelligence. Russell sincerely hoped that Giminich was not intending to use his incarceration as a declaration of war.

'Your loyalty does you credit,' Giminich said stiffly, moving out from behind the chair, and over to the window. 'Would you like to see George Welland?' he asked over his shoulder.

'Of course,' Russell said automatically, his mind scrambling in search of an explanation for this sudden turn in the conversation. George Welland was one of the younger American journalists, a New Yorker who had grown increasingly disgusted with his Nazi hosts. He had said so often and publicly, been warned, and said so again. His final crime had been to smuggle out a story about the little-known farm in Bavaria which supplied Hitler – and only Hitler – with a constant supply of fresh vegetables. Welland's American editors had compounded this folly by attaching his by-line to the printed article, and two days later the Gestapo had been waiting at the Promi doors when the journalists were let out. Welland had not been heard of since.

Russell neither knew nor liked the young man very much, but found it hard to fault his choice of enemies.

'He's in the basement,' Giminich said – a simple enough statement, but one which did little for Russell's peace of mind. The last time he had been down there was in the summer of 1939, and on that occasion he had been visiting Effi. Then too, someone upstairs had been trying to make a point.

A Rottenführer was summoned to take him down, carpet giving way to stone as they burrowed deeper. The final corridor had not changed in two years and Welland, it transpired, was locked in Effi's old cell. Hardly a coincidence, Russell guessed.

The young American was sitting on a wooden bunk. One eye was a mess of dried blood but there were no other obvious bruises. He didn't seem surprised to see Russell, and the look he gave him with the one good eye seemed more resentful than relieved. He offered a hand to shake, without getting up. Even lifting the arm made him wince.

'How are you doing?' Russell asked unnecessarily.

'Not well,' Welland said shortly.

'I can see that. Look, I was upstairs, and they asked if I wanted to see you, so of course I said yes. The Gestapo have refused to give out any information since they arrested you. The Consulate's been trying to kick up a fuss, but they couldn't even find out where you were being held. Have you been here the whole time?

'Yes, I must have been.' He massaged his forehead with his fingers. 'They take me up every day for questioning. Sometimes twice a day. Hours and hours of it.'

'What do they think you know?'

Welland's laugh was utterly devoid of humour. 'They don't think I know anything. The interrogations, the beatings – they don't have any purpose. They're just for fun.'

Russell knew why he'd been offered this meeting , but what did it mean for Welland? They would assume that Russell would report the prisoner's condition to the Consulate, that there would be more and bigger protests. Was war between the two countries so close that they no longer cared? 'I'll let the Consulate know where you are,' he said. 'Are there any personal messages you want to send?' he asked.

'My father, back in the States.'

Russell took it his notebook. 'What's his address? What shall I tell him?'

'That I'm alive. That I love him.'

'And the address?'

Welland told him, stretching out the words in such a way that Brooklyn sounded like another planet.

After writing it all down, Russell looked up to find tears streaming down the young man's cheeks. 'They'll let you go soon,' he offered. 'They've made their point.'

'You think so?' Welland retorted bitterly.

Russell had rarely felt so helpless. He reached across and put a hand on the young man's shoulder. 'We'll get you out of here,' he promised, but the hollowness of his words was reflected in the other's despairing expression.

'You'd better be quick,' Welland replied. He was still crying, and once the cell door had closed behind him Russell heard the young American begin to sob. The sound stayed with him as he walked up the stairs, and it was a struggle to keep his anger under control.

Giminich was no longer there – his point made, he had left Leitmaritz to close out the demonstration.

'You may tell the American Consulate that espionage charges are being prepared against Herr Welland,' the Hauptsturmführer said. 'It does not pay to abuse the hospitality of the Reich,' he added with a pointed stare at Russell. 'Now you may go.'

On his way back down to the main entrance, Russell tried to make sense of what had just happened. The visit to Welland had obviously been arranged to scare him, but to what end? Had all the stuff about Zembski and his communist past only been used to put him off guard, make him nervous? It was much more likely, he realised, that the Zembski business had brought his name to someone's attention, and that that someone had looked through his file and seen the possibility of using him against Canaris. If that was indeed what had happened, then going down to Neukölln in search of Zembski had been a serious mistake. Serving time as a cat's-paw of competing Nazi intelligence services was no one's idea of a good time.

Outside it was raining again, more heavily this time, and Russell had neglected to bring an umbrella. His greatest need, though, was for a drink, and these days the most reliable sources of alcohol were the two foreign press clubs. Russell preferred the Foreign Office-sponsored club in the old Anglo-German Society building on Fasanenstrasse, but that was only a short walk from Effi's flat in the West End. The Propaganda Ministry version, by contrast, was just around the corner from the Gestapo, in the former Bleichröder Palace on Leipziger Platz.

Arriving drenched, he left a message – 'still free' – at the studio number Effi had given him, then called Dallin at the Consulate. He passed on Welland's location, described his poor condition, and reported Leitmaritz's message. None of it seemed to interest the American very much. Either Dallin had too much else on his mind or Welland had pissed off his own Consulate almost as much as he'd pissed off the Nazis.

Duty done, Russell headed for the bar. This was closed, but he managed to persuade one of Goebbels' minions that his future good health depended on an immediate brandy, and the heating in the club rooms soon dried him out. With no other journalists around, he had his pick of the foreign newspapers, and spent a couple of hours wading through them. Their assessments of Germany's military prospects were generally less rosy than those of the Nazi press, but the difference was much less dramatic than Russell had hoped for. It seemed as if everything, and particularly Moscow, was still up for grabs.

The rain was beating against the windows, trams splashing their way through one large puddle in the corner of Leipziger Platz. He would give

Ribbentrop's press conference a miss, he thought, and lunch where he was. There was plenty of paper, and it was time he produced some copy. He decided to take the official German briefings as gospel, and share his hosts' belief that the capture of Moscow was imminent. Who knew – it might get the Americans off their backsides.

After writing a first draft he brooded awhile on what Giminich might be planning, before abruptly deciding that second-guessing Obersturmbannführers was only likely to make one anxious. Once Ribbentrop's press conference was over the Press Club would rapidly fill with correspondents in search of lunch, and with pleasant odours already drifting up from the kitchens, he headed for the dining-room. A couple of Ministry officials were already there, sitting at different tables with nothing in front of them, waiting for conversations to influence or report on. Goebbels was a thorough bastard in both meanings of the phrase.

Welland's other colleagues received the news of his sighting with resigned shrugs. There was nothing any of them could do to help him, or anyone else foolish or unfortunate enough to end up in the basements of the Gestapo.

Effi sat on the sofa in Ansgar Marssolek's enormous office, watching the producer rummage through an overfull in-tray for whatever it was he was looking for. Outside it was raining in earnest, lakes forming in the empty car lot and torrents gushing from the down-pipes on either end of the sound stage opposite. Two actors in eighteenth-century costume were leaning on either jamb of an open doorway, both smoking cigarettes and staring out mournfully.

She had known of Marssolek for a long time, but had never met him before. Before the Nazis seized their industry by the throat, he had been known as a producer of interesting films, but these days, reduced like the rest of them to the effective status of a state employee, he was best known as one of Goebbels' more reliable disciples. He could be relied upon to get a film made, on time and on message.

'Have you worked with Karl Lautmann?' he asked, still searching, glasses perched precariously on the end of his nose.

'Yes. I did *Mother* with him a couple of years ago.'

'Of course. I remember now. That must be why he wants you.'

'For what?'

'Ah, here it is,' Marssolek exclaimed, gingerly extracting a script from a teetering pile. 'The working title is "Betrayal", but we need something better.' He came out from behind his desk and joined her on the sofa, the script resting across his thighs. 'My dear, there's one I thing I have to tell you before we proceed. And this comes from the Minister Goebbels himself. Given the nature of this particular role, you are under no professional obligation to accept it.'

A child-molester was her first thought.

'We want you to play a Jewess,' Marssolek said apologetically.

She paused before replying. 'Why me?'

'Well, there are two reasons. Forgive me, my dear, but you have the right skin tone and hair colour. And it has to be admitted that some Jewesses are, like you, exceptionally beautiful. Secondly, you are a wonderful actress, and this will be a very difficult part to play. One that has to be performed just right. And Lautmann is convinced you could do it justice.'

She felt both repelled and intrigued. 'Tell me the story.'

'It's still in the formative stage – you have *GPU* to do first, and this other film won't start shooting until at least February. Yours is one of the two central characters – your husband will be the other, and he hasn't been cast yet. He's an SS Standartenführer. The film begins with the two of you meeting. You are beautiful and full of life, and neither he nor the audience has any idea that you're Jewish. He takes to you immediately, and so do his friends. You seduce him – though it doesn't become clear until later how manipulative you have been – and get pregnant. He almost begs you to marry him, and the child is born. The years go by – the film starts in 1933, by the way – and you're enjoying the high life to the full, in fact rather too much for his taste, but he's still willing to forgive you almost anything. He dotes on his son, or at least wants to – there's something wrong there, but the only reason he can think of is that he's away so much on the Führer's business, preparing for the war in the East. In the meantime you use his absences to conduct affairs with other men. And then, out of the blue, someone from your past turns up, a Jew who demands money for not exposing you. Twice you get the money from your husband, telling him it's for other things, but on the third occasion he refuses, suspecting, wrongly as it turns out, that you're having an affair. The Jew then goes to him, tells him he's married to a Jewess and has a *mischling* son, and demands money for not disgracing him. Your husband gives him the money, and of course realises what's been happening. The whole history of your relationship suddenly makes sense – the distance he feels from his son, your inveterate flirting and love of material things. The writers haven't decided how it ends. You'll have to die, of course. Either the husband will kill you in a fit of rage, or you'll die in a suitably appropriate accident.'

Effi was almost lost for words. 'What happens to the *mischling* child?'

'The writers haven't decided, but they're leaning towards killing him in the same accident.'

Effi raised one hand, fingers splayed. 'I can't do a film like this,' she almost shouted.

He was all sympathy. 'I understand. As I said at the beginning – you don't have to take this part. We do appreciate how risky it would be for you.'

Risky? Oh God, she thought, he was worried that playing the part would damage her career, that the great German public would see her as a Jew, and assume she really was one. What greater sacrifice could anyone make for their art?

She placed a hand over his. 'I'm sorry,' she said. 'I know I must think of the wider picture. Of my country. Let me have some time to think this through.'

'Of course, my dear,' Marssolek agreed. 'But I do hope you will do it.'

Russell finished his article around four. With an hour and a half to wait before the afternoon press conference at Promi, another visit to the bar seemed in order.

It was crowded with correspondents who had made the same calculation, and there was only one available seat – opposite Patrick Sullivan at one of the tables for two. Russell hesitated, but decided what the hell – of all the American nationals who staffed Goebbels' USA Zone, Sullivan was probably the least offensive.

Since long before the war Radio Berlin had been broadcasting Goebbels' messages across the world from its transmitter at Zeesen, some thirty kilometres south of the city. The stars of the 'USA Zone' were the small collection of American nationals who provided their countrymen and women across the Atlantic with a German's-eye view of the world. At present, if Russell remembered correctly, there were six of them, four men and two women. He knew them all by sight, but like all the real American correspondents – and most of the neutrals – he avoided them whenever possible. All but Sullivan were Americans of German ancestry, and their betrayal, if that was indeed what their activities amounted to, seemed at least understandable. But listening, as he occasionally did, to their broadcasts, Russell felt an instinctive revulsion. They made the obvious points – why, for example, should Americans join sides with the oppressive British Empire against a Germany merely seeking its own rightful place in the world? – but that was about all. Their arguments were usually glib, their humour always cheap, their eagerness to jump on Hitler's anti-Semitic bandwagon downright inexcusable.

Sullivan was different. His ancestry was Irish-American, but his support for the Nazis had little or nothing to do with any traditional Irish hatred of the English. His hate figure was Franklin Delano Roosevelt, whom he saw as the father of the appalling socialist New Deal, and whom he considered an inveterate warmonger. Sullivan saw himself as an ally of those great Americans – men like Henry Ford, J. Edgar Hoover and

Charles Lindbergh – who were desperate to keep their country out of the war, particularly now that Germany was doing civilisation's work in the East, subduing the Bolshevik monster.

He had been a small-time Hollywood actor in his twenties and a pulp novelist in his thirties, but despite his lack of journalistic training he had a good eye for a story. He had a regular Saturday spot which he filled with word-pictures of ordinary German life that stressed how well everything was going. The last time Russell had listened to him, Sullivan had been telling Americans how good the food still was in Berlin, and how useful his cigarette ration could be when it came to attracting young frauleins. But Sullivan was far from stupid, and Russell found himself wondering whether he was beginning to have second thoughts about tying his future to the Nazi cause.

Sullivan, as he soon discovered, was more than a little drunk. Though well into middle-age, with thin brown hair greying and receding at the temples, he still conveyed an impression of substance. The pugnacious jaw looked ready for a fight; the restlessly intelligent eyes seemed more than capable of choosing the right opponents. On the last few occasions that they had met, Sullivan had been particularly friendly, and Russell had wondered whether his work for the Abwehr had somehow reached the American's ears. On this occasion too Sullivan's eyes lit up at his approach, and not for the first time Russell found himself wondering about his own post-war reputation. In reality, he had done nothing to help Nazi Germany and several things to impede it, but the number of people who could actually testify to that fact were decidedly thin on the ground. If all of them dropped dead before the war's end he would have some difficult explaining to do.

'How's it going, comrade?' Sullivan asked as he sat down.

'Not so bad. And you?'

'Fine, fine,' he said distractedly, as the waiter loomed over them. 'What can I get you?'

'Whatever beer they have.'

'Okay. And another whisky for me,' he told the waiter. 'Who knows when they'll get another shipment?' he confided to Russell.

'Maybe the war will be over in the New Year,' Russell suggested. 'Moscow before Christmas, a surrender in January?'

Sullivan didn't look convinced. 'Maybe. We can only hope.' He leaned forward. 'Should have been there already, if the truth were known. Those idiots in Rosenberg's department have buggered the whole thing up. If they'd marched in and set up an independent Ukraine straight away... well, it would all have been over weeks ago. Such a wasted opportunity.'

'It's not irretrievable, is it?'

'I don't know, old man. If Roosevelt can buy enough support in Congress to bring us in...'

'If the Japs give him a good excuse he won't need to buy anyone off.'

'That is true, very true. But joining the war will be such a mistake. For America, for Germany, for everyone. The Soviets will be the only winners.'

'I expect Ribbentrop's pestering the Japs.'

'Yes, but to what end? The man's a complete fool – everyone knows that. Everyone but Hitler, apparently.'

Russell wondered how close they were sitting to a minion or a microphone, but didn't suppose it would matter. Goebbels would be delighted with Sullivan's description of his arch-enemy Ribbentrop. 'You think Ribbentrop might be encouraging the Japs to attack the Americans? That would be insane.'

Sullivan laughed. 'Wouldn't it? But I've heard some of his officials argue that such a move would keep the Americans off Germany's back, at least until the Russian campaign has been put to bed. The Americans will be so busy in the Pacific that they'll have to cut right back on their activities in the Atlantic, and on their support for the British and the Russians.'

'You don't buy it?'

Sullivan snorted. 'They haven't got a clue how powerful the American war economy will be. You know, before the war, everyone underestimated Hitler. Now it's the other way round.'

'You don't sound very optimistic.'

'I'm not.'

'So why do you carry on working for them?'

Sullivan smiled. 'A good question,' he almost whispered.

There was no sign of Goebbels at the Ministry of Propaganda, a sure sign that there was no real news. As usual, the overall tone of the press conference was friendlier than at the Foreign Ministry equivalent, but the answers offered to questions were no less vacuous for being politely put. There had been no fresh news from the Moscow Front for several days, Russell realised, which had to mean something. Were the Germans stuck? Had the Russians even managed to push them back? Or were the Germans still advancing? Russell wouldn't put it past Goebbels to store up a few days of small advances and add them all together for dramatic effect.

After wiring off his article he headed for the tram stop on Leipziger Strasse. The rain had finally stopped, but clouds still wreathed the city and the blackout was intense. The first tram was full to bursting, the second even fuller, and Russell decided that walking would be less stressful. In any case, he needed time to think, something he always did better in motion.

Sullivan's hint that he might turn on his masters had been interesting. Would those masters just wish him well – 'Here's your final pay cheque, see you after the war' – or would they get nasty? Russell suspected the latter, and Sullivan was bright enough not to expect any help from the US Consulate. Even if the Nazis surprised themselves and everyone else, he could hardly expect prodigal son treatment from the administration in Washington that he'd been paid to vilify. Refusal would be risky.

It usually was. Russell had hoped that Knieriem moving or dying would save him, at least temporarily, from saying no to Dallin, but some people were born selfish. He certainly had no intention of saying yes. Since his tête-à-tête with Giminich and his Gestapo stooge that morning, the idea of visiting anyone with the slightest connection to the German war effort was the last thing on his mind. The Americans would just have to whistle for their bomber intelligence. If the choice was between saying no to them and yes to a concentration camp, not much thought was required.

The Americans might even take no for an answer, which was more than he could say for the Germans. Giminich hadn't yet asked him for anything, but Russell had little doubt that he would. It was beginning to look as if an early American entry into the war, and an indefinite period of fraught internment, was the best of several poor futures staring him in the face. In that event the peculiar mix of national and political loyalties which had made him attractive to so many intelligence services would no longer be relevant – he would just be one more enemy alien, and proud of it.

But how many years would it be before he saw Effi and Paul again? If he ever did. People died in wars, civilians included. And if the British could drive Berliners to their shelters on a regular basis, imagine what the Yanks could do.

Effi was waiting for him, intent on eating out. 'We should celebrate your escape from the Gestapo's clutches,' she said, regretting her levity the moment she saw his expression. 'I'm sorry; was it bad?'

'No, not really.' He saw no reason to bring up Welland. 'Just another reminder of how thin the ice is. Where do you want to eat?'

'Let's try the Chinese. They're better at drowning out the taste of chemicals.'

'You're right. Let's go.'

As they walked down Uhlandstrasse he gave her a brief account of his interrogation that morning. She listened in silence, struck as usual by his knack for ordering information. 'They'll be back, won't they?' she said when he had finished.

'I'd be amazed if they weren't.'

On the Ku'damm a surprising number of people were out enjoying the newly clear sky, their phosphorescent badges reflecting in the still-wet pavements. Away to the west the yellow glow of a rising moon was silhouetting the stark lines of the Memorial Church.

The Chinese restaurant was fuller than usual, but a table was quickly found for such old and regular customers. There was nothing to drink but tea, and for once that seemed enough. Looking round, remembering the many times they had eaten there, with each other, with relatives and friends, Russell felt his spirits rising. In eight years together they had shared so much personal history – enough, surely, to carry them through the separation that the war was about to impose.

'Guess what part I got offered today?' Effi asked him.

'Magda Goebbels?'

'A manipulative Jewess married to an SS Captain.'

'Does he know she's Jewish?'

'Oh no.'

'Did you accept it?'

'Not yet. My first instinct was to brain the producer with the script. Or something heavier. But you, my darling, have taught me that every now and then – once in a very blue moon – it actually pays to think before opening one's mouth.'

'Is that what I've been teaching you?'

'Amongst other bad habits. And it seemed to me that this might be one of those times. Because the first thing that occurred to me was that if I didn't do the wretched film then someone else would, someone who wouldn't have my interest in sabotaging the whole disgusting project.'

Russell was unconvinced. 'Can a storyline like that be sabotaged? I mean, I know you could give this woman different layers of feeling and motivation, but in films like that doesn't the message come through in what happens, rather than in what the people are feeling?'

'Maybe. That's what I want to think about.'

'Okay, but I don't want to think that I've given birth to a monster. You, my darling, have taught me that every now and then – in fact, much of the time – it pays to go with your first instinct.'

'Have I really?' She placed a hand on one of his. 'We must be the best-balanced couple in Berlin by now.'

'Other than Magda and Joey.'

'Wash your mouth out.'

Aces low

The noon press conference at the Foreign Ministry saw Paul Schmidt replace his underling von Stumm, and Russell's first glimpse of the fat young Prussian as he made his confident entrance was enough to tell him that something bad had happened. Schmidt wasted no time in telling the assembled press corps what that was: Rostov – 'the gateway to the Caucasus' – had fallen to the Wehrmacht. A collective sigh was audible, the appreciation of Germany's allies mingled with the scarcely-concealed despair of the supposed neutrals. For the Caucasus, as Schmidt delighted in explaining at length, contained enough oil to keep the panzers and Stukas in almost perpetual motion. It was, he said, a crucial step on the road to inevitable victory.

The allied journalists wanted more tales of triumph, but Schmidt was more interested in goading the neutrals. Perhaps the warmonger Roosevelt would think twice about dragging his countrymen into a war that few of them wanted; perhaps even Churchill might stop preening himself for a few hours, and acknowledge that Britain's position grew more hopeless by the day. Questioned about British claims that their new offensive in North Africa was going well, Schmidt offered a disdainful smile and a smug invitation to wait and see. One side was clearly kidding itself, and Russell had a sinking feeling it might be his own.

After the conference he walked up to the Adlon, expecting to find a message from Ströhm confirming the arrival of Monday's train at Lodz. The lack of one was probably insignificant, but added to Russell's sense of frustration. Lying in bed the previous night it had suddenly occurred to him that Ströhm, with his presumed KPD connections, might know what had happened to Zembski. But Russell had no way of contacting the man. He would have to wait for Ströhm's next call, which added a somewhat sinister note – that the corollary of setting his own mind at rest was the dispatch of another trainload of Berlin's Jews into the dark unknown.

Effi met her older sister Zarah for lunch at Wertheim's, or Awags as it was now officially called. The restaurant was quite full, but the clientele had not been attracted by the quality of the food, which seemed noticeably worse than on their previous visit in October. The department store, as Zarah had already discovered, was in no better shape – half the cage-lifts were permanently out of order and there was absolutely nothing worth buying.

Over the last year or so, Effi's relationship with her sister had become increasingly constrained. Once her son Lothar had started school Zarah had found herself with a lot of time on her hands, and little idea of how to use it in an increasingly austere Berlin. Her husband, Jens, seemed to spend most of his waking hours working at the Economic Ministry, and those that remained poring over his coin collection. He was almost always in a bad mood, which enraged Zarah. What did he have to be depressed about? – he had something worthwhile to do. And, whenever Effi tried to describe how she felt about making films for Goebbels' propaganda machine, she received short shrift from her older sister. What was Effi, a film star for heaven's sake, complaining about? She had a wonderful career and a man that she loved who spent time with her; how much better could it get?

Effi, for her part, felt bad that she could no longer confide in Zarah. Before the war they had told each other everything, had in fact been more honest with each other than they were with their respective partners. But all that had ended for Effi when she and Russell had decided on resistance. A safe-as-they-could-make-it kind of resistance, admittedly, but beyond anything that Zarah would understand or want to share. She had never been interested in politics, and Jens, though a decent husband and a doting father, was also a long-time Party member with an important job in the Nazi administrative machine. The things that kept Effi awake at nights were no longer things she could share with her sister, and these days their conversations revolved around less essential topics – Lothar's progress at school, their aging parents, the latest shortages, the movies that Zarah saw in her thrice-weekly trips to the cinema.

This particular meeting was no different. Lothar was loving school, their mother was already worrying about Christmas, the dentist down Zarah's street had started using aluminium for fillings. How was Jens? She hardly ever saw him, and when she did his mind was somewhere else. This war was having a terrible effect on family life.

Effi loved Zarah, but sometimes she wanted to shake her.

As he wiled away the hours in a Press Club armchair waiting for the Promi briefing, Russell overheard one of his colleagues offering long odds on them all still being around at Christmas. The man was probably right, he thought. If he was going to get presents for his son, then now was the time to do it. Christmas shopping, moreover, seemed a much better use of his time than listening to Goebbels gloat over the capture of Rostov.

In pre-war days Paul's favourite toyshop had been Schilling's on Friedrichstrasse, just beyond the station. Last time they had visited the spacious emporium – just before his son's birthday the previous March – the shelves had been almost empty, but Russell could think of nowhere better to try.

A tram got him there just before closing time, but he was soon wondering why the shop had bothered to open. The only items suitable for boys of Paul's age were cheaply-made board games with names like 'Bombs over England' and 'Panzers to Moscow.' The Third Reich might be short of most things, but cardboard was obviously plentiful.

Disappointed, Russell walked back under the bridge and climbed the stairs to the elevated platforms. With no toys, no meat and precious little alcohol, a merry Christmas seemed somewhat unlikely, although Goebbels' hacks had done their best to evoke the true Christmas spirit, re-writing 'Silent Night' as a paean to the Führer. *He* would be standing guard over them all. *He* would have no time for fun.

The Stadtbahn train rattled in over the bridge, full of rush-hour passengers and smelling as bad as usual. Russell clung to a strap as it crossed and re-crossed the wintry-looking Spree, and wondered whether Effi would be there when he got home. Stepping out onto the platform at Zoo Station, the first thing he noticed was the sound of barking dogs.

There were two of them, both Alsatians, slavering and straining at their leashes. Two young *Ordnungspolizei* – Orpo, as they were universally known – were pulling on the other ends, and looking round nervously for further instruction. The leather coats were clearly in charge, and three of them were half dragging, half kicking, a young man out of the next carriage. One of the Gestapo men wrenched the youth's coat open, and a large number of leaflets cascaded down onto the platform.

Treason, Russell thought. Punishable, like so many things in the Third Reich, by death.

The youth was a head shorter than his captors, with tousled blond hair and gold-rimmed glasses. He looked like he belonged in a Grunewald academy for the sons of the privileged. He was no more than seventeen.

The train pulled out. Most of the alighting passengers had disappeared down the stairs, but some, like Russell, were finding it harder to tear themselves away. One leather coat tried an intimidatory stare, and several Reichsbahn officials made coaxing motions towards the exit, but all to little effect. Across the tracks, a large crowd of waiting passengers watched from the other local platform.

The young man shrugged himself free of the one man still holding him. In lunging to refasten his grip, the Gestapo man lost his footing and went down heavily on his back, evoking several cheers from the audience on the opposite platform.

This was too much to bear. As his colleague grabbed the boy, the leather coat pulled a gun from his coat pocket and crashed it into the side of the boy's face. Russell expected the young man to go down, but he was wrong. The boy staggered, but then hurled himself at his attacker, pulling him to the ground. After a second's hesitation, the other two leather coats joined the fray, kicking and punching like men possessed, while the Orpo men just stood there, unable to release their hysterical dogs for fear that they might shred the wrong victim.

Barely a minute or so later, the three Gestapo men were back on their feet, breathing heavily. The young man lay still on the ground, his glasses a few feet away. They looked broken, but just to make sure one of the leather coats ground them under his shoe.

There were no cheers now, only an accusing silence.

A Gestapo man said something to the Orpo officers, who both shrugged their shoulders at him. Russell guessed they had been asked to carry the victim down and were pointing out that someone had to hold the still-slavering dogs. Acting as bearers was obviously beneath the dignity of the Gestapo, who began scanning the platform for likely 'volunteers'.

The young man must have heard it before Russell, the sudden shift of his spread-eagled body anticipating the sounds of the approaching train by a few seconds. As Russell turned to look, it passed the end of the platform, the locomotive steaming furiously, the line of laden flat-cars still snaking round the curve above Kantstrasse. Turning back, he found the youth already in motion, running, half stumbling, away from the screaming Gestapo.

Oh no, Russell thought.

The young man ran diagonally across the platform and launched himself into the face of the oncoming locomotive. A silent flurry of limbs, a splash of crimson, and he was gone.

The locomotive thundered by, the unknowing driver on the other side of the cab. The long line of flat-cars rattled through, their draped loads bound for the East and other, less accidental, encounters with death.

The platform was full of stunned faces. Even the dogs seemed shocked.

As the train cleared the platform, Russell found himself drawn to the edge. A headless body was lying between the rails about twenty metres on from where the youth had jumped. The head was nowhere to be seen.

The dogs were whining now, the three leather coats staring down at the mutilated corpse. Even they seemed subdued by the turn of events. Russell was probably imagining it, but their expressions seemed those of children, up early on a Christmas morning, who had just broken a much-anticipated toy.

He turned on his heel and made for the stairway. Half-way down he found one of the leaflets the youth had been distributing. 'In whose name?' was the headline; that of the German people, the text insisted, had been taken in vain.

Too true, Russell thought. But who gave a Führer's fuck for the wishes of the German people?

Back home that evening, Russell listened as Effi recounted her depressing lunch with Zarah, and decided against making things worse by sharing his experience at Zoo Station. Thinking the BBC might raise their spirits, they risked a joint listening session, seats pulled up close beside the wireless. But for once the Oxbridge-vowelled spokesman sounded strangely unsure of himself. They scoured the German wavelengths for some cheerful music, but all they could find were variations of central European gloom. The idea of going out was swiftly abandoned when the rain began beating on the blacked-out windows.

'A day to forget,' Effi said, as they settled for an early night.

Which was easier said than done. As Russell lay there unable to sleep, the train thundered on in his mind.

Next morning at ten, they met Paul at the main entrance to the Friedrichstrasse Station. Since his fourteenth birthday that March, Russell's son had been allowed to navigate his own way across Berlin, and the novelty had obviously not worn off – he clattered down the stairs from the elevated platforms in his *Hitlerjugend* uniform, looking very pleased with himself. Noticing how happy his son was to see Effi, Russell congratulated himself on overcoming her objections to attending. 'Why would I want to stand in the rain for God knows how many hours just to watch some dead Nazi roll by on a flag-covered cart?' had been her first reaction to his suggestion.

The actual ceremony was a bigwigs-only affair – the Führer had apparently arrived overnight from his eastern military headquarters – but thousands of Berliners were thronging the streets, heading for vantage points on the route of the procession. The rain had finally moved on, and the sky in the west showed definite signs of brightening. The wind remained brisk, lifting and shaking the legions of swastikas that flew at half-mast from poles, roofs and facades.

'I thought the Marschall Bridge,' Russell suggested to Paul.

'Good idea,' his son agreed, with the sort of smile that Effi imagined she used on Zarah. Perhaps her sister had a point about families and war.

They walked along the front of the station, crossed over the river, and continued down past the Electricity Works to the Marschall Bridge. A lot of people had had the same idea, but the three of them found a good vantage point on the downstream side, up against one of the parapets.

'The service should be over by now,' Russell said, looking at his watch. The crowd around them was growing by the minute – soldiers, sailors and airmen on leave, bureaucrats in suits and secretaries in high heels, lots of mothers with children, a large sprinkling of older men wearing their Great War medals.

'There are lots of people, aren't there?' Paul said. 'People must have known how good he was.'

'I'm sure they did,' Russell agreed.

He might just as well have disagreed, Effi thought, watching Paul's face. She understood what Russell had meant when he begged her to come. The boy did seem to be looking for a fight, although whether or not he was aware of it was another matter. 'I hear you've been getting yourself into trouble,' she said lightly.

He shrugged. 'Not really.'

'Well, I know how easy it is. I got arrested for making a joke, remember? And I've been really careful ever since.'

'I'll be careful.'

'Promise?' Russell asked playfully.

'Didn't I just say so?'

'Yes...'

'They're coming,' Effi said, hoping that Udet's funeral procession was indeed responsible for the signs of movement on the distant Wilhelmstrasse.

It was. A few moments later a snatch of music arrived on a momentary change of the wind; a few minutes more and the strains of the funeral march were clearly audible. It grew louder as the small object in the distance slowly grew into a gun-carriage with a swastika-draped coffin, flanked by an honour guard, followed by rank after rank of men in Luftwaffe uniform. As the carriage crossed onto the bridge, the hands in the crowd swept up in the familiar salute, Paul's among them. After only a moment's hesitation Effi followed suit, but Russell resisted. He was English, he told himself, and therefore excused.

His son thought differently. 'The England football team gave the salute,' he almost hissed at his father.

Russell raised his arm, feeling more foolish than for many a year. Paul gave him one last reproachful look, and turned back to the procession. Another famous pilot, Adolf Galland, was one of the honour guard, but Russell didn't recognise any of the others. On the other hand the fat man padding along behind the gun-carriage was easy to identify – the *Reichsmarschall*, resplendent in red-brown boots and gold-braided pale grey uniform. Goering was already breathing heavily, and Russell wondered whether he'd make it to the Invalidenfriedhof cemetery. He wasn't yet halfway.

The top-ranking Luftwaffe officers marched behind him, along with all those pilots who had won the Knight's Cross. 'There's Walter Oesau,' Paul whispered excitedly, more to himself than any audience. 'And Hans Hahn. And there's Gunther Lützow! But where's Mölders?'

Where was Germany's other famous ace? Russell wondered. His shoulder was beginning to ache, and now that the bigwigs had gone past most people were lowering theirs. Russell happily followed suit. But Paul held his aloft for several minutes more, waiting until the gun carriage had disappeared under the Stadtbahn bridge and the crowd had slowly begun to disperse.

By the time they'd had lunch and – at Paul's suggestion – revisited the stamp exhibition at the Central Library, it was time for Russell to head off for the afternoon press conference. Effi suggested to Paul that the two of them walk back across the Tiergarten to Zoo Station, and Russell stood for a few seconds on the corner of Wilhelmstrasse and Unter den Linden watching them head off towards the park, hoping that she would come back with a clearer idea of what exactly was eating at his son.

The press conference was getting underway as the door guards checked his credentials, and he could already feel the triumphalist mood as he climbed the marble stairway to the main auditorium. Goebbels was holding forth in his usual manner, suave, persuasive, never far from a cynical smile. *Taifun*, the attack on Moscow, had apparently been resumed, and with startling success. Curtains parted with a theatrical flourish to reveal the latest positions, and the assembled journalists all leaned forward to make them out. A host of arrows were closing on the fortress towns of Klin, Istra and Tula, the lynchpins of Moscow's final ring of defences. According to the map the latest attacks had seen the Army advance a third of the remaining distance to the Soviet capital.

'In how many days?' someone wanted to know.

'Five,' was the reply, the implication clear – another ten and Moscow would be taken.

A stillness pervaded the room, and Goebbels' lips twitched in a knowing half-smile. Over the next ten minutes he answered questions calmly, wittily, with what seemed palpable frankness. What reason to lie or exaggerate, his smile seemed to say, when the truth was such good news?

Only once did the smile disappear. Like Paul, Ralph Morrison had noticed Werner Mölders's absence from Udet's honour guard, and his request for an explanation was, Russell guessed, only intended as a minor spoke in Goebbels' free-running wheels. If so, he got more than he intended.

'An official announcement has not yet been released,' the Propaganda Minister said gravely, 'but Oberst Mölders was killed earlier today in a flying accident. In Breslau, on his way to today's funeral. I have no other details at present.'

The room seemed stunned. Mölders had been one of Nazi Germany's more acceptable heroes, and there was something ridiculously sad about dying on the way to someone else's funeral. Another dead man on his son's wall, Russell thought. Poor Paul.

Later that evening, Effi sat at a beautifully-laid dining table in the most exclusive district of Grunewald, sipping the best wine she had tasted in several months, listening to her host and a fellow dinner guest enthuse over the latest cinema attendance figures. As a celebrity of sorts, she had rarely lacked for such invitations, but in pre-war times she had politely refused ninety-five per cent of them, and took John with her when she chose to accept. Once the war began, however, she and John had realised how much secret information could be leeched from such gatherings of the rich and influential, and those percentages had been reversed. So, since his presence, as a foreigner and journalist, tended to inhibit her companions, she almost always went alone. Effi had no intention of selling her body for secrets, but flattery and flirting were something else again.

This particular evening, she had realised on meeting her fellow guests, was unlikely to provide anything more than a good meal. Her hosts were Max and Christiane Weinart, he a personal friend of Goebbels and leading shareholder in the Babelsberg studio, she an ex-starlet who had caught her future husband's attention in a film extolling the joys of physical exercise. The other five guests were the camera manufacturer Alfred Hoyer and his wife Anna, two hotshots from the Ministry of Propaganda named Stefan and Heinrich, and a blonde young actress whom she had never met, Ute Fahrian. Effi guessed that Weinart and the Hoyers were in their mid-fifties, Ute in her mid-twenties, and everyone else in or around their thirties. She hoped the food would make up for the conversation, which had turned to the growing problems of actually getting films made. Promi, conscious of rising attendances and the opportunity they represented, had set a target of a hundred a year, but this year, as last, it was unlikely to be met.

The first of several courses arrived, and over the next hour Effi concentrated on the food, speaking only when spoken to. There were vegetables other than potatoes to be eaten, and they hadn't been boiled or fried in chemicals. The meat, which tasted suspiciously like real beef, came with a richly succulent sauce. The bread wasn't battleship grey; the butter was a pale, unthreatening shade of yellow. Her fellow actress kept glancing wide-eyed round the table, as if she could hardly believe such food still existed, but the others clearly took such quality sustenance for granted. Most Berliners might be suffering from skin rashes, yellowing eyes, biliousness and appalling flatulence, but how would her fellow diners know that? They wouldn't be using the U-Bahn, their servants would be doing the shopping, and they'd all have their own private air raid shelters. As John had said the other evening – if the RAF ever worked out how to hit a military target, the war would pass the rich by.

Her anger, she realised, was in danger of spoiling her meal. She concentrated on the Black Forest gateau which had just been placed in front of her.

Still engrossed in the world of films, the men were now talking about the *Die Grosse Liebe*, and the political row it had unleashed. The movie starred Viktor Staal and Zarah Leander as a Luftwaffe pilot and the woman he meets and sleeps with while on leave. Some people at Promi had apparently considered this theme a little too daring for public consumption, and senior Luftwaffe figures had condemned Staal's character as reflecting dishonour on their service. Goering, on the other hand, had reportedly asked what else a Luftwaffe officer was supposed to do on leave. Weinart, Hoyer and the two Promi men could all see his point.

Stirring her small but wonderfully fragrant cup of black coffee, Effi decided to give them something real to play with. 'I've been asked to play a Jewess,' she announced at the first convenient moment, 'and I must admit to being torn.'

Ute Fahrian let out a heartfelt 'Oh', shook her blonde curls, and said: 'I'm glad I'll never have to face that problem!' Then, as if suddenly hearing her own words, she flushed deeply. 'I'm sorry, I didn't mean…'

'Don't distress yourself, 'Effi said. 'I can hardly deny that, in outward appearance, I could pass for a Jewess.'

'Some Jewesses are very beautiful,' Alfred Hoyer said gallantly, raising an expression of faint surprise from Christiane Weinart.

'It is a dilemma,' Anna Hoyer said with the slightest of ironic smiles. She was brighter than she looked, Effi decided. And drinking more than she should.

'If we wish to make films that reflect real life in our country then we need Jewish characters,' Weinart insisted.

'And we can't have them played by real Jews,' his wife chipped in.

'Of course not,' Stefan agreed. 'If you decide to take the part,' he told Effi with a smile, 'then I suggest you give interviews explaining how hard it was for you, but how satisfying you found the experience. Emphasise how difficult it was for you, a German actress, to create a convincing Jew, but how necessary it is for the good of the Reich that the Jewish peril be realistically presented in films.'

'Yes, that sounds right,' Weinart agreed.

'Mmm,' Effi said.

'The people will admire you for your honesty,' Stephan went on, 'and thank you.'

Effi offered him a grateful smile. 'I think you may have solved my dilemma.'

'All in a day's work,' he said, giving her a slight bow. 'And it has been a wonderful day. Has everyone heard the latest news from the East?'

They had not.

'We are closing in on Moscow,' Heinrich explained. 'It should be all over in two weeks. Three at worst.'

Anna Hoyer laughed. 'Now let's not get carried away. We were told it was all over a month ago, and look what happened.'

'A mistake,' Heinrich admitted coldly, 'but an understandable one. If it hadn't been for a sudden change in the weather, it really would have been over.'

'What if the weather suddenly changes again?' Frau Hoyer wanted to know.

'That sounds perilously close to defeatism, my dear,' her husband interjected, with an apologetic look at the Promi men.

'I do think we need to be realistic,' Effi said, coming to her aid. 'Your wife is only pointing out how dangerous wishful thinking can be. And it would be terrible to suffer October's disappointment all over again.'

'I have a brother in the East,' Ute Fahrian revealed. 'He's only eighteen.'

So many of them are, Effi thought, remembering the rows of young faces in the Elisabeth Hospital.

After the press conference Russell joined most of his fellow correspondents in heading for the Press Club on Leipzigerplatz. Two black cars were parked in the rapidly darkening square, each with the traditional pair of leather-coated Gestapo officers occupying the front seats. They made no move to get out, but the expressions on their faces as they scanned the foreign journalists were almost absurdly hostile. Russell had a sudden memory of a pantomime that his parents had taken him to, somewhere in London's West End before the first war, and how much he had enjoyed hissing at the villains.

Upstairs, dinner was already being served. It was decent enough by current standards, but he toyed with the food, his mind on Paul and how much easier being a father had once seemed. An evening of reckless drinking beckoned, but he tore himself away, heading home on foot under a clear sky. It looked a great night for bombing, which probably meant that they wouldn't come.

The press conference had also depressed him. Had his feeling that the Germans had shot their bolt been over-optimistic? If Moscow and the Caucasus fell, and the Soviets were taken out of the equation, then Hitler's hold on the continent would surely be secure. Invading Britain might prove beyond him – he had given Churchill over a year to strengthen the island's defences – but invading Europe would be equally beyond his enemies. A stalemate would ensue, while each side raised new armies and developed new weapons and Hitler let his soul-dead acolytes loose on Europe's helpless: the Jews, the disabled, the Reds and the queers, anyone who deviated from Promi's ludicrous travesty of what a human being should be. Russell would get to stay with Effi and Paul, but only in the worst of futures.

He got home soon after eight. Effi would be hours yet, which gave him time to translate two technical articles from the American press which the Abwehr's Colonel Piekenbrock had given him a couple of weeks earlier. He mistranslated the occasional word when it suited him – and when the mistake was easily explainable – but usually there seemed no harm in giving the Abwehr what it wanted. These were not secrets he was dealing with.

He wasn't totally convinced that his translations were ever read. They might be commissioned, at least in part, to satisfy the German hunger for completeness, but Russell suspected that Canaris and his subordinates were simply thinking up something for him to do, something that would keep him on board, an asset-in-waiting for a situation that hadn't yet arisen. With any luck it never would, Russell thought, as he spread out the papers on the kitchen table.

An hour or so later, with one article finished and the kettle waiting to boil, he turned on the radio. The latest BBC news bulletin had just finished, so he turned the dial in search of Radio Berlin and found Patrick Sullivan's laconic voice in full flow, describing an imaginary Axis attack on the United States. The intention was to ridicule, and after a fashion it worked – U-boats carrying fleets of bombers, aircraft carriers fuelled on corn that could sail up America's rivers and navigate the Niagara Falls, a veritable 'Sixth Column'. But was Sullivan's heart really in it? It didn't sound like it to Russell, but perhaps he was reading too much into one chance remark.

He turned off the radio, made his tea and went back to work, one ear cocked for the sound of Effi's feet on the stairs.

She arrived home just before midnight, the self-satisfied purr of the studio limousine sounding unnaturally loud on the otherwise silent street. 'The food was wonderful, the company boring,' she told him, throwing her coat across the back of a chair. 'With one slight exception.' She told him about Anna Hoyer. 'I'm meeting more and more people like her – people who can see what's happening, but only ever say so when they're drunk. And they'd never dream of doing anything. It wouldn't even occur to them that they could.'

'Did you get anything out of Paul?' Russell asked.

'No, I'm afraid not. I tried, believe me, but he's not stupid. He knows that anything he says to me will get passed on to you. I told him he seemed really angry with you, and he simply denied it. More or less implied I was imagining things. He was very polite about it, of course. He just denies there's a problem.'

'Maybe I should talk to Ilse.'

'It won't help. He's punishing you – I don't think he knows what for. It's not for anything specific that you've done, I'm sure of that.'

'Is that good or bad?'

She smiled. 'Probably neither and both. Look, John, there's nothing you're doing that you could do any differently. And explaining yourself won't help – fourteen-year-olds aren't interested in motives, just in how things affect them.'

'So what can I do?'

'Nothing. Just be patient. You know he loves you.'

'Sometimes I… no, I do know, of course I do.'

'Come here.'

Enfolded in her arms, he suddenly felt on the verge of tears. Everything seemed to be cracking apart. Everything but him and her.

Later, lying awake and cradling her sleeping head, he found himself thinking about Zembski, and the thoughts that must have raced through the Silesian's mind as the Gestapo broke into his studio. He'd have known he was a dead man, and that the only decision left to him lay in the timing. Die now, and take some of the bastards with him, or in a few weeks' time, after enduring agonies of pain and betraying his comrades.

How many people could he give up himself, Russell wondered. He went through the list, arranging them in the sequence of betrayal. How many people in Germany had made such macabre calculations – hundreds? Thousands? Calculations that in all probability would be instantly forgotten in the panic of the moment.

But he would never give her up. Never.

A broken egg

First thing Monday morning, Russell took the elevated U-Bahn towards Silesian Gate on his way to visit Ilse's brother Thomas. His mood remained dark, and the panoramic spread of hospital trains stabled side by side in the yards outside Anhalter Station did nothing to lighten it. He wondered how Thomas, who took this train to work each day, and whose son Joachim was fighting in the East, coped with this daily reminder of all too possible loss.

The previous day he and Effi had tried to leave the war behind and enjoy a normal pre-war Sunday. The effort had been a dismal failure. The outdoor café where they had once shared breakfast and newspapers had been closed, the tables folded away and the terrace littered with shrapnel. The Tiergarten was sunny for once, but it was impossible to ignore the wretched monstrosity of a flak tower, which seemed to loom above them whichever way they turned. Those of their favourite restaurants which remained open displayed menus that repelled rather than enticed, and Thomas and his family, whom they often visited on Sunday afternoons, had selfishly refused to answer their telephone. Thomas, Russell eventually remembered, had said something about visiting his wife's family in Leipzig. A last-ditch tour of the cinemas on the Ku'damm hadn't helped – everything on offer from Joey's dream factory seemed designed to depress them even further. Defeated, they had eaten badly at a restaurant full of dull-eyed soldiers on leave, and gone home to the BBC's unwelcome admission that the situation in North Africa was 'still confused.'

Russell wondered what Paul Schmidt would make of the situation at the noon press conference. He had never yet heard a Nazi official admit to confusion.

He walked from the Silesian Gate U-Bahn station to the Schade factory, crossing the Landwehrkanal as a long flotilla of coal barges passed under the bridge, heading for the Spree. Turning into the factory gates, the sight of the familiar black saloons brought him to an abrupt halt. What were the Gestapo doing here? After wondering for a moment whether his arrival would make matters worse, he decided that Thomas might need some moral support.

Both cars were empty of people, but a toy wooden fortress sat somewhat incongruously on the back seat of the second. Even the Gestapo had children.

Russell walked in through the front entrance and turned left into the outer office, where two of the visitors were chatting to the young woman whom they thought was the book keeper. Russell knew better – her name was Erna, and she was one of Thomas's many nieces, recently apprenticed to the family business. The actual bookkeeper, Ali Blumenthal, would have disappeared through the door leading to the printing rooms the moment the cars appeared in her window. By this time Ali would be wearing a star-adorned overall and wielding a broom. Jews were not allowed to do clerical work.

'Who are you?' rapped out one of the men. 'And what do you want?'

'I'm the owner's brother-in-law,' Russell said. This didn't seem the moment to admit that he was no longer married to Thomas's sister.

'Well you'll have to take your turn. Sit there.'

Russell did as he was told, straining his ears to hear the conversation taking place in the inner office above the usual clatter of the presses. Thomas seemed to be doing most of the talking. 'I have explained all this to Groening,' he said with exaggerated patience. 'I cannot fill my government orders if you people keep threatening to decimate my work-force. If I were to lose all the people on this list I dread to think what my output would shrink to.'

A softer voice interjected, one that Russell could not quite decipher. The one word he recognised was *juden*, and only because it was repeated several times.

'That's nonsense,' Thomas replied, raising his voice a little. 'The Jews I employ are treated as they should be. They have separate toilets and washrooms, and they work the sort of hours which such people should work. You and I could argue for hours about how these particular Jews managed to make themselves essential to the running of this business, but that would not make the slightest difference to the fact that they are. Once the war is won, and I am not up to my ears in urgent government contracts, I will happily take them down to the station and load them on a train for the East myself. But until that day comes…'

The Gestapo man was not convinced. The Reichsminister had decreed that Berlin should become *judenfrei*, and the process was now underway. It was irreversible. If one factory owner was granted exemptions, they would all want them, and nothing would be achieved. Herr Schade would simply have to find other workers. He would have no trouble getting hold of Russian prisoners, and they could learn anything that Jews could learn.

'If you persist with this nonsense,' Thomas told him, 'I shall have to take the matter up with Gruppenführer Wohlauf.'

This name induced a few moments' silence, and even pricked the ears of the two Gestapo men in the outer office. When their superior in the next room resumed talking it was in a quieter, more conciliatory tone. Russell was impressed. He knew that Thomas had been deliberately widening his circle of influential acquaintances, but Wohlauf was one of Heydrich's protégés, and hardly a name to be taken in vain.

Two Gestapo officers emerged, the older one thin with glasses and a pale angry face, the younger one plumpish and harassed-looking. The former gave Russell a passing glare, and half paused in his stride, as if the need for a scapegoat had been both recognised and deferred in a few split seconds. All four of them passed out through the door, and seconds later the engines of their two cars burst into simultaneous life.

Russell walked into the inner office, and found Thomas at the window, a fist massaging his left temple.

'Wohlauf?' Russell asked with mock incredulity.

Thomas gave him a wry smile. 'Would you believe I had dinner with him and his wife last week? Lotte is in the same *Bund Deutscher Mädel* group as his older daughter, and she found out a few months ago that Papa has a passion for sailing. I eventually dug up a mutual acquaintance and engineered a chance meeting. We may be going up to Rugen Island together in the spring.'

'The sacrifices we make.'

'He's not such a bad chap really. Well, he is; but for a Gruppenführer in the SD he doesn't come across too badly. There's none of the usual obsession with Jews – he seems to despise all races more or less equally.'

'Will he play ball if you need him to?'

'God knows. I hope I don't have to ask.'

'What was it about this time?'

'A list of our Jewish workers for deportation. You know some of them live on the premises? Eleven single men, all over fifty. They were thrown out of their apartments in Wedding and Moabit so we put up some bunks in one of the old storehouses. Nothing special, I'm afraid – I have to keep convincing the Gestapo that I hate the Jews as much as I need them. Anyway, some bright spark down at Prinz-Albrecht-Strasse dug up some regulation forbidding Jews from staying overnight at their workplaces, and decided it was a good excuse for putting my lot on the next train.'

'But you've saved them?'

'For the moment. Untangling all the relevant red tape will take me the rest of the morning, but it should be okay. For my eleven, that is. All it really means is that eleven others will be chosen in their place.'

There was no reply to that.

'Is this just a social call?' Thomas asked.

'Yes. We tried to ring you yesterday before I remembered that you were away. How are Hanna's family?'

'Good.'

'No news from Joachim?'

'Nothing for weeks,' Thomas said breezily. 'Look, John, I've got to deal with this business. Why don't we have lunch – how about Wednesday? The Russischer Hof, like we used to. One o'clock.'

'Make it one-thirty. And don't bring along any Gruppenführers.'

'Everyone needs a Gruppenführer, John.'

Seeing Thomas almost always lifted Russell's spirits, and watching the Gestapo sweep out in a collective temper-tantrum had lifted them higher than usual. And despite sitting for the better part of an hour on a hard wooden seat in a tram that probably pre-dated Bismarck, he still felt like smiling when he reached Wilhelmstrasse.

Dr Schmidt soon brought him back to earth. Klin had fallen, Ribbentrop's spokesman announced with a repulsive smirk, and the map behind him, though less crowded with sweeping arrows than Promi's version, showed how important that might be. The left wing of the German forces closing on Moscow would soon be due north of the city, and poised to sweep around behind it. Another 'biggest encirclement battle of all time' seemed on the cards.

The main business of the day, to which Schmidt turned with some reluctance, was the conference to renew the Anti-Comintern Pact. It was due to begin on the following day, and delegations from all the allies, both willing and reluctant, would be arriving today or tomorrow morning. The official renewal ceremony was tomorrow afternoon, and Foreign Minister Ribbentrop would be making the keynote speech on Wednesday. This would also be broadcast on the radio and printed in full in the newspapers.

'The word "ubiquitous" springs to mind,' Ralph Morrison whispered to Russell.

'Not to mention "unavoidable".'

The Führer, Schmidt continued, would be arriving on Thursday for important consultations with the various presidents and prime ministers.

'He's only just left,' an American further down the table muttered.

Schmidt glared at the guilty party, and concluded with the announcement of a special European postage stamp, released to celebrate the continent's new-found unity.

'United in despair,' Morrison said as he got up. 'You know it's Thanksgiving on Thursday. I wish to Christ I was back in the States.'

Russell was still staring at the map, and the red dot marked Klin. 'They might still do it, you know,' he said quietly. 'And God help us if they do.'

After the press conference was over, he avoided the Press Club, settling for a bowl of potato soup in one of the Potsdam Station buffets. Lately, he was finding the company of his fellow journalists harder and harder to stomach, probably because he saw his own cynical impotence reflected in theirs. What was he going to send off today? Anything resembling the truth was *verboten*, and he, like his colleagues, had turned into as much of a propagandist as Dr Goebbels, cherry-picking whichever publishable stories suited his own agenda. He liked to think he was pursuing a deeper truth, but in the here and now it was all about manipulation. Would the American people be more likely to support intervention if the Russians looked close to defeat, or if it looked as if the Germans had been stopped? He wasn't at all sure. In fact, he suspected that at this particular moment it didn't matter a damn what story he filed.

His next stop was the Abwehr building on Tirpitz Ufer. He was simply hoping to drop off the translations, but Colonel Piekenbrock, catching sight of Russell through his open office door, beckoned him in. 'Good,' he said. 'Saved me the trouble of sending for you. The Admiral wants to see you.'

'What for?' Russell asked with some irritation. He didn't like the idea of being 'sent for', and it was hard to imagine such an invitation boding well.

'You will hear that from him,' Piekenbrock said calmly, picking up the internal phone. 'Let me see if he's back from lunch.'

He wasn't, and Russell was left to cool his heels in one of the conference rooms. The windows overlooked the canal, where another long chain of coal barges was chugging slowly westward. Unless of course it was the same one going round in circles, intent on convincing Berliners that fuel supplies for the winter were plentiful.

Perhaps the Admiral wanted to thank him for his services, and wish him well in American exile.

Perhaps Hitler had a mistress named Sarah Finkelstein.

Russell reminded himself of his golden rule, that official requests should never be met with a definite yes or no.

It was almost three o'clock when an aide came to fetch him. The ancient lifts were out of order, so they walked up three flights to the top floor, where Canaris had his spacious office. He was sitting behind a huge desk, but got up to shake Russell's hand, gesturing him towards one end of the large black leather sofa. After Russell had refused the offer of a cigarette from a carved wooden box, Canaris sat down on the other end.

He looked older than his fifty-four years, his face lined by a sailor's long exposure to the sun. He also had a way of glancing sideways at those he addressed which was slightly unnerving. Russell's first impression of the Admiral, from their only previous meeting, had been of a man who knew a lot more than he actually understood, and who wasn't particularly sharp on the uptake. But Canaris had kept Heydrich and his rival *Sicherheitsdienst* at bay for almost seven years, which if nothing else suggested a certain talent for bureaucratic in-fighting.

'Herr Russell, we are pleased with your work for us. Your liaison work with the Americans, that is. I'm sure your translations are also excellent, but they do not concern me.'

Russell nodded his appreciation of the compliments.

'Now, it seems very likely that Japan is about to expand its operations in the Pacific. Exactly how and where we do not know, but it's hard to think of any meaningful Japanese move which the United States will not regard as a *casus belli*. And if America is drawn into a war with Japan, I am certain that Roosevelt will see to it that war is also declared on Germany.' He paused for a second, inviting Russell to comment.

'I can't argue with that,' Russell agreed.

'So your time in Germany is coming to an end?'

'So it would seem.'

'Well, I have a proposition for you. I would like you to consider continuing with the work you've been doing – that is, acting as a liaison between the Abwehr and the United States government.'

'But there will be no American government presence in Berlin.'

'Of course not. You will have to leave Germany. But I do want to stress how important your role might be. There are many Germans who would welcome an understanding with the Western powers that allows them to continue the war in the East. You must remember the Führer's offer of peace to Great Britain last summer. It was genuinely meant, I assure you.'

'So where?' Russell wanted to know.

'Switzerland is the obvious choice – easy access for both us and the Americans. You will have to leave your current job, and set yourself up as an independent – I believe "freelance" is the English word. Zurich would be best, but Basle or Berne if you insist. We will pay all your living expenses, and...'

'But that...'

'And of course we would ensure that your friend Fraulein Koenen was allowed to visit you on a regular basis.'

Russell was suddenly lost for words.

'This would be a secret arrangement,' the Admiral went on. 'It would be vital to ensure that other intelligence services – even other German services – were unaware of your role.'

Like the *Sicherheitsdienst*, Russell thought. Them and them alone, in all likelihood. Which was one good reason for saying no. Looking like a well-paid German stooge was another, but if the Americans also offered financial support he could claim independence. And not to be separated from Effi for however many years the war went on – that had to go in the yes column. He might even be able to get her out on a permanent basis – the Nazis would still have her family as hostages to her good behaviour. 'When would this happen?' he asked.

'Two weeks, maybe three.' Canaris shifted in his seat, as if his back was giving him trouble. 'First, I would appreciate your help in another matter.'

Russell's face must have betrayed him.

'There is no need for concern. This only involves a trip to Prague and the delivery of a message. Much the same task as you performed in Copenhagen a year or so ago.'

'I was already going to Copenhagen. And the message was for my own government. Is that the case this time?'

'No, it is not. This message will be in code, and I cannot divulge its contents. I can assure you that it has no bearing on the outcome of the war. You will not be compromising any loyalty you might feel to England or America.'

'But why me?' asked Russell. 'And who's the message for?'

'His name is Johann Grashof,' Canaris said, ignoring the first question. 'He runs the Abwehr office in Prague responsible for Hungary and the Balkans. A good and honourable man,' he added, surprising Russell. 'I have known him for many years.'

'You haven't explained why I've been chosen.'

'Because I believe I can trust you in this matter,' Canaris said. 'Your status as an outsider raises you above the fray, so to speak. You understand?'

Russell thought he did. This was a message that Canaris, for reasons unknown, could not trust to any of his own agents. Which was hardly encouraging. Russell asked the obvious question: 'Is the Swiss arrangement contingent on my delivering this message?'

Canaris looked away, but his words were equally direct: 'Yes, I'm afraid it is. We will fly you there and back,' he added, as if Russell's main objection to the mission might be the number of hours he would have to spend on a train. 'With any luck you'll be back within twenty-four hours.'

'Have you a date in mind?'

'A week today. December the first.'

Russell considered for a moment. 'Would there be any chance of my son visiting me in Switzerland?'

'I don't see why not.'

'It's a tempting offer,' Russell admitted. 'Can I have a few days to think it over?'

'Not too many. I need an answer by Wednesday.'

They shook hands again, and Canaris himself took Russell to the top of the stairs. He descended slowly, wondering what to do. The prize seemed great, the level of risk, for all of Canaris's blandishments, essentially unknown.

Outside the building, he turned left along the canal. What risks could there be? What could a message from the chief of German Military Intelligence to one of his officers contain that might threaten its bearer? Details of a plot to assassinate Hitler? Unlikely. Details of a scheme to undermine Heydrich? More likely, particularly since the destination was Prague, now the capital of Heydrich's own little fiefdom.

It wasn't somewhere Russell wanted to go. His last trip to the old Czech capital had seen him fleeing down alleys with the local Gestapo in close pursuit, suspected by the local resistance, and forced to depart the city with what seemed like undignified haste. Prague might be beautiful, but over the last few weeks Heydrich's crackdown had reportedly turned it into the most dangerous city in occupied Europe. If there were corpses swinging on the Charles Bridge lamp-posts, Russell wouldn't be at all surprised.

But – and it was a big but – when Canaris had offered him the chance of seeing Effi on a regular basis, he had suddenly realised how afraid he was of the alternative, of a separation that might last years, or even decades. Avoiding that fate was surely worth a few risks.

Shooting for *GPU* began on the following Monday, so Effi had stayed at home that day, studying an early draft of the script for *Betrayal* which Marssolek had sent her. It was depressing in the extreme, and seemed – as Russell had suspected it would be – almost immune to interpretation. The thought of it even being made filled her with anger, as did the realisation that most of her fellow actresses would play the part exactly as the makers intended.

Was she being over-sensitive? Surely most of her fellow countrymen would see through this evil nonsense as easily as she did. Her friends would find the storyline laughable. But then her memory slipped back to the conversation with Annaliese Huiskes in her hospital office, and the hundreds of Jews being shot by ordinary German men in Russia. Those men must have found the demonisation of the Jews believable, or they wouldn't be able to act the way they did. And movies must have played a part, however small, in that process, in making such terrible crimes not only possible but almost, it seemed, a matter of routine. The cost might come later, chorusing 'I can't do it anymore' in a Berlin hospital ward with your fellow criminals, but by then it was too late for everyone, murderers and victims alike.

She couldn't do this film, Effi realised. And she couldn't explain her refusal on the grounds that it would harm her career. She would have to tell Marssolek the truth, or something very like it. If they stopped offering her parts, then so be it. She would rather get a job on the trams than play Goebbels' idea of a Jewess.

When Russell got home he found Effi on the sofa and their living room littered with paper aeroplanes. 'You were right,' she said. 'This particular script was not susceptible to a human interpretation.'

'But it makes good paper aeroplanes?'

'Excellent paper aeroplanes.'

'Don't they want it back?'

'I shall say I left it on a tram. What can they do?'

Russell lifted her bare feet and sat down with them in his lap. 'I've had an offer,' he said. '*We've* had an offer,' he corrected himself. He explained the arrangement that Canaris had in mind, and was pleased to see the gleam of hope in Effi's eyes.

'That would be wonderful,' she said. 'I love Switzerland.'

'You may have to actually visit me, you know.'

'All right. But I learnt to ski there when I was sixteen, and I've never been back.'

'Well you can teach me.'

'There's a catch, isn't there?' she asked, suddenly serious.

'Only a small one.' He told her about the planned trip to Prague.

'John, you mustn't do it,' was the instinctual response.

'Why not?'

'Remember what happened the last time.'

'Yes, but...'

'I have a bad feeling about this, John.'

'I have a bad feeling about not seeing you for years.'

'Yes, of course, so do I...'

'Is it anything more than a bad feeling?' he asked. 'Is there something obvious I've missed? As far as I can see, all Canaris wants is for me to put a letter in someone else's hand. And I can't think of any reason why he should want to set me up. If...'

'Are you sure?'

'As sure as I can be. And if some enemy of Canaris's – which I suppose means the SD – if they catch me with the letter, it'll be sealed and in code. I'm just the postman. An innocent dupe.'

She gave him a reproachful look. 'That's not how the SD will see it, and you know it as well as I do.'

'Perhaps. But I'm also a foreign journalist, and someone they believe has done them a few favours in the past. I almost got a medal a couple of years ago. And if the worst came to the worst, I could always offer to work for them against Canaris. They could join the ranks of my visitors in Swiss exile.'

'And then what?'

'Play it by ear.' Russell shrugged. 'What else do I ever do?'

'I'm not convinced,' said Effi.

'Neither am I,' Russell admitted, 'but I think I'm going to risk it. Canaris chose the right reward.'

The following morning he decided on another day's consideration before delivering his answer. Maybe something would turn up, and push him one way or the other. He had, he realised, become another soldier in Berlin's growing army of Micawbers.

The Foreign Ministry press conference followed the recent pattern, only this time it was Solnechnogorsk that had fallen, twenty kilometres on from Klin, and only sixty from the Kremlin. Russell tried to find comfort in the unspoken – but obvious – fact that Tula, defending the southern approaches, had clearly not succumbed to the German onslaught. At least one of the pincers was not converging.

That afternoon the Ministry held a lavish reception for the foreign conference delegates, all of whom had now arrived. The foreign press was not allowed in, so Russell and his colleagues retreated to the Adlon bar, hoping to waylay the delegates en route to their rooms. It proved a successful ploy. Gestapo eavesdroppers were out in force, but as one of the Finns rudely remarked, few of them could speak German properly, let alone a foreign language. The delegates happily shared their thoughts with their own country's correspondents, while the latter, in a rare display of solidarity, happily shared what they'd heard with all of their colleagues. Ribbentrop's new Europe was not, it seemed, wholly united. The Hungarians were not speaking to the Romanians, the Slovaks or the Bulgarians – there were even rumours that a duel with pistols had been arranged for the following sunrise between Hungarian and Romanian colonels. This proved false, unlike the ongoing spat between Italy and Croatia, and the Italian delegation's outrage at being given similar ranking to the Spanish. No one had understood a word the Chinese or Japanese had said, and everyone thought Ribbentrop was an overbearing idiot. Most sensational of all, one Danish delegate revealed that anti-government – and anti-occupation – riots were taking place in Copenhagen at that very moment.

It was almost like old times in the Adlon bar, albeit with two major differences – the quality of the alcohol and the depressing fact that nothing they heard would ever see a front page.

Around seven, Russell realised he had time to pick up Effi at the hospital. He walked down Hermann-Goering-Strasse – or 'Meyerstrasse' as many Berliners now called it, following Goering's boast that they could call him Meyer if a single British bomb dropped on the capital – and around an eerily empty Potsdamer Platz, once the German equivalent of Times Square. Reaching the Elisabeth Hospital, he had trouble finding the military wing, but eventually found Effi sitting in a ward office with a small and tired-looking blonde in nurse's uniform. Both were drinking what looked like pink schnapps, Effi looking decidedly shaken.

She introduced Russell to Annaliese Huiskes, who offered him a drink.

He declined, admitting he'd already had enough for one evening.

They chatted for a few minutes, until Annaliese was called away. 'Take her home,' the nurse told Russell. 'She's had a bad evening.'

'It wasn't any worse than it usually is,' Effi told him as they walked to the tram stop. 'I've usually managed to let it all go by the time I get home. There's just so much of it, so many stories, so much anguish. One boy tonight, he kept on and on about this friend who'd been killed, and how it had been his fault. I told him I couldn't see why he should blame himself, and he just lost his temper – I thought he was going to hit me. He really needed it to be his fault, and I just hadn't realised...'

They had reached the tram stop, and Effi burrowed into Russell's arms, her shoulders shaking with grief. He stroked her hair, and thanked the blackout for their near-invisibility. In a very similar situation before the war, two middle-aged women had practically demanded her autograph.

She wiped her eyes and kissed him. 'Just another day at the office.'

The tram, when it finally arrived, was less crowded than usual. An elderly gentleman offered his seat to Effi, but she refused it with a smile. There were several middle-aged men in *Arbeitsfront* uniforms – shop stewards in the Nazi-controlled unions – standing close to the doors and talking with what seemed drunken abandon. Men to avoid, Russell thought, just as he caught sight of the two young women huddled in a dark corner, wearing yellow stars. It was only a few minutes from their curfew, and judging by the frequency with which the older one consulted her watch she was aware of that fact.

One last look, a word in her younger friend's ear, and the two of them sidled toward the doors as the tram approached the stop outside the closed Ka-de-We department store. The younger girl, Russell noticed, was carrying something rolled up in a piece of cloth. As she neared the door one of the uniformed men – a stereotypical Party man if Russell ever saw one, with his red piggish face and overflowing stomach – deliberately bumped her with an ample hip, causing her to stumble. A raw egg fell out of the cloth and broke on the floor.

The girl stared at the mess, resisting the tug of her older companion, heartbreak written all over her face. The man responsible yanked off her headscarf and thrust it at her: 'Now clear it up, you Jew bitch.'

'Where did a Jew get hold of an egg?' someone else asked indignantly. The doors had now closed, and the tram was in motion.

So was Effi, pushing her way past other passengers to place herself between the Jewish girls and their tormentor. 'You made her drop it, you clean it up,' she told him in cold, calm voice. 'People like you make me ashamed to be a German,' she heard herself add.

His contorted face looked almost fiendish in the dim yellow light. 'Mind your own fucking business,' he shouted. 'Who the fuck do you think you are? You look like a fucking Jew yourself.' He flicked out a hand, making contact with her left breast. 'Where's *your* fucking badge?'

'Back off, you bastard,' Russell said, giving the man a solid shove in the chest. He had no doubt that he could knock this one down, but the other three might prove more of a problem. 'What's the matter with you? Is this your idea of a good time – bullying women?'

'They're Jews, for fuck's sake,' the man shouted, as if that rendered all other considerations null and void.

'So fucking what?' Russell shouted back.

Effi had rarely seen him so angry. The tram, she noticed, had almost come to a halt. 'Go,' she told the Jewish girls, and they needed no second bidding. The elder one pulled the doors open, and they both tumbled down to the street and out into the darkness.

Russell and the *Arbeitsfront* official were still eyeball to eyeball, glued in place by their mutual loathing. 'John, let's go,' Effi said peremptorily, holding the door with one hand and tugging at his sleeve with the other.

It broke the spell. Russell beamed at the still-raging face in front of him, and turned to follow her. Stepping off, he heard a woman's voice inside the tram say, 'I'm sure that was Effi Koenen.'

Improvisations

Russell told Thomas the story at lunch next day, although not before checking the underside of their tables and chairs for listening devices. The ceilings in the Russischer Hof dining rooms were exceptionally high, so the chandeliers at least were free of bugs.

'I'm amazed that I didn't slug him,' he told Thomas. 'I don't know what stopped me. When he punched Effi in the breast... But I'm glad that I didn't, because God knows what would have happened. I'd have been flattened by his friends, and Effi would have joined in and probably been flattened too. And the two Jewish girls might have been caught and arrested and put on the next train out.'

'You said it was Effi who blew up first.'

'Yes, but I'm usually there to calm things down, not make them worse.'

'That would seem to work better than the two of you egging each other on,' Thomas said with a wry smile. 'Still, it doesn't look like you'll be around for much longer.'

'What have you heard?'

'Oh, nothing specific. Only the usual sources,' he added, meaning the BBC. 'It just looks like things are coming to a head.'

'Hitler might distance himself from a Japanese attack. After all, what would he gain from joining them? There's no way he could help them fight the Americans, but if he keeps out of it, the Americans might reward him by moving most of their forces from the Atlantic to the Pacific.'

'That makes perfect sense,' Thomas agreed, 'but does it sound like our Führer?'

'Perhaps not,' Russell admitted. 'I've been doing a lot of straw-clutching lately.'

'Who isn't?'

His friend was looking noticeably older, Russell thought. The wrinkles around his eyes and the grey in his hair were both spreading. The strain of having a son at the front must be bad enough, without the need to fight an endless rearguard action against the Gestapo in defence of his Jewish workers. 'No word from Joachim?' he asked.

'Oh yes, I meant to tell you. There was a letter yesterday. Just a few words – no specific news. But he's all right. Or at least he was a few days ago.'

'Hanna must be relieved. '

'Yes, of course. Though it gives her more space to worry about Lotte. Our daughter has suddenly decided, for reasons that neither of us can even begin to fathom, to become an exemplary – and I do mean exemplary – member of the *Bund Deutscher Mädel.* Three weeks ago she was a normal healthy sixteen-year-old, interested in boys and clothes and film stars. Now she has *his* picture over her bed. I mean, I suppose it's harmless enough, at least for a while; but why, for God's sake? It's as if some malign spirit has taken over the poor girl's brain.'

'At least the Gestapo won't be coming for her,' Russell said.

Thomas laughed. 'There is that.'

'And did you sort out Monday's difficulty?'

'Yes, but they'll be back. It's like building sandcastles – sooner or later the tide rolls over them. Unless there's some basic change of heart, my Jews will be sent away to whatever horrors are waiting for them. And what could provoke one? I sometimes wonder which would be better for the Jews – a quick victory in the East or a bloody stalemate that lasts for years. Victory might endow our leaders with a little magnanimity, whereas defeat would probably make them even nastier. So here I am,' he concluded, raising his glass in mock salute, 'longing for total victory.'

'No one finds a cloud in a silver lining better than you do,' Russell agreed.

They were halfway through dessert – an applecake seriously lacking in apple – when the waiter came round warning the diners that the broadcast was about to begin. He had hardly disappeared when inspirational music began pouring from the speakers.

'Ribbentrop's speech,' Russell remembered. 'Into every life…'

They were onto their ersatz coffees by the time the Foreign Minister began his peroration. Continuing their own conversation proved impossible. 'It's impossible to tune him out,' Thomas said. 'I've actually been thinking about him lately…'

'Why, for God's sake?'

'I've come to see him as the essential Nazi. The absolute distillation of Naziness. And that's why you can't get away from his voice – it's as if the whole system is doing the talking.'

'I would have thought the Führer would take the starring role.'

'He would, he would. No, Ribbentrop isn't a star, much though he'd like to be. He's the Nazi everyman. He loves himself to death, he's not very clever but he thinks he is, he prides himself on his logic and reeks of prejudice, and above all he's crushingly boring.'

'After the war you should write his biography.'

Thomas's laugh was cut short by something he saw over Russell's shoulder. 'Behave,' he whispered, and rose from his chair, hand outstretched. Russell turned to see a tall, greying man with a chiselled face in the uniform of an SS Gruppenführer.

Thomas introduced them, and invited the Gruppenführer to share their table. Much to Russell's relief, the man was with his own party. Russell listened as the other two made arrangements for an afternoon's sailing on the Havel, Ribbentrop's voice droning away behind them.

'It was good to meet you, Herr Russell,' the Gruppenführer said, shaking his hand again. 'You are not a sailor like your brother-in-law?'

'No, but I can see the attraction.'

'You must join us one weekend. Perhaps in the spring when the weather is kinder.'

'Perhaps,' Russell agreed with a smile. He watched the man walk back to his table, where two other black-uniformed officers were waiting for him. 'What powerful friends you have,' he murmured.

'I'll probably be needing them,' Thomas replied. 'Believe it or not, once you get that man out of his uniform and onto a boat he's a decent enough chap.'

'Some of them are.'

'Not that it matters much,' Thomas said. 'Decent or not, the lever that works is self-interest. And since things started looking iffy in Russia, people like the Gruppenführer have started worrying about the world after the war. They're still not expecting defeat, mind you, but they do sense the possibility, and they're looking for some sort of insurance. Being nice to people like me, who've never had anything to do with the Nazis, is one way they can keep a foot in the other camp. Just in case.'

'And that gives you names to wave at the Gestapo.'

'It does. I don't like most of these people, in or out of uniform, but being nice to them doesn't exactly cost me anything.' He looked at his watch. 'I'd better be getting back. I doubt they'll visit us again this week, but I like to be on hand.'

As they stood on the steps outside prior to parting, Thomas looked up at the clear blue sky. 'The English will be back tonight,' he predicted. 'They won't miss the chance of embarrassing Ribbentrop while his guests are in town.'

Thomas headed for the U-Bahn at Friedrichstrasse Station, while Russell went towards Unter de Linden and the Adlon. Ribbentrop's voice rose and fell with each loudspeaker he passed, like ripples of an intermittent headache. Until only a year or so ago people had gathered beside speakers at moments like these, but nowadays they just hurried by, as if the voice was driving them onwards. In the Adlon bar there was no escape, and people were simply shouting above the speech. Russell talked to a couple of his Swedish colleagues, who confirmed his opinion that no other news would be allowed to challenge the Foreign Minister's speech that day. Since he had the entire text in his pocket – copies had been handed out at the noon press conference – there seemed little point in waiting around. He sat himself down at a vacant table and wrote a simple summary of the speech interspersed with ample quotes. An honest evaluation would not be allowed, but should in any case be superfluous. If Russell's readers on the other side of the Atlantic were dim enough to take Ribbentrop's fantasies seriously then he could only wish them a speedy recovery.

His job as a Berlin correspondent was over, he decided. Some time in the next few days he should take the trouble to resign.

Other work beckoned. He stopped off at the Abwehr headquarters on his way home, and was taken straight to Canaris's office. The Admiral seemed slightly surprised that he was willing to visit Prague, a reaction which set faint alarm bells ringing in his mind. Russell told himself it was only Canaris's diffident manner, and chose to ignore them. The arrangements for his meeting with Johann Grashof had still not been finalised, and he was told to see Piekenbrock on Monday morning, prior to catching the overnight train. The promise of air travel was unfortunately rescinded – the Luftwaffe had nothing to spare.

Arriving home before dark, he found Effi memorising her *GPU* lines, and an unusually aromatic casserole simmering on the stove. 'It's nearly the end of the month, so I went mad with our ration coupons,' she explained. And there was a message from the American Consulate. 'A man named Kenyon wants to see you tomorrow, at ten if you can make it. He said it was about contingencies,' she added. 'Whatever that means.'

Russell had no idea. He had met Kenyon a couple of times: once at the American Consulate in Prague in the summer of 1939, and again a few months later after the diplomat's transfer to Berlin. As far as Russell knew, the man had nothing to do with American intelligence, although that might have changed. Or perhaps Dallin had asked for Kenyon's help in persuading Russell to contact the Air Ministry official Franz Knieriem. If so, he'd been wasting his time.

They did, however, have excellent coffee at the Consulate. After ringing and leaving a message for Kenyon that he'd see him the following morning, Russell decided to phone his son. Paul seemed happy to talk for a change, albeit mostly about his growing proficiency with guns. That Saturday, it turned out, he was taking part in a *Hitlerjugend* shooting tournament, and wouldn't be able to see his father. Russell was surprised and upset by the momentary sense of relief this news caused, and almost welcomed the more lasting feelings of guilt which swiftly followed.

Effi, he decided, had heard enough of his agonising in recent days. 'Are you still feeling okay about that script?' he asked.

'It's wonderful,' she said. 'It's a comedy, and either no one's noticed or no one dares to say so. My only worry is that fifty years from now people will think I was taking it seriously. I was thinking – you know those people who dig deep holes in the ground and bury a box of typical things with the date...'

'Time capsules.'

'That's it. Well, I thought I could bury this script with my comments on it.'

'Why not? Let's just hope there are no Nazis around in fifty years to dig it up, particularly if we're still here and the film's become a classic.'

She stuck her tongue out at him.

'I don't think you ever told me the storyline.'

'I did, but you were half asleep at the time.'

'Tell me again.'

'All right. I am Olga...'

'A Russian.'

'A *White* Russian. I think they must be further up the race table. Anyway, my parents were killed by the GPU...'

'Which has been the NKVD for almost ten years.'

'That sounds like the sort of detail the writers would have missed. But stop interrupting.'

'Okay.'

'Whatever they're called, they killed my parents. Or one of them did, and I've joined the organisation with the secret intention of tracking him down. I'm also an amazing violinist, by the way, and as the film begins I'm in Riga to give a recital for the International Women's League. I'm in mid-performance when some old man in the audience starts shouting that the League is financed by Jewish interests in Moscow. His proof is that a top GPU agent named Bokscha is also in Riga. Get it? Jews and Bolsheviks hand in glove!

'It gets less subtle as it goes on,' she went on. 'Needless to say, Bokscha is the man who killed my parents. He falls in love with me of course, and we roam around Europe with him organising sabotage and murders on the Kremlin's behalf and me waiting for the perfect moment to betray him. All his meetings are in the same dark cellar, which has portraits of Lenin and Stalin on the walls. The people he's plotting with are almost always Jews, and they laugh a lot together about how stupid and vulnerable everyone else is. Do you detect a theme here? Oh, and there's a sub-plot about this Latvian couple whom I befriend. They're forced to spy for the Soviets, and eventually end up imprisoned in Rotterdam, purely, as far as I can see, so that they can be set free by our invading army. By this time Bokscha and I are both dead. First I tell Moscow that he's a traitor and get him shot, and then I admit to joining the GPU under false pretences and get myself shot. Clever, eh?

'I see what you mean about a lack of subtlety.'

'It's complete nonsense from beginning to end, and I can hardly wait to start shooting.'

'Monday, yes?' Russell asked, dipping a spoon into the casserole.

'Yes.'

'Any location stuff?'

'All indoors for the first few weeks. Mostly the cellar, in fact.'

Russell laughed. 'This is ready,' he said, taking the casserole off the stove.

They were still eating when the air raid warning sounded, and Effi insisted on clearing her plate before they walked to the local shelter. This was a very different type of district to the one where the Blumenthals lived, and the local warden was as obsequious as theirs had been officious. Most of the adults had pained expressions on their faces, as if they found it hard to believe that such inconvenience was really necessary. Their children were better behaved than their Wedding counterparts, but seemed to laugh a lot less. It was after midnight before the all-clear sounded, freeing them all to grumble their way back up to the street.

On Thursday morning, Russell's tram downtown passed evidence of the previous night's raid, the wreck of a three-storey building like a broken tooth in an otherwise healthy row, roofless and gutted, surrounded by shards of broken glass. A few wisps of smoke were still rising from the ruin, and a sizable crowd was gathered outside, watching as the civil engineers made the neighbouring buildings safe. It was a sign of how little impact the RAF campaign was having, Russell thought, that one bombed house could still attract so much interest.

He had not been inside the American Consulate for several months, and was struck by how empty it seemed. Now that voluntary emigration was forbidden, the long Jewish queues had disappeared, and with Germany and the US fighting an undeclared war in the Atlantic the Consulate's diplomatic business had shrunk to almost nothing. Many diplomats had presumably been sent home.

Russell could smell the coffee as he waited for Joseph Kenyon, but that was the closest he got. The young bespectacled diplomat came down the stairs in his overcoat, and ushered his visitor back out onto the street. 'We keep finding new microphones,' he explained, 'so these days we just use the building for keeping warm. All our business is done outdoors.'

They walked up to the Spree, which at least made a change from the

Tiergarten. The sun was out, but the brisk wind sweeping in from the east more than cancelled it out, and both men were soon rubbing their gloved hands and hugging themselves to retain a little warmth. They followed the river to the left, walking past the Reichstag and around the long bend opposite Lehrter Station. Kenyon seemed hesitant about raising whatever it was he had in mind, so Russell asked him if he had any inside dope about the negotiations with Japan.

'Off the record?'

Russell nodded.

'There are no real negotiations. Tokyo wants more than Washington can give, and vice versa. Sooner or later the balloon will go up, probably sooner. I don't know this for certain, but I imagine Washington is playing for time, because with each month that goes by our re-armament programme makes us a little stronger and the economic embargo makes them a little weaker. They know this as well as we do, of course, and I don't think they'll wait for long. I expect an attack before Christmas.'

'But on whom?'

'That's the big question. If oil's as big a problem for them as we think it is, they have to attack the Dutch East Indies – it's the only source within reach. And if they attack the Dutch they're bound to attack the British – you can't expect to take Sumatra without taking Singapore first. Which raises the big question – could they afford to leave us alone in the Philippines, knowing that we could cut their new oil lifeline any time we chose? I don't think so. They'll have to go for us as well.'

Russell thought about it. Most of what Kenyon had just said seemed like common sense, although he still couldn't quite believe that the Japanese would be foolhardy enough to attack America. But then maybe countries in desperate corners really did behave like men in similar plights – they just lashed out and hoped for the best.

'How well do you know Patrick Sullivan?' Kenyon asked him out of the blue.

'Not well. We're not exactly political allies. I must have spoken to him about half a dozen times since the war began. I actually had a conversation with him last week.'

'He said.' Kenyon pulled a packet of Chesterfields from his pocket. 'You don't, do you?' he asked.

'No.'

Kenyon lit his cigarette with a silver lighter, took a deep drag, and exhaled with obvious pleasure. 'It's Sullivan I want to talk to you about. Off the record, of course.'

'Of course,' Russell echoed, curious as to what was coming.

'The man's had a change of heart. Or at least that's the way he put it.' Kenyon smiled inwardly. 'I guess he's suddenly realised which way the wind is blowing.'

'He's very pessimistic about the war in the East.'

'Exactly. If the Soviets survive this winter and we come in, then Hitler is finished. It might take years, but the end result won't be in doubt.'

'Let's hope,' Russell concurred. They must have walked about one and a half kilometres by this time, and were skirting the northern edge of the Tiergarten. Across the river a leaning pillar of smoke from the Lehrter Station goods yard was rising above the massive Customs and Excise building.

Kenyon tapped off his ash. 'You know that some American corporations are still doing a lot of business with Germany?'

'You mean like Ford, working through their German subsidiaries?'

'Ford, Standard Oil, GM, even Coca Cola. It's a long list, and there are also the American subsidiaries of German corporations like IG Farben. Some of these links are downright crucial to the German war effort. Without Ford trucks they'd be a hell of a lot further from Moscow.'

'But none of it's illegal, right?

'At the moment. But Sullivan claims that several of these corporations have made secret arrangements for business as usual even after we enter the war. Which would be treason in most people's eyes. It certainly would in mine,' Kenyon added, grinding out his cigarette. 'And Sullivan says he has proof.'

'What does he want in return?' Russell asked.

'He wants to go home to Chicago, with enough money for a nice house and immunity from any future prosecution.'

'Why should he need that? He hasn't done anything illegal, has he?'

Kenyon shrugged. 'Probably not. But whether American Jews will see it that way is another matter. I can see why he'd like some insurance.'

'So where do I come in?'

'He wants you to act as a go-between. He doesn't trust us; he thinks we'll just take his proof and throw him back out to the wolves.'

'Would you?'

Kenyon shrugged. 'We might. He hasn't exactly endeared himself to anyone at the Consulate.'

'Okay, so why me?'

'He likes you for some reason.'

'I'm probably the only American journalist left who doesn't leave a room the moment he walks into it. So how's this supposed to work?'

'He wants to meet you and show you his proof. You'll then report back to us, and verify that he's got what he says he's got. But he'll still have the documents we would need for court cases back in DC.'

'But he'll have to hand them over at some point.'

'Not until he's on the ship, he says, though as far as I can see there'd be nothing to stop us taking them then and dumping him back on the quayside. Maybe he has something else up his sleeve. Perhaps he thinks using a journalist as a go-between will shame the US Government into keeping its part of the bargain.'

'He has a higher regard for the power of the press than I do, then.'

Kenyon smiled, and lit another Chesterfield. Ahead of them, a Stadtbahn train rattled over the river, slowing as it approached Bellevue Station. 'So will you meet him?'

'Why not?' It sounded like a story, and Kenyon could hardly insist that Russell's conversation with Sullivan was off the record. 'Where and when?'

'The buffet at Stettin Station. Saturday at noon.'

Russell was about to object when he remembered that he wasn't seeing Paul. 'Fine,' he said.

They turned back. It had growing noticeably colder in the last hour, and they upped their pace, chatting as they walked about the situations in Russia and the Balkans, and the wildly conflicting reports from the battlefield in North Africa. Russell liked the way Kenyon's mind worked. Unlike most American diplomats of his acquaintance, Kenyon was not burdened by a sense of inherent American superiority. He was doubtless proud of his country, but had no difficulty accepting that other men could be equally proud of theirs, and for equally valid reasons. He would make a good academic, Russell thought, particularly with the worldly experience he had now accumulated.

He asked Kenyon if he had any recent news from Prague, without mentioning his own forthcoming visit.

Kenyon had none, but couldn't resist inserting an aside about the *Reichsprotektor* – 'of all the people I could imagine running a country, Reinhard Heydrich is far and away the most frightening.'

As they walked across Unter den Linden towards the Consulate, Russell asked if Scott Dallin was in that morning. 'I just need a few minutes, ten at most.' Kenyon didn't know, but went in to find out. A couple of minutes later Dallin appeared, well wrapped for the cold.

They strode up one side of Unter den Linden as far as Friedrichstrasse, then back along the other side. Russell told Dallin about the Abwehr's offer to install him in Switzerland and, after some hesitation, decided to also come clean about the job Canaris wanted doing in Prague. Everyone seemed to be mentioning insurance that morning, and he thought Dallin knowing about Prague might provide him with some; against what, he wasn't too clear, but if Effi came to the Consulate to report his non-return it would be nice if someone there had a clue as to what she was talking about.

Dallin was clearly struck by the potential importance of the Swiss arrangement, but not so much that he forgot to press Russell on the 'other business'.

For a second or so Russell wondered what he was referring to, then remembered Franz Knieriem. 'No, not yet,' he said as non-committally as he could manage.

'It is important,' Dallin insisted.

'I know,' Russell said disingenuously. Even if it was, which he seriously doubted, ensuring his own survival seemed rather more important.

Thirty minutes later he was climbing the Foreign Ministry stairs. He had decided that morning that he would at least attend the press conferences, and save himself some money on newspapers.

The first item on Schmidt's agenda was the Führer's return. All that day Hitler would be receiving a long line of foreign ministers at the Chancellery: those from Finland, Hungary, Bulgaria, Denmark... Schmidt rolled his tongue around each country's name as if he wished to eat it. Well, the army had already had done that. Russell wondered whether Hitler had the same speech for each of them. That, of course, would depend on his noticing when one man left and another arrived.

More ominously, Istra had fallen. Russell had visited the town's New Jerusalem Monastery with Ilse in 1924, only a few days after their first meeting in the international comrades' dormitory. On that summer day the drive from Moscow in an old Ford taxi had taken them about two hours. How long would it take a Panzer IV in late November?

After lunch at the Adlon he hunkered down in the bar to write what he hoped was a cry of alarm – a map-in-prose of the rolling forested countryside outside the Soviet capital and the battles now engulfing it. He wanted his readers to hear the Kremlin bells ringing out across Red Square, summoning the last defenders to man the last ditches, as they had done in centuries past when other barbarians were at the gates. He wanted Americans to feel how close to the edge their world was inching.

Once finished he sent it off, confident that the Nazis censors would see nothing more than a simple paean to their coming victory. Effi was out at the cinema with Zarah, so he decided to stay for the Promi press conference, walking down Wilhelmstrasse, only slightly inebriated, as dusk fell. Goebbels was elsewhere, his minions as lacklustre as ever, and the guest speaker – an IG Farben manager with a speech defect – was unable to convince anyone that recent synthetic rubber breakthroughs would decide the war.

After visiting both press clubs in a vain search for a game of poker, he reluctantly headed home. His coat was only half off when the telephone rang.

'Klaus, there's a game tonight,' the familiar voice intoned. 'Number 21, at –' he paused, and Russell could almost see him checking his watch '– at eight-thirty.'

He put down the phone, got out his S-Bahn map and counted the stations off. The twenty-first station running clockwise from Wedding was Westkreuz – which was only two stops west of Savignyplatz on the Stadtbahn. He probably had plenty of time, but with each week that passed the trains seemed less reliable. He should probably leave immediately.

He had not gone a hundred metres down Carmerstrasse when he heard footfalls behind him. Glancing back over his shoulder he could just make out two human shapes walking behind him, some twenty metres away. He slowed, stopped, and bent to re-tie a shoelace, feeling faintly ridiculous at resorting to such an obvious stratagem. The two men kept coming, as of course they had to – stratagems became obvious because they worked. Once they were twenty metres ahead of him, Russell began walking again, keeping the distance between them until they reached Savignyplatz. When his potential tails turned right onto Kant Strasse he watched until the darkness swallowed them, then crossed the square and climbed the stairs to the elevated station. He was getting paranoid, he thought. One thing you could say for the blackout – it made the Gestapo's job much more difficult, particularly at this time of the year, when there were only nine hours of daylight. During the other fifteen hours of the day Berlin was cloaked in the sort of darkness that only burglars and rapists loved. Any sort of mobile surveillance was practically impossible.

He waited on the elevated platform at Savignyplatz for the best part of half an hour, hunched up against the bitter cold, trying to remember which stars were which in the firmament above. It was a struggle getting aboard the train when it came, and he spent the next six minutes with a tall soldier's elbow pressing into his neck. Westkreuz was the two-level station where the Stadtbahn and national lines crossed over the Ringbahn, and numerous travellers changing lines were busily bumping into each other in the starlit gloom. Russell went downstairs and up again, just in case. It then took him several minutes to find the street exit, and several more to be absolutely sure that Ströhm was not lurking in one of the darker corners.

He settled down to wait, and five minutes later a Ringbahn train pulled in below. Ströhm appeared a minute or so later, walking past Russell without a word, but discreetly tugging at his sleeve. Once outside, he walked a short distance down the dark road and stopped. 'We'll wait for a few minutes and go back in,' he said. 'There's nothing for you to see tonight, and the end of a platform's as good a place as any for talking.'

His voice sounded unusually flat, Russell noticed. Bad news was coming.

They walked to the furthest end of the eastbound Stadtbahn platform, where a large swathe of Berlin spread darkly away from them under the starry sky. 'The train that left last Monday was scheduled for Riga,' Ströhm said quietly. He expelled a small blue cloud of warm breath. 'They're building a new concentration camp there with a capacity of 25,000.'

It crossed Russell's mind that many football stadiums were smaller.

On the platform opposite an embracing couple were silhouetted against the southern horizon.

'But it's not ready,' Ströhm went on. 'The Jews were taken off at Kovno in Lithuania, and taken to one of the old Czarist forts on the outskirts.

That was on Saturday. On Sunday a second trainload of Jews arrived from Frankfurt, on Monday a third from Munich. On Tuesday all three thousand were taken out and shot.'

Russell closed his eyes. 'Why?' he asked. 'On whose orders?' One mental picture of Leonore Blumenthal's Aunt Trudi, in front of a mirror, smiling as she adjusted her hat, gave way to another, of the same woman standing beside a freshly-dug pit, with trembling lips and untidy grey hair.

'We're not certain,' Ströhm replied, 'but the decision was probably taken locally. We think that the authorities in Kovno were just told to look after their unexpected guests in whatever way they deemed appropriate.'

A steam locomotive was approaching on the fast line, the sound of its passage rapidly increasing in volume. It hurried through the station, pulling a long line of efficiently darkened carriages, an orange glow seeping from the roughly blacked-out cab.

'So they just killed them,' Russell said, once the noise had sufficiently abated.

'That's what they've been doing in Russia,' Ströhm said. 'The fact that these were German Jews doesn't seem to have made any difference.'

'But it doesn't seem as if there was a pre-arranged plan to murder them,' Russell said, as much to himself as Ströhm. 'And that does make a difference. If the Riga camp's ready when the next trains are sent, then presumably the Jews will end up there. Why would they be building it otherwise?'

'Perhaps,' Ströhm agreed.

He didn't sound convinced, and Russell could hardly blame him. He asked if the leaders of Berlin's Jewish community had been told.

'They will be, if they haven't been already. But they often refuse to believe such news. Some of them at least. They thank us kindly for the information, but you can see it in their eyes. It doesn't surprise me. Knowing that something bad is about to happen is only useful when there's something you can do to avert it.'

'Are any more trains scheduled?'

'Not at the moment. There are none available.' Ströhm smiled for the first time. 'The train that took the Jews to Kovno was commandeered in Warsaw by the Quartermasters.'

'Well I suppose that's good news.'

'That and the damage the Soviet partisans are doing to our trains in Russia. There's one thing I have for you: a driver who's willing to talk about what he's seen in the East. He was badly injured several weeks ago in a partisan attack, and now he's convalescing at home. Are you interested?'

'Of course.'

'His name is Walter Meltza. His address is Flat 6, Spanheimstrasse 7. It's near the Plumpe, the Hertha ground. You know where that is?'

'Does the Führer like vegetables?'

Ströhm smiled again. 'One day we must have a talk about football, and which is the best Berlin team to support. Have you memorised the address?'

'Yes.'

'Please be careful, for everyone's sake. Only visit after dark. I'll make sure he knows you are coming.'

'At the end of next week,' Russell suggested. He had Sullivan and the Admiral's message to deal with over the next few days.

A local train could be heard approaching from the west. 'I'll tell him.'

They shook hands, and Ströhm faded into the darkness as the thin blue headlight glided into the station. This train was almost empty, not to mention strewn with copies of the same leaflet. 'War with America?' was the bold headline, but reading the small print beneath was impossible in the negligible light, and he stuffed the leaflet in his pocket. The war might be European, he thought, but all eyes were now on America. It occurred to him that his own day had revolved around four Americans – Kenyon, Sullivan, Dallin and Ströhm. And four more different Americans were hard to imagine: a cosmopolitan diplomat, an ex-actor turned Nazi, a would-be spymaster from California and an essentially German communist. Not to mention himself, the American who had only ever spent six weeks in his supposed homeland. Yet here they all were in Berlin, waiting with their eighty million German hosts for their government in Washington to take the plunge, with or without a Japanese push.

The train pulled in to Savignyplatz station. There were a few signs of movement in the square, but it had an empty sound, as if the residents had already tucked themselves away for the night. Walking up Carmerstrasse, he found himself thinking about the Blumenthals. If they didn't already know, should he tell them? How would it help them to know?

He would ask Effi, he decided, as he climbed the stairs to her apartment. She was lying on the sofa, a script laid flat across her stomach, stretching her arms in the air. 'I heard the outside door,' she said. 'Where've you been?'

'Meeting my railwayman. He had...'

The swelling of sirens interrupted him.

'Oh, not again,' Effi lamented. 'I need some sleep!'

She was still sleeping when Russell left the next morning. Either the raid had been protracted, or those in charge of the all-clear had inadvertently dropped off, because it hadn't sounded until a quarter past four. Two possible chains of circumstance that any local Sherlock Holmes could have deduced from the bleary eyes of his fellow passengers on the Route 30 tram.

Russell remembered how quickly Paul had fallen in love with Holmes and Watson. How old had he been? Nine? Ten? One day at the Funkturm they had invented German equivalents – Siegfried Helmer and Doctor Weindling. They lived at Kurfürstendamm 221, over an actual tobacco shop.

How would Paul react if he told him what had happened in Kovno? He had told Effi on their way back home from the shelter, and she had not wanted to believe it. She had, but only after desperately searching through the facts for a more acceptable interpretation. Paul would simply deny it. His father's source must be mistaken, or simply inspired by hatred of the Reich.

And Russell was almost glad that Paul would think that way, because denial was infinitely preferable to acceptance.

His tram ground to a halt in the shadow of the Brandenburg Gate. The sky was mostly clear, but was expected to cloud over in the afternoon and thereby offer Berliners some respite from the attentions of the RAF. That was the good news. The bad was that Effi had accepted an invitation for dinner at her sister's house for them both. The food might be good, but only until Zarah cooked it; and sharing several hours with her punctilious Nazi husband was hardly Russell's idea of an enjoyable Friday evening, even in war-time Berlin. In fact, now that he thought about it, the turn in the weather was somewhat unfortunate. An air raid might have shortened the torment.

Neither newspaper nor coffee improved his mood. The latter seemed worse than ever, a cold brown soup that bore no relation to the real thing, and the former was full of self-congratulatory coverage of the recently-concluded, so-called conference. *Völkischer Beobachter* readers were invited to imagine a world in which England rather than Germany had enjoyed two years of victories: 'Instead of being able to face the world united, having as its centre a Reich immeasurably greater in power and potentialities, Europe would now be split into fragments consisting of nothing more than a small heap of non-organic separated parts…'

'Let's hear it for small heaps,' Russell murmured to himself. A long article in the same paper revealed the 'secret last testament' of Tsar Peter the Great, a template for expansionism which the Bolsheviks had taken for their own. The journalists concerned seemed unaware that the testament in question had been revealed as a forgery more than thirty years before.

After attending two press conferences and writing one uninspired article, he met Effi at the Zoo Station buffet. Zarah and Jens Biesinger lived on the border of Grunewald and Schmargendorf, a kilometre or so east of his son Paul's home. It was an important kilometre in social terms, and the Biesinger house, though ample in size for a family of three, was considerably less spacious than the small mansion which Matthias Gehrts had inherited from his industrialist father. There were also, as Russell had noticed on previous visits to collect Effi, many more swastikas waving in the less leafy street.

The promised cloud cover had arrived, deepening the blackout, and they stepped down from their tram into a river of dancing blue lights, as phosphorescent-badged Berliners crowded the pavements on their way home from work. Effi remembered one of her soldiers in the Elisabeth Hospital describing Russian skies awash with coloured flares. She tightened her grip on Russell's arm. 'John, be nice this evening.'

'I'm always nice.'

'Who are you talking to? I'm serious. Zarah's not doing well at the moment, and from everything she says I don't think Jens can be either.'

'I thought he'd been promoted.'

'He has. But I don't think... This is the street, isn't it?'

'It's Karlsbaderstrasse,' a passing voice in the dark said helpfully.

'Thank you.'

'You were saying?' Russell said, once they'd found the white kerb.

'Zarah says he's drinking more than he used to.'

'That wouldn't be difficult. The last time I came to dinner here the wine was in thimbles.'

'That was years ago. And I thought you promised to be nice.'

'I am. I will be. But what problems do they have? A Party favourite with a prestige job and a wife who doesn't have to work. Is Lothar okay?'

'It's not that simple,' Effi retorted. Sometimes she wondered how someone so intelligent could also be so obtuse.

'Is Lothar okay?' Russell asked again

'He's fine,' Effi replied. 'A bit strange perhaps, but fine.'

'Strange how?' Two years ago Zarah and Jens had been worried that their child was mentally sub-normal, not something they wanted to publicise given the Party's attitude to handicapped people of any age or type. Russell had escorted Zarah and the boy to London for a clandestine assessment. Lothar, it turned out, was just a little disconnected from the rest of humanity. There was nothing to worry about.

'Oh, I don't know,' Effi said. 'Just little things. One of Jens's sisters bought him a stunning set of toy soldiers for his birthday, and he just refused to play with them. Wouldn't say why, just put them back in their box and left them there.'

'Sounds very sensible to me.'

'You wouldn't say that if it was Paul. Remember how overjoyed he was when Thomas bought him that set of dead soldiers. He went on and on about how realistic they were.'

'True,' Russell conceded. He didn't want to talk about Paul.

'Lothar says the strangest things sometimes,' Effi went on. 'He asked me the other day whether pretending to be other people at work made me confused when I wasn't. It's not an unreasonable question, but from a six year-old?'

'I see what you mean.'

They were almost there. Effi pulled them to a halt at the gate, and put her hands on his shoulders. 'It hurts me that Zarah and I aren't as close as we used to be. This war will end one day, and I want to still have a sister when it does.' She stared him in the eye, making sure he understood her. 'We may not like how they think or what Jens does, but they're part of our family.'

'I get it,' Russell said. He did.

It was Lothar who answered the door, smiling happily at Effi and earnestly shaking hands with Russell. Zarah appeared, looking much the same as ever, a full-figured woman with wavy chestnut hair which now hung past her shoulder. She gave him a bigger smile than he expected, and kissed him warmly on the cheek. Jens emerged last. He looked at least five years older than he had in 1939, although much-thinned hair perhaps exaggerated the effect. He was out of uniform for once, unless the enamel swastika in his lapel could be counted as such.

A surprisingly wonderful smell was coming from the kitchen. Perhaps the quality of the ingredients had transcended the quality of the cook, Russell thought unkindly.

Jens seemed eager to get them drinking, and appeared slightly disappointed when Lothar commandeered both guests for a look at his latest acquisition – an atlas of world animals. He had the book open at a map of the Soviet Union, a double-page spread full of wolves, black bears and Siberian tigers. The Red Army and Wehrmacht were nowhere to be seen.

With Zarah announcing that dinner was fifteen minutes away, Effi took Lothar upstairs for a bedtime story and Russell was able to oblige Jens's desire to share his excellent wine. The two of them swapped opinions on the military news from Africa – a safe option in that neither had any real idea what was happening – and Russell offered a vaguely optimistic view of events in the East, which he assumed would please his host. All he got was a frown. 'We must hope for the best,' was all Jens would say.

This was a surprise, and made Russell want to dig deeper. What did Jens know that Dr Schmidt and Dr Goebbels did not?

Effi's reappearance prevented it. 'Lothar is ready for his goodnight kiss,' she told her brother-in-law. 'How's it going?' she asked Russell once Jens had disappeared up the stairs.

'Splendidly,' he told her.

She disappeared into the kitchen, leaving him to stare at the framed Führer above the mantelpiece. 'How's your war going?' Russell muttered at him. 'As well as you hoped, or are the cracks beginning to show?'

'Second sign of madness,' Effi said at his shoulder.

'What's the first?'

'Talking to portraits of Goering. It's time to sit down.'

They went through into the dining room. Zarah had lit candles, but resisted Effi's suggestion that they turn off the lights – 'There's too much darkness these days.' Jens returned and topped up their glasses – his, Russell noticed, was already empty. He and Effi shared knowing glances.

The food – a sausage casserole with unmistakably real sausage – was excellent, and Russell said so.

'You needn't sound so surprised,' Zarah told him with a nervous smile.

'I'm not,' Russell protested, but he did wonder whether their hosts knew how few people in Berlin would be enjoying a dinner as good as this. He knew better than to ask, though.

'These days any good meal is a surprise,' Effi interjected diplomatically.

As they ate, the conversation meandered through the current Berlin topics – the sudden shortage of shoes, the irritating air raids, the recent avalanche of leaflets criticising the government, the errant behaviour of youth. 'Two boys were caught throwing stones at the trains last week,' Zarah said. 'Near Halensee Station, I think it was. They were on their way home from a *Hitlerjugend* meeting.'

Jens said little, and even then only when his wife appealed to him directly. He seemed distracted, Russell thought. He was drinking steadily, and had sunk well over a bottle of wine before they turned to the brandy.

'How's work?' Russell asked, more out of politeness than from any hope of learning anything useful.

'Hard,' Jens said, and smiled rather bleakly. 'Hard,' he echoed himself. 'Just between us,' he said, waving a hand to embrace them all, 'the job is becoming impossible.'

Russell couldn't resist asking: 'Which job?'

'Feeding everyone,' Jens said simply. 'In peacetime it was a challenge, but one we could meet. In wartime – well, you can imagine. There are fewer men available for farm work, so production has suffered…'

'Aren't there enough Land Girls?' his wife asked.

'A lot of them are getting married just to avoid farm work,' Effi offered.

'We can feed our cities and countryside,' Jens went on, as if no one else had spoken. 'But the Wehrmacht is more of a problem. We now have almost four million soldiers and half a million horses to feed, and most of them are more than eight hundred kilometres from the old borders of the Reich.'

'And there aren't enough trains,' Russell murmured. He was, he realised, about to learn something.

'Exactly. So they must live off the Russian countryside. They will consume the agricultural surplus that used to feed the Russian towns.'

'And the Russian towns?' Effi asked.

'As I said, it is hard. We must be hard.'

He looked anything but, Russell thought. In fact, he might be imagining it, but there seemed to be a glint of tears in Jens's eyes.

There was a sudden silence around the table.

Russell thought through the implications. Most of the Russian peasantry would survive – they'd been hiding food from invaders and governments since time began. The towns would indeed suffer, but not as badly as the millions of Soviet prisoners. What would they be fed with? And then there were the Jews, trainload after trainload travelling east, into this man-made famine. What would they eat? They wouldn't.

'You can only do your best,' Zarah was telling her husband.

He looked furious, but only for an instant. 'Of course. The men at the front are the ones who really suffer. I just work in an office.' He got up. 'Excuse me for a moment. I thought I heard Lothar.'

'He worries about the boy,' Zarah said.

He should worry about himself, Effi thought. He was as close to a breakdown as any of her soldiers in their hospital beds. 'He's a good father,' was all she said.

'That's something, isn't it?' Zarah replied. 'I was thinking the other day – so many boys are going to be without their fathers when all this is over.'

There was no air raid that night, but Russell was woken by the sound of Effi crying. He found her wrapped in her old fur coat, curled up on the sofa with her knees up under her chin. 'I'm sorry,' she sobbed. 'I didn't want to wake you.'

He took her in his arms, and asked what the matter was.

'It just gets worse and worse,' she said.

He knew what she meant.

A valued friend of the Reich

They woke later than usual, and Effi cooked the eggs that Zarah had insisted on giving them. 'What time are you meeting Paul?' she asked.

'I'm not,' Russell said, realising he hadn't told her about the *Hitlerjugend* shooting tournament.

'Don't they allow fathers?'

'If they do, Paul forgot to tell me.'

'Oh well, you can come shopping with me. I need some new boots.'

'You'll be lucky.'

'Ah, I've been told about an old man in Friedrichshain who still makes them. He must get the leather on the black market.'

'Wouldn't it be simpler to borrow some from the studio wardrobe department?'

'Of course, but not half as much fun.'

It occurred to Russell that he hadn't mentioned his rendezvous with Sullivan either. 'I've got a meeting at noon,' he told her, 'but it won't take long. We could meet after that. Two o'clock at the stop in Alexander Platz?'

'Fine. But I thought you'd given up on Ribbentrop's press conferences.'

'I have. It's something else. I'll tell you later,' he added, touching his ear to indicate that they might be overheard. It was several weeks since their last hunt for listening devices.

'Nothing too dangerous, I hope,' she said lightly.

'I can't see why it would be,' he told her, but half an hour later, standing on the Zoo Station platform, he didn't feel quite so sure. The way Kenyon had presented it, Russell was just meeting Sullivan for a friendly chat and a peek at the latter's *bona fides*. The latter might be corporate secrets rather than state secrets, but was the Gestapo bright enough to know the difference? Although to be fair to the leather-coated brigade, he wasn't sure there was much of a difference anymore. The industrial corporations hadn't been nationalised in any official sense, but they were, to all intents and purposes, controlled by the state. And poring over documentation of their darkest secrets in the Stettin Station buffet might well be considered a crime.

Russell was reasonably certain that he wasn't being followed, and it wouldn't be hard to make absolutely sure. In any case, it seemed much more likely that Sullivan would be followed, since any doubts about the Radio Berlin broadcaster's continuing loyalty to the Reich would have stemmed from his own behaviour. The man had to know that, and would be taking the necessary precautions.

Or would he? Sullivan was intelligent, but in Russell's experience intelligent people just had bigger blind spots.

How could he be sure that Sullivan wasn't being followed? He couldn't trail the man from his home because he didn't know where he lived. He could hope to watch him arrive at Stettin Station, but the number of entrances – at least three from the street and one from the U-Bahn – made missing him much more likely. There were even two entrances to the buffet, although the street one was little used. His best bet was to find a spot on the concourse with a good view of the buffet, hope Sullivan used that entrance, and watch for anyone following him in.

But first things first. He left the Stadtbahn train at Lehrter Station, and remained for several minutes on the elevated platform, staring down with apparent interest at the throat of the terminus below. All but two of the other alighting passengers took the steps down to the mainline platforms, and those two were already out of sight when Russell followed them down the walkway to Invaliden Strasse. Reaching the main road, he could see the man walking west past the old guards' barracks, the woman crossing the road to his right, with the apparent intention of entering the District Court building. She disappeared through the doorway.

Russell walked eastward, turning once or twice to check that the woman hadn't re-emerged. It was about a kilometre to Stettin Station, and he had over half an hour to spare. Crossing the Hohenzollern Canal he could see the Invalidenfriedhof Cemetery stretched out along the eastern bank, a conveniently short journey from the huge military hospital which rose behind it. A steam barge was disappearing into the grey distance, the rust-coloured water rippling in the breeze.

Ten minutes later, he was walking in through the western side entrance of Stettin Station. It was one of Berlin's older and smaller termini, with half a dozen platforms hosting services to Stettin, Rostock and Danzig, and local trains serving Pankow and the outlying suburbs beyond. A spacious glass-roofed concourse lay between the buffers and the booking office, with the buffet and other facilities lining the sides. After buying a newspaper at the kiosk, Russell took up position near the entrance to platform 1, where the steady stream of passengers looking to board the Stettin express offered a modicum of anonymity. He had a clear view of all three street exits, the steps down to the U-Bahn, and the concourse entrance to the buffet. It was eleven forty-five.

The minutes ticked by. Two young women in black walked past him, heading for the Stettin train, and following them with his eyes Russell saw one of several waiting coffins being loaded into a luggage van. Outside it had begun to rain – with some abandon if the loud drumming on the station roof was any guide. A local train pulled in on the far side with a squeal of tired brakes, and soon a procession of arrivals were crossing the concourse towards the various exits. Sullivan was not among them.

It was five to twelve, and Russell wondered when he should check the buffet – the outside entrance was only really convenient for railwaymen coming from the goods yard, but there was always a chance that Sullivan had slinked in that way. He would give it another ten minutes.

The last few passengers for Stettin hurried by, the whistle sounded, and the distant locomotive went into a momentary fit, blasting steam in all directions before finding its feet and easing its load away. The drumming on the roof seemed louder in the subsequent silence, and Russell blessed the fact that the U-Bahn would take him to Alexanderplatz. By the time he met Effi the rain might have stopped.

Suddenly he saw Sullivan, cutting across the concourse from the same direction as the arriving local passengers some ten minutes earlier. Had he been on that train? It seemed unlikely that he would have chosen to live north of the city when Radio Berlin was situated thirty kilometres to the south. And if he had, where had he been for the last ten minutes? In a toilet?

Not that it mattered. Russell watched Sullivan walk into the buffet without a backward glance – the broadcaster clearly had no qualms about a possible tail. He would give it a minute, he decided, and only set himself in motion once the second hand of the station clock had stuttered its way around the dial. He was about ten metres from the buffet doors when two young men hurried in through the main station entrance, eyes flashing in all directions, clearly searching for someone or something. They were wearing neither leather coats nor formal uniforms, but Russell was willing to bet they knew people who did. He adjusted his route and speed accordingly, walking slowly past the open buffet doors towards the main entrance. As he passed the doors he caught a glimpse of the two men bearing down on an unsuspecting Sullivan.

Russell walked on through the wide archway of the main entrance, and stopped among the people waiting for the rain to slacken or stop. There was a Mercedes 260 parked in front, its busy windscreen wiper offering pulsatory glimpses of the man behind the wheel. He seemed to be studying his manicure. When several footfalls sounded behind Russell, he didn't turn his head, just waited until the three men were past him, splashing their way across to the parked car. He only saw Sullivan's face as one of the young men hustled him into the back seat. The broadcaster looked more angry than frightened.

The car pulled away and, as it turned towards the forecourt exit on Invalidenstrasse, Russell had a clear view of the rear numberplate. Stepping further back into the archway, he jotted it down in his notebook.

It was still raining when he emerged from the U-Bahn at Alexanderplatz, still raining when Effi's tram arrived at the stop twenty minutes later. Russell made to get on, but she urged him back off again. 'I've lost the boot-maker's address,' she said. 'I know which street he lives on, but this doesn't seem like a day for knocking on lots of doors.'

'No,' he agreed.

'I've also lost my umbrella,' she added plaintively. 'I thought you could take me somewhere nice for lunch instead.'

'How about the Adlon? I have to call in at the Consulate.' As they waited for a tram back up Königstrasse he told her about Sullivan, the arranged meeting and the events at Stettin Station.

'Thank God they didn't catch you with him,' was her first reaction. 'But what if he tells them he was there to meet you?'

'Why should he? He'd only incriminate himself. No, I'm safe enough. They'd have had to catch us in the act, flash bulbs popping as the documents were handed over.'

'Yes?' she half asked, as if not quite convinced.

'Yes,' he insisted, hiding the fact that he wasn't either.

The tram arrived and dropped them a few minutes later on Behrenstrasse, several hundred very wet metres from the Adlon. A waiter fan of Effi's insisted on bringing towels for their hair, and took their coats away to be dried while they ate. 'I thought you said this place had gone downhill,' Effi whispered.

'Look around you,' Russell told her. There were only about twenty people in the huge dining room, and most of them were in uniform.

'And the food is somewhat variable.'

But today was one of the better days, and being there with Effi brought back fond memories of pre-war times, when the Adlon had still functioned as a cosmopolitan island in a cheerless German sea.

After eating they moved into the bar, where some of Russell's colleagues were already ensconced. The Foreign Ministry press conference had yielded fresh news of Soviet reverses, with Tula supposedly surrounded and Moscow threatened from the south. By contrast, the latest releases on the situation in North Africa had seemed less confident, as if the authorities were preparing the ground for possible failure. Dr Schmidt had spent most of the briefing rubbishing British claims that the allied delegations now departing Berlin were mere 'puppets' of the Germans, but in vain. 'You could see that part of him really liked the idea of their being puppets,' one of the Americans explained, 'so his denials weren't that convincing.'

Russell left Effi with a colleague and a bilious-looking cocktail, and made a dash through the rain to the adjacent Consulate.

Kenyon came down to meet him, and invited him back out into the shelter of the portico. 'I can't see any suspicious wires,' he said, examining the column-supported roof. 'Can you?'

'Not even one,' Russell agreed. The rain was still falling steadily, running in sheets down the side of the Brandenburg Gate.

'So?' Kenyon asked, one hand emerging from one pocket with a packet of cigarettes, the other from the other pocket with the silver lighter.

'He was arrested,' Russell said. 'At least I assume so.' He went through the sequence of events. 'I didn't see them show him any identification, but that would have happened in the buffet. There was no struggle of any kind, no guns. Sullivan looked furious, but he went with them willingly enough.'

Kenyon exhaled a lungful of smoke, and thought for a few moments. 'Was he carrying anything?' he eventually asked.

'Only a newspaper. He must have had the documents in an inside pocket.'

'Whatever they were,' Kenyon murmured, apparently to himself. 'And I don't expect we'll ever find out now. Which sticks in my craw. If American businesses really are planning on supplying the enemy after an official declaration then I'd happily see their bosses taken out and shot.'

'Those guys always survive.'

Kenyon stubbed out his cigarette and stared out at the rain. 'They do, don't they? But let me dream. If Sullivan does get back in touch, and if by some miracle he still has those proofs he was talking about, I'll fix up another meeting.'

'Okay,' Russell said, shaking his hand. Back at the Adlon he found Effi deep in conversation with the waiter who'd provided the towels. They were talking about the film she'd been making when Russell first met her. 'They don't seem to write such good stories these days,' the waiter admitted. 'Too much politics,' he added in a whisper.

The telephone rang at six in the morning, which was rather early for a Sunday. Russell decided to ignore it, but Effi was worried it might be Zarah, and leapt out of bed to answer. Much to her disgust, it was for him. Rainer Duhnke was a German journalist whom Russell had known since the early thirties, and the two of them had made a habit of passing on stories which suited their own national readerships.

'I've just had a tip-off from a friend at the Alex,' Duhnke said, 'and you seemed like the right person to tell. They've just found Patrick Sullivan's body in the Tiergarten.'

Russell felt a momentary pang of sadness. 'Do you know where exactly?'

'Between the Neuer See and the Landwehrkanal. It's still there – nothing can happen until it gets light. So if you get down there now…'

'Thanks, Rainer.'

'What is it?' Effi wanted to know.

He told her as he dressed.

'Be careful,' she said.

'No need. I'm only wearing my journalist hat.'

It still seemed very dark outside, but as he turned onto Hardenberg Strasse a pale grey glow was noticeable in the eastern sky, and by the time he reached the bridge over Landwehrkanal the world was taking visible shape once more. Three black cars were already lined up on the Tiergartenufer, with one uniformed policeman standing guard. As Russell walked towards them he heard the sound of other cars approaching from the west. Turning, he saw headlights cleaving their way through the dawn twilight with the sort of abandon that only high-ranking officials could afford. And as the leading car materialised into a swish limousine generously bedecked with swastikas, it became apparent that Joseph Goebbels himself had come to examine the corpse.

Hoping to escape attention, Russell stayed where he was on the canal side of the road. Goebbels emerged from the limousine, straightened the large peaked cap that always made him look even shorter than he was, and strode energetically off across the grass in the direction indicated by the uniformed officer. In the meantime, the other cars in Goebbels' convoy had begun discharging their passengers, and these, Russell delightedly realised, were colleagues. Most seemed to be German, but he recognised at least one Swede. The press had clearly been invited.

After working his way around the line of cars Russell joined the rear of the procession. The light was rapidly improving now, the bare trees sharply outlined against the grey dawn, the flak tower behind them a well-defined block in the southern sky. It only took about three minutes to reach the crime scene, which lay just beside a footbridge carrying a path across a narrow arm of the Neuer See. Around a dozen policeman were already at work, most of them Kripo officers in plain clothes. Sullivan's blanket-covered body lay in the middle of the path, and Goebbels was standing over it, staring down with what looked like a calculated mixture of grief and anger. He was clearly itching to lift the blanket, and a few seconds later did so, briefly revealing blood-encrusted hair and a badly beaten face.

The Propaganda Minister asked a question of an acolyte, who gestured towards one of the plain clothes men. Obviously under instruction to fetch him, the acolyte trotted across the glistening grass, laid a proprietary hand on his quarry's arm and said something in his ear. The detective turned his eyes in Goebbels' direction, giving Russell a first glimpse of his face. It was Uwe Kuzorra.

If memory served him well, Kuzorra had resigned from the police force in 1933, a few months after the Nazi takeover. He had worked as a private detective for five years, and Russell had met him during that period, whilst engaged in writing a freelance piece on Berlin's growing army of shamuses. In the summer of 1939 he had persuaded Kuzorra to help him hunt down a missing Jewish girl named Miriam Rosenfeld, but old Nazi colleagues in the Kripo had pressured the detective into withdrawing from the case. Now it seemed he was back in his original harness. Russell had heard that the police were re-engaging retired officers as replacements for those lost to the military, and presumably Kuzorra was one of them.

He was talking to Goebbels at this moment, or at least listening. His face wore a neutral expression, but Russell would have bet money that Kuzorra was secretly enjoying his height advantage. He had always loathed the Nazis.

Goebbels turned away from the detective, eyes searching and finding his audience. The journalists dutifully arranged themselves in a semicircle.

'A valued friend of the Reich has been brutally murdered,' he began. 'And no effort will be spared in the search for his murderer. Kriminalinspektor Kuzorra' – he indicated the detective beside him – 'will lead the investigation, and will be given all the resources he deems necessary for bringing it to a rapid conclusion. Patrick Sullivan will be sorely missed by his colleagues at Radio Berlin, and, of course, by his millions of listeners in the United States, who looked to his broadcasts for the sort of no-nonsense truth-telling which their own newspapers have long since abandoned. Herr Sullivan also offered a constant and welcome reminder to Germans that not all Americans have fallen for the lies of their President and his British cronies.'

Goebbels paused, perhaps for effect, perhaps for inspiration. He was, Russell noted with reluctant admiration, making it up as he went along.

'It may turn out that Herr Sullivan was the victim of a random crime,' the Minister continued, 'that he was assaulted by one of those despicable criminals who use the blackout as a cover for their robberies and murders. That may be the case. But it is also possible that Herr Sullivan was killed for political reasons, because he was prepared to speak out for fairness and plain speaking in German-American relations, and prepared to speak out against the Jews, who work day and night in their attempt to poison those relations. Herr Sullivan was a committed enemy of the Jewish-Bolshevik alliance, and his murder is bound to increase the anxiety of ordinary Berliners about the large number of Jews still living in their midst.'

Goebbels paused again. 'That will be all for the moment. Any developments in the investigation will be reported at this afternoon's press conference.' He turned to shake Kuzorra by the hand, then strode towards his limousine, the acolytes falling in behind him like a squadron of geese in flight.

Russell headed back in the same direction. He didn't think Kuzorra had noticed him, and he wasn't at all sure that re-introducing himself at this moment was a sensible idea. It was theoretically possible that one of Goebbels' two suppositions were right; that Sullivan, once released from custody, had chosen to celebrate this fact by going for a winter's night stroll in the blacked-out Tiergarten, and had accidentally bumped into either a homicidal maniac or an outraged Jew. But it seemed more likely that the broadcaster had been murdered by the men who picked him up at Stettin Station, and then dumped in the Tiergarten after it got dark. Why was another question. Assuming they'd found the illicit documents, then several more obvious options sprang to mind. They could have blackmailed Sullivan into continuing his broadcasts; they could have arrested and promised to try him; they could have dropped him in the concrete foundations of the new flak tower in Friedrichshain.

All of which made more sense than dumping his body in a public park and inviting a thorough police investigation.

Goebbels obviously had no idea that state minions were responsible, or he wouldn't have ordered Kuzorra to force open what was certain to be a huge can of worms. Of course, Russell couldn't know for sure that the men he'd seen at Stettin Station were state minions, but these days who else got to drive cars? Only big businessmen – like the German heads of American subsidiaries – and perhaps their enforcers.

It was more than possible. In Russell's experience, few governments could match big business when it came to the ruthless pursuit of self-interest. But it didn't really make any difference – in 1941 Berlin both government and business belonged to the Nazis. The only question was how deeply Kuzorra would delve before someone informed him that the investigation was off. For the detective's sake, Russell hoped that it wouldn't be too deep; he liked Kuzorra. He thought about warning him, but could think of no way of doing so without exposing himself. In any case the detective had never struck him as someone who had trouble looking after himself.

Back at the apartment, he found Effi already up, sitting at the kitchen table with a cup of Chinese tea. 'Zarah did call,' she said by way of explanation. 'Was it gruesome?'

'Not particularly, not in the way you mean. Goebbels turned up, which is always a bit on the gruesome side.'

'What on earth for?'

'Oh, one of his soldiers in the great propaganda war has made the ultimate sacrifice, etc etc. You know how they love swearing vengeance on anyone who crosses them.'

Effi suddenly worried. 'Will they want to talk to you?'

'Perhaps. The Consulate won't say anything, so it depends on whether Sullivan told anyone else that he was meeting me. He might have put it in his diary, I suppose. "Meeting John Russell to hand over state secrets" – something like that.'

'Fool. Are we still going to see the Blumenthals today?'

'I thought so.'

'When?'

'Around three o'clock?'

'That's good. Zarah wants to meet me at eleven, at Café Palmenhaus. She sounded really upset on the telephone.'

When Effi arrived at the café on Ku'damm, the reason for her sister's distress was immediately evident – Zarah's left cheek was purple with bruising. 'What happened?' she asked, already guessing the answer.

'Jens hit me. Last night. After Lothar had gone to bed, thank God.'

'Why? Not that there's any excuse, but what set him off?'

'Oh, I was nagging him about his drinking. I shouldn't do that...'

'It's no reason to hit you.'

'No, I know, but... on the tram coming here there was a young woman in mourning with two small children... and Jens lashing out just once... well, it's nothing is it?'

'It is *not* nothing, and you know it.'

'He was so sorry afterwards. He was nicer to me this morning than he has been for months. And he's under so much pressure at work.'

'I know.' Effi could see Jens at the dinner table, the slight tremble of his lips as he described what was happening in Russia. She took her sister's hand and squeezed it, wondering what she would do if John ever hit her. She would show him the door, simple as that. But Zarah would never do that to Jens. Where could she go? Back to their parents with Lothar? 'You must tell Jens that if he ever hits you again, you and Lothar will be gone,' she said.

'But I couldn't leave him...'

'He doesn't know that. However bad it is at work, he has no right to take it out on you.' Though you could be doing more to help him, Effi thought but didn't say. Jens had crossed a line, and for today at least her sister should feel herself blameless.

They talked for an hour or more, going over and over the same ground, Effi's frustration kept in check by the obvious comfort this was giving her sister. On the pavement prior to parting, Zarah revealed how terrified Jens was that Effi would never speak to him again.

'Don't disabuse him,' Effi told her. 'Not for a while.'

Russell had stayed home to write up the story. He had his doubts as to whether a report of Sullivan's death would ever see the light of day, but where Nazi government circles were concerned there was always a reasonable chance that the left hand was in utter ignorance of the right hand's activities. And, if no one whispered a few cautionary words in Goebbels' ear before Russell's copy deadline, then the story might slip through.

Soon after one o'clock he arrived at the Press Club on Leipziger Platz, and after handing the article over to the censors climbed the stairs to the dining room. Sullivan's fate was one topic of conversation among the foreign correspondents, but not the most prominent: that honour belonged to the German Army's unexpected ejection from recently-conquered Rostov. This news had been aired by the BBC on the previous evening, and grudgingly confirmed by Braun von Stumm at the Foreign Ministry press conference only an hour or so ago.

This was important news. Rostov was the first city the German Army had been forced to surrender in over two years of war. Rostov was the gateway to all that oil which the Wehrmacht so desperately needed – a gateway now apparently closed. His *sauerkraut* was tasting so much sweeter, Russell realised. After lunch he used Bradley Emmering's notes from the press conference to write an appropriate piece, and submitted that to the censors.

His good mood ebbed away as he waited for Effi at the tram stop on Budapester Strasse. He had decided to pass on Ströhm's terrible news, but found himself hoping that the Blumenthals had already heard it from other sources. Effi had argued for complete disclosure from the start, and was utterly unimpressed by his argument that the news might unleash a violent reaction from the Jewish community, one which would seal its fate more swiftly and surely than might otherwise have been the case. 'They deserve to know,' she had said with her usual trenchancy. 'You know they do.'

He did. Maybe not knowing was something he craved for himself.

Her tram arrived, and ten minutes later they were alighting close to the old synagogue on Oranienburgerstrasse. Once inside the Blumenthals' crowded apartment it immediately became apparent that the terrible news had preceded them. The welcome was warm as ever, but the eyes of mother and daughter held an underlying bleakness which was new. 'Someone came round from the Jewish community office,' Leonore explained, 'and asked if we could pass the news on. They would have called a meeting, but meetings are forbidden.'

The whole story had been reported: the unfinished camp at Riga, the 'improvised' response at Kovno. All the Blumenthals' friends were hoping that the latter was an aberration – Martin Blumenthal was even hoping that the guilty parties would be punished – but a majority also feared the worst. Knowing what Jens had told him and Effi over a candlelit dinner in Grunewald, Russell was afraid they were right, and that the survival of Berlin's remaining Jews was dependent on the continuing inefficiency of the Reichsbahn. But he refrained from saying so.

'If I'm on the next list, I'm not going,' Ali said abruptly.

The announcement obviously surprised her parents. 'You won't be on the list,' was her father's reaction. 'Why would they send a good worker like you? Herr Schade will see to it, you'll see.'

'What would you do?' her mother said.

'Go underground. More of us are doing it every day. You take off the star and you become invisible again. That's why they insist on us wearing them.'

'But how would you live?' her mother wanted to know.

'I'll manage somehow. I'll have a better chance here in a city I know than I would on a train to the East.'

'This is foolish talk,' her father said heatedly. 'We're not going on a train to the East. You and I, we both have important jobs, and your mother must be here to look after the house. Why would they send away workers they need? It's the old they are sending, God spare them.'

Ali walked over and put an arm around her father's neck. 'I hope you are right, Papa.'

He smiled at her, and looked out of the window. 'A beautiful day for a walk in the park,' he said wistfully. 'Maybe in Lodz there are still parks where Jews are allowed to walk,' he added quietly, almost as if he was talking to himself.

'They are *starving* in Lodz,' his wife muttered angrily.

Travelling home together, Effi and Russell sat mostly in silence, lost in their own thoughts. Effi was thinking about Zarah's troubles, how insignificant they seemed when compared to those of the Blumenthals, and how irrelevant such contrasts always were. Russell watched the familiar streets go by, streets which would soon no longer be familiar. His evacuation train would not be heading east into lands wracked by famine and war, but north or south to Denmark or Switzerland, havens of relative peace and prosperity. He thanked providence for not making him a German Jew, and wondered what had happened to his sense of shame.

The knock on their door came soon after dark, and as he went to answer it Russell realised that his unconscious had registered the arrival of a car a minute or so earlier. The visitors would be official.

The first face he saw – both boyish and bookish – belonged to a tall young man in an SS Obersturmführer's uniform. The second, half hidden behind the first man's shoulder, belonged to Uwe Kuzorra. 'Herr John Russell,' the Obersturmführer stated rather than asked.

The man had lost an arm, Russell realised. 'That's me,' he said, without unblocking the doorway.

'We need to ask you some questions. Inside, if you please.'

Russell stepped back to allow them in, and pushed the door shut. Effi had retreated to the bedroom doorway, and the Obersturmführer was staring at her with obvious recognition.

'I'll leave you to it,' she said with a smile, and closed the door behind her.

Russell offered the two men seats, his mind racing. They must have discovered that he had an appointment to meet Sullivan on the previous day. What could he safely tell them? Certainly not that Sullivan had secret information to hand over – Russell had no desire to face an espionage charge.

Kuzorra lowered himself onto the sofa with obvious pleasure. The detective would have had a long and busy day, and he was well into his sixties by now.

The Obersturmführer remained on his feet, tapping his right thigh with his hand.

'You know who I am,' Kuzorra told Russell. 'This is my assistant, Obersturmführer Schwering.'

The younger man reluctantly accepted Russell's offer of a handshake.

'I noticed you this morning,' Kuzorra went on. 'I was rather surprised to find that you were still in Berlin.'

'I live here,' Russell said with a shrug. Saying as little as he could seemed a good guiding principle where this conversation was concerned.

'We have discovered that our victim arranged a meeting with you,' the Obersturmführer said accusingly. 'Stettin Station at twelve o'clock, I believe.'

'Who told you that?' Russell asked pleasantly.

'That is neither…' Schwering began.

'His wife,' Kuzorra cut his subordinate off. 'His widow,' he corrected himself.

'It's true that I had arranged to meet him,' Russell admitted. 'But I was late. If he ever turned up, he was gone by the time I got there.'

The Obersturmführer looked unconvinced, but let that go for the moment. 'So what was this meeting for?'

'He said he had some information for me. As I'm sure you know, most journalists get their information from a variety of sources.'

'Was he giving or selling?' Kuzorra wanted to know.

'Selling. Patrick Sullivan was only ever interested in the truth as a commodity.'

'What was this information?' Schwering asked.

Russell shrugged. 'I've no idea. Sullivan obviously thought it was worth something, but he wouldn't tell me anything in advance. He was probably afraid that spreading a few clues would allow me to dig the story up myself.'

The Obersturmführer was far from happy. 'We shall be checking your story,' he said, as if knowing that fact would persuade Russell to come clean.

'I'm sure Herr Russell is aware of that,' Kuzorra said, getting to feet.

'How is your wife?' Russell asked, hoping to move matters onto a more convivial footing.

'She died last year,' Kuzorra told him, a moment of bleakness apparent in his eyes. 'A sudden illness. She didn't suffer.'

Unlike you, Russell thought. He remembered how well suited the two of them had seemed. 'I'm sorry,' he said. 'How long have you been back at work?'

'Since that time.' He managed a thin smile. 'I needed something to do.'

Russell showed them out, and leant back against the door with some relief.

'Trouble?' Effi asked as she emerged.

'I don't think so.' He filled in those bits of the conversation which she had been unable to follow from the other side of the bedroom door.

'That's sad,' she said of Kuzorra's loss. She had not met the detective before, but remembered Russell's description of him and his wife Katrin.

'She seemed the one with the energy,' Russell recalled. 'And she made a wonderful cup of coffee.'

'Let's go out to eat,' Effi said. 'In case they come back. I don't want to share my last free evening before filming with an overgrown boy in a black uniform.'

They followed the white kerbs to the Ku'damm, and walked slowly west along the wide boulevard. This was also blacked-out, but the sheer number of phosphorescent badges and masked headlights provided sufficient illumination for seeing their way and recognising restaurants. Most of the latter were doing good business, Berliners having just received their December ration tickets.

They opted for the Chinese. The meat in the chow mein didn't taste much like chicken, but then it didn't taste much like anything else either. Russell wasn't even sure it was meat. Watching the members of the extended family who owned and ran the restaurant hurrying to and fro, he wondered, not for the first time, what on heaven's earth had persuaded them to set up shop in Hitler's Reich.

After they had finished eating someone stopped at the table to ask for Effi's autograph, and she obliged with her usual good grace. 'Are you looking forward to tomorrow?' Russell asked once the happy fan had returned to her own table.

'First days are usually fun,' she said. 'Everyone's trying to make a good impression on everyone else, even the director. And a masterpiece still seems possible, especially if you've only read your own part of the script. Of course, the first scene usually shatters that particular illusion.'

'Not the first scene of *GPU*, surely?'

'That may have the whole cast in stitches. I hope so. If everyone knows what rubbish it is, then we really can have some fun with it. But if the director thinks he's making an important statement, then God help us.' She smiled a quite dazzling smile at Russell. 'But I do love it most of the time. If it wasn't for the getting up at four-thirty in the morning, and the fact that we hardly see each other when I'm filming…'

'I know. Particularly now, when I may be whisked out of the country at a moment's notice.'

She reached a hand across the table. 'I've been meaning to tell you. Just in case you don't know. I shall be waiting for you, however long it takes. Though I can't guarantee that I'll still have my film star looks. '

'I love you too,' he said. 'And with any luck at all we'll soon be enjoying regular conjugal visits in Switzerland, courtesy of the Abwehr.'

'Conjugal, eh?'

'I was hoping.'

'I shall miss our bed, though.'

'It is an excellent bed.'

'And waiting for us right now.'

'I'll get the bill.'

Russell was still half asleep when he heard the knock on the door, and his first thought was that Effi had returned, having forgotten her keys and God knew what else. He was almost at the door when he noticed the clock, and realised that she would be in front of the cameras by this time.

It was Kuzorra, and this time he was alone. Russell stood aside to let the detective in, and offered him a cup of coffee.

'Real coffee?' his guest asked.

'I'm afraid not. Even we pampered foreigners have trouble getting that.'

'Then I'll pass.'

Kuzorra took the seat he had occupied the evening before. 'There's a phrase you journalists use when you want a quote, and the person concerned doesn't want anyone to know that it came from them…'

'Off the record.'

'That's the one. Well, I'd like you to tell me what you know about this business – off the record.'

'What makes you think I know anything more than what I've already told you?'

Kuzorra smiled. 'A journalist who loathes the Nazis meets a journalist who loves them for unexplained reasons. And before you can say "Joseph Goebbels" the second journalist is apparently beaten to death. It's hard to believe there's no connection.'

'I didn't kill him.'

'I didn't say you did. But I do think you know more about this than you're telling me. Hence the unofficial visit. Without my new assistant.'

Russell considered. 'These are strange times we live in,' he said finally, 'when the police are asking questions off the record.'

'These are strange times.'

'Why can't it have been a robbery?' Russell asked, still prevaricating.

Kuzorra smiled again. 'According to the Luftwaffe weather people it only stopped raining around two in the morning on Sunday. The body was wet underneath but dry on top when it was found an hour or so later.'

'So he was killed during that hour.'

'He'd been dead for well over twelve hours when the pathologist examined him at eight this morning.'

'Ah.'

'Ah indeed. He was killed just a few hours after your missed appointment, and placed in the park a lot later, between two and three in the morning.'

'And I don't suppose you're looking for a gang of Jewish-Bolshevik cut-throats?'

'They're thin on the ground these days.'

Russell had run out of wriggle room. 'Off the record,' he began, 'I didn't lie to you yesterday, but I didn't tell you the whole truth either. I didn't meet with Sullivan, but I did see him arrive at Stettin Station.' He paused, wondering how to explain his preliminary surveillance. 'I was a bit worried about meeting him in public,' he went on, improvising heroically. 'Sullivan was a Nazi, after all, and I could imagine him agreeing to help trap me in some sort of indiscretion. Anyway, I watched him go into the buffet and then waited a few moments to make sure that he wasn't being tailed. No one appeared, and I was just about to join him when two goons in suits beat me to it. They took Sullivan out to their car and drove off with him. I had no idea why, and I still haven't. I try and stay out of arguments between Nazis.'

'What did these men look like?'

Russell described them, and the car.

'I don't suppose you noticed the number.'

In for a penny, Russell thought. He collected the notebook from his jacket pocket, and read the number out.

'Anything else?' Kuzorra asked, once he had noted it down.

'Nothing.'

'Did Sullivan say, or hint, that he had something for you? Something material, I mean. Documents perhaps, or photographs.'

'No. But if he had brought something to show me, then presumably his killers will have it now.'

'Perhaps.' Kuzorra ran a hand across the grey stubble which passed for his hair, a personal habit which Russell remembered from their previous meetings. 'This is a strange case. While we're off the record – I presume this works both ways?'

Russell nodded, intrigued.

'The officer who was with me yesterday evening – Obersturmführer Schwering – was appointed as my assistant less than two hours after Sullivan's body was found. He's on secondment from the *Sicherheitsdienst*. The first thing he suggested was a thorough search of Sullivan's apartment in Dahlem, and when he got there he seemed very insistent on conducting it himself. I let him get on with it, but kept an eye on him. He seemed rather put out when he didn't find anything.'

'Interesting,' Russell murmured.

'He may insist on searching this flat,' Kuzorra added.

'He won't find anything here,' Russell said flatly. Having their home ransacked by the SD was not a welcome prospect. Particularly if only Effi was here to receive them. 'I'm off to Prague this evening,' he told the detective, 'and I'll be gone for a couple of nights. So if you want to search the place, I'd be grateful if you'd do it now. '

Kuzorra gave him a lengthy stare. 'Consider it searched,' he said at last, and got to his feet. 'I'll give Schwering the car number, and tell him I got it from a witness at the station. It should keep him busy for a day or so.'

'Busy failing to trace it?'

'If it's a car from the SD pool. If it isn't, then he'll be the hero of the hour.'

'Depending on whom it does belong to. I don't envy you this particular job.'

Kuzorra paused with his hand on the doorknob. 'It beats chasing blackout robbers. And the expression on Goebbels' face when the penny finally drops should be something to behold.'

An hour or so later, Russell walked down to Zoo Station. Searching through the *Völkischer Beobachter* over the usual unsatisfactory breakfast, he found no mention of Sullivan's unfortunate demise. Someone had given Goebbels pause for thought, and sufficient reason for delaying his planned publicity blitz around the manhunt for Sullivan's killer. By tomorrow, Russell guessed, it would all be over. Sullivan's death would be fictionalised in a suitably edifying light, his killers on to their next mission of mercy. Kuzorra would be off the hook, and so would he.

It was a two-kilometre walk down the Landwehrkanal to the Abwehr headquarters. Yesterday's clear skies had persisted, and the low sun was frequently in his eyes as he walked south-eastwards along the towpath. It was suitably cold for December the first, and hopefully colder outside Moscow. The coal traffic seemed busier than ever, barge after laden barge puttering down the ice-edged canal towards the factories and generating stations in the north-western outskirts. The men at their helms all looked like the Ancient Mariner, dragged out of retirement in the Reich's hour of need.

With the Abwehr building looming in the distance, Russell used the Graf Spee Bridge to switch banks. As he approached the entrance on

Tirpitz Ufer, he noticed the usual Gestapo Mercedes 260 parked on the opposite quay. In pre-war days foreign agents of all descriptions had lurked in this vicinity, hopeful of overhearing some useful tidbit of military information, but the real war had put paid to such boyish games, and Russell could only assume that the men in the car were Germans spying on their own countrymen.

At reception he was told to report to Colonel Piekenbrock, and for once the Section 1 chief didn't keep Russell waiting outside. Piekenbrock invited him in, sat him down and even suggested a cup of coffee. Russell accepted the latter, more in hope than expectation, and was only mildly disappointed when a pretty brunette arrived with the usual slop.

Piekenbrock gulped his down with almost inhuman gusto. 'This is Grashof,' he said, handing across a photograph. 'That was taken quite recently.'

Russell studied the picture. A tall-looking man with a gaunt face and short dark hair was standing on Prague's famous Charles Bridge, the Little Quarter and Castle rising behind him. Grashof was wearing glasses, and his lips were slightly curled in the beginnings of a smile. This is a clever man, Russell thought, and wondered what it was in the photograph that led him to that conclusion.

He handed it back.

'Your meeting will be at the Šramota Café. It's on the river, close to the Smetana Bridge. Grashof will be sitting on the terrace, the very last table along from the entrance. You should arrive at exactly two o'clock, with the latest issue of *Signal*.'

'What if it's raining? Or snowing even?'

'It's a glassed-in terrace.'

'What if someone beats us to that table?'

'They won't. This is all taken care of; you just have to be there. Greet Grashof like he was an old friend, order a coffee, sit and chat for ten, fifteen minutes. Before you arrive, you will have hidden this letter –' Piekenbrock passed a wax-sealed and unaddressed envelope across the desk '– in your magazine. Grashof will have his own copy, and it should not prove difficult to switch them over.'

'Elementary,' Russell murmured. The Admiral's penchant for the old traditions had scuppered his plan to steam the missive open. 'Will there be anything in his copy?'

'No.'

Russell put the envelope in his inside jacket pocket. 'Is that it?'

'You will need your train tickets and visa,' Piekenbrock said, handing over another envelope. 'You will find some local currency for your expenses. More than enough, I'm sure. Do you have any questions?'

He had several, but none that Piekenbrock could or would answer. He shook his head.

'Then have a good journey.'

Russell resumed his walk along the Landwehrkanal for another few hundred metres, before climbing the steps at the Potsdamer Strasse Bridge and strolling northward at a leisurely pace towards Leipziger Platz and the Press Club. He felt unreasonably cheerful, and could only assume it was the play of sunlight working its usual magic.

A couple of dozing Italians and one self-important Romanian were the press club's only customers, and Russell had the English-language newspapers all to himself. Not that they offered any real enlightenment. Some thought the battles in Russia were going well for the Germans, with the battles in North Africa going better for the British; while others thought the opposite on both counts.

He walked up Wilhelmstrasse to the Foreign Ministry. Braun von Stumm was again presiding, a sure sign that the regime was short of good news. The subject of Rostov's fall – and the unknown extent of the subsequent German retreat – was evaded with all the usual finesse: von Stumm simply refused to talk about it. The attack on Moscow was still said to be going well, but there were no new towns in the 'captured' column – German troops were simply 'closer to the capital'. Leafing back through his notebook, Russell found more of the same. The previous day they had 'taken more ground', the day before that 'further progress had been made'. The fall of Istra provided the last specific tidemark, and that had been five days ago. Were they hoarding news of advances for maximum later effect, or had they really run out of steam? His mind said the latter, his heart feared the former.

He headed homeward, stopping off at the Press Club to file a near-perfect copy of the Germans' own official release. There were no caveats he could add which the censors would pass, and the gaps in the German version hardly seemed to need pointing out.

Back at the flat, he packed an overnight bag. A pair of trousers had gone missing – Effi must have taken a sack of washing to the laundry without telling him, and then forgotten to collect it. He rescued the half-read *Tristram Shandy* from under the bed and eventually dug up the street map of Prague he had bought in 1939. The flat felt cold and empty, and he hung on later than he should, hoping that Effi would arrive home. She didn't, and the slowness of the tram to Anhalter Station would have caused him to him miss his train, had it not been delayed by an hour. Russell asked a convenient Reichsbahn employee whether dinner on the train would be better than dinner in the Anhalter buffet, and was told to draw his own conclusions from the prominent sign regretting the lack of a dining car. Others had obviously bothered to read it, and the station buffet was packed. Ordering took forever, leaving the time for eating seriously curtailed. Forced to run for the train, Russell quickly realised that every seat was taken, and that even space in the corridors was at a premium. He finally squeezed himself into a small corner beside a draughty corridor connection, feeling slightly nauseous and very out of breath.

It was not a very auspicious beginning. But at least he wasn't carrying anything for the comrades on this trip. Canaris might have occasional problems remembering who his country was fighting, but the Abwehr was still one of the most powerful organisations in Germany, and working for it should be relatively risk-free. He would, he admitted, be happier if he knew what was in the letter, but removing and invisibly replacing the Admiral's seal was beyond him. And whatever it said, it wouldn't have anything to do with him. Or so he assumed – for all he knew the message concealed within was a simple 'Shoot the messenger'. Unlikely, though. It would have been easier to shoot him in Berlin.

The blackout screens on the windows were firmly fixed in place, and Russell was suddenly reminded of a long coffin, rumbling south towards a distant funeral.

The Petschek Palace

Soon after eleven the train reached Dresden, where most of the passengers got off, and Russell was finally able to stretch his limbs on a very cold platform. Several carriages were detached from the rear of the train and, much to his astonishment, replaced by a Czech dining car. There were no meals on offer, but the range of alcoholic drinks seemed wider than that found in Berlin's better hotels. Russell treated himself to three glasses of slivovitz, and sat for the better part of an hour enjoying the views of moonlit mountains in the unscreened windows.

Finding a line of unoccupied seats to lie down on proved surprisingly easy, and he dozed off for a couple of hours. Woken at the Sudeten junction of Usti by the slamming of doors, he noticed that some but not all of the station signs bore the new German name of Aussig. A trip to the waterless toilet indicated that the train was now virtually empty – visas for Heydrich's Protectorate were either hard to come by or in low demand. He was almost asleep again when the train reached the essentially meaningless border, and officialdom required a long and overly suspicious perusal of his papers.

The next few hours were spent in that unsatisfying netherworld between sleep and wakefulness, and as light began filtering around the blackout screens he made his way back to the dining car, where the fields of the Protectorate were now visible. The counter was closed, but Russell could smell the coffee, and a short burst of abject begging persuaded the old Czech in charge to supply him with a cup. It was the best he had drunk for several months, and would prove the undisputed highlight of his trip to Prague.

The train pulled into Masaryk Station – now renamed Hiberner Station – almost two hours late. Russell was supposed to be returning that evening on the same train, but had decided to take a hotel room in any case – after his adventures in Prague two years earlier he had no desire to spend his day wandering the streets, where someone might recognise him. The same risk applied to the Europa Hotel, but any of the other establishments on the long and inappropriately-named Wenceslas Square should prove safe enough. He was just wondering what the new German name might be when he saw the two leather coats waiting at the ticket barrier.

He told himself they were waiting for someone else, but didn't really believe it.

'Herr Russell,' the shorter of the two stated.

There seemed no point in denying it. 'That's me.'

'Come this way please.'

Russell followed, conscious of the other man walking behind him, and of the scrutiny of their Czech audience. He felt an absurd inclination to start goose-stepping, but managed to restrain himself.

They walked through one office and into another. The latter was obviously home to the local transport police, but none were there. Perched on the edge of one desk, arms folded across his stomach, was Obersturmbannführer Giminich of the *Sicherheitsdienst*. On the edge of the other, in probably unconscious imitation of his superior, was a younger man. He was also wearing a smart dark suit, but the classy effect was spoiled by his gingery blond hair, which several litres of grease had failed to flatten.

'Good morning, Herr Russell,' Giminich said. 'Welcome to the Protectorate.'

'Good morning,' Russell replied.

'Please give me the letter which Admiral Canaris entrusted you with.'

Russell took the envelope from his inside jacket pocket and handed it over.

Giminich examined the Admiral's seal with interest. 'You have no idea of the contents?'

'None whatsoever. As you can see, the seal is unbroken.'

Giminich broke it, and removed what looked like a single sheet half-covered in type. After reading it through he passed the letter to his junior.

'What does it say?' Russell asked, intent on emphasising his ignorance of the contents.

Giminich ignored the question. 'This is Untersturmführer Schulenburg,' he told Russell. 'You will be spending the morning with him.'

'Why?'

'Ah. Perhaps we should begin at the beginning. Please, take a seat,' he added, indicating one of the upright chairs. 'Your meeting with Johann Grashof is at the Šramota Café, at two o'clock, the furthest table from the entrance. Yes?'

'You are well informed,' Russell said dryly.

'Much better than yourself, I imagine. What do you know about Johann Grashof?'

'That he's an officer in the Abwehr. Apart from that, absolutely nothing.'

'But you know what he looks like?'

'Yes, I was shown a photograph.'

'Would it surprise you to know that Grashof is a traitor to the Reich?'

'It would.'

Giminich brought his two palms together and balanced his chin on the ends of his fingers. 'Earlier this year certain information was leaked to the British Embassy in Belgrade, information that only three people had access to. Two were away when the leak occurred, but the third – Grashof – was considered above suspicion by Berlin. Then, two months ago, a captured Czech terrorist admitted that he and his organisation had been receiving information from a Wehrmacht source. He had not met this source himself, but he claimed that another terrorist – one that we already had in custody – had met the man. This terrorist was questioned, and eventually produced a vague description – he said he had only met our suspect in the blackout. As before, the description and the information passed on pointed to one of three men, and, as before, two of those men were quickly able to prove their innocence. And once again the third man was Grashof.'

'So why is he still at large?'

Giminich nodded, as if conceding a point. 'The case is not quite complete,' he admitted. 'Herr Grashof has several influential supporters, and they have found it extremely difficult to believe in his treachery. But now, with your assistance, we will soon have enough evidence to convince even the most sceptical.'

Russell couldn't help grimacing.

'You will keep your appointment with him, but deliver a different message. You will tell him, using these exact words: "The Admiral says that you're in danger, and advises you to run".'

'But...'

'You will then ask Grashof if he has any final message for the Admiral. Do you understand?'

Only too well, Russell thought. If Grashof accepted the instruction, he would be condemning both himself and Canaris. And once the two men were revealed as traitors, then those who carried messages between them were unlikely to receive any favours; Russell's own hopes of a comfortable Swiss exile would certainly be over, along with any chance of seeing Effi while the war lasted. And worse than that was a distinct possibility. 'I understand what you'd like me to do,' he said, 'but as I'm sure you can see, this puts me in a very difficult position. I have no personal knowledge of this man Grashof, but I find it hard to believe that Admiral Canaris is a traitor to the Reich...'

'There is no difficulty here,' Giminich interrupted. 'As a resident of the Reich you are obliged, like everyone else, to obey its laws, and treason is most definitely against those laws. If Canaris and Grashof are innocent then that will become clear, and no harm will be done, while if they do prove to be traitors, you will have done the Reich a useful service. What is the problem?'

They had him, Russell thought. He had only one more card, and it was a low one. 'When we met at Prinz-Albrecht-Strasse you said my loyalty did me credit.'

Giminich smiled. 'And so it did. But the situation has changed. Where treason is concerned, loyalty becomes a very risky business, something to weigh very carefully. Your cooperation in this matter would certainly remove any doubts about your own position.'

'And if I refuse?' Russell asked.

Giminich shrugged. 'Would threats help you make up your mind?'

'Let's just say I like to know exactly where I stand.'

'Very well. You may have thought that we had forgotten about you since 1939. Your file is a long one, Herr Russell, well-researched and very up-to-date. Your girlfriend, your son, your Jew-lover of a brother-in-law and his son – their lives could all get a lot more difficult. You yourself would forfeit any chance of leaving Germany, and, at best, undergo imprisonment as an enemy alien for the duration of the war. I think we can agree, here, just between us, that this will be a long war. The United States will doubtless join in eventually, but the Atlantic is very wide, and they will find it as hard to cross as we shall. A stalemate seems very likely, and many years for you to regret refusing your services in this matter.'

'No' was not an option, Russell thought. It very rarely was where the *Sicherheitsdienst* was involved. 'You've convinced me,' he told Giminich. Maybe something would occur to him over the next few hours, some devious means of sabotaging the intended trap that could not be blamed on him, but it didn't seem very likely.

'Excellent,' Giminich said. 'We have reserved a room for you at the Alcron Hotel. Untersturmführer Schulenburg will take you there now, and then to the Šramota Café for your *treff* with Herr Grashof. Anything you require, please ask. Once your part is over, your time is your own. The hotel room is yours until tomorrow, though I believe your return ticket is for this evening.'

'It is. And I do need to be back in Berlin tomorrow.' He didn't, but insisting that he still had an agenda of his own made him feel slightly less helpless.

Schulenburg led him outside to where an ancient-looking black saloon was waiting. Two more men in suits were sitting in the front seats, both of whom looked like Czechs. The Untersturmführer had not opened his mouth in the station office, and his directions to the driver revealed a surprisingly deep voice. He ushered Russell into the back seat and joined him there, absent-mindedly pressing down on his unruly ginger thatch.

The streets of Prague seemed sombre to Russell, but that might just have been the overcast sky. According to the BBC, Heydrich's executioners had hardly enjoyed a moment's rest since early November, but as Russell knew only too well from Berlin, the sufferings of a small minority could pass almost unnoticed by their fellow citizens.

They had reached Jindřišská Street, which now bore the name Heinrichsgasse. As in 1939, giant swastikas adorned the upper façade of the Post Office and nearby Deutsches Haus, but traffic was noticeably lighter. There were a couple of trams in the distance, but no cars beyond their own. As they turned onto Wenzelsplatz another black saloon could be seen parked further up the slope, but that was all – this piece of occupied Europe had apparently exhausted its petrol ration.

Lepanska Street had also been re-christened, but Russell failed to catch the new name. The dark, rectangular and depressingly modern Alcron seemed unchanged from 1939, when he had eschewed it and its predominantly German clientele in favour of the Europa.

Once inside the impression improved, although sharing the small lift with two violently sneezing SS officers was hardly conducive to good health. His room, it turned out, was actually two – a sitting room, with a child's bed, leading into a large bedroom. Both had large windows overlooking the canyon-like street.

Russell looked at his watch – it was ten to ten. He had just over four hours to figure some way out of his and Grashof's predicament. Breakfast would be a start.

'I'd like some coffee,' he told Schulenburg. 'And something to eat. A couple of rolls will do.'

The Untersturmführer seemed momentarily upset by the audacity of this request, but managed to recover himself. He opened the door, relayed the request to someone outside, and shut it once more.

'Have you been in Prague long?' Russell asked him cheerily.

'That's no business of yours,' was the surly reply.

'Just trying to be friendly,' Russell said lightly.

'We are not friends.'

No indeed, Russell thought. Silence it was. He sat down in a convenient armchair, stretched out his legs and waited for breakfast to arrive. Thinking was always hard work without coffee.

He suddenly realised that they hadn't provided him with the requisite copy of *Signal*. Had Giminich slipped up? Surely Grashof would notice if he turned up without one, but what would he do?

The coffee arrived, along with rolls, real butter and real jam. Russell could hardly believe it, but the Untersturmführer, clearly used to such luxuries, left most of his on the plate. The coffee was no better than Berlin's – but then Prague was just as far from Brazil.

Feast over, Russell asked if he could lie down in the adjoining room. Schulenburg took a long look round, presumably to make sure there were no telephones, semaphore paddles or carrier pigeons available for Russell's use. He then granted permission, contingent on the door remaining open.

Russell laid himself out on the bed, closed his eyes, and tried to think. What was Giminich expecting to happen? Grashof would accept the legitimacy of the fake message without query, and perhaps incriminate himself still further by sending an indiscreet message back to Canaris. All of which would be overheard by the SD – a listening device under the table in all likelihood. Knowing which table the meeting was arranged for, they only had to bug the one.

But unless the relevant technology had improved out of all recognition there was no way the SD could record the conversation. So why not just make one up? Why go to all this trouble to get real evidence of guilt? Because, he realised, they needed the real evidence to convince Grashof's 'influential supporters' in Berlin. There would be someone with 'neutral' credentials listening in with the SD operatives, Russell guessed. Someone from the Foreign Office or Wehrmacht.

Once Grashof had incriminated himself, he would be immediately arrested, and the focus would shift back to Berlin. Moving against Canaris would take time – someone of his stature couldn't be arrested without the Führer's agreement, and the latter was notoriously difficult to get hold of, what with his bizarre sleeping hours and penchant for military briefings that lasted longer than the campaigns concerned. And despite Giminich's promise, Russell couldn't see himself being set free until Canaris was beyond warning.

How could he break this chain of events? He would get no chance of warning anyone ahead of time – Schulenburg would be sticking to him like a ginger limpet.

Was there any way of presenting the message that would cause Grashof to smell a rat, yet not cast suspicion on Russell himself? By making faces? Kicking the man's leg under the table? It was hard to imagine that Giminich had neglected such possibilities. There would be people watching, probably droves of them, all with high-powered binoculars. There might even be lip-readers in case the microphones failed.

Could he remain faithful to the script provided, yet undermine the words with inappropriate tones and emphases? It would be risky. An inadequate grasp of the German language would be the only possible excuse, and Giminich knew only too well that he spoke it like a native.

But what else was there? Could he warn Grashof with his eyes? He tried a warning look at the ceiling, and found his mouth was hanging open. Ridiculous.

What was left – telepathy?

There was nothing. Should he have refused? He still could. If he followed Giminich's orders he would, in all likelihood, be condemning a man to death. Against that, Grashof and Canaris were likely to remain firmly fixed in Heydrich's crosshairs with or without his own involvement. Not a noble argument, but a reasonable one. And why should he sacrifice his own future – not to mention those of his extended family – for Grashof and Canaris, who must have known the risks they were taking, and who were apparently betraying a regime they had freely chosen to serve? When it came down to it, he had no real idea whether these two men were enemies of the Reich or just enemies of Heydrich. The evidence for Grashof being a genuine friend of the resistance seemed strong, but Russell still found it hard to imagine Canaris actually working against his own country. The best bet was that Heydrich was using Grashof's real guilt to smear his real adversary.

Not that it really mattered, because Russell had no intention of risking his own future for theirs. There was no honourable way out of this particular predicament. If a risk-free chance to help Grashof came up, he would take it. Maybe even a low-risk chance. Very low-risk. But that was all. He would have to play it by ear, hope that something went wrong, and live with himself if it didn't. The Abwehr was not his family.

He got up off the bed to explore the adjoining bathroom. A turn of the tap produced hot water, and he decided that taking a bath might cheer him up. The suspicious Schulenburg explored the room for secret exits, then left him to it. It felt like a victory, though he knew it was nothing of the sort.

Drying himself off with a huge soft towel, he felt renewed pangs of hunger. With rolls that good, who knew what Prague had to offer in the way of real meat and vegetables? Like all Berliners in recent months he had, he realised, fallen in thrall to his taste buds. 'What about lunch?' he asked Schulenburg.

The Untersturmführer was unsympathetic: 'You can eat afterwards.'

Russell went back to waiting, and the search for a flaw in Giminich's plan. None occurred to him. His thoughts wandered, taking him back to his last time in Prague, and his clandestine contacts on Washington's behalf with the still-gestating resistance movement. He had no idea whether those contacts had borne lasting fruit, or whether any of those involved were still alive. The resistance would be hard-pressed now, and those still at large would be lying low, waiting for Heydrich's storm to blow over. He remembered the execution he had witnessed, the lifeless corpse collapsing into the sand.

'Time to go,' Schulenburg said from the doorway.

Collecting the man in the corridor, they went down to the car, where the fourth member of the original party was half asleep behind the wheel. Jerked awake by Schulenburg's sarcastic greeting, the driver started the engine and roughly released the clutch, causing the car to take off like a frightened horse. Russell found himself wondering whether his guards would be stupid enough to drop him off at the café door.

The answer was no. They drove to the eastern end of the Legií Bridge, which now bore the name of the Czech composer Smetana. At a quarter to two Schulenburg pulled a copy of *Signal* from his briefcase, handed it to Russell and set him in motion. He would walk the remaining distance – across the bridge and a short way along the opposite bank – on his own. He would also, as Schulenburg made amply clear, be under constant observation.

The bridge was a long one, crossing two arms of the charcoal-coloured river and the island of bare trees that lay between them. It was on this island that Russell had met his first resistance contact in the summer of

1939, but today the paths were as empty as the trees, and the sun nowhere to be seen. In fact it was beginning to rain, and the dark forbidding castle high to his right was rapidly disappearing behind a curtain of mist.

Once beyond the island Russell could see the line of establishments on the far bank, their illuminated interiors brightly glowing in the overall gloom. The Šramota Café was the last in line, its outside terrace covered by an awning of ironwork and glass. Russell felt a faint stirring of hope – the clatter of rain on such a roof might hide their conversation from Giminich's microphones.

It was still only ten to two when he reached the steps leading down from the bridge to the quay. He stopped and leaned on the parapet, only too aware that he was getting wetter, but determined not to miss a single trick. The more time he gave the SD for making mistakes, the more likely they were to make one.

A man appeared in the distance, walking down from the direction of the Charles Bridge. Identification was impossible in the gloom, but the general build was consistent with Grashof's. The man entered the Šramota Café.

With enormous reluctance Russell resumed his journey, descending the slippery stone steps and making his way along the cobbled quayside. The rain was now swirling above the dark river, masking the far bank from view. It had turned into what the English called a 'filthy day' – the SD would need more than high-powered binoculars to see through this lot.

Assuming that the watchers were far away. They might be in the back of the café, or sitting at a nearby table.

Russell reached the outer door and swung it open. There were several customers visible in the warmer interior of the café, but only one man, wrapped in raincoat and scarf, at the far end of the covered terrace. Johann Grashof.

Russell walked slowly towards the Abwehr officer. The windows to his left offered those in the café proper an excellent view of those on the terrace, and there were several obvious hiding places for microphones – on the bottom of the table, inside the suspiciously early bunches of Christmas holly, among the decorative ironwork which supported the glass roof. The patter of the falling rain was depressingly muted.

'Good day,' Grashof said politely.

'Good day,' Russell echoed, sitting down and placing his sodden magazine beside the other man's copy. Grashof's expression invited him to say more.

There was no way out of it.

'The Admiral says that you're in danger, and advises you to run.'

Grashof's lip curled slightly, as if he found the message amusing. 'I don't understand,' he said, though his eyes told a different story. 'In danger from what? Run where? What does he mean?'

This wasn't in the script, and neither was the Luger which Grashof suddenly brought into view, leaving the hand that held it resting on the metal table.

'Who are you?' Grashof asked.

'I am John Russell. The man you came here to meet.'

'I came here to meet a man of that name. Can you prove that you're John Russell?'

Russell took out his papers and handed them across the table, wondering what the SD eavesdroppers were making of this unexpected turn.

'These look like forgeries,' Grashof announced. 'Who are you really?'

'John Russell.'

'I don't think so. Are you a foreign agent?'

'Of course not. I…'

'Then I can only assume that you're an impostor in the pay of the *Sicherheitsdienst*, and that this is all part of some preposterous scheme to expose me as a traitor.'

'I know nothing of…'

'Well, please tell whoever hired you that their scheme has failed. As all their attempts will, for one very simple reason. I am not and never have been a traitor.'

Grashof was enjoying himself. He had been tipped off, of course, an eventuality which hardly seemed surprising in hindsight. A lot of ordinary Czechs had witnessed Russell's virtual arrest at Masaryk Station, and several members of the Czech resistance whom he'd met in 1939 had worked at the nearby depot. News of the SD's intervention had been passed on to Grashof, and the Abwehr officer had made up his own little speech for the hidden microphones.

Of course the very fact of a tip-off had treason written all over it, but Grashof had certainly made the best of a bad situation. Russell felt like congratulating him, but decided to wait until after the war. Giminich would be furious.

Moments later, the man himself emerged from inside the café, trailing leather coats and SS uniforms in his wake.

Grashof's fingers momentarily tightened on the Luger's butt, and for one dreadful second Russell expected to die in the crossfire. Then the fingers relaxed and retreated from the weapon, with Grashof settling for an ironic smile. 'You must be the ringmaster of this particular circus,' he said, addressing Giminich.

'You are required for questioning,' the latter said, gesturing two of the uniforms forward.

'By whose authority?'

'That of the *Reichsprotektor*.'

'Then of course I am happy to oblige.' Grashof got to his feet. 'May I take my gun?'

'No,' Giminich said. 'The Petschek Palace,' he told the uniforms, who escorted Grashof out onto the quay.

'I tried,' Russell told the Obersturmbannführer.

'He was forewarned,' Giminich said. 'And we shall find the men who forewarned him.'

Bully for you, Russell thought. 'So I'm free to go?'

'Not quite. Admiral Canaris must not hear of this. Your report to him will be very simple. You came to the rendezvous, but Grashof did not show up. That is all. If the Admiral discovers what really happened I will hold you personally responsible. Is that clear?'

'Very,' Russell agreed. He seemed to have got off lightly. 'My bag is still at the hotel,' he added.

Giminich was already on his way. 'Collect it and return to Berlin,' he snapped over his shoulder.

At least the rain was easing. His appetite returning, Russell walked up to the central square of the Little Quarter and found a small restaurant filling the street with enticing odours. The food was indeed good, but the staff and the other customers seemed unfriendly. He should have ordered in English rather than German, he eventually realised.

The rain had fully stopped when he emerged, and there was even a hint of blue in the sky above the castle. As he walked across the Charles Bridge he sense that he was being followed, and sure enough, fifty metres or so behind him, there lurked a small bespectacled man in raincoat and hat. He told himself that he was imagining things, that if he turned his head on any street in the world he was likely to find someone bringing up his rear, but the small man still looked suspicious. Reaching the tower at the eastern end of the bridge, Russell stood in a recessed doorway and waited. The small man, now walking a bit faster, seemed surprised to see him, but kept on going, disappearing into one of the streets that led into the heart of the Old Town.

Russell took a different route, trusting on a combination of memory and instinct to reach Na Príkope, and the foot of Wenceslas Square. From there he had no trouble finding Lepanska Street and the Alcron Hotel, but securing his possessions proved rather more difficult. The Czech receptionist refused to let him upstairs, and it took several phone calls to some unspecified authority and the helpful intervention of a passing SS officer before a busboy could be sent to retrieve his bag.

This accomplished, Russell still had several hours to waste before his train was due to depart. He considered a long sojourn in the well-stocked bar, but was deterred by the number of black uniforms on display. It also occurred to him that finding Masaryk Station in the blackout would be far from easy. Better to get there while it was still light, and camp out in the station restaurant for the duration.

Picking up his bag, he sauntered out of the front doors and began walking towards Wenceslas Square. He would later have a vague memory of a car engine bursting into life, but in the here and now the vehicle was almost level with him when he first became aware of it. Slowing his stride as he turned to look, Russell noted, in very swift succession, a flash in a window, a searing pain in the side of his head, and a loud echoing boom which went rolling down the narrow street. As the car sped away he fell backwards against the stone side of the building, and slumped to the pavement feeling more than a little foolish. The Resistance, he thought, as consciousness faded.

On her way to the studio that afternoon Effi remembered she had some shopping to do, and asked the driver to drop her off on the Ku'damm. She had hardly walked ten metres when she noticed Ali Blumenthal stepping down from a tram outside the Universum Cinema. There was no yellow star sewn into her coat.

'I'm going to the cinema with a friend,' Ali explained, once Effi had caught up with her. 'But I'm half an hour early.'

'Let's have a coffee,' Effi suggested. 'There's a place just round the corner.'

'Are you sure?' Ally asked. 'If they ask to see my papers…'

'They won't. They know me, and I'll say you're my baby sister.'

'If only I was,' Ali said wistfully.

The café was full, but empty tables just seemed to appear when celebrities arrived, and on this particular occasion Effi decided not to feel too guilty about it. She ordered coffees and cakes, and hoped that they wouldn't be noticeably better than those served at the adjoining tables.

The two of them chatted about films until the women at the next table left, and there was no longer any danger of their being overheard. Effi asked after Ali's family, and received an earful of the girl's frustration with her parents. 'My dad is such an *innocent*,' Ali complained, 'but my mother's even worse. She knows better, and she's not afraid to say so, but she won't actually stand up to him. When they get the letter they'll just bicker with each other all the way to the train, and they'll still be bickering when they get wherever it is they're sent to.'

'You won't go?'

'Absolutely not. I shall stay in Berlin. You know –' she lowered her voice to a whisper '– I heard a wonderful story yesterday about a Jewish woman who wanted an Aryan work permit. She waited for an air raid, and then looked for a block in which the Party office and all of its records had been destroyed. Then she went to the report centre for people who've been bombed out and gave them a false name, a real photograph and the number of one of the houses which had been destroyed. They had no way of checking her story so they gave her the permit. And some emergency money! The welfare service fed and housed her for several weeks, and then evacuated her to Pomerania. And now she's got a job working as a housekeeper for a Party bigwig!'

Effi couldn't help smiling.

'I know there's not enough bombing at the moment,' Ali went on, 'but Kurt says – he's my boyfriend,' she explained, blushing slightly – 'he says it will get worse and worse once the Americans come into the war. There'll be more and more record offices bombed, and it'll be harder and harder for them to keep track of people. More and more Jews will be living as Christians – hundreds of them, I wouldn't wonder.' She looked at her watch. 'I must go. Do I look all right?'

'You look gorgeous,' Effi said, and meant it. She watched the girl go, thinking of herself at seventeen. She'd been every bit as headstrong, but the possible consequences of her youthful exuberance had not included years in a concentration camp.

The next face Russell saw belonged to Obersturmbannführer Giminich. Someone else's fingers were playing with his hair, causing shooting pains across his scalp.

'Not serious,' a voice behind him said in Czech-accented German. The fingers did one more painful dance. 'Water, disinfectant, bandage,' the voice added. 'That is all.'

'Do whatever you have to, doctor,' Giminich said curtly. 'You have been extremely fortunate,' he told Russell, in a tone that implied someone else would have made a more deserving recipient of such luck.

Russell recognised his surroundings – he was back in the original hotel bedroom. He asked how long he'd been out.

'About half an hour,' Giminich grudgingly revealed.

'This stings,' the doctor told him, a second before dousing his head with what had to be neat alcohol.

He wasn't exaggerating. The shock took Russell's breath away, and for a second he thought he was losing consciousness again. 'Christ,' he murmured, as the pain slowly subsided.

The doctor began wrapping a long bandage around Russell's head. He was younger than he'd sounded, a short Czech in his late twenties or early thirties man with a shock of curly dark hair and a cadaverous face.

'What did you see of your assailants?' Giminich wanted to know. He was pacing up and down, a lit cigarette clamped between finger and thumb. Schulenburg, Russell now noticed, was standing by the blackout-screened window.

'Nothing really. The car was an Adler, but I didn't see any faces.'

'The car was stolen,' Giminich said, as if someone had asked him to explain the motorisation of the Czech resistance. 'It was abandoned outside Hiberner Station,' he added unnecessarily.

Russell was wondering why he'd been so stupid. The men who had tipped off Grashof had assumed that Russell was in league with the SD, and Russell himself had done nothing to shake that assumption. He had made no protest when taken away at Masaryk Station, and he had said nothing at the Šramota Café to suggest he was an unwilling participant in the entrapment process. Grashof's friends in the resistance had assumed Russell was one of the enemy, and following Grashof's arrest they had sought the obvious retaliation. He could hardly fault their logic, painful as the consequences still were.

'Did you see anything suspicious on your way back to the hotel?' Giminich asked him.

'I thought I was being followed on the Charles Bridge,' Russell said incautiously. 'But I wasn't,' he added quickly. Think before speaking, he told himself.

'What made you think you were not?' Giminich asked, his pacing momentarily suspended.

Russell went through the story, concluding with the disappearance of his supposed tail in another direction.

'They work in pairs,' Giminich told him.

'There was no one else,' Russell insisted, although it now seemed likely that there had been.

Giminich looked dissatisfied, but then that was who he was. The doctor had finished with his bandaging, and looked only too ready to depart. 'You must see a doctor when you reach Berlin,' he told Russell. 'But you will be fine.' Like Giminich, he seemed less than ecstatic about this outcome.

Russell thanked him anyway.

'You will come to headquarters now,' Giminich told him. 'Where your protection can be assured.'

The prospect of several hours cooped up in the Petschek Palace was appalling, but Russell very much doubted that he could refuse. What Giminich had just said was depressingly true – Heydrich's men in black were all that stood between him and the righteous wrath of the Czech Resistance. Irony was too short a word.

He slowly levered himself off the bed, and was pleasantly surprised by the lack of any sharp reaction inside his skull. The doctor had been right;

the bullet had caused little more damage than a sudden blow from a sharp instrument. He had seen many such wounds in Flanders, where they had often been welcomed as a relatively painless ticket away from the front line.

The trip down in the lift made him feel slightly woozy, but the cold night air soon put that right. Night had fallen, and the car waiting outside had the usual thinly-slit covers over its headlights. 'Has Prague been bombed?' he asked his companions.

'Of course not,' Schulenburg told him.

Then why a blackout, Russell wondered but didn't ask. The Resistance was probably grateful.

The streets were virtually empty, only one darkened tram squealing its way past them as they neared the top of Wenceslas Square. In less than five minutes they were drawing up outside what Russell could only assume was the Petschek Palace. He had seen the building by daylight in 1939, a vast block of huge stones which reminded him of the Inca capital Cuzco in Paul's much-loved *Wonders of the World* book. It had five main floors, with two more in the roof and an unknown number below ground level. Several, if Russell knew the Gestapo and SD. They loved their cellars.

Inside the hanging lights seemed permanently dimmed, walls and stairs receding upwards into apparently depthless shadow. A uniformed SD officer was waiting for Giminich, and instructions.

'Take ten men from the Cinema,' Giminich told him. 'And make sure there are reports in tomorrow morning's Czech newspapers. A list of names, and the reasons for their execution.'

Russell had a terrible notion of what this was all about. 'You're not going to kill ten prisoners in retaliation for the attack on me?' he blurted out, realising as he did so that protest would only anger his hosts. 'I don't want that sort of blood on my hands,' he added, as if Giminich would care a damn what he wanted.

'It's nothing to do with you,' Giminich snapped, waving his surprised subordinate away. 'Whatever you want and whatever your sympathies, those who tried to kill you considered you a representative of the Reich. Such attacks must be deterred.'

'And you think killing ten innocent men will weaken the will of the Resistance?'

'I do. But I repeat, this is not your concern.' He turned to Schulenburg. 'Willi, take Herr Russell to the reception lounge.'

'This way,' Schulenburg ordered, as Giminich strode away down a corridor. The reception lounge was in the opposite direction, and surprisingly well-furnished for a police headquarters. A place to park visiting dignitaries, Russell assumed, not to mention foreign journalists on the run from the Resistance. 'You will remain here,' Schulenburg ordered.

'One question,' Russell said, although he wasn't at all sure he wanted the answer. 'What is the Cinema?'

Schulenburg smiled, which was scary in itself. 'It's the room downstairs where prisoners wait for their interrogations. The walls are bare, and several months ago one of them told his interrogator that he had seen his worst imaginings projected onto them. Like a horror film. It has been called the Cinema ever since.' He closed the door behind him.

Russell lowered himself into the nearest armchair. A vehicle was in motion outside the blacked-out window, but that was all he could hear – the building might have been empty for all the sound its other occupants were making. The walls didn't look as if they'd been sound-proofed, but they were probably already thick enough for the Gestapo's purposes. For all he knew there were men and women screaming their heads off a few rooms away.

He looked around him. The armchairs, polished wooden table and eighteenth-century desk, the fleur-de-lys embossed wallpaper, ornate cornices and bucolic oil paintings – all the trappings of moderate affluence, anywhere in Central Europe. It all looked so ordinary, in a faded, antiquated sort of way. Like the anteroom to an outmoded version of hell.

His head was throbbing, which might or might not be a good sign. He placed a hand over the wound, and found the bandage was sticky with blood. Not wet, though. He walked across to the mirror, but no amount of twisting his head could provide him with a decent view. Another two inches to the left, he thought, and his brains would have been splattered all over Lepanska Street. Perhaps he was destined to survive the war.

Unlike the ten men from the Cinema. Their deaths were not down to him, not in any real sense. He hadn't attacked them himself, hadn't ordered reprisals. But if he hadn't been seduced by the promise of Swiss weekends with Effi, those ten men would not be living their last few hours.

He shook his head, and pain coursed through it.

The door opened, revealing Schulenburg. 'Come,' he said.

Russell reached for his bag, noticing for the first time the neat line of blood droplets which adorned it.

'Leave that,' Schulenburg ordered.

'We're not going to the station?'

'Not yet.'

They walked down a long corridor, turned left, and descended a flight of worn stone steps. With each step down the weight of the building seemed to grow, and Russell felt the kernel of fear in his stomach begin to expand. He told himself not to worry. What could they possibly want from him? Silence was the obvious answer, one that chilled him to the bone. He had a sudden picture of himself, knelt down, his executioner holding the pistol to the back of his neck.

Two head shots in one day seemed excessive.

They were, he guessed, two floors below street level. A shorter corridor, an ominously reinforced door, and they were entering one end of a long narrow room. It was spotlessly clean, and the metallic smell of blood was probably all in his imagination. Or emanating from his own head wound.

Obersturmbannführer Giminich was waiting, along with two uniformed men with machine guns, several other Germans in plain clothes and a line of Czech prisoners. Seven of them. One was the man who had followed him across the Charles Bridge.

'Do you recognise any of these men?' Giminich asked.

Russell took his time, walking slowly down the line, scrutinising each face with apparent thoroughness. Most were bruised, some cut as well, and a couple of eyes were swollen shut. The open eyes were full of defiance. Not to mention loathing.

The man from the bridge was not the only one he recognised. A second man, younger, with a pugnacious face and longish blond hair, also seemed familiar, but not from today. Russell realised he must have come into contact with him during one of his two trips in 1939, but he couldn't remember which, let alone what the circumstances had been. He was fairly sure that the man had recognised him.

'No,' he told Giminich, 'I don't recognise any of them.'

'Are you certain? Take another look.'

Russell took another slow walk along the line-up. Had the man on the bridge already confessed? Was Giminich using the man to trap him?

He wasn't going to give the man up, but… 'I can't be sure,' he said, hedging his bets.

'But you have an idea?'

'No, not really. Nothing that I'd risk an innocent man's life on.'

'They tried to kill you,' Giminich reminded him.

'Someone did,' he agreed. And I can't say that I blame them, he thought to himself. Judging by the looks on the Czech faces, he would be well-advised to avoid post-war Prague.

Rather to Russell's surprise, Giminich did not seem disappointed. 'Very well, ' he said, consulting his watch. 'You will be taken to the station now. You will be well looked after until the train leaves, and a compartment has been arranged for your personal use as far as Dresden. I'm sure I don't need to remind you of our earlier conversation, about the wording of your report to the Admiral.'

'No,' Russell agreed, 'you don't.'

Walking up the stone stairs seemed infinitely preferable to walking down, as if the weight of the building was sloughing off his back. They collected his bag from the guest lounge and made their way out to the interior courtyard, where a combination of masked headlights and ill-fitting window screens cast everything in a thin blue light, as if the world was wreathed in cigarette smoke.

Schulenburg got in the back with him, but said nothing on the short drive to the station. The concourse was unusually empty, and Russell felt sadly reassured by all the uniforms and guns in evidence – leaving Prague like a Nazi celebrity might not prove a treasured memory, but it definitely seemed preferable to dying in a hail of Resistance bullets.

The train was already at the platform. Schulenburg rapped out a few orders and walked away without a word of farewell, leaving two uniformed *Ordnungspolizei* to stand guard outside Russell's compartment until the train departed. It began drawing out of the station at precisely nine o'clock. It was his third departure from the Masaryk Station in two years, and all three had been accompanied by a decided whiff of desperation.

He headed for the bar, where the blackout screens had not been lowered. They were just passing the locomotive depot where Russell had witnessed a more successful Resistance execution, and it suddenly occurred to him that the face he had vaguely recognised in the line-up had belonged to the young man standing guard outside the sand-dryer building on that long-ago night.

No warning

The train pulled into Berlin's Anhalter Station soon after nine, and Russell let it empty out before alighting. As on the outward trip, both corridors and vestibules had been packed with standing passengers between Dresden and Berlin, and only the lack of heating had prevented the rank atmosphere from becoming truly unbearable. If the Third Reich was going to last a thousand years it needed more soap and less flatulence-inducing food.

It was a cold, grey day, with gusts of an easterly breeze tugging at the swastikas above the station's main entrance. Russell bought a paper from the forecourt kiosk and asked whether there had been any air raids over the last two nights. There had not, the proprietor told him, gazing with blatant curiosity at the blood-encrusted bandage still wrapped around Russell's head.

'A falling brick,' he offered in explanation, and headed for the tram stop. He had never acquired the hat-wearing habit, but several years ago Effi had bought him a very smart fedora, and this seemed like a good time to break it in.

He reached the flat around ten. It was empty of course – Effi would be into her third day of shooting by now – but a note on the pillow announced her intention of being back around five. The bed still held a trace of her warmth, and he lay there for a few moments wondering what to do. His head was sore, but not so much that medical attention seemed urgent. He would get the Abwehr over with first. The quicker he told his lie, the less chance that the truth would get there before him.

But first a bath, and a change of clothes. As the water ran, he removed both bandage and dressing without causing a haemorrhage, and with the help of two mirrors managed to get a decent look at the furrow in his head. Considering its origin it seemed healthy enough, but a visit to the hospital would probably be wise. After taking his bath he dug some gauze and an old roll of bandage out of the medicine cabinet, re-dressed the wound, and went in search of the fedora. It looked very stylish, the more so when worn with clothes. He left Effi a note promising to be back by five, and started out for the Abwehr headquarters.

He was halfway there when a flaw in Giminich's story occurred to him. It was all very well claiming that Grashof had failed to make their appointment; the problem was, Canaris would want his letter back. The same letter which Giminich had casually torn open and pocketed. How could he explain its disappearance?

On the train home he had considered, and then dismissed, the option of defying Giminich and telling Canaris the truth. Now, walking along the bank of the ice-edged Landwehrkanal, he considered it again. He would be giving Canaris reason to trust him, and reason to proceed with the Swiss arrangement. But the latter would have to happen before the SD got wind of his betrayal, which wasn't very likely. The fact that Giminich had already known all the details of his *treff* with Grashof pointed to an SD mole in the higher reaches of the Abwehr. No, he couldn't tell the truth.

So what lie should he tell? He reached a final decision as the aide led him up to Piekenbrock's office. The Colonel seemed busy as ever, endlessly shuffling papers in an apparently vain attempt to secure some workable order. He listened to Russell's brief account, shrugged, and warned that the Admiral might have further questions at a later date. Russell asked the Colonel to remind Canaris of the Swiss arrangement which they had discussed the previous week. He was halfway to the door when Piekenbrock remembered the letter.

'I burned it,' Russell admitted. 'When Grashof failed to appear I became worried that someone might know of the letter, and try to steal it. Since the Admiral wrote it I didn't think he would need reminding of its contents.'

Piekenbrock considered this explanation for a few worrying moments, but then accepted it. 'You destroyed it completely?'

'Of course. I flushed the ashes down a toilet,' he added, hoping that he was not overdoing it. Or that Giminich would post it back to Canaris.

'Excellent,' Piekenbrock said absent-mindedly, as if he had suddenly realised how easily an outbreak of arson could clear his own desk.

Outside the building, Russell's immediate sense of relief soon turned to something more ambivalent. He had managed to avoid betraying Giminich, but that might just encourage the SD man to come back with another daring wheeze from the SS Book of Adventures. The Abwehr might still agree to set him up in Switzerland, but time was probably short, and they didn't seem in much of hurry. It was beginning to seem as if a swift American entry into the war offered him his best chance of safety, albeit one that neither included Effi nor guaranteed a prompt exit from the Reich.

Of course, much might have happened since he last heard or read an uncensored news report, and, given that he was still employed to write the stuff, he supposed he should bring himself up to date. The Foreign Press Club on Leipziger Platz was the nearest source of relatively uncensored news, and if that failed to provide, one could always find a journalist or three in the Adlon Bar. Even if they were only Italians.

The Press Club was deserted, the foreign newspapers four days old. He walked up Hermann-Goering-Strasse, wondering what had happened outside Moscow in those four days, and remembering a Sunday years before, waiting with an anxious Paul for the evening papers to arrive at the local kiosk with the football results. Hertha had lost.

The Russians, apparently, had not. Ralph Morrison was in the Adlon Bar, typing noisily away at a corner table on his brand new portable and ignoring the dirty looks being cast in his direction. 'They've hit real trouble,' he told Russell in what could only be described as a joyous whisper.

'The Germans?'

'Of course the goddamned Germans. They're up to their necks in snow, their tanks won't move, their planes won't fly... It's Napoleon all over again.'

'What's the source?'

'Wehrmacht. It's the goods, believe me. There are whole divisions coming down with frostbite.'

Russell felt a warm glow spreading up from his stomach, and fought back the desire to cheer out loud. 'What are their press people saying?'

'Oh, the usual crap. "Heavy fighting", "titanic struggle", you know the stuff. But they've given up claiming advances. And you can see it in their eyes. They *know*.'

'What about North Africa?'

'Harder to say. If I were a cynical man...'

'Perish the thought.'

'...I'd say neither the British nor the Germans have any idea who's winning. And I mean the ones who are fighting, the ones who you might think *would* know.'

'And the Pacific?'

'A matter of days. I'm packed, and I advise you to do the same. If we're not out of here by the middle of next week I'll be really surprised.'

'What's actually happened?'

'It's what hasn't happened. The Japs made a last offer, which Washington turned down flat. Now Roosevelt's made a counter-offer, one that requires the Japs to slice off their own balls and eat them. And guess what? They haven't replied. Unless you count the various armadas heading down past China.'

'They started the Russo-Japanese War with a surprise attack.'

'Well, this one won't be much of a surprise.'

A drink, Russell thought, but he was only halfway to the bar when Uwe Kuzorra filled the doorway leading to reception.

'I'd like a few words,' the detective said. 'Not here though. My car's outside.'

'No assistant today,' Russell noted as they crossed the pavement. The police Opel was empty.

'No,' Kuzorra agreed. 'How was Prague?'

'Stimulating.'

'Somebody hit you?' the detective asked, staring at the bandage.

'Don't ask,' Russell said, and somewhat to his surprise Kuzorra didn't.

They settled into the front seats and Russell gazed through the windscreen at the Brandenburg Gate as the detective searched his pockets for matches.

'So how's the case going?' Russell asked. He was still smiling inside at the news from Moscow.

'Not so good. Stimulating, though. I gave Schwering the number of the Mercedes, and he came back about half an hour later with some ridiculous story about it being burnt out in an accident on the Avus Speedway. I gave one of my own men the same job – without telling Schwering, of course – and he tracked the car down in fifteen minutes.'

'SD?'

Kuzorra blew out smoke. 'No, as it happens. It's registered to Fordwerke, the German subsidiary of the American corporation.' He turned his head to look at Russell. 'Now why would people like that want Herr Sullivan dead?'

'I don't know,' Russell said, 'but I could offer a guess.'

'Be my guest.'

Russell ignored the sarcastic tone; in Kuzorra's shoes he would probably have found himself a pain in the arse. 'Sullivan knew most of the German business leaders with American ties. He was called in – or called himself in – whenever Americans came over for meetings, either here or in Switzerland.

You know, nice hotels, good food, the high life in general. He helped with the interpreting, particularly when one side or another was anxious to keep the discussion under wraps. Mostly the language side of things, but the cultural stuff too – making sure they all understood each other.'

'I get the picture.'

'Well, imagine a few things. One, those American businesses with interests in Germany are afraid that American entry into the war will seriously dent their profits. Two, they reach some sort of secret deal which allows them to carry on doing business with their German subsidiaries, and Sullivan's there when they reach it. Three, Sullivan decides he's had enough of the Nazis and wants to go home. But given that he's been defecating on the United States from a great height for several years he badly needs a sweetener, something that'll buy his way back into the good graces of the US government.'

'With you as the go-between.'

'He asked to meet me. I do know he wanted to go home, but the rest is guesswork. I don't know what sort of deal he had in mind.'

Kuzorra thought about it. 'The American Government cares about this stuff?' he eventually asked.

'So I'm told.'

'So the German subsidiaries of these American businesses killed Sullivan to stop him blowing the whistle on them.'

'German, American – it doesn't matter. This is just money talking. These people don't let national loyalties get in the way of making a profit.'

'Hmm.' Kuzorra began another search for his matches.

'I don't think you want to solve this one,' Russell told him.

'Oh, but I do.'

'Pressure from above?'

'You heard the Reichsminister the other morning.'

'Can't you have a private chat with him?'

Kuzorra grunted. 'And say what? He won't be satisfied with guesses. If I'm going to accuse one of Germany's biggest industrial concerns of murder then I'm going to need some proof. There are no forensics, no witnesses, and the motive you've just offered me sounds like Soviet propaganda.'

'What about the car?'

'I imagine it *has* been burnt out by now.'

They stared at the Brandenburg Gate for a little bit longer. 'I still think there's something to find,' Kuzorra said at last. 'Schwering's bouncing round the office like a man who's terrified of missing something.'

'What'll you do if you find it first?'

'I'll take it to Goebbels, have the satisfaction of wiping the smile off the little rat's face, and humbly agree with whatever plan he comes up with for saving his own reputation.'

'Little victories,' Russell said, reaching for the door.

'The only ones we get,' Kuzorra agreed, turning the key in the ignition.

Back inside the hotel, Russell decided lunch was more pressing than the Foreign Office press conference. The quality of the food gave him reason to regret the decision, but the briefing, as he discovered on reaching the Press Club an hour or so later, had been equally dire. Von Stumm had offered no new information worth the name, and had treated the assembled foreign journalists to twenty minutes of pathetic bluster. 'I almost felt sorry for him,' one of the Americans admitted, as if that alone was cause for bitterness.

The hubbub in the bar made Russell's head hurt, reminding him that he still hadn't seen a doctor. The Elisabeth Hospital was only a ten-minute walk away, and he had just decided to pay it a visit when a member of the Press Club staff appeared in the doorway, holding a letter. Spotting Russell, he walked across to deliver it. 'This arrived yesterday,' he said.

The envelope was addressed to John Russell, c/o the Foreign Press Club, Leipziger Platz. The letter was from Frau Marianne Sullivan. She had 'vital information', and wanted to meet him for their 'mutual benefit.' A telephone number was attached.

Russell headed for the booth on the ground floor, but changed his mind at the last moment. Collecting his coat, he walked across Potsdamer Platz to the main line station and found a booth there. The phone rang three times before she answered. Her voice sounded tired, almost cynical, but perked up a little when he told her who he was. Yes, she could meet him that afternoon. She lived in Dahlem, but he couldn't come to her flat. Did he know Wilmersdorf? There was a coffee shop named Werner's on the Hohenzollerndamm, about a hundred metres from the Fehrbelliner Platz U-Bahn station, going towards the city centre.

He said he could find it.

'At three o'clock,' she stipulated. 'I'll be carrying one of Patrick's books.'

'I'll be there.'

Another broken-down tram was gumming up the tracks, and he arrived almost fifteen minutes late. The coffee shop had clearly seen better times, but it wasn't alone in that, and an aura of middle-class respectability still clung, somewhat shabbily, to the mostly female clientele. None of the women had books on display though, and he was beginning to wonder whether he'd been stood up when she finally appeared in the doorway, one of Sullivan's novels clasped to her chest. She was younger and prettier than Russell had expected – a small thin blonde of about thirty-five with large blue eyes and a born-to-pout mouth. She was wearing black.

He introduced himself, let her choose their table in a lonely corner, and murmured 'an accident' in response to her questioning look at his bandaged head. His expressions of regret for her recent loss were shrugged aside – either she was putting a very brave face on widowhood or she was less bothered than he was.

'How long were you married?' Russell asked, purely out of curiosity. Sullivan had never mentioned a wife.

'Almost two years,' she answered, once the waitress had taken his coupons and gone off in search of coffee and cake. 'He was very good to me,' she added almost grudgingly. 'He was taking me to Italy once he had the money from those papers.'

Russell managed not to look surprised. 'Italy?' he asked.

'Away from the war,' she explained. 'And winters like this.'

'So what information do you have for me?' Russell asked.

The waitress arrived with their coffees and a creamy-looking confection that IG Farben had probably created between batches of synthetic rubber.

She took a bite and made a face. 'I think you already have the information,' she said, after wiping her lips. 'You do have Patrick's papers, don't you? Well, I want my share of whatever it is they're worth. I *was* his wife.'

'I don't have his papers,' Russell told her.

She wasn't convinced. 'Look, I'm sorry I told the police that Patrick was meeting you at Stettin Station. I was flustered.'

'I still don't have any of your husband's papers. What makes you think I do?'

She gave him a hard stare. 'Well, the police turned our flat upside-down looking for something, and what else were they looking for? So they weren't on the... you know, when they found him...'

'The people who killed your husband must have taken them.'

'I don't think so. If they did, why are they watching me?'

'What? How do you...'

'There are men watching me. There's a car outside our building all day. I called that Kriminalinspektor and he said it wasn't his people. So who else can it be?'

A good question, Russell thought. Was this why Kuzorra thought there was still something to find? 'Did they follow you here?' he asked, looking round. He couldn't remember any suspicious-looking characters entering the café since her arrival.

'No,' she said. 'I left by the back entrance, and I made sure no one followed me onto the U-Bahn.'

She was, Russell realised, smarter than she looked.

'Look,' she said, 'I don't know whether to believe you or not. When Patrick left home that morning he had the briefcase with him, so he must...'

Russell stopped listening. The strange direction from which Sullivan had appeared at Stettin Station – it suddenly made sense. The ticket… he must have found a chance to drop it, or more likely swallow it.

She was looking at him, expecting an answer.

'Your husband wasn't carrying anything when those men led him away,' he said truthfully. And Kuzorra, he realised, had made no mention of it. 'Did you tell the police about the briefcase?'

'No, of course not. They wouldn't let me sell the papers. They might even arrest me for knowing about them.'

'Maybe he left them in safe keeping at one of the foreign press clubs,' Russell improvised. 'I'll make some discreet enquiries. What does it look like?'

She said nothing, but the suspicion in her eyes was eloquent enough.

'I won't cut you out,' he said reassuringly. 'If I find the papers, and if we can sell them, then we'll split the proceeds 50-50. Fair enough?'

She wanted to protest, but was clever enough to know that he held all the cards. 'All right,' she said grudgingly.

It was a brown leather briefcase with two straps. Sullivan's initials were embossed in gold above the lock.

Russell walked her back to the U-Bahn station, watched her disappear down the steps, and sought out a public telephone. Over recent months the Gestapo had taken to cutting off the American Consulate whenever the mood seemed right, but on this particular day they must have been harassing other innocents. He got straight through, and persuaded the telephonist to summon Joseph Kenyon.

'I need to see you and Dallin,' he told the diplomat.

'Now?' Kenyon asked.

'Tomorrow morning will do,' Russell said, remembering his promise to be home by five.

There was a pause. 'Say ten o'clock,' Kenyon said. 'I'll try and round up Scott.'

'Good.'

Russell only realised that he'd forgotten to visit the hospital as he let himself into the flat. Effi was not yet back, but his son would be home from school. He unhooked the phone and dialled the Grunewald number. Paul himself answered, and sounded genuinely pleased to hear from his father.

Their usual Saturday afternoon get-together had, however, once again fallen victim to the insatiable appetite of the *Hitlerjugend*. The whole day had been taken over for a 'terrain game' in Havelland, and, as if that wasn't enough, four further hours on Sunday morning had been set aside for training in the laying of telephone cables. Russell sometimes wondered if Germany's youth would have any energy left by the time they were called up, but Paul seemed unfazed by the fullness of his weekend. 'Could we go to the game on Sunday afternoon?' he asked. 'I should be finished in time.'

Russell was delighted. They hadn't been for a while – Paul had not seemed keen, and Russell found it hard to feel enthusiastic about football in the middle of a war, though this was not a view shared by his fellow Berliners. Attendances had swollen over the last year, despite the fact that many of the best players and a high proportion of the regular fans were strewn across Europe at the Wehrmacht's bidding. 'I'd like that,' he said.

'So would I,' Paul agreed, and their goodbyes were imbued with the sort of simple father-son camaraderie that both had once taken for granted.

A few minutes later Effi walked in, and was suitably shocked by his bandaged head. 'What...'

'It's nothing,' he reassured her. 'Someone took a shot at me. Just a crease. I'm fine.'

'Someone took a *shot* at you?'

'In Prague.'

'Have you seen a doctor?'

'In Prague. A Czech doctor. I meant to go today but...'

'Let me look at it.'

'There's no need...'

'Sit down!'

He did as he was told, and she began unwinding the bandage.

'How's the filming going?' he asked.

'I don't want to talk about it. Not until I've had a drink anyway. And I'm afraid I still haven't got to the shops; we'll have to eat out.' The bandage was off, and the wound seemed clean enough. She felt relieved, but also frightened at the closeness of the shave. 'And stop trying to change the subject. Who was it shot you? And why?'

'The Czech Resistance.'

'Well, they're rotten shots. This doesn't look too bad.'

'The worst bit is having to explain the bandage to everyone I meet.'

She smiled in spite of herself, and went into the bathroom. 'One of those woolly ski caps we bought in Innsbruck would cover it up,' she said, rifling through the medicine cabinet.

'Yes. And add a hint of sartorial *joie de vivre* to Ribbentrop's press conferences.'

She emerged with a new dressing. 'Now tell me the whole story.'

He gave her a detailed précis of his twelve hours in Prague.

'You were lucky,' she said when he was finished. 'And I don't just mean with the bullet.'

'Not that lucky. Canaris made the Swiss arrangement conditional on my delivering the message.'

'So that's off,' she said, failing to hide her disappointment.

'Not necessarily,' Russell told her. 'I have another idea.'

At ten the following morning he was ringing the doorbell at the American Consulate. A sprinkling of snow had fallen overnight, and both Kenyon and Dallin were waiting in Russian-style overcoats. The three of them walked across Pariser Platz, past the Brandenburg Gate and into the festive-looking Tiergarten.

'Any news?' Russell asked, as three fighters flew past a half-kilometre or so to the north. The BBC news of the previous evening had reported 'rising tension' in the Far East, but nothing more specific.

'No,' Kenyon told him, pausing to light one of his cigarettes. 'But we're still thinking days rather than weeks.'

'What about you,' Dallin asked. 'Have you seen Knieriem yet?'

'I tried,' Russell lied. 'I went round to his house last night, and there were two official cars outside. I think Herr Knieriem has thrown in his lot with the Nazis.'

'That doesn't necessarily follow,' Dallin insisted. 'He could be...'

'I know he could,' Russell interjected. 'But it didn't seem like the right moment to find out.'

They all fell silent as a well-wrapped nanny walked by with her two charges, one still in a pram, the other clasping a snowball and clearly itching to throw it.

'So when are you going back?' Dallin asked, looking warily over his shoulder.

'Maybe tonight, but that's not what I wanted to see you about.' He stopped and turned to Kenyon. 'I think I may know where those documents are, the ones Sullivan was going to give us.'

'Where?' Kenyon asked, his eyes lighting up.

Russell ignored the question and turned to Dallin. 'But I need something from you in exchange,' he told the Intelligence man. 'Remember the idea of setting me up in Switzerland as a channel between you and the Abwehr, and the job I was supposed to do in Prague for Canaris as proof of my usefulness and loyalty? Well, the SD torpedoed the job, and Canaris is probably less fond of me than he was. So I need you to push my case from your end, tell Canaris how useful it would be for you and him to have me there in Switzerland.'

Kenyon was smiling, Dallin frowning and shaking his head. 'I can't do a deal like that,' the latter said.

'Of course you can. You liked the idea when I first told you about it, and it's in your government's interest – a channel to the Abwehr would be useful, particularly if Canaris falls out even further with Heydrich. And it's in the Admiral's interests too. All you have to do is insist that I'm the man you want as the go-between. Put it in writing, and I'll deliver it. What could that cost you?'

'And when do you think you can recover Sullivan's papers?' Kenyon asked. Away in the distance a train was rumbling across the Spree bridge outside Bellevue Station.

Russell worked through a mental timetable. 'Saturday,' he suggested. 'Maybe Sunday.'

'I don't know,' Dallin said stubbornly.

As Russell had hoped, the senior diplomat was not about to be denied. 'We'll work something out,' Kenyon assured him.

Dropping in at the Adlon to check for messages, Russell found most of the foreign press corps strewn around the bar like passengers waiting for a train. Some had even taken the precaution of bringing small suitcases with them, just in case. Several were enjoying a late and decidedly alcoholic breakfast.

Around eleven forty-five they set off *en masse* for the Foreign Ministry, rather in the manner of schoolboys and girls resenting a disagreeable outing. The briefing proved even less enlightening than usual – with the battles in Russia and North Africa apparently still raging, all von Stumm wanted to talk about was a heinous attack by terrorists on a German officer in Paris. For once, Russell thought, the German spokesman might have got his priorities right, albeit not in the way he intended. As finite German power was spread ever more thinly across an expanding empire, an ever-swelling tide of resistance seemed inevitable.

The briefing concluded in the traditional way, with one of the Americans asking a question that the Germans either wouldn't or couldn't answer. 'Would the spokesman like to comment on Turkey's decision to accept lend-lease aid from the United States?' Ralph Morrison asked. Von Stumm looked at the table, said for the hundredth time that year that this particular question was 'not worthy of an answer', and made the usual abrupt exit, sucking minions into his wake as he swept from the chamber. There was a brief and thoroughly sarcastic ripple of applause.

The press corps adjourned to the Press Club for a long and highly alcoholic lunch, before attending their second circus of the day at Goebbels' Big Top. One of the Americans was leaving for Switzerland soon thereafter, and a farewell party had been planned for the station platform. Russell didn't know the man well, but joined his drunken colleagues in their stumbling progress to the nearby Potsdam Station. Out on the platform, the party turned into a multinational singsong, with a fine rendition of 'Lili Marlene' sandwiched between equally melodic takes on 'Swanee River' and 'Pennies from Heaven'. Several colleagues had come armed with rolls containing real sausage for the traveller, and insisted that their later consumption be suitably ostentatious – if at all possible, sizable chunks of meat should be casually jettisoned in front of watching Germans.

The whistles finally blew, and as the train moved off into the darkness the journalists all waved white handkerchiefs at their departing colleague. It was quite ridiculous, and annoyingly moving.

After sobering himself up with a strong and thoroughly disgusting coffee at the station buffet, Russell descended the steps to the U-Bahn platforms. The normal rush hours were over, but the trains were still packed, and he stood all the way to Alexander Platz, where he changed lines. The Gesundbrunnen train was almost as full, but a seat opened up after a couple of stops. He was tired, he realised, both physically and mentally. Tired of waiting for some sort of axe to fall.

Emerging from the U-Bahn terminus, he turned down Behmstrasse. Ahead of him, the dark rectangle of Hertha's Plumpe Stadium was dimly silhouetted against the clear night sky. The locomotive driver Walter Metza lived a couple of streets to the north, in one of the old apartment blocks that housed many of the local Reichsbahn workers, and Russell found the street without much difficulty. This was not the sort of area the Gestapo would visit on foot, but for Metza's sake Russell was careful to make sure that he wasn't being followed.

The woman who answered the door was initially suspicious, but managed a thin smile of welcome when he explained who he was, and swiftly ushered him inside. She was a tallish blonde in her early thirties, with one of those plain faces that would sometimes slip into beauty. As she shut the door Russell noticed a Reichspost cap hanging behind it.

'I'm his wife,' she said, squeezing past him. 'Ute.' She opened another door. 'Walter's in here.'

Metza was in an armchair, with one heavily strapped leg resting on a cushioned upright chair. The left side of his face was a mass of healing lesions, and the hair on that side of his head was still growing back. He was at least ten years older than his wife, but the two young girls examining Russell with great curiosity clearly belonged to both of them – the older one looked like him, the younger one like her. The wife quickly shooed the two girls into the other room and shut the door behind the three of them.

Russell explained who he was, who he worked for, and how he was trying to build up a picture of what was really happening in Russia before the outbreak of German-American hostilities caused his deportation. Metza nodded his understanding, and asked for reassurance that his name would not be mentioned.

'No. And I'll make damn sure that no one could deduce my source from reading the story.'

'Then fire away.'

Russell began running through the questions he had prepared. The driver answered them in a slow but confident voice, often thinking for several moments before speaking. He was, Russell guessed, one of the many workers who had benefited from the KPD's sponsorship of adult education classes in the late 1920s.

Metza had mostly been employed on the main line to Moscow through Brest, Minsk and Smolensk, which, as Russell knew, was the principal supply route for Army Group Centre. The whole line had needed re-gauging for German locomotives and rolling stock, the driver explained, and most of it had been. The continued use of Russian locomotives and rolling stock complicated matters, but those problems were proving surmountable. Others were not. Every Reichsbahn district manager in Germany had volunteered his worst workers for service in the East, and Reichsbahn equipment had proved utterly inadequate for the conditions. 'The Soviets have their steam pipes inside the boiler on their locomotives, so that they do not freeze up,' Metza explained. 'Ours are outside, and of course they do. And that's just one of the differences. Their tenders carry more water, so their water towers are further apart, too far apart for ours. There are so many problems like that. Our trains are just not built for Russian conditions.'

And then there were the partisans. 'At first we thought, "Ah, this is just a small nuisance that we'll have to get used to", but the attacks grew more frequent very quickly, and now they are a major problem. Lines are blown up, bridges too – there are so many long stretches of track running through empty forests. Not that the partisans stick to the countryside – sabotage attacks are common in cities like Minsk and Smolensk.'

'I know it's an impossible question,' Russell said, 'but how much is the Army getting of what it needs? Are there just difficulties, or is there a real supply crisis?'

Metza thought about that for a moment, idly scratching at his side where less visible injuries were presumably itching. 'In early November, when I was wounded, there were serious difficulties. And from what comrades have told me since then, I would guess that those difficulties have turned into a real crisis. Even three weeks ago the yards in Brest and Baranovichi were full of supplies which couldn't be moved, and from what I hear the blockages are now backed up as far as Warsaw.'

'How were you wounded?' Russell asked out of curiosity.

'A partisan attack.' He had seen the blown bridge in time to stop, but his stationary train had immediately come under fire. 'And not just from rifles. It was a mortar that got me. It landed in the tender.' Metza smiled ruefully. 'They'd obviously fired a few before we arrived to get the range.' He flexed his leg in remembrance. 'Nothing that won't heal. I was lucky. My fireman was killed outright, and about twenty others. If a troop train hadn't pulled up behind us it would have been a lot worse.'

'How do you feel about going back?'

'Not good. I mean, no one wants to die or get maimed in a good cause, and our cause stinks. I was a member of the Party before the Nazis came to power, and I'm still a communist at heart. Why would I want to see the Soviet Union destroyed? But what choice do I have, a married man with two daughters? We lost in '33, and we'll have to keep paying the price until someone else brings the bastard down.'

Russell had more specific questions about fuel and food supplies, but Metza couldn't help him – 'All the people at the forward depots ever complained about was the lack of winter clothing.' The driver did have more information about the Jews. Special SS squads called *einsatzgruppen* were combing the occupied territories, and rumour had it that Jews in small villages and towns were simply being shot. In big cities like Minsk they were only being forced into the ghettoes. There were no large-scale transports, either east or west, although that might be down to a simple shortage of trains.

Metza was visibly tiring, although he managed a smile when a sudden burst of high-pitched laughter erupted in the other room. Russell put his notebook away, and got to his feet. 'I have a favour to ask. I need to talk to Gerhard Ströhm, and I have no way of contacting him. I know he works in the Stettin Station yards but it's always been him getting in touch with me, not the other way round. Could you get word to him, tell him I need to speak to him? It is urgent.'

The driver nodded. 'I can do that. But not until the morning.'

'That'll do. Tell him he can telephone me tomorrow evening, any time after six.'

They shook hands, and Russell let himself out. As he steered his way back through the blackout to the U-Bahn station, he imagined the mother and daughters reoccupying the room he had just vacated, pushing back the war with their laughter.

Effi usually left work early on a Friday, and today it was even earlier – a sudden row between director and writer had been won by the former, necessitating a weekend rewrite and the postponement of shooting. John being already home was a nice surprise; the news that they had to stay in and wait for a call from his railwayman was most definitely not, particularly since the call itself would probably result in her spending the rest of the evening alone. Seeing her disappointment, Russell suggested they went out immediately for an early dinner. If Ströhm called in the meantime, he would doubtless call again.

As it happened, the German-American called ten minutes after their return. 'Klaus, I heard you were trying to reach me.'

'Yes. Thanks for calling. There's another game tonight at Number 21. Same time – 8.30. Can you make it?'

There was a moment's pause. 'Yes, I can,' Ströhm said. He was, Russell guessed, somewhat mystified by the request for a meeting.

Half an hour later he left Effi curled up on the sofa and walked down to Savignyplatz. This time a westbound train drew in almost instantly, and he arrived at Westkreuz with almost half an hour to spare. The sky was as clear as yesterday's, the temperature probably lower, and after enduring twenty minutes of the chilling breeze the only way he could find to warm himself was by stamping up and down the steps between the station's two levels.

At least Ströhm was on time. They went through the same charade as before, leaving the station, returning, and retreating to the end of a platform.

'I need your help,' Russell told the other man. He explained about Sullivan – the putative deal, the arrest and murder, the still-missing papers. 'He must have put them in the left luggage. He was coming from that direction when I saw him, but I didn't make the connection until his wife told me he was carrying a briefcase. I've got a description and I need to get in there and look for it. Are there any comrades working there who can let me in? Or someone else who'll take a bribe to look the other way?'

'I don't know,' Ströhm said. 'I suppose you've thought of just turning up and saying you lost the ticket?'

'I have. But Sullivan's initials are on the briefcase, and I have no papers to prove that I'm him, even if I wanted to try. And if either the police or Sullivan's murderers have a similar brainwave about the left luggage, they'll end up getting my description from whomever I talk to, which I definitely don't want. No, in this instance, the illegal way seems the safest way. I want whoever helps me to have a personal motive for keeping quiet. Loyalty to the cause would be best. I mean, think about it. These papers will prove that American and German capitalists are determined to carry on sharing out profits while Germans and American workers are dying on the battlefields. It's perfect propaganda because it's so fucking true.'

Ströhm grunted. 'I'll see what I can do. When can I call you?'

'Tomorrow between five and seven?'

'All right. If I can arrange something I'll give you a time and day for a movie, and we'll meet at Stettin Station. If I can't I'll ask for Wolfgang, and you can tell me I've got the wrong number.'

Back home, Russell found Effi in bed, almost asleep. 'Sorry,' she said. 'It's these five o'clock starts. Come and hold me.'

He did for ten minutes or so, finally disentangling himself when her breathing grew heavier. His brain seemed to be humming with possibilities, most of them dire, and listening to the nine o'clock news on the BBC engendered boredom without inducing calm. He wondered whether he should pack. He probably should, but what? His books were mostly still in boxes, and his only other prized possession was an unusable car. Clothes, he supposed, but how many of those would he need? Was he supposed to take all his underwear into exile?

Rummaging through a drawer he came across a collection of Paul's pictures from his first school, and one in particular – a collection of stick-figured Hertha Berlin players wildly celebrating a goal – caught his eye. On impulse he folded it up and tucked it into his wallet. A photograph of Effi was already there, a head and shoulders shot that Thomas had taken during a boating day on the Havel four, five years ago. Her face was turned towards the camera, an impish smile warring with the seriousness in her eyes. Thomas had caught both the child and the adult, which was no mean feat.

Russell picked up the phone and called his ex-brother-in-law. 'How are things?' he asked, once Thomas had picked up.

'As good as can be expected. You're not out on the town, then?'

'No, Effi's gone to bed. Early mornings and all that.'

'Ah.'

Why had he rung? Russell didn't really know. 'I'm just rummaging through my worldly possessions, wondering what to pack,' he said. 'It could be any day now, and, well, if anything should happen to Ilse and Matthias, you will…'

'Of course,' Thomas said, sounding almost hurt that Russell would ever doubt it.

'I know you will. Sorry.'

'And make sure to tell Effi that we want to keep seeing her,' Thomas added.

'I will.'

'If you are still here next week, let's meet for lunch. Tuesday at the usual time and place?'

'Why break the habits of a lifetime?'

'Why indeed?'

'I'll see you then.'

'Goodnight, John.'

Saturday morning they slept in, then walked down to the Ku'damm for a late breakfast. The sun was shining, and pre-war numbers of well-wrapped Berliners were sitting at outside tables, sipping their ersatz coffee and smiling at each other. Everyone seemed in good spirits – it was wonderful what two clear nights without an air raid could do.

'And the forecast for tonight is cloudy,' Russell read aloud from his half of the newspaper. 'There is a God.'

'There's also Goebbels,' Effi murmured. 'He has a whole trainload of women's fur coats ready for shipment to the front.'

'The troops'll look very fetching,' Russell observed.

She laughed and looked at her watch. 'I have to go,' she said, but made no move to do so. 'I do love Zarah, but… I assumed you'd be spending the day with Paul.'

'Not a good assumption these days. The *Hitlerjugend* has first call.'

She picked up her cup, realised it was empty, and put it down again. This, Russell thought, is how she always ends up being late. 'I've got to go too,' he said encouragingly, and she reluctantly got to her feet.

They parted at the tram stops outside the Universum, she heading west towards Grunewald, he travelling east towards the old city and what would probably prove a long and futile afternoon attending to business. His first stop was the table of foreign newspapers at the Press Club, his second the Adlon bar, where his fellow-American journalists seemed to be waiting, drinks in hand, for someone to shout 'Last orders' on their Berlin sojourn. It felt to Russell as if everyone was holding his breath, or at least waiting for some sign that the wind had decided which way to blow. Who was winning outside Moscow? Who was winning in North Africa? Where and when would the Japanese strike? The war seemed at a tipping point, yet refused to tip.

He was back home in time to hear the six o'clock news from the BBC, but an encouraging tone was all that London had to offer. Effi's key was just turning in the lock when the telephone rang. It was Ströhm.

'That film you asked about,' the familiar voice began. 'It's showing at the Metropole at five o'clock tomorrow afternoon.'

'I'll meet you there,' Russell told him. The Hertha game would be over by four – he'd just have to put Paul on the U-Bahn.

'The railwayman?' Effi asked.

Russell nodded and reached for his newspaper. 'It's on for tomorrow evening,' he said, scanning the cinema listings. The film at the Metropole was indeed opening at five. Ströhm was thorough. 'How was Zarah?' he asked.

Effi made a face. 'She's all right. Jens is still trying to atone. How long that will last is anyone's guess. She needs to help him, but I'm not sure she knows how. I'm not sure I do.' She sighed. 'But enough. Let's have some fun. Can we leave the war behind for a few hours?'

'We can try.'

They did. A better than usual meal at one of their pre-war favourite restaurants was a good start, and only slightly spoiled by a tall, thin and very insistent SS officer, who leaned over their table like a black heron and gushed his way through an account of Effi's career that would have embarrassed her old agent. As a *pièce de resistance* he took off one black leather glove, revealing an index finger encased in plaster which Effi was required to sign.

'I dread to think how he got that injury,' Russell remarked once the man had gone.

They thought about taking in a show, but the only entertainments on offer were those revues that so shocked provincial visitors to the capital. The newspapers had been full of indignant letters for months, but nothing had been done – their enormous popularity with soldiers on leave obviously overrode the old Nazi puritanism.

Effi found nothing thrilling in 'flashing sequins and bouncing breasts'. She wanted to dance.

That was harder to arrange than it had been, but they eventually located a joint behind Alexanderplatz Station which one of Russell's colleagues had recommended. The music in the expansive cellar was hardly audible from the street, which was just as well since the band was playing unmistakably forbidden material, albeit interspersing it with syncopated versions of German folk tunes and *Deutschland Uber Alles*. The air was thick with cheap cigarette smoke, the cocktails all variations on the same mixture of industrial alcohol and grenadine, but they had a wonderful couple of hours, alternating dances with watching others enjoy themselves. They even tried something called 'jitterbugging', which Effi did a hundred times better than him.

When they stumbled back out around midnight a light shower of sleet was falling, and it took all their semi-drunken enthusiasm to steer a straight course through very dark streets to Alexanderplatz Station. The train home seemed full of other revellers, all beaming at each other and ignoring the myriad leaflets which someone had scattered around the carriage. 'A Christmas without honour' was the headline, and Russell felt no need to read the rest.

At around a quarter to two on the following afternoon he and his son shouldered their way through the packed western terrace at the Plumpe to reach their habitual spot, halfway up and opposite the edge of the penalty area. Paul was in plain clothes for once, but his commitment to the *Hitlerjugend* was evidenced by yet another vividly bruised cheek, the alleged result of a collision with a tree while 'terrain-gaming.' Russell didn't believe the explanation, but his son seemed in a good mood, and he didn't want to spoil it by playing the nosy and over-protective father.

Instead they talked football. Hertha were playing SV Jena, and the latter's recent record suggested a difficult ninety minutes for the home team. But, as Paul jubilantly pointed out, Jena had recently seen three of their first-choice defenders drafted into the army, so the teams were probably well matched.

The home team emerged to rousing cheers and the usual chants of 'Ha! Ho! He! Hertha BSC!' The stadium was almost full, the crowd well wrapped and, as many a wafting breath amply demonstrated, fortified with alcohol against the cold. Mittened hands lifted loosely-packed cigarettes to chapped lips, sucked in smoke and exhaled with obvious satisfaction.

A Hertha player drafted in the previous year had just been reported killed in action, and the team were all wearing black armbands in his memory. They should probably make them part of the normal strip, Russell thought sourly.

The Jena team followed Hertha out onto the frosty pitch, several players craning their necks to examine the heavens. The sleet had stopped overnight, but a dark and ominously-coloured sky seemed heavy with more.

The game began. Paul was standing to his father's left, and when play was at that end of the pitch, Russell found himself taking surreptitious glances at his son. The boy was only a few inches shorter than he was, and seemed noticeably older each time Russell saw him. Ilse had always said that he looked like his father, but Russell couldn't see it – they had the same coloured eyes, but that was about it.

The game seemed faster than usual, as if the players were all working overtime at keeping warm. Lacking permission to hare up and down the pitch, the two goalkeepers were both walking brisk circles inside their penalty areas, occasionally stopping to run on the spot. But all the frenetic activity failed to produce a decent chance, let alone a goal, in the first forty-five minutes.

Halfway through the second period it began to snow. This seemed to galvanise both teams, who shared four goals between them in an exhilarating last ten minutes, Hertha scoring a second equaliser with only seconds remaining. 'A fair result,' Russell murmured, as the players trudged off the now white pitch.

'I suppose so,' Paul admitted. He was still staring at the players, as if willing them to return and settle the matter. 'But what good is a fair result?' he muttered to himself.

Maybe his son did take after him, Russell thought.

They headed slowly for the nearest exit, eventually emerging onto Bellermanstrasse. 'Can we come to the next game?' Paul asked.

'If I'm still here,' Russell said without thinking.

'You will be, won't you?'

'I don't know. My influence over the Japanese, American and German governments seems somewhat limited these days. I hope so,' he added, wondering as he did so whether that was true. Some small part of him wanted a clean break, for his son's sake as much as his own.

Paul walked in silence for a while, a sure sign that he was pondering an important question. 'You will come back, won't you?' he finally asked, the tone almost accusative, his voice pitched slightly higher than usual. 'After the war, I mean.'

'Of course I will,' Russell said, putting a hand on the boy's shoulder.

'You won't decide to live in England or America?'

'No. I'm a Berliner. And so's my son.'

'Yes,' Paul said, as if realising that fact for the first time. 'We are, aren't we?'

They joined the crowd funnelling into the U-Bahn entrance, and waited on the densely packed platform for the next train.

'You'll be all right getting home?' Russell asked anxiously as the train neared his stop.

'Dad!' Paul said indignantly, and they both laughed. Russell stayed on the platform to watch the train leave, and saw his son's face seeking his own as the wheels started turning. It was a comforting moment, one he would treasure in the years to come.

Out on Bernauerstrasse the snow was already several millimetres thick. Daylight was almost gone, an eerily pallid darkness taking its place. A few army lorries swished their way past on the other side of the wide road; a tram clanked by on the near side, full of swaying shadows.

It took him fifteen minutes to reach Stettin Station. Behind the blackout screens that hung from the entrance archways there was just enough light to run a railway, but not that much activity. One train looked set for an imminent departure, and a steady trickle of people were heading for it. People returning home after a weekend in the capital, Russell guessed, their overloaded bags a sure sign that Berlin's shops were still better stocked than those of provincial towns like Stettin and Rostock.

No other meeting place had been specified, but it was still too early to head for the left luggage office. Entering the buffet where he and Sullivan had planned to meet, Russell saw Ströhm sitting with a newspaper and beer on the far side. He was wearing a long overcoat, and had placed his hat on the table in front of him. Russell took a careful look round, saw nothing to rouse his suspicions, and walked across to join him.

Ströhm gave him a quick smile of welcome and, as usual, wasted no words on pleasantries. 'The shift changes at five o'clock,' he said. 'Two men come off, and our man comes on. The Stettin train leaves at 5.10, so we'd better give him until then to deal with last-minute collections.'

'Is our man a comrade?' Russell asked in a suitably low whisper.

'Yes. He knows this is for the Party.'

'Good. I'll get myself a beer.'

He sat and sipped while Ströhm read his paper and the buffet clock worked its way past the hour-mark. There were few other customers, and the only new arrivals were a pair of young army officers, who came in laughing happily and bore all the hallmarks of men starting their period of leave.

'If you ever need to contact me again,' Ströhm offered, 'I nearly always take lunch at Johann's on Gartenstrasse. It's a working man's café, about two hundred metres from here, just past the Lazarus Hospital on the same side. I'm usually there between twelve and twelve-thirty. Just come in, get something to eat or drink, and make sure I see you. When I leave, follow me onto the street. All right?'

'All right.'

After a flurry of whistles and steam had signalled the departure of the Stettin train Ströhm folded his paper, carefully placed his hat on his head, and got to his feet. 'I won't be hanging around,' he told Russell as they crossed the thinly populated concourse. 'I'll just introduce you and leave you to it.'

'Fine,' Russell agreed. He couldn't believe how loud their steps sounded. 'And thanks,' he added. Assuming the briefcase was there, he planned to examine its contents as thoroughly as the circumstances permitted, then deposit it again under a new and false name. He certainly had no intention of carrying anything home.

The left luggage office was about twenty metres down platform one, part of the long building which lined the eastern wall of the train shed. An open doorway led into a small waiting area with a wide counter. The man behind it was probably in his fifties, with a round, cheerful-looking face and a seemingly bald head under his uniform cap. A faded naval tattoo was visible on his lower right arm. Behind him, lines of luggage shelves could be seen through another open doorway.

'This is Herr Russell,' Ströhm told him.

The man opened the counter-flap and gestured Russell though.

'Good luck,' Ströhm said as he left.

The room behind was bigger than Russell had expected, but the shelves were far from crowded.

'When was the article deposited?' the man asked him.

'A week ago. Saturday the 29th.'

'This way then,' the man said, leading him down one aisle and turning into another. 'This is the section.'

There were several hundred items – suitcases, canvas bags, burlap sacks, even a barrel – but only a few briefcases, and Russell noticed the one on the top shelf which matched his description almost instantly. It was not locked, and the two leather straps were all that stood between Russell and the contents. He took out the sheaf of papers and scanned the one on top. The English words 'Standard Oil' stood out amidst the German.

'This is it,' he told his accomplice. The light was good enough in this corner, and he couldn't be seen from the doorway. 'Can I spend a few minutes here looking through these papers?' he asked.

The man looked doubtful, but only for a second. 'All right. But don't be too long. The bosses only make the rounds once in a blue moon, but they do make them.'

'I'll be as quick as I can.'

The man headed back to his counter. Russell pulled out a suitcase to sit down on, and started leafing through the papers. They were, he quickly realised, exactly what Sullivan had said they were. Most were carbon copies of official minutes, a meticulous recording of meetings in the year soon ending between representatives of German and American industry. The majority were unadorned, but Sullivan had added explanatory notes in a few of the margins.

Most of the big names were mentioned. Here was Standard Oil promising shipments of oil to Tenerife on Panamanian-registered tankers, making secret deals to secure patents against wartime seizure, banking German payments for oil not yet extracted from its Romanian fields. Here was Ford making sure that everyone benefited from its new French plant, with German-American messages flowing via Vichy and Lisbon, ensuring that American shareholders would get their profits from the lorries now supplying the Wehrmacht in Russia. Here were General Motors and its Opel subsidiary, communicating in secret through a Danish sub-division.

There was a lot more. Russell leafed through the pages, marvelling at how wide Sullivan's access had been, and the thoroughness with which he had made use of it. If the man hadn't loved the Nazis so much, he would have been a damn good journalist.

And then, at the bottom of the sheaf, he found it. Sullivan's ace in the hole. A journalist's dream, a people's nightmare.

The final document contained the minutes of a meeting in Milan the previous May, in which representatives of IG Farben and their American partners arranged to use a supposedly unconnected South American firm as the middleman in their continuing shipment of pharmaceuticals. Attached to this document, and only connected to it by the corporation involved, was a sheet in Sullivan's own handwriting. It was, he claimed, a record of a conversation he had overheard in the executive dining room at IG Farben, between a corporation lawyer and the director of another company, Degesch, which Farben part-owned. The conversation concerned one of Degesch's most profitable products, a pesticide gas by the name of Zyklon-B, which was used to combat rat and insect infestations in premises like barracks and factories. The gas itself was odourless, the Degesch man had explained, and a chemical 'indicator' had always been added to warn humans of its dangerous presence.

But in early November the SS had placed a huge order for Zyklon-B, and insisted that no indicator should be added. This order had created a major problem for Degesch because, although the company still owned the patent on the indicator, its patent on the gas had now expired. Negotiations at the highest level had been required to sort the matter out, and Degesch had only agreed to accept the SS order once its production and sale monopoly had been guaranteed for a further ten years.

Russell stared into space for a few seconds. Could there be any other explanation? He couldn't think of one. He just sat there for a while, caught in the grip of a terrible sadness. He remembered walking alongside Albert Wiesner in Friedrichshain Park more than two years before. 'Some of my friends think they'll just kill us,' Albert had said, almost daring him to disagree. The friends had been right.

The sound of an arriving train shook him out of it. He put the papers back in the briefcase, fastened the straps and made his way back to the outer office.

As he reached it, Uwe Kuzorra walked in from the platform.

The detective's eyes took in the briefcase. 'Patrick Sullivan's?' he asked.

There was no point in denying it. Russell passed the briefcase across the counter. 'It only occurred to me this afternoon,' he said, as Kuzorra began unfastening the straps. 'But I did claim it was mine. I said I'd lost the ticket. My friend here was just being helpful.'

Kuzorra looked unconvinced. He opened the bag, briefly rifled through its contents, and closed it again. The expression on his face was more disappointed than angry. 'How did you know what to look for?' he asked.

'His wife. She let slip he was carrying a briefcase when he left home.'

'I think we'd better have a talk down at the Alex,' Kuzorra decided. 'It's time I heard the whole story in one go. Having you read me a new chapter every few days is getting more than a little tiresome.'

Russell opened his mouth to say something, but thought better of it.

The car was outside, Kuzorra's driver enjoying a cigarette in the falling snow. They skidded their way out of the forecourt and headed east on Invalidenstrasse before turning south onto Rosenthaler. It took only ten minutes to reach the Alex, and almost as long again tramping corridors and stairs to reach Kuzorra's office on the police building's top floor. The room was crowded but not cluttered, and a framed photograph of the detective's late wife stood on the shelf behind the main desk, allowing her to look out over his shoulder.

Kuzorra took his own seat, gestured Russell into the other, and reopened the briefcase.

'If you read the first one you'll get the idea,' Russell said helpfully.

The detective said nothing in reply, but did look up after working his way through the first document. 'Are they all like this?'

'All except for the last page.'

As Kuzorra read that, Russell watched the sequence of emotions crossing the detective's face – curiosity, anger, disgust, a bottomless grief. At last he looked up, and their eyes met.

The telephone rang.

Kuzorra listened, glanced briefly up at Russell, said 'Very well', and broke the connection. 'Stay here,' he said, 'I'll be back in a few minutes.'

What now? Russell wondered. Would he be handed over to the Gestapo or the SD? He reminded himself that he hadn't done anything seriously illegal. And Kuzorra would help if he could – not because he liked Russell, but because they hated the same people.

The minutes stretched by. He listened to the low hum of the building, the occasional footfalls in the corridor outside. The snow was still falling past the window, the courtyard below a square of ghostly light. He was supposed to be meeting Effi at the Chinese restaurant at seven, which was less than half an hour away. He was going to be late, at the very least. He considered using Kuzorra's phone, but had no idea how to get an outside line.

It was almost seven when the detective finally reappeared. He closed the door firmly behind him and leaned back against it. 'They have you, John,' he said quietly.

'What?' Russell asked, his stomach in freefall.

'I was called downstairs because they know you've been involved in my case,' Kuzorra continued. 'The Gestapo are out looking for you. At your home, the press clubs, the hotels...'

'Why?'

'Espionage.'

Russell was reminded of the day in Flanders, more than twenty years earlier, when he had first understood the expression 'almost choking with fear'.

'Your trip to Prague, someone recognised you. An informer, I think. He tied you to the communist resistance there, and the Gestapo have been showing your picture to communists they have in the camps. One man's refusal to recognise you wasn't very convincing, and they eventually got him to talk about things that happened more than two years ago. A meeting you had in the Tiergarten, naval papers you were supposed to collect in Kiel and pass on to the Reds.'

Russell remembered that day in the Tiergarten, the young man with the shaking hands who said his name was Gert.

'They showed your photograph around in Kiel as well, and someone else recognised you, a woman who was there when the papers were handed over.'

Geli, her name had been. Russell just stared at the detective. His mind seemed reluctant to work.

'What were you going to do with the papers in the briefcase?' Kuzorra asked.

Russell shook his head, hoping to set his brain in motion. 'There's a man at the US Consulate who wants them. He doesn't like big business types who betray their country. The last page I thought I'd keep for myself, and tell the world when I got out.' He managed a wry smile. 'Not that that seems very likely now.'

Kuzorra gave him a long hard look. 'I can probably get you out of the building,' he said eventually, 'but that's all I can do.'

'It sounds like a start,' Russell said. He could hear the brittleness in his own voice. Where the hell was he going to go?

Rolf and Eva Vollmar

Kuzorra inserted the sheaf of papers, fastened the straps on the briefcase, and handed it across. 'Your chances of making use of this are better than mine,' he said. 'Are you ready?'

'As I'll ever be,' Russell told him. His mind was still straining to catch up.

Out in the blissfully empty corridor, Kuzorra hesitated for a second, then chose a direction. 'Try to look less like a hunted animal,' he murmured as they walked towards the distant stairwell. A typewriter was clacking behind one door, voices audible behind another, but that was all.

They reached the top of the stairs at the same time as another uniformed officer. He brushed past them, offering Kuzorra a cursory greeting but hardly glancing at Russell. If questions were asked, the latter realised, the detective would find it difficult to explain why he had chosen to escort a wanted man off the premises. 'I do know the way out,' Russell said, as they hurried down the stairs. 'There's no point in us both being caught.'

'If that was true, I'd still be in my office,' Kuzorra said bluntly. 'You won't get out the way we came in.'

'If you say so.' He had counted eight flight of stairs when Kuzorra turned off down a brightly-lit corridor and headed, if Russell's directional sense was still functioning, for the interior courtyard. Another couple of turns and they seemed to be heading back towards the main frontage on Dircksenstrasse. A man in a long white coat and rubber gloves suddenly emerged in front of them, gave them an indifferent glance, and disappeared through an opposite doorway. A faint whiff of formaldehyde told Russell that they were close to the morgue, and he suddenly recognised the seating area where he'd waited more than two years previously with Eleanor McKinley before viewing her brother's body. The lost property department beyond was unstaffed, the No.2 door to the main street bolted shut for the night.

'Do you know where you are?' Kuzorra asked, as he gently pulled back the bolts.

'Yes. And thanks,' Russell said, offering his hand

'Good luck,' the detective said, shaking it firmly but briefly. As he opened one side of the double doors, a flurry of snow blew in.

Russell stepped out into the darkness, heard the door shut behind him, and fought back a rising sense of panic. One step at a time, he told himself. Turn right. Walk down to the square. Catch a train or a tram.

Each step along the front of the police building seemed fraught with danger, those that carried him across the front of the No.1 entrance almost impossibly so; but no voices suddenly cried out, and no car suddenly screeched to a halt beside him.

A train, he told himself, as one rattled its way along the elevated lines to his left. He had to get out of Berlin, and trains from Alexanderplatz Station served all corners of the Reich. He had enough money on him, and he had his papers. They would surely be good for a few hours more – the Gestapo wouldn't know that he'd been warned. There would be men waiting at the flat, maybe at the press clubs, at the Adlon. And probably at his son's home, he thought with a sinking heart.

And Effi. Could he leave without at least trying to say goodbye? He couldn't read his watch in the darkness, but she would probably still be waiting for him at the Chinese restaurant. He could telephone her there, he thought, and hurried his pace towards the station.

The public booths on the street level concourse all seemed occupied, but a woman emerged from one just as he arrived. He picked up the still-warm receiver and, after another moment's panic, remembered the number. He dialled it, hoping that Ho Lung would answer. The young man's Chinese-accented German might be barely decipherable, but it was the only German on offer.

He was in luck. 'This is John Russell,' he said, as slowly and distinctly as he could manage. 'Is Fraulein Koenen there? We were supposed to meet at seven.'

'I go see,' Ho Lung said, and there was a loud thunk as he put the mouthpiece down.

As he stared out through the glass door at the milling people, the concourse clock caught Russell's eye. It was a few minutes past eight. Surely Effi would have gone home by this time.

He heard Ho Lung pick up the earpiece. 'She go,' the young man said. 'One minute, maybe two.'

Russell took a deep breath. 'Ho Lung, please, can you do me a big favour? Go after her, and bring her back. I need to talk to her. A matter of life and death, believe me.'

'Oh. But where? Which street?'

'She will be walking east, past the Universum, towards the Memorial Church. Please.'

'Okay.'

Russell sank down onto the booth seat. He had a mental picture of Ho Lung leaving the restaurant, hurrying down the snow-covered boulevard, cursing himself in Chinese for agreeing to this mad search in almost total darkness.

The telephone demanded another infusion of cash, and Russell leapt back to his feet, frantically rummaging through his pockets for the necessary pfennigs. Several coins fell to the floor, but there was enough in his hand to prolong the call. He squatted down to retrieve the others, and rose to his feet just as an impatient-looking woman tapped on his door. He raised five fingers and turned his back on her.

'John,' Effi said, in the tone of someone who'd been kept waiting for an hour.

'The Gestapo are after me,' he said without preamble. 'Kuzorra tipped me off, and I assume they're waiting at Carmerstrasse. I've got to get out of Berlin, but I want to see you before I go…'

'Why are they after you?' she asked, wondering as she did so where such a sensible question had come from. 'How serious is it?'

'The business two years ago. It couldn't be more serious.'

'But where can you go?'

'I've no idea, but…'

'Where shall we meet?' she interjected.

They were both about fifteen minutes from Zoo Station. The buffet would be crowded at this time of night, but it was also well lit. 'Zoo Station, the eastbound platform,' he decided.

'Where are you?' she asked.

He told her.

'I've got a better idea,' she said. 'You remember that bar on Friedrichstrasse, just up from the station? Siggi's. Let's meet there.'

'But…'

'I'll explain later. Trust me.'

'All right.'

'I'll make sure I'm not being followed.'

There was a click as she hung up the phone. Why Friedrichstrasse, he wondered. He hung up his own earpiece, and thought about calling Paul. He felt an intense need to tell his son, to prepare him for what was coming, to say how sorry he was. But he knew he couldn't. The Gehrts' line might be tapped by now, and the less he implicated them the better.

The same applied to Thomas.

A different woman was now raising a hand to tap the window. He acknowledged her and exited the booth, scanning the concourse for uniforms and leather coats. There were none in sight, but if they were watching the main line stations they would be at the entrance to the platforms. Was that why Effi had vetoed Zoo Station? If so, she was proving a lot quicker on her feet than he was.

He could take the S-Bahn to Friedrichstrasse, but a tram would probably be safer. Back out on Alexanderplatz he waited impatiently for one to arrive. Behind him the huge bulk of the police building was screened by snow and darkness, but he could almost feel its presence, as if the energy of all those men engaged in tracking him down was sweeping out across the city like a psychic searchlight.

The tram came. It wasn't full, and everyone on board had the opportunity to examine him and raise the alarm. No one did. He was just another German heading home.

The tram rumbled slowly down Königstrasse, its thin blue headlights revealing nothing but rails and snow. With no visual clues as to location, the passengers were all cocking their ears for familiar sounds, like the echoing rumbles provided by the bridges across the Spree River and Canal. Thinking he had made out the vague silhouette of the Französische Church, Russell got off at the next stop and found himself close to Friedrichstrasse.

He walked north towards the station, passing Café Kranzler and crossing the snow-swept Unter den Linden. Continuing up Friedrichstrasse, he passed under the iron railway bridge and eventually singled out Siggi's Bar from the line of blacked-out premises beyond. The light inside was momentarily blinding, but his eyes soon adjusted and took in the usual Sunday evening customers – a group of older men playing skat, several individual soldiers with female company, a couple of men in a corner who looked to be holding hands under the table.

Assuming Effi was taking the S-Bahn, the trip should take her about half an hour, which meant another ten minutes. He ordered whatever was passing for schnapps, and drank it down in one gulp. He ordered another, and took that to one of the tables, ignoring the middle-aged barman's obvious desire for a chat. He looked like one of those men who were always recognising Effi.

Not that this would matter unless Russell's own name, and his association with hers, had already been broadcast on the radio. It didn't seem likely, but the possibility had obviously occurred to Effi as well – she arrived with hat pulled almost over her eyes, scarf wrapped round her mouth and nose.

'Let's go,' she said through the scarf, before Russell had time to offer her a drink. Outside on the pavement she grabbed him tightly by the arm and began steering him back towards the station.

'Where are we going?' he asked, amused in spite of himself.

'Wedding,' she said succinctly.

'Wedding?' It was north Berlin's most down-at-heel area, full of factories and old apartment blocks. Before the Nazis it had been a KPD fortress.

They reached the wide bridge which carried the Reichsbahn and S-Bahn tracks across the street, and Effi pulled him into a niche beside the closed newspaper kiosk. 'There's something I've kept from you,' she said, placing a hand on each of his shoulders. 'I have an apartment in Wedding. On Prinz-Eugen-Strasse.'

'You what?'

'Well, it's not mine. I rent it. Since the end of last year actually.'

'But...'

'I thought this day would come,' she said simply.

He looked at her, dumbfounded. 'But aren't the neighbours a bit surprised to have a film star living in their block? And won't they...'

'They don't know I'm a film star,' Effi said patiently. 'I don't rent it as myself. I rent it as a fifty-five-year-old woman who spends most of her time with her children on their farm in Saxony, but who wants somewhere to stay in Berlin, where all her old friends are. I didn't go through all those lessons in make-up from Lili Rohde for fun. No one on Prinz-Eugen-Strasse has seen me out of character, and we have to pray that no one sees us going in tonight.'

For the second time that evening, Russell was lost for words.

'We can't hide there for ever,' Effi continued, 'but it should give us a breathing space while we work out what we're going to do.'

'We?'

'Of course "we". But we can discuss all that when we get there. Let's get on the U-Bahn.'

There was no watch on the U-Bahn entrance, but the train was just crowded enough to inhibit further conversation, and neither spoke again before they reached their Leopold platz stop. Russell was still struggling to adjust. How had she arranged all this without his noticing? He had always known that Effi had many strengths, but he had never thought that strategic planning was one of them.

Back on the surface, it seemed noticeably darker than downtown, but Effi picked their way through the grid of streets without apparent difficulty. 'It's not the Adlon,' she said, as they reached the end of Prinz-Eugen-Strasse, 'but there *is* a private toilet. I thought we should see as little of the neighbours as possible. The concierge is old and deaf, which has to help, and the original block warden seemed like a nice man. He was one of my reasons for choosing this place, but he died in the summer. I haven't met his replacement, but the woman across the landing doesn't like him. Her husband is in Russia by the way. From the way she talks I'd say he was a Red in the old days.'

She stopped by the entrance to a courtyard. 'This is it,' she said, pulling her keys from her coat pocket, and heading for the doors on the left hand side. The walls of the buildings rose up into darkness, leaving Russell with the impression that he was standing at the bottom of a deep well.

The key turned smoothly, and Effi pushed into the dimly-lit interior. There was no sight or sound of the *portierfrau*, and they climbed the two flights of stairs to the first floor. Another door, another key, and they were safe inside the apartment.

It was better than Russell had expected. The block's heating was obviously adequate, and the flat, though decidedly cramped, seemed pleasant enough. The living room had space for two armchairs, a side table and two upright chairs. The kitchen, though essentially a passage leading to the small bathroom, had an electric stove and several wall cupboards well-stocked with provisions. 'A film star's perks,' Effi explained. In the bathroom itself, the various elements of her make-up kit were laid out on another narrow table.

The bedroom was just large enough to accommodate a double bed and wardrobe. Opening the latter, Russell was surprised to find a selection of his own clothes, including several of the items he had given up for lost.

'I brought all the photographs of you,' she said behind him. 'I'm afraid they won't have any trouble finding ones of me.'

He turned to embrace her. 'You're absolutely unbelievable,' he said.

'And I bought the Rugen Island jigsaw which we never got round to doing,' she added once their hug had loosened.

He didn't know whether to laugh or weep.

'I'll boil some water,' she said.

He sat down, ran a hand through his hair. He had to convince her to go back, but the thought of losing her seemed scarier than ever. Too much had happened too quickly. Much too much. He got back to his feet intent on pacing, but the room wasn't big enough. A look around the edge of the window screening revealed only darkness.

She brought in two tin mugs of tea. 'No milk, I'm afraid.'

He took his and held her eye. 'Effi, they're only after me. You had no part in the business two years ago, and there's no way they could prove otherwise. Tomorrow morning, you should go back to Carmerstrasse and… in fact, the best thing you can do is go to the Alex and report me missing.'

She smiled and shook her head. 'John, you know as well as I do that they'll arrest me. And I'm not going back to the Gestapo, not voluntarily. The last time was bad enough, and this time they'd want to know where you are. I'd have a choice between telling them, and wasting all the effort I've put into this place, or not telling them, and having them do God knows what to me. I'm not doing it, so forget that idea right now. We're in this together – if you get out then I get out; if you don't, then I don't want to either.'

'But you're making yourself an accessory,' Russell argued. 'Helping an enemy of the Reich, that's treason. They could execute you. At the very least, they'll put you in Ravensbrück.'

'I know that. And I'm scared. I expect you are too.'

'What about your career?' he asked stupidly.

'I used to enjoy it,' she admitted. 'All of it – the work, the money, being recognised. But not any more. Either it changed or I did. Or both. Whatever it was, it's over now. *GPU* will have to soldier on without me. And you have to think up some way of getting us out of the country. I know you can. It's the sort of thing you're good at.'

Russell wasn't so sure, but decided to play along. A discussion of the difficulties might make her see sense. 'All right,' he agreed. 'But we have to look at all the options. One,' he began, tapping his left thumb with his right index finger, 'we can give ourselves up. Two, I can try gate-crashing the American Consulate and you can go back home.' He raised a palm to stifle her protest. 'We're looking at all the options, and that's one of them. The bastards have nothing against you, and if they know where I am, then there's no need for them to question you.'

'You're not listening to me,' she said quietly.

'I am,' he insisted. 'I'll try to find a way to get us both out. But if there's no way to do that, then I'd rather go down alone than take you with me.'

'But you said yourself – there's a good chance they'd just walk into the Consulate and drag you out.'

'They might. They might not. But I'll take the chance. Effi, I'm not going to let you sacrifice yourself for no good reason.'

'Love is a good reason.'

'Okay, but love should be a reason to live. And if I'm going down anyway, I'd feel a lot happier knowing that you weren't. Wouldn't you feel the same way?'

'I don't know.'

'Look, let's get back to the options. If we're not giving ourselves up, we're left with two – either spend the war in hiding inside Germany, or find some way of getting out. A life in hiding doesn't look too promising – how would we eat, for a start?'

'I'd rather get out,' she admitted.

'Okay, we could try and get across a border. Switzerland is the obvious choice, being neutral, and I have a feeling we could survive in Denmark if we got there. Going east would be suicidal, going west… well, Holland, Belgium and France are all occupied, and we wouldn't be safe until we got to Spain, which is a hell of a long way away. So, Switzerland or Denmark. But how do we get there? We can't use our own papers, and neither of us – as far as I know – has any facility at forging documents.'

'No,' she agreed, walking into the bedroom and rummaging under the bed. 'But I do have these,' she said, pulling out an apparent pile of brown paper. She spread the paper out, revealing the uniform of an SS Sturmbannführer. 'I also have a Luftwaffe pilot, a *Reichfrauenschaft* official and a nurse,' she added.

Russell shook his head in amazement. 'From the wardrobe department?' he guessed.

'I was spoilt for choice,' she confessed.

'They might come in useful,' he said, 'but without new papers… Any long distance train journey, there are checks every hour or so. And the moment someone asks for ours, we're done for. We wouldn't get a second chance.'

'Oh.'

'We'll have to get some papers from somewhere,' he said. Precisely where was another matter. Zembski's demise, while always unfortunate for Zembski, now also seemed fatal to their own prospects. Russell couldn't look up another Comintern forger in the Berlin telephone directory.

But he did still have a line to the comrades. Ströhm could – and probably would – pass on a request for help.

Would they help? Russell felt he was owed – it was, after all, his passing of naval secrets to the Soviets which had put the Gestapo on his tail. Then again, Stalin and his NKVD were not known for their nostalgic sense of gratitude. But he would have to try them. There was no one else. Kenyon would want to help, if only to get his hands on Sullivan's papers, but now that the Gestapo had abandoned all pretence of following the diplomatic rules there was nothing he could actually do.

'I'll go to Ströhm,' he said. 'My railwayman,' he added, remembering he had never told Effi the name. 'He may be able to help us, either with getting hold of some papers, or even with getting us out of the country.'

'That sounds good,' she agreed, deciding to share in his confidence. They had to remain positive, or they were lost. She took a peek round the corner of the window screen. 'There's not going to be an air raid tonight, is there?'

'Not unless the British have completely lost their senses.'

'Good. We can wait until morning before turning you into my older brother…'

'Your brother!?'

'My husband died some years ago, and I'm much too old for a fancy man.' She thought for a moment. 'We should probably leave something to suggest that you're sleeping in here, just in case we have visitors.'

'Can't we just bolt the door?'

'We can at night. But it'll look a bit suspicious during the day.'

'You're probably right,' he admitted.

'You know your English saying about clouds having a golden lining?'

'Silver.'

'Whichever. Well, I don't have to get up at half past four in the morning. The limousine driver will bang on our door in vain.'

'The neighbours will be ecstatic.'

She laughed, the first time she had done so that evening. 'I think I'm ready for bed,' she said. 'Not that I think I'll sleep.'

She did though, much to Russell's surprise. If the truth were told, she had amazed him almost daily since their first meeting almost eight years before. He lay awake in the dark unfamiliar room, marvelling at her resourcefulness, fearful of what the future held for them both. At least they still had each other. He told himself how lucky he had been to meet and know her, to be loved by her. All in all, he decided, he had enjoyed a fairly charmed forty-two years on the planet. He had grown up in a rich country at peace; he had, unlike so many of his friends, survived the horror of the trenches with both body and mind intact. He had been there in the thick of things after the war, when the world seemed dizzy with the hope of something better. That dream might have died, but he wouldn't have missed the dreaming. He had mostly enjoyed his work; he had her and a wonderful, healthy son.

The trouble was, he wanted another forty-two years.

He could just about envisage an escape, but the chances were thin. Better of course than those of the Jews, now that Heydrich and Co. were ordering indicator-free pesticides in vast quantities. Europe's Jews looked doomed. Even if Moscow survived, if the Soviets held out and the Americans entered the war against Germany before the year was out, the Nazis would still have time for a killing spree that sane people would struggle to find imaginable. He thought about the briefcase sitting in the other room, and Sullivan's handwritten postscript to all the proof of corporate perfidy. Would the governments in London, Washington and Moscow be convinced? And even if they were, would they care?

They woke together, a sign of change if ever there was one. He made them cups of ersatz coffee and told her what he'd found in Sullivan's briefcase. She sat there, staring into space and wondering at her own lack of surprise.

'We need a newspaper,' Russell announced, once they'd done the usual ablutions and eaten their usual breakfast. 'We need to know if all Berlin is looking for us, or only the Gestapo.'

She greyed his hair and eyebrows, lined his face, and fixed the small moustache, assuring him that the latter wouldn't fall off if he sneezed. 'When we do come to take it off, you'll realise how firmly it's attached,' she added ominously. She also insisted on his wearing gloves and the woolly hat. His head wound was healing faster than he expected, but the tiny lawn in his meadow of hair was something of a giveaway.

'I'll do myself while you're out,' she said, handing him a pair of keys. 'You remember who you are?'

'Rolf Vollmar. From Gelsenkirchen,' he said promptly. 'My house was bombed out by the British, and I'm staying with my sister Eva until I'm fully recovered.'

'Good,' she said. 'Do you know how to get back to the U-Bahn station?'

'I'm sure I can find it.'

'Right outside the door. Then left, right and left again.'

He let himself out and descended the stairs, feeling more than a little nervous. He knew how good Effi was at make-up, how long she had practised the difficult art of using theatrical make-up outside the theatre, but he still found it hard to believe that people would be taken in by his disguise.

There was no sign of the *portierfrau*, and no one on the snow-covered street. There were plenty of footprints though, large ones for the workers now ensconced in the factories, small ones for the children now at their school desks. There was also a strong smell of bread being baked, which presumably came from a nearby bakery. The odour was actually enticing, which raised the interesting question of what happened to the loaves between factory and shop.

He walked towards the first turning, taking care not to slip on a patch of ice – this was no time for breaking a bone. Effi's insistence on sharing whatever fate had in store had meant a lot to him, but in the cold light of morning he found himself wondering how selfish he was being. Should he just take off, take a local train away from Berlin, and try working his way towards a border in short and hopefully inconspicuous leaps? He might get near enough to try a night crossing on foot. It was possible.

But would it save her? Probably not. They would probably arrest her and torture her. If by some miracle he got out, the Gestapo wouldn't just smile, admit defeat, and move on; that wasn't their style. They'd want someone to punish, and she would be available.

Or was he just frightened of striking out alone?

He didn't know. He would try with Ströhm, but he wasn't hopeful. He thought Ströhm would agree to carry the message, but the chances of a swift reply, let alone a positive one, seemed remote. The most likely outcome was a long and dangerous wait culminating in refusal. Why would the comrades rush to help him? Unlike two years ago, he had nothing to offer them. They weren't interested in the perfidy of American corporations; they took that for granted.

Reaching the wide Müllerstrasse, he could see the kiosk outside the Leopoldplatz U-Bahn station. The level of traffic reminded him of a pre-war Sunday, and only a handful of pedestrians were out on the pavements. A stiff breeze was funnelling down the street, and he instinctively placed two fingers over the false moustache to hold it in place.

When he reached the kiosk the proprietor, an old man wearing a woolly hat remarkably similar to his own was deep in conversation with what looked like a regular customer. He paused to serve Russell, who remembered at the last moment that the *Völkischer Beobachter* was unlikely to be the paper of choice in an old Red stronghold like Wedding. He asked for *Der Angriff* and the Berlin edition of the *Frankfurter Zeitung*, and thumbed anxiously through them in search of his former face.

'You won't find the latest news in there,' the regular customer volunteered, causing Russell to look up with something approaching alarm.

'The Japanese have attacked the Americans,' the old proprietor said mournfully.

'In Hawaii,' the customer added. 'Their big naval base there.'

'When?' Russell asked.

'Yesterday, I think. The man on the radio wasn't too clear. I mean, it's probably the middle of the night there now, but whether it's yesterday night or tomorrow night I couldn't tell you.'

Russell couldn't help smiling – he had never got the hang of the International Date Line himself. 'But the Americans haven't declared war on us?'

'Not yet,' the customer said cheerfully.

Effi was going through the normal motions, bathing in what seemed ample hot water, but feeling far from normal. After drying herself, she carried the wall-mirror into the living room, propped it up on the table, and began turning herself into Eva Vollmar. Dabbing away with the make-up brush, she told herself that anticipating a turn of events was not the same as being ready for one. The very real possibility that she would never see her sister, parents or nephew again was hard to accept. Impossible, in fact.

She got up abruptly and switched on the People's Radio, hoping for some music to lift her spirits. It was Wagner, who always left her feeling more depressed. She turned him off, and resisted a sudden urge to throw the radio across the room.

Her transformation complete, she pulled back the screening from the street and courtyard windows, letting the sunlight in. What she could see of the street was empty, and she found herself wondering what she would do if Russell was arrested and didn't come back. Go back home and start clamouring for his release, she supposed.

And then he hove into view, paper under his arm, ridiculous woolly hat on his head, exhaling clouds of life into the cold air. Watching him walking towards her, she felt love well up inside her.

'The Japanese have bombed Pearl Harbour,' were his first words on entering, before her new appearance left him temporarily speechless.

'Where's that?' she asked.

'In Hawaii, in the middle of the Pacific. It's the main American naval base.'

'So America is in the war now?'

'It's at war with Japan. They might not want to take on Germany at the same time. I don't know.'

'Oh,' she said, disappointed. For a moment an end had seemed in sight.

'But I can't see how they'll be able to keep the two wars separate,' Russell added thoughtfully. He imagined the scene in the Consulate on Unter den Linden. They would be destroying all the papers, preparing themselves for internment. Any lingering chance of help from that quarter was well and truly gone. He wondered whether George Welland would ever get out now.

'What about us?' Effi asked. 'Are we in the paper?'

'No, not yet. This evening perhaps, but I think it'll only be me. I don't think Goebbels will be keen to let on that one of his favourite actresses has gone over to the enemy.'

'But I haven't,' she said instinctively. 'I'm not against Germany. I'm against *them*.'

'I know you are,' Russell admitted. 'But they think they *are* Germany.'

'They're not.'

'I know. Look, I've got to try and see Ströhm, and it might as well be today. There's no point in waiting.'

'No,' Effi agreed, hope rising in her eyes.

Seeing that hope, Russell wished he had something to justify it. How could he convince the comrades to help them?

It only took him a few minutes to remember Franz Knieriem.

The sky was clouding over again as he walked down Gartenstrasse, the vast bulk of the Lazarus Hospital rearing up in front of him, the long low buildings of the Stettiner Goods Station lining the other side of the street. Johann's Cafe was sandwiched between a closed cobbler's and a barber's, its steamed-up windows as effective as curtains at concealing the interior. He pushed open the door and walked in.

The café was larger inside than he expected, a long narrow room some four metres wide and over twenty long, with tables for four and eight flanking a single aisle that stretched into the gloomy interior. Almost all were occupied by men, most of them in overalls, a few in suits. Three waitresses were taking and delivering orders, flitting to and fro between the tables and a small counter area halfway down, which was obviously connected by dumb waiter to the floor above or below.

Russell walked two-thirds of the way down and then retraced his steps. There was no sign of Ströhm, and a table near the entrance seemed his safest bet. He took an empty seat on one of the large tables, smiling back at the curious glances of the five men already sitting there. The food looked less than inviting, but then he hadn't really felt hungry since Kuzorra's revelation. When the waitress – a pinched-face girl of about fourteen – arrived to take his order, he just asked for a bowl of whatever soup was on offer. It was potato and cabbage, but when it came he detected few signs of the latter.

He ate slowly, and by the time he was finished the café clock read almost twelve-twenty. On his way there he had fretted over whether Ströhm would see through his disguise, but with each passing moment it seemed increasingly unlikely that the German-American would show up. The crowd was gradually thinning out, as if this particular shift was drawing to a close.

He ordered a coffee he didn't want and sat with it, hoping against hope. It was twenty-five to one when his prayers were answered, and Ströhm walked in with three other men. Russell tried to catch the other man's eye, and thought he'd succeeded, but Ströhm simply looked through him. His disguise was obviously effective.

The newcomers occupied a four-seater two tables down, Ströhm next to the aisle with his back to the door. Now what? Russell asked himself. Should he just sit there and wait, and hope that Ströhm noticed him on the way out? What if he didn't?

No, he had to make the running somehow. Ströhm would probably recognise his voice.

He sipped at his coffee as they ordered, received and began eating their meals, then strode past their table to the counter and bought a packet of the cheapest cigarettes. He then walked slowly back down the aisle, apparently intent on opening the packet, actually willing Ströhm to look up and notice him.

He didn't.

Russell played his last card, 'accidentally' scattering pfennigs alongside Ströhm's table, and then sinking to his knees beside the German-American in order to retrieve them. 'I'm sorry about this,' he said, and thought he could feel the man beside him stiffen. Gathering up his last coin, Russell got to his feet, looked Ströhm straight in the eye, and walked back to his table. He knew he'd been recognised. If only for a split second, Ströhm's eyes had widened with surprise.

Ten minutes later Ströhm left the café, making some excuse to his colleagues, and walked off alone up Gartenstrasse. Russell walked faster to catch him up. When he did so, Ströhm eyed him with some amusement. 'Is this for a story?' he asked.

'I wish it was. The Gestapo are looking for me,' Russell announced without further preamble. He had spent most of the morning working out exactly what he needed to say in order to enlist Ströhm's support.

'That's not good,' the other man said, taking a quick glance over his shoulder.

'I'm not being followed,' Russell told him. 'You didn't recognise me yourself when you walked into the café,' he added reassuringly.

'True,' Ströhm said, with only the faintest hint of a smile. 'So how can I help you?'

'It's a long story, but I'll make it as short as possible. Two years ago – almost three now – I did some articles for the Soviet press at the request of the NKVD. Then, when I asked them for help in getting a Jewish boy out of Germany, they asked me to bring some secret papers out for them. We both kept our sides of the bargain – the boy got out, they got the papers, and everything seemed fine. Until now. The Gestapo have finally gotten hold of the whole story, and my part in it. So I need to get out, with my girlfriend. The comrades promised to get us out if things went wrong in 1939, and I'm hoping they'll help me now. And I'm hoping you'll know who to ask.'

'Of course I can ask, but…'

'I have something to offer in return,' Russell interrupted him. 'Back in June, Hitler told Mussolini that he would have bombers capable of hitting New York by the end of the year. If such bombers exist, they would also be capable of reaching Siberia, and bombing all the arms factories that the Soviets have just moved heaven and earth to relocate there.'

'Do they?' Ströhm asked ingenuously.

'I don't know,' Russell said truthfully. 'But I can find out,' he added with more confidence than honesty.

'Ah.'

'I also have an answer to the question that we have been asking ourselves for the last month. They really do mean to wipe out the Jews.' He told Ströhm about the Degesch pesticide and the SS ordering huge quantities without the usual indicator.

That stopped Ströhm in his tracks. 'You have proof of this?' he asked, as if he still couldn't quite believe it.

'Yes,' Russell said, stretching the truth somewhat – Sullivan's hearsay was hardly proof in the usual sense of the word. 'And when I get out, I can tell the whole damn world what's happening.'

'I'll see what I can do,' Ströhm promised him. 'How can I contact you now?'

Russell hesitated at the thought of giving out their new address, but it was a risk he had to take. He gave Ströhm the details.

'And what name are you using?'

Russell's mind blanked for a moment. 'Rolf Vollmar,' he said eventually.

They went their separate ways. Now that the efficacy of his disguise had been proven, Russell felt confident enough to lengthen his walk home in search of an early evening paper. He found one on Müllerstrasse. Thumbing through it, he came upon a most unflattering picture of himself, along with the information that he was armed, dangerous and urgently wanted for questioning on matters 'vital to the security of the Reich'. Though American by birth, 'Mister' John Russell had learned to speak German like a native, presumably with espionage in mind.

More disturbingly, a recent studio photo of Effi accompanied his own. She had gone missing in suspicious circumstances, the writer claimed, before dropping a few heavy hints to the effect that she had been kidnapped by the American villain.

As Russell walked back, he found himself wondering how the *portierfrau* at his old digs in Hallesches Tor would be taking the news of his treachery. He could just see Frau Heidegger skulking in her doorway, newspaper in hand, waiting to discuss the story with any passing tenant. Would she believe the worst of him? Probably not. They'd always got on pretty well, and no one with half a brain trusted official stories any more.

Effi was not pleased with the photo – she thought it made her look like a simpering idiot – and the notion that she'd been abducted was laughable. 'No one who knows us would believe that you've carried me off against my will,' she said incredulously. 'And I can't imagine anyone else believing it – it all sounds like one of those white slaver romances they used to make in the twenties.'

'Goebbels' kind of film,' Russell murmured. He was rather pleased by the newspaper story – they were clearly offering Effi a possible alibi, if only to preserve appearances.

Over an early supper he told her how it had gone with Ströhm and the comrades. She agreed that they had little to lose by approaching Knieriem, but still felt queasy at the prospect. 'What do you really know about him?' she asked.

'He's a forty-three-year-old Berliner with a high-placed job at the Air Ministry. He was a Social Democrat until 1933 and, according to one of his old friends who now lives in America, he always despised the Nazis. He married in the twenties, divorced in the early thirties. His older brother Kurt was sent to Dachau in 1933 after one of the round-ups in Neukölln, and died there a few days later, supposedly in a fight with other inmates. The Americans found nothing to suggest that Franz was hungry for revenge, but he has access to really important information, so they thought he was worth a shot. Particularly since it was my head they were raising above the parapet.'

'If I had to guess,' Effi said, 'I'd say his brother's death scared him into permanent submission.'

'It's not unlikely.'

'So what if he says no?'

'Then I beat a hasty retreat.'

'How big is he?'

'Big, but in the fat sense. I don't think I'll have any trouble getting away from him.'

'He might recognise you.'

'Ströhm didn't. And what if he does?'

'He'll have the police swarming all over the place.'

'They'd be lucky to catch me in the blackout. But we shouldn't assume the worst – Knieriem may welcome the chance to betray his bosses. He was a Social Democrat once.'

Effi snorted. 'Wasn't it you who used to say that Mussolini was a communist once?'

'He was.'

'I rest my case.'

She might be right, Russell thought later as he lay there unable to sleep. Perhaps they were being foolish in trusting to Knieriem's former allegiances. And asking for information was not the only way of obtaining it.

Lying there, listening to Effi's breathing and the faint hum of the city outside, a plan began to take shape.

The next three days were spent in waiting. Neither of them was used to spending much of the day at home, let alone a home with so few possibilities for diversion. There was only uninspiring food, the radio, the jigsaw and each other, and by Wednesday the picture of Rugen Island had been completed. Effi insisted that it was her turn to go out for a newspaper, and overrode Russell's argument that she was more likely to be recognised. 'The neighbours know I'm here,' she said, 'and it would be suspicious if I never went out.'

She returned with a *Völkischer Beobachter* which contained fresh pictures of them both, along with news from the family. The well-known industrialist Thomas Schade had expressed his 'astonishment' at the charges facing his former brother-in-law, and earnestly entreated him to give himself up. Russell smiled at that, but not at the mention of his 'equally astonished' son, an exemplary member of the *Hitlerjugend*. Paul really would be shocked, if only at the seriousness of the alleged crime. He didn't like to think what else the boy might be feeling.

Zarah, too, had been interviewed. She was 'sick with worry' for her sister, and refused to believe that Effi had done anything wrong.

Effi, Russell noticed, was fighting off tears. 'We can't afford to waste the make-up,' she said angrily.

That evening the sirens sounded. They had debated the pros and cons of going down to the shelter, and decided that incurring the wrath of the block warden would be more dangerous than testing their disguises. The thought of being bombed didn't come into it – if they lost the bolthole, they were doomed in any case.

In the event, the three hours spent with the rest of the building's inhabitants passed uneventfully. The block warden seemed suspicious of them, but only, they quickly realised, because he was suspicious of everyone. Most people dozed or fussed over their children, and the light was dim enough to hide a circumcision ceremony, let alone their brilliant disguises. Watching the way Effi climbed the stairs after the all-clear sounded, Russell was almost convinced that she had aged twenty years in a couple of days. He was also quite pleased with his own simulation until she put him right. 'You're walking like an eighty-year-old with gout,' she told him once they were back in their room. 'I'll have to give you some lessons.'

The Führer's return to Berlin had been announced the previous day, and on Thursday afternoon he spoke to the Reichstag. The whole nation was obliged to listen: turning their own radio off for a few seconds, they could still hear the voice in the distance, emanating from so many street and factory loudspeakers that it seemed to be seeping out of the earth and sky. The speech lasted for an hour and a half. Hitler began with a long, triumphalist report on how the war was going, though details of the current position were noticeably sparse. He claimed that the German war dead now amounted to 160,000, a figure which astonished and appalled Effi, but which Russell thought was probably an under-estimate. The second half of the speech was a long diatribe against Roosevelt, a man backed by the 'entire satanic insidiousness' of the Jews, a man bent only on destroying Germany on their behalf. It ended, predictably enough, with a list of the provocations that Germany had been forced to endure, and their necessary corollary, a formal declaration of war on the United States.

'He's done it,' Russell murmured with deep satisfaction. If ever the prospect of another nation entering a war was cause for celebration, then this was that moment. It was all over bar the dying, he thought.

Next morning a letter arrived for Rolf Vollmar. Its message was short and extremely sweet – 'The Kaiser Bar, Schwedter Strasse, 7pm on December 13. Ask for Rainer.'

Russell took a deep breath. Perhaps they would get out after all.

'That's tomorrow,' Effi pointed out.

'I'll go to Knieriem this evening. Just after dark.'

'Tell me if I'm being stupid,' Effi said, 'but surely the best you can get from this man is information. I mean, he's not going to have official documents at his home, is he? So there'll be nothing to show the comrades. You might just as well make something up.'

'That had occurred to me,' Russell admitted. 'If the worst comes to the worst, and Knieriem won't cooperate, that's what I'll have to do. But the real facts will come out eventually, and if it turns out that I've given false information to the Soviets there will be consequences. If Hitler loses this war, then Stalin will win it, and the NKVD will be settling a lot of old scores. I don't want us to be one of them. So while there's a chance of getting them the right information I think we should take it.'

'I suppose that makes sense,' she agreed reluctantly.

'Besides,' he added with a smile, 'I'd like to do something for the war effort.'

Franz Knieriem lived in Charlottenburg, about halfway between the S-Bahn station of that name and the Bismarckstrasse U-Bahn station. It would have been quicker to take the overground train, but Russell felt safer in the overcrowded U-Bahn. He also needed a public toilet without a resident attendant, and the only one he knew in central Berlin was secreted away next to the suburban platforms at Potsdam Station.

The first leg on the U-Bahn was uneventful. He got a seat, wedged the large travel bag between his legs, and hid behind his paper until the time came to change at Leipzigerstrasse. Another stop, and he was soon wending his way across the Potsdam Station concourse. Reaching the chosen toilet, he shut himself in a cubicle, waited until the man next door had departed, and pulled the SS uniform from the bag. The *Sicherheitsdienst* were as likely to wear plain clothes as uniforms, but someone like Knieriem would probably ask to see identification if he was wearing the latter. The uniform spoke for itself.

Back at Prinz-Eugen-Strasse he had tried it on, and discovered that the sleeves and trousers were overlong. Effi had shortened the former, and the latter now disappeared into the shiny boots. He placed the peaked cap on his head, rammed his own suit jacket and trousers into the travel bag, and waited a few minutes, hoping to ensure that anyone who had seen him arrive would not be around to watch him depart.

He flushed and walked out, just as another man entered the toilet. The latter saw him and instantly looked away. Russell admired himself in the mirror, and couldn't help noticing that the new arrival was suffering a little stage fright at the adjoining urinal. 'Heil Hitler,' he murmured spontaneously, inducing a strangled echo from the other man.

If the Nazis didn't get him, his sense of humour would.

He walked back out onto the concourse, and down the steps to the U-Bahn platform. His fellow-passengers seemed disinclined to jostle him, and some even managed ingratiating smiles. Two trains and twenty-five minutes later he was climbing out onto Bismarckstrasse. It was fully dark now, and the overcast sky blotted out moon and stars. He had memorised the way to Knieriem's house before leaving, but checked it with a kiosk proprietor before heading off into the even darker side streets. What he most looked forward to in the world beyond Germany was a night full of bright lights and laughter.

It took him about ten minutes to find the street and the house. Rather to his surprise, a young woman in a *Nachrichtenhelferinnen* uniform answered his knock on the door.

'I wish to see Herr Knieriem,' Russell said, with the air of someone who expected compliance.

She flushed for no apparent reason. 'Oh, I'm just going out. Is my father expecting you?'

'No,' he said, walking past her and into the spacious hallway. 'Please tell him Sturmbannführer Scheel wishes to see him.'

She disappeared, leaving Russell to congratulate himself for not trusting an old Social Democrat. Anyone with a daughter keen enough to join an army auxiliary unit was unlikely to be handing out military secrets.

Franz Knieriem emerged, kissed his daughter goodbye, and invited Russell through to a spacious, well-heated room at the back of the house. He had lost weight since Russell had last seen him, but he still didn't look like a fighter. Thinning hair, neatly parted down the centre, topped a head that seemed too large for its features – piggy eyes, a knob of a nose, and a small fleshy mouth. Your typical Aryan.

He offered Russell a moist grip, but looked somewhat wary. 'How can I help you, Sturmbannführer?'

Russell lowered himself into a plush armchair. 'Please shut the door, Herr Knieriem. This is a security matter.'

'There's no else in the house.'

'Very well. I belong to the *Sicherheitsdienst*, Herr Knieriem. You know who we are and what we do?'

'You...'

'We protect the Reich from its less visible enemies – spies, Bolsheviks, dissidents of all kinds.'

'But what has that to do with me?'

'Please, Herr Knieriem, do not be concerned. I did not mean to imply that you were such an enemy. The reason for my visit is this – we have information that you are about to be approached by a foreign agent. This man is a German, but he works for the Reds. You yourself were a Social Democrat, I believe?'

'A great many years ago,' Knieriem protested.

'Of course. But the Reds no doubt believe that they can play on past sympathies, and on family loyalties of course – your brother was a communist, was he not?'

'He was, but I can assure you...'

'Of course. You would no more pass on secrets than I would. The point, however, is that this misapprehension on the part of the enemy has presented us with a golden opportunity to mislead him.'

'I don't understand.'

Russell's hopes rose. Knieriem was clearly not the brightest spark in the blackout. 'The information which the Reds are interested in concerns our long-range bomber force. Which you, of course, are in a position to tell them about. If you tell them we will soon have a long-range capability they will believe it. And if you tell them we will not, the same will apply.'

'So what should I tell them?'

'We think dishonesty would be the best policy. You understand?'

'You mean I should tell them that such bombers will soon be ready?'

Russell breathed an inner sigh of satisfaction. 'Exactly. But you'll have to say more than that. The more details you can offer, the more convincing the lie will be.'

Knieriem thought about it. 'Well, there *are* plans,' he said. 'The Me264, for example, and there are several other prototypes. The Ju390 looks promising. But none of them will be ready before 1943 at the very earliest, and only in very small numbers even then. I suppose I could speed up the development times for our Red friend, and multiply the production orders.'

'That would be ideal. You could outline the real difficulties that we are having, but then assure him that they have all been overcome. The more details the better.'

'Well, the main difficulty is the lack of resources. The need for more fighters and shorter-range bombers is considered more urgent, so they have a higher priority.' Knieriem smiled almost wistfully.

Russell frowned. 'Perhaps too much detail would be counter-productive. Perhaps it would be better if you simply told the agent that our long-range bombers are almost ready. Give the Reds something to worry about, eh? They can use up all their resources moving their factories another thousand kilometres to the East.'

'When should I expect this man to approach me? He won't come here, will he?'

'Probably not. But once he has contacted you, you must report to me at Wilhelmstrasse 102.'

'And if he doesn't?'

'Then do nothing,' Russell said, levering himself out of the armchair. 'He may be watching to make sure you are not in contact with us. That's why I came here after dark,' he added, as the obvious question dawned in the other man's eyes.

Russell got to his feet, placed the peaked cap on his head, and did up the buttons on his outside coat. 'We are relying on you, Herr Knieriem,' he said by way of farewell. 'Do not fail us.'

Back on the street, he managed to walk twenty metres before virtually exploding with laughter. He was pummelling an adjacent wall with glee when a uniformed man loomed out of the darkness and shone a torch in his face.

'Oh, pardon me,' the man stuttered, extinguishing his torch and hurrying away in the darkness. There were few more disturbing sights than a hysterical Sturmbannführer.

Saturday morning dawned clear and cold. The several centimetres of overnight snow showed no sign of succumbing to the primrose-coloured sun, and children too young for the *Jungvolk* were happily hurling balls of the stuff at each other. Their triumphant peals of laughter and joyous squeals of dismay drifted up from the street like echoes from another world.

Effi insisted on breakfast in bed, but the urge to get up soon proved irresistible. While she agonised over what they should take, he wrote an account of what Knieriem had inadvertently told him, and added those sheets to the ones from Sullivan's briefcase. It was still only hearsay, but it seemed more authoritative in black and white. That done, he went out and reconnoitred the route they would take that evening. The thought of getting lost in the dark and missing their appointment was too dreadful to contemplate.

Returning an hour and a half later, he found Effi content to leave almost everything behind. Neither of them could make up their mind about the SS uniform, but its bulk eventually told against it. They also decided to leave most of Effi's cash in its hiding place under the floorboards – having that much money on them would rouse suspicion in even the dimmest official. In the end they packed only the slim sheaf of papers, enough food for a few meals and a single change of clothing for each of them. It didn't seem much to be leaving Berlin with, particularly if one was a successful film actress, and Russell lamented Effi's probable loss of a lifetime's earnings.

'I'll get most of it back after the war,' she said. 'Zarah and I opened an account in her name about a year ago, and I've moved a lot of my savings into that.'

Russell shook his head. 'Please don't tell me you've been taking flying lessons, and that there's an aeroplane waiting somewhere nearby.'

'Unfortunately not.'

The afternoon dragged on, the sun finally disappearing behind the school on the next street. They sat by the window with the blackout screens pulled back, watching the city slowly darken as the minutes ticked by. As the time for leaving approached, a pale light on the roofs opposite reflected the rising of the moon. Would that help or hinder their escape, Russell wondered. There was no way of knowing.

They left at a quarter past six. Effi had seen no point in taking the keys to the apartment, but Russell thought it far from certain that the comrades would agree to help them. No promises had yet been made. All they had was a meeting. They might be back in a couple of hours.

The walk took them past block after block of run-down apartments, past the bakery that filled the air with its nostalgic odours, past still-humming electrical works and an abandoned-looking chocolate factory. By the time they reached Gesundbrunnen Station a three-quarter moon was hanging over the Plumpe and, as they crossed the bridge overlooking the locomotive roundhouse, the snow-covered roofs to the east stretched away in a jumble of luminescence.

The Kaiser Bar was huddled in deep shadow on the eastern side of Schwedter Strasse. The interior looked as if it hadn't been decorated since before the first war, and the old, leather-lined booths that stretched along one wall were as faded and worn as the only customers – two old men playing dominoes at a table on the other side of the room. Pride of place behind the sparse-looking bar belonged to a group photograph of Hertha's championship-winning team of 1931.

The middle-aged man behind the bar wished them welcome in a less than welcoming tone.

'We're here to see Rainer,' Russell told him.

After lifting an eyebrow in apparent surprise, the barman disappeared through a door at the back. He re-emerged only seconds later with finger beckoning.

Walking through, Russell and Effi found themselves in a large windowless room. There was a second door on the far side, and most of the available floor-space was occupied by upright wooden chairs in various states of decrepitude. A Party meeting room, Russell assumed. Like the Party, it had seen better days.

Two men were waiting for them. One was about Russell's age, a burly, balding man with worn hands and a leathery face that had spent most of its days outdoors. The other was probably in his early twenties, wiry and snub-nosed with a shock of dark hair. Given Ströhm's job and known connections, it seemed fairly certain that both were Reichsbahn employees.

The older man invited them to sit. 'This is John Russell,' he said, as if others were present who needed to know. 'And this is Effi Koenen,' the slightest edge of distaste colouring his intonation. 'An excellent disguise,' he added.

'That was the intention,' she said coldly.

Russell gave her a warning glance.

'I believe you have something for us,' the man said to him.

'And you are?' Russell asked.

The man offered a thin smile. 'You know whom I represent. You don't need a name.'

Russell shrugged, removed the folded sheet of paper from his inside jacket pocket, and handed it over.

The man read it through twice, and reached the same conclusion as Effi. 'You could have made this up.'

'I could,' Russell agreed. 'But I didn't.'

'Why would this official reveal this information to you? Was it for money?'

Russell told the whole story – its American genesis, his visit to Knieriem in SS guise, the trick he had played on the ministry official.

'Very ingenious,' the other man responded, with the air of someone who considered ingenuity a bourgeois affectation.

Their fate was hanging in the balance. 'Not really,' Russell told him with a self-deprecating smile. 'Luckily for me, the man was a fool. But the information is genuine. If it were false, I would not be staking my future on it.'

The older man was clearly torn. His own future might also be resting on the validity of Russell's report.

'You have nothing to lose by helping us,' Russell argued. 'Even if I have made all of this up – which I haven't – you would gain nothing by sending us back into the arms of the Gestapo. On the contrary, you know and I know that sooner or later we would talk, and more comrades would be lost.'

'A dangerous argument,' the man said, reaching for his pocket. Russell half expected a gun to appear in his hand, but it was only a wodge of pipe tobacco.

'This is ridiculous,' Effi interjected. 'We are all enemies of the Nazis. We should be helping each other. Those papers will help the Soviet Union.'

'I saw you in *Sturmfront*,' the man said.

She gave him an incredulous look, then sighed. In that film her husband had been beaten to death by communists. 'I was just playing a role,' she said. 'I didn't write it.'

'Some roles should be refused.'

'I didn't know that then. I'm afraid it takes some people longer than others to see what is happening.'

He smiled. 'You were very convincing. You still are. And you are right,' he said, turning to Russell, 'your departure from Berlin is in everyone's interest.'

'What has been arranged?' Russell asked.

'You are travelling to Stettin tonight.'

Russell felt relieved, but didn't want to make it too obvious. 'And when we get there?' A ship, he guessed. Sweden, with any luck.

'You will be taken care of. I know nothing more.'

'What time do we go?'

The man looked at his watch. 'The train is scheduled to leave at ten, but the sooner you get on board the better. The comrade here' – he gestured towards the younger man – 'will take you across.'

They all stood up, and the older man shook hands with both of them. Out on the moonlit Schwedter Strasse a lorry was disappearing in the direction of the city centre, but otherwise the road was clear. The open gates to the Gesundbrunnen goods yard were almost opposite the Kaiser Bar and, as they followed the young man through them, the sounds of shunting in the sidings beyond were suddenly audible. Away to the south several planes were crossing the moonlit sky, heading west.

'What happens if there's an air raid?' Russell asked.

'That depends,' the young man said, but failed to elucidate.

They walked down the side of a seemingly endless goods shed, worked their way round its northern end and started out across the fan of sidings. The yard lights were on, but hardly bright enough to compete with the moonlight. After crossing the tracks ahead of several lines of open wagons, the young man led them into the gap between two trains of covered vans. 'You're in luck,' he told them. 'The last lot travelled in an empty ore wagon. They'd have been really cold by the time they reached Stettin.'

They were only three boxcars from the end when he stopped, grabbed hold of a rail with one hand, clambered up two steps, and pulled the sliding door open with the other. Jumping back down, he explained that the vans had brought paper from the Stettin mills, and were going back empty. 'The guard knows you're on board,' he told them, 'but the loco crew doesn't. When you get to Stettin, just stay where you are and wait for the guard.' He took the heavy bag from Russell's hand, swung it onto the floor of the boxcar, and unexpectedly offered Effi a helping hand. She took it, and gave him a smile of thanks once she was aboard. Russell followed her up and turned to say goodbye, but the young man had already left. There was nothing to see inside the van, so he pulled the door shut, and they helped each other blindly to the floor.

It had to be at least half-past seven. They had two and a half hours to wait.

'Who'd have guessed it would end like this,' Effi said after a minute or so.

'My grandmother once told me I'd come to a bad end,' Russell admitted. He hadn't remembered that in years – his father's mother had died when he was eight years old.

'What had you done?' Effi asked.

'I ate the cherries off the top of a trifle.'

Her laugh reverberated round the empty van, and he joined in.

'Let's talk about our childhoods,' she suggested eventually, and they did, chattering the time away with what seemed like reminiscences from two other people's lives. Russell was thinking that at least two hours had passed when the floor shook beneath them – a locomotive was being attached to the front of the train. Only seconds later air raid sirens began to wail not far away.

What should they do? Yards like this were a prime target, but the British rarely hit one of those. Would the train leave in the middle of an air raid? If so, they couldn't afford to get off. But then, why wasn't it moving?

For twenty minutes or more nothing happened, no bombs, no movement. Then suddenly there was an enormous bang, and the van rocked on its wheels, as if an army of men had given it a great push. Russell pulled the door open just in time to see another bomb explode, this one beyond the line of the goods sheds, and probably Schwedter Strasse as well. The orange flash lasted only a second, and a column of debris rose up, glittering in the moonlight. At that moment the train clanked into motion, jerking Russell backwards and almost out of the open doorway. He recovered his balance and tugged it shut as two other bombs exploded in quick succession away to his left.

The train quickly gathered speed, violently rolling its way through the switches, as if the driver's only concern was to get it out of Berlin. The bombing continued, but none fell as close again, and the sound of the explosions soon began to fade. They lay entwined on the dusty floor, their bodies prey to each jolt of the wheels, their minds still straining to cope with the fact of leaving Berlin.

The fan in the mirror

It took the train almost nine hours to cover the hundred and twenty kilometres between Berlin and the port city of Stettin. The breakneck pace of their initial escape from the RAF's attentions soon gave way to slow and desultory progress across the rolling Pomeranian fields, with long, frequent and mostly inexplicable stops in what seemed, through the cracks in the door, to be variations on the middle of nowhere. Sleep would have been welcome, but it was soon evident that the appalling suspension and plummeting temperatures ruled out any such respite. They huddled together and shivered.

It was still dark when the wheels beneath them began rattling through points with increasing frequency, suggesting their arrival in Stettin. Easing the door back a few inches, Russell got a glimpse of what was probably the main station, and a few moments later they were rumbling across the huge swing bridge he remembered from his previous visit.

The river disappeared, replaced by the backs of apartment blocks, and the train began to slow. Another long bridge across water, and the tracks began multiplying, with stationary rakes of carriages and wagons stretching into the distance. Their train wove a path through several crossings before straightening itself out in a siding and finally wheezing to a halt. Russell eased the door ajar and stuck his head out. The yard was lit with amber lights mounted on high poles, yellowing the snow which lay across the tracks and casting the whole scene in a sepia glow. The guard was hurrying towards him.

'Stay where you are,' he whispered on reaching their boxcar, his eyes fixed on the distant head of the train. Looking forward, Russell could see a small figure climbing up into the cab, and after a few seconds several bursts of yellow steam rose into the air as the locomotive pulled away. 'Come,' the guard said. 'Quickly.'

They climbed down, wincing as they gripped the icy handrails. The guard examined them closely, presumably to make sure he had the correct escapees, and couldn't suppress a private smile at recognising the film star behind the half-eroded make-up. 'Follow me,' he said, turning back in the direction of his brake van. At the end of the adjacent train they started zigzagging their way across the fan of tracks, keeping as close as possible to the cover of other rolling stock, and finally reaching the side of a goods warehouse. Following this, they eventually came to a road transshipment area, where a line of darkened lorries was parked.

A man loomed out of the dark, making them jump. 'This way,' he said, leading them to the lorry at the end of the line. 'In the back,' he ordered, offering Effi a hand up and briefly illuminating the inside with a flashlight. Large crates took up most of the space, but a passage had been left between them. Effi and Russell ensconced themselves at the far end, and listened as their helpers shifted crates across the opening. 'It's like being a child again,' Effi murmured, mostly to herself. The sense of being completely dependent on others was almost comforting.

The back doors slammed, and a few moments later the engine sprang to life. They moved off, bumping their way across what felt like tracks before finding the smoothness of a real road. From what Russell remembered of Stettin's geography, he guessed they were somewhere to the south and east of the city's centre, close to the main dock area. Where they were going he had no idea, but the journey seemed to take forever, and when the doors were finally opened the grey light of dawn flooded their hiding place. The crates, Russell saw, each contained a single huge glass bottle of some chemical or other.

They climbed down onto a street of working-class apartment blocks and small industrial premises. Lights were showing in some windows, as the occupants got ready for the day ahead. 'Where are we?' Russell asked the driver, who now had a partner in tow, a younger man with pockmarked cheeks.

'Bredow. You know where that is?'

'To the north of the city?'

'That's right. Kurt will take you in. And good luck,' he added over his shoulder as he headed for his cab.

'This way,' the young man told them, heading for the entrance to the nearest block. 'It's the top floor,' he added, almost apologetically.

They twice met men coming down, but neither paid them much attention, and their companion seemed unworried by the fact that they'd been seen. Was the whole block dependable, Russell wondered. He sincerely hoped so.

On reaching the top floor, the young man led them to the right and knocked softly on the nearest door. A woman opened it, beckoned them in, and introduced herself as Margarete Otting. She was about forty-five, with a tired face and short blonde hair. 'We're both working Sunday shifts, and my husband has already left,' she said. 'And I am late. Please make yourselves at home. We shall be back soon after four.'

'Thank you for...' Effi started to say, but Frau Otting was already halfway through the door. 'I must go too,' Kurt told them. 'Someone will come to see you this evening, after Margarete and Hans return from work. In the meantime, please don't go out, and make as little noise as possible.'

The door closed behind him, leaving Russell and Effi to share a look of surprise.

They explored the apartment. It was not much bigger than the one on Prinz-Eugen-Strasse, with a small book-lined sitting room and two bedrooms, one of which clearly belonged to Margarete and Hans. The other had twin beds, and showed traces of adolescent occupation. A photograph in the sitting room showed a happier-looking Margarete sitting beside an impishly-smiling Hans, with two serious-looking young men in army uniform standing behind them. The books that lined the walls were a mixture of detective novels and European history, with one thinned-out shelf of philosophy and political theory. Glancing along the latter, Russell reached the conclusion that all the Marxist tomes had been removed.

Effi was standing in the doorway, rubbing her eyes. 'I guess we can lie down in the boys' room,' she said.

Hans Otting arrived home first, and seemed almost over-pleased to meet them. He was one of those truly generous people, Russell realised, with all the joy and heartache that implied for his more practical wife. They were, as Effi put it later, like a goyish version of the Blumenthals. He worked in the docks as a stevedore, she on the local trams, and their one surviving son was serving with Rommel in North Africa. The elder boy had been killed in Russia the previous July.

Margarete Otting seemed more worried by their presence than her husband, but was careful to show no obvious signs of resentment. She was clearly delighted by the food they had brought from Berlin, and with the large supply of ration tickets which they would probably be leaving behind. The Gestapo might descend on her flat, but she wouldn't starve.

The four of them had just finished eating when the promised visitor arrived. A short, bald, tough-looking character in his fifties, and clearly an old comrade of the Ottings, he asked after their son in Africa before introducing himself to Russell and Effi. 'I am Ernst,' he said, 'and I am in charge of the arrangements for your… I suppose "escape" is the only word that really fits.' He offered them both a smile, which Russell wanted to find more convincing. 'The plan is to get you aboard a ship for Sweden. An iron ore ship. There's one due to dock on Wednesday evening – it will be unloaded during the next day and then leave as soon after dark as possible. Now the authorities watch these boats very carefully in the hours before sailing, but hardly at all before that, so we plan to get you aboard and well hidden on Wednesday evening. Do you understand?'

'Of course,' Russell said, his hopes rising.

'The voyage will take about forty hours,' Ernst said. 'You should reach Oxelösund on Friday morning. Someone from the Stockholm embassy will meet you there, and take charge of the documents you are carrying. '

The next two days seemed replete with more than the usual number of hours. During the day they had the apartment to themselves, and read until their eyes could no longer cope with the inadequate light. There was no radio, but Russell scoured the morning paper, which Hans brought back each evening, for news of themselves and the war's progress. The same pictures of him and Effi were repeated, but the accompanying words had shrunk to a simple demand that any sighting be immediately reported. Hans seemed almost amused by it all, but his wife, staring at the offending photographs, looked almost stunned, and Effi found herself praying that the Ottings would not suffer for their generosity.

After Russell had mentioned in passing how unused he was to staying indoors all day, Hans took him and Effi down the corridor, through an unmarked door, and up a single flight of stairs to the roof, where a host of washing lines were waiting for better weather. The smell of the sea, thirty kilometres to the north, was faint but unmistakable.

An almost full moon was rising in the east, bathing the city and its river in pale light, and after Hans went back down the two of them stayed out in the bitter cold for as long as they could endure it, taking in what might be their last real sight of Germany.

'What are we going to do when we get to Sweden?' Effi asked, snuggling up against him. 'Are we going to England or America?'

'It may take some time to get to either,' Russell told her. 'I suppose Sweden's still trading with the outside world, but I've no idea whether there are any ships to Britain or the States. We may have to stay in Sweden for the duration.'

'I could cope with that. In a way it would be nice – we'd still be close to our family and our friends. Or at least not too far away.'

Wednesday was another long wait. They were unlikely to meet anyone between flat and docks, but Effi applied their make-up with great care, determined that nothing should be left to even the slightest chance. By the time she had finished, their supply was almost gone, but it seemed unlikely they would need any more – once they left the flat, either the ship or the Gestapo would be taking them away, and there would be no need of disguises in either Sweden or a concentration camp.

So went the theory. Margarete and Hans had been home only a few minutes when a tap on the door announced the arrival of Ernst. Bad news was written across his face. 'The ship has been sunk,' he said without preamble.

'By whom?' Effi asked, surprise and indignation in her voice.

'A Soviet submarine,' Ernst told her. 'We should rejoice of course.'

'Of course,' Russell agreed dryly. He supposed they should: there was no reason why his and Effi's war with the Nazis should take precedence over everyone else's.

'I hope the crew got off,' Hans said.

'Oh, of course,' Effi agreed, momentarily ashamed that she'd only been thinking of herself.

'So what happens now?' Russell asked Ernst. As the news sank in, he could feel the stirrings of panic. The Germans had one of their all-engrossing words for it – *torschlusspanik*, the burst of terror that accompanies a closing door.

'I don't know,' Ernst was saying. 'There will be other ships, of course. For the moment, you must stay here,' he added, looking at Hans and Margarete as he did so.

'Of course,' Hans agreed, and his wife nodded her acceptance of the fact. But she didn't look thrilled at the prospect, and who could blame her?

Later that night, as she tried to fall asleep, Effi imagined herself on a torpedoed ship, the screams of the wounded, the lurching deck, the cold immensity of the dark sea. The sailors from the sunken ship – were they German or Swedish? – were probably out there still, desperately trying to keep warm as their lifeboats bobbed in the chilling Baltic swell. Why, she wondered for the umpteenth time, would anyone sane start a war?

It was only seven-thirty, and still completely dark, when they heard the knock on the door. The softness of the knock boded well – the Gestapo had a propensity to hammer – and Russell allowed himself the absurd hope that their ship had not been sunk after all. He left their room to find Hans admitting Ernst.

Though clearly out of breath from climbing ten flights of the stairs, the comrade's first priority was a cigarette. 'More bad news,' he told them tersely through a cloud of smoke. 'There have been arrests in Berlin. Many comrades. Twenty at least. And one of them –' he looked at Russell and Effi '– is the man who sent you here.'

'What happened?' Hans wanted to know.

Ernst shrugged. 'We don't know. A traitor, I expect. It usually is. But these two will have to be moved. Tonight, after dark. They should be all right until then.'

Which meant, Russell thought, that the arrests had probably happened the previous evening, and that those arrested were expected to hold out until the same time today, to endure a minimum of twenty-four hours' suffering before coughing up the first name. The guard on the train, he thought. The next link in the chain. He remembered the collapsing wooden bridge in an adventure movie he had seen with Paul, the hero racing to cross the chasm as the trestles collapsed behind him.

Margarete was looking deathly pale.

'If we see their cars in the street,' Russell told her, 'we'll get out of the apartment. Onto the roof. They won't know where we came from.'

She gave him a look of disbelief, as if unable to comprehend such naivety.

'You'll get plenty of warning,' Ernst confirmed. 'They only ever come up here in force. But I don't think it'll be today.'

'Where are we going this evening?' Effi asked him.

'I don't know yet. All I know is Moscow wants you out, and I'll do my best to oblige them. Someone will be here after dark.'

After indicating to Hans that he wanted a private word with Ernst, Russell followed the Party man out into the stairwell. 'Can you get me a gun?' he asked. He wasn't at all sure he would use one, but it would be nice to have the option. 'I don't want them to take us alive,' he said in response to the other man's hesitation. He found it hard to imagine sharing a suicide pact with Effi, but he knew that Ernst would like the idea – dead people stayed silent for a lot longer than twenty-four hours.

'I'll see what I can do,' Ernst told him.

The sitting room window faced south, overlooking the street below and offering a panoramic view of central Stettin. They shared the watch, dreading the sound of approaching motors yet perversely eager for any relief from the tension and boredom. When he told Effi about his request for a gun, she looked blank for a moment and then simply nodded, as if accepting that some point of no return had finally been passed.

'But could you hit anything with it?' she asked after a while.

'I'm actually a pretty good shot,' he retorted. 'Or at least I was in 1918.'

The sky was overcast, but they could tell from the fast-vanishing snow that the temperature was rising, and when the clouds opened later that afternoon it was rain mixed with sleet that obscured their distant view of the city. As the hours went by,. Russell found it hard not to dwell on unwelcome outcomes, both for them and their hosts. He hated the idea of the Ottings paying with their lives for a few days' hospitality, but there was nothing he could do about it. If he and Effi disappeared at that moment there would still be the men who had brought them from the goods yard to the flat. They were the last link in the chain from Berlin, and the Ottings' only real chance was for those two men to either escape the clutches of the Gestapo or die in the attempt.

Darkness finally began to fall, and soon after five Margarete returned home. She was clearly upset to find them still there, and suddenly burst into tears when Effi offered to help with the cooking. 'I'm sorry,' she said eventually. 'It's not your fault. I keep thinking of my son in Africa, and him coming home to find he has no family.'

Effi encased her in a hug. 'We're sorry,' she said. 'We…'

'You are just trying to survive,' Margarete interrupted her. 'I know that. And I hope you get out. I really do.'

A few minutes later Hans returned, took one look at his wife's tear-stained face, and reached out to embrace her. Effi and Russell left them on their own for a few minutes, and when Russell returned to the sitting room he found Hans staring at his books with the air of someone who doubted he'd ever see them again. 'We might as well eat,' Margarete said from the kitchen doorway with a rueful smile.

They were just about finished when a loud and confident knock sounded on the outer door. Hans went to answer it, and returned with a tall, smiling young man. 'Are you ready?' he asked Russell and Effi. 'I'm Andreas,' he added, offering a large and calloused hand to each of them in turn. 'I know who you are,' he told Effi with a big grin.

He insisted that they hurry, and their goodbyes had to be brief. Clattering down the stairs ahead of them, he announced almost casually that the Gestapo were 'all over the town'. Two older men sharing a chat on the next landing down clearly heard the remark, and watched them go by with expressions that mingled sympathy and alarm. In the dimly-lit ground-floor lobby, a young couple embracing in a corner showed considerably less interest in their plight.

Outside, an icy rain was falling. The ground was slippery underfoot and the darkness almost complete.

'My van is two streets away,' Andreas told them, as they made their way across the open courtyard. 'I didn't want to park right outside.'

They reached the street just as two pinpoints of lights swung towards them a few hundred metres away. Another two followed, and another two, as the sound of motors rose above the usual hum of the city.

Andreas broke into a run, yelling 'This way!' over his shoulder. The car headlights were muted by the rain, but just bright enough to show them where they were going, straight across the street and onto the gravel path between workshops that Russell had noticed from the Ottings' window. Once off the street it was hard to see more than a few feet ahead, but Andreas obviously knew where he was going, and the path was less slippery than the street had been. Behind them car doors were slamming, a voice shouting orders. 'Just in time,' they heard Andreas murmur. But not for the Ottings, they both thought.

The sounds faded as they moved on, crossing another street and entering another path. The large factory to their right was still working, the sound of machinery drowning out any noise of pursuit, the glow of fires within rising from chimneys like illuminated gold dust in the falling rain. In her mind, Effi could see the men in leather coats hammering on the door, the last hurried farewells as the Ottings' world caved in.

Andreas was waiting at the exit to the next street. A line of lorries was parked on either side of the road outside the main factory entrance, a small van just beyond them, as if it was part of the same fleet.

'I'm right in thinking you have no false papers?' Andreas asked.

'You are.'

'Then you'll have to get in the back.' He opened the rear doors, and showed them the inside with a well-masked flashlight. The pencil-thin beam revealed various metal trays, a large number of paint tins, a bucket full of brushes and a large expanse of crumpled cloth. 'If we're stopped, you'd better get under the dust-sheet,' he advised. 'Just cover yourselves and pray.'

'Where are we going?' Russell asked.

'The docks. And I have something for you,' he added, heading for the front of the van. He returned a few moments later with a gun wrapped in oilcloth. 'It's only an M1910, but it's the best we could do at short notice.'

Russell unwrapped and grasped it, the metal cold in his hand. He had handled one of these guns before, one he had bought from a German officer after the November armistice, on the ridiculous assumption that any self-respecting class warrior needed his own personal firearm. He was later told that Gavrilo Princip had set the whole bloody mess in motion with an M1910, when he used it to assassinate Archduke Franz Ferdinand in June 1914.

'We should go,' Andreas told him.

Effi and Russell crawled into the back of the van, ending up with their backs to the driving compartment and the dust-sheet roughly draped across their legs, ready for pulling up over their heads. It wasn't nearly voluminous enough, Russell realised. It would take someone half-blind and wholly stupid to fall for such a ruse.

The van's engine started, and they moved off down the street. They could see nothing in the back, but Andreas kept up a running commentary on their progress, as much for his own reassurance, Russell thought, as for theirs. The first name he recognised was the Königsplatz, which he had walked round during a visit some years before the war. He also remembered Breitestrasse, and could picture their journey down it, passing the Nikolaikirche and taking the bridge across the Oder to Lastadie. 'Almost there,' he whispered to Effi, as the rain hammered a little harder on the van's roof.

He had spoken too soon.

'Someone's shining a red light at me,' Andreas told them, suddenly sounding much younger. 'There's a barrier across the road,' he added a few moments later. 'And at least two men. They look like Gestapo.' As the van began slowing they tried to burrow beneath the dust-sheet, but it was too dark to see how well they had succeeded in covering themselves. The fact that they were tugging it in opposite directions didn't bode well.

Andreas pulled the van to a halt and wound down his window. 'A miserable night,' they heard him say cheerfully. 'So what's this about?'

The man he was addressing seemed uninterested in friendly banter. 'Gestapo,' he said curtly, and asked for Andreas's papers. A long silence followed as he checked them.

Let that be enough, Russell silently pleaded.

The Gestapo officer asked what Andreas was doing out so late.

Andreas explained with a laugh that one of the local Party bigwigs was desperate to have his offices redecorated in time for Labour Minister Robert Ley's imminent visit.

It was the wrong tone, Russell thought. The man asking the questions didn't sound like a lover of the common people. But how many colleagues did he have with him? Russell had heard no other voices.

'What's in the back?' the Gestapo man asked.

'Just my gear.'

'Turn off the engine and get out.'

The van gently rocked as Andreas climbed out. They heard footsteps, and a sliver of light appeared through the crack between the rear doors. 'Open them up,' the Gestapo officer ordered, his voice now coming from behind the van.

Russell took what seemed, in that instant, their only chance of survival. Throwing off the dust sheet, he took aim at the doors, hoping and praying that Andreas, knowing he had the gun, would have the sense to keep out of the line of fire.

He heard the door handle turn, waited for the light to shine in, and blindly pulled the trigger.

The light spun downwards as the boom of the gun echoed in the van, drowning out the sound of the falling body. He heard Effi gasp as he scrambled feet first towards the open doorway, and half-ordered, half-begged her to stay where she was.

The Gestapo man's torch was still on, illuminating a puddle in the road and throwing a faint reflective glow. As Russell kicked it away, his standing foot slipped on the icy cobbles, throwing him onto his back and quite possibly saving him from the shot which rang out at the same instant. A few feet away, scarcely visible in the darkness, two grunting shadows were locked together.

So there were there at least three of them.

As Russell inched towards the two men struggling on the ground, he scanned the darkness for sight or sound of the man who had fired the last shot. There was nothing – the knowable world had shrunk to a lightless bubble, leaving him blind, deaf and prey to any lucky bullet. He told himself that his opponents were in the same position, but fear still rose in his throat, tightening his finger on the pistol's trigger.

A flashlight suddenly flared into life, illuminating the rain and the road, the two men struggling by the stationary van. As the beam whirled to pick out Russell himself, he raised the gun and fired, bracing his body for the bullet that was surely on its way. But none came. A second torch fell to the ground, and there was a muffled splash as something heavy hit the ground.

There was another shot, this time much closer, an accompanying grunt of surprise, and then only the sound of the falling rain.

Russell raised his gun as a silhouette struggled to its feet. 'Andreas?' he asked.

'I'm here,' the shape said.

'Were there only three of them?' Russell asked. His hand was shaking, he realised.

'That's all I saw.'

'John?' Effi enquired anxiously from the back of the van.

'Stay there a moment,' he told her, and walked across to where the body was lying beside the still-lit torch, the face half-buried in an icy puddle. He picked up the torch and examined the man, who seemed far too youthful for his *ordnungspolizei* uniform. Russell's bullet had passed straight through the throat, as lucky a shot as he could have wished for. The young man's fatal mistake had been to switch on his torch, but Russell, remembering his own moment of terror in the darkness, understood what had caused him to make it.

Behind the body, parked up against a wall, was the Gestapo car.

He walked back to the van, and pointed the torch beam at the other two bodies. Both were wearing leather coats, and Russell's victim had lost most of his face. 'Is yours dead?' he asked Andreas.

'Yes.'

Russell took a deep breath. He had just killed as many men in thirty seconds as he had managed in ten months of the Great War, but at least he wouldn't have to finish anyone off.

'Oh God,' Effi said quietly, as she stepped out past the first victim.

'We should be getting out of here,' Andreas urged.

'No, wait,' Russell said, turning off the flashlight and staring out into the darkness. There were no lights heading their way, no distant voices, and he doubted whether the sounds of gunfire had travelled far in the rain. The buildings that surrounded them were obviously not houses. 'Are we at the entrance to the docks?' he asked.

'Yes.'

'And we were going into them?'

'There's a disused warehouse the Party uses for storage. It was the best we could come up with at short notice.'

'Of course,' Russell muttered. 'But after they find these men I should think they'll scour every inch of the dockyards.'

'Yes, but...'

'We could have been leaving,' Effi interjected. 'How would they know?'

By the position of the bodies, Russell thought. Create a mirror image of the current configuration on the other side of the barrier, and maybe, just maybe, the wrong assumption would be made. He explained the idea to Andreas, and the two of them dragged a body each under the barrier, leaving them lying in the equivalent position on the other side. Both had shed flesh and blood where they fell, and Russell did his best to scatter the solids, trusting the rain to wash everything away. The young man by the barrier was left where he was.

It was the best they could do. Once Effi had clambered into the back, Russell lifted the barrier for Andreas to drive the van through, lowered it once more and climbed into the front seat, gun at the ready. Every bridge behind them was broken now.

They drove on into the docks, bumping across inlaid rails, moving slowly for fear of driving off one of the quaysides. They met only one other vehicle, a lorry moving at a similar speed, which gave them a friendly toot of its horn as it passed. It was probably heading south, Andreas told Russell, and would not be using the Lastadie entrance. Hardly anything did at this time of night. 'Which is why I thought it would be safe to use,' he added wryly.

As they ventured further in, visibility seemed to improve, and an angular pattern of cranes loomed out of the darkness. Soon the sky seemed infused with pale light, and as they passed the end of a warehouse they found the source – a well-lit ship and quay on the far side of a basin. 'Ball bearings from Sweden,' Andreas guessed. 'They're allowed to relax the blackout for those.'

That view was soon cut off by more low buildings, and Andreas finally pulled up alongside a warehouse on the opposite side of the road. He led them to a corrugated iron door, and only turned on his flashlight once they were all inside. His thin beam darted round the interior, a wide space between windowless walls, empty save for a few broken crates, some broken glass and the odd length of frayed rope. The scurrying sound had to be rats.

Russell could almost hear Effi shudder.

'This way,' Andreas said, heading towards the rats. About fifty metres further in, a series of offices had been mounted on stilts against one wall, with long windows overlooking the warehouse floor. Access was by a metal staircase, which led up to a door marked 'Quaymaster'. The rooms were lined with what looked like postal sorting shelves, but devoid of furniture.

'This is it,' Andreas said apologetically.

'It'll have to do,' was all Russell could think to say.

'I should be on my way,' Andreas told them. 'I'll be back in the morning. Or whenever I can.'

They watched until his torch flickered out, then held each other tight for several moments.

'Oh John,' was all Effi could say.

'Anyone would think we were going down in the world,' Russell said, plunking down their bag and turning on the torch he had taken from the dead *ordnungspolizei*. He shone it around the office. Despair was like a physical weight pressing down on his shoulder blades. 'I'm sorry,' he said. 'I can't tell you how sorry.'

'I'm sorry too,' Effi said. 'Sorry that it looks like the bastards have beaten us.'

'We're not beaten yet,' he said mechanically. He had failed her, he thought.

'No,' she said, 'but John, I'm frightened. I don't want to die, but if we're caught... we'll be executed, won't we?'

'I will be. Both of us, probably,' he added, thinking that this was hardly the moment for a white lie.

'I'd rather die with you,' she said emphatically. 'Can we do that together? If the Gestapo surround this place or come bursting in can we just end it here?'

'We can if you want.' Paul would be better off without him, he thought.

'We've had a good life,' she said, as if that made ending it more palatable.

It was a long night. They had a little food, but no water, and after a few hours both were so thirsty that Russell went outside to collect what he could in the bottom of a broken bottle. They found a ragged rug in one of the offices, but even folded in four it did little to soften the floor, and when morning light started seeping into the warehouse neither of them had enjoyed more than a few minutes' sleep.

They found a long-disused toilet for their morning ablutions, ate a sparse breakfast, and explored their surroundings. The warehouse was about two hundred metres long, with another set of raised offices towards the far end. Doors on the eastern side led to the street, those on the west to the quayside with its rusted rails and cranes and an apparently abandoned dock basin. Beyond the water and the low roofs of Lastadie, they could see the elegant spires of Stettin against the grey sky, a vision of tranquillity at odds with the fear churning inside them.

Each moment they expected the rising sound of motors on the street outside, and their relief at seeing Andreas come through the corrugated door was profound. He had come on foot, and not alone. Another, older man was with him, whom he introduced as Hartmut.

Hartmut unpacked a camera and collapsible tripod from the canvas bag he was carrying and began setting them up in the brightest available pool of light.

'They know you came to Stettin,' was Andreas's first devastating remark. 'Let me tell you what has been decided. There will be no more ships for at least a week, which, given the situation in the city, is much too long for you…'

'What is the situation?' Russell asked.

'Many arrests. Your friends Hans and Margarete, many others.'

A wave of sadness and guilt washed through Effi's brain.

'And Ernst?' Russell was asking.

'Ernst is safe for the moment.'

'They must have found the men we killed.'

'No,' Andreas said with a hint of a smile. 'The bodies were moved last night. They were put back in their car and the car was pushed into one of the deeper docks before first light. It was a committee decision,' he added, as if that were explanation enough. 'The bodies will never be found, and later this morning one of our people inside the local Kripo will tell the Gestapo about a tip-off he has received, that someone saw two cars in a high speed chase on the Stargard road late yesterday evening. Which should get them looking in the wrong direction altogether.'

'I'm ready,' the other man shouted across. He was unfolding a large sheet of dark red cloth.

'You need new papers,' Andreas said in reply to Russell's questioning look. 'Which means photographs.'

'We need to fix our make-up,' Effi said, tearing her thoughts away from Hans and Margarete. She still wore most of her last application, but the previous night's rain had removed most of Russell's. The moustache, though, showed no sign of loosening its grip on his upper lip.

'As quick as you can,' Andreas urged them.

'We're almost out in any case,' she told Russell, as she worked on the area around his eyes.

'Then save it for yourself,' he said. 'You're the one who'll be recognised.'

'There's enough,' she told him. 'And I can't leave you with one side of your face looking twenty years older than the other.'

Preparations completed, they each had their photographs taken standing in front of the red material that Andreas held up as a backcloth. The photographer grumbled about the light, but thought the resulting pictures would probably do.

'Who'll be looking at them?' Russell asked Andreas. 'Where are we going?'

'Riga.'

'Riga?!'

Andreas sighed. 'You can't stay in Stettin, and Riga's the only other place with regular sailings to Sweden. We have people there who'll look after you, and it's the one direction the Gestapo will not expect. These days no one travels east out of choice.'

'A train?' Russell asked.

Andreas nodded. 'Trains. It'll take about two days. You'll need to change in Danzig and Königsberg, perhaps in Tilsit as well. Don't worry,' he said, noticing their expressions, 'you will have excellent papers. Your chances are good. Certainly much better than they would be here.'

'Who do we contact when we get there?'

'I'll tell you that this evening. The overnight express for Danzig leaves at eight-thirty, and we will find a way to get you there before then.'

'How?'

'I don't know yet. Your papers will be for a husband and wife, by the way. Herr and Frau Sasowski. Werner and Mathilde.'

'What happened to them?' Russell asked.

'They committed suicide after the Gestapo killed their son.'

More dead people, Effi thought. They were being lifted out of Germany by the arms of the dead.

'Married at last,' Russell said to her, as Andreas and the photographer walked away across the warehouse floor.

She put an arm round his waist and leant her head on his shoulder.

Andreas had brought water with him, enough to last them the day. There was still some food, but neither of them felt hungry, and they spent most of the daylight hours curled up on the folded rug, drifting in and out of uneasy sleeps. Russell had wondered whether one of them should stay awake, and decided there was no point. If the Gestapo roared up outside, there would be enough time to follow through on their pledge of the night before. More than enough.

Strange as it seemed, Effi felt safer by day. The night might hide them, but not from fear or surprise, whereas daylight, which rendered them visible, also seemed redolent of life – the distant sounds of unloading elsewhere in the docks, the ships' horns like mournful animals seeking a place to rest. If this was where her life ended, in a derelict corner of a city she had never seen before, then she wanted her final moments in the light, conscious of every last cobweb that hung from the ceiling, of every piece of rubbish which the breeze blew along the warehouse floor.

Dying in darkness would be so... so completely *wrong*.

She thought about the Ottings and what they must be going through, and struggled to conceal her own sense of dread.

Andreas returned soon after six. 'All the entrances to the docks are being watched,' he announced with his usual smile. 'The roads and ferries.'

'So how will we get out?' Russell asked calmly, wondering what the young man had up his sleeve this time.

'By boat,' Andreas said triumphantly. 'A small boat will come to the quay outside at seven. It will take us out of the docks, and up the Oder to a small landing stage close to the railway station. You will only have a five-minute walk. That's good, eh?'

Russell admitted it sounded so.

Andreas handed over their new documentation, which looked convincing enough. Had they still been alive, Werner and Mathilde Sasowski would have been fifty-four and fifty-two, roughly the ages which he and Effi looked in the photographer's grainy pictures. There were no obvious signs that the latter had just been added to the frayed and grimy papers.

'And here are your tickets,' Andreas added, handing them across.

'How much do we owe you?' Russell asked, reaching for his wallet. It seemed like weeks since he'd spent any money.

Andreas made a gesture of refusal. 'We didn't pay for them,' he said. 'Now, once you reach Riga, you must go to 16 Satekles Street – it's near the station – and ask for Felix. You must tell him that you have a message from Stettin. Have you got all that?'

Russell repeated it.

'Good. Now all we all have to do is wait.' He looked at his watch. 'Forty-two minutes.'

Effi asked Andreas about himself. How long had he been a painter? Was he married?

He wasn't married and he wasn't a painter – the van was his father's. He had worked in the docks since he was sixteen, and been a Party member almost as long – since 1932, in fact. Both his uncles had been killed the following year, one in a street fight and one in a concentration camp. So had many others. But the Party was still strong in Stettin, and particularly in the docks. Seven iron carriers had been sabotaged over the last two years, all sent to the bottom of the Baltic with explosives which the Gestapo and their sniffer dogs had failed to find. Things were certainly bad at the moment, but the cells had all shut down – 'like the compartments of a U-boat'. A few would be prised open, but most would survive. And after the war… well, Effi would return to a communist Germany, and make a movie about her own escape and the comrades who helped her. 'We will all play ourselves,' Andreas decided.

At five minutes to seven they walked out onto the darkened quay, Andreas guiding them to a ladder of iron rungs which led down to the water. The faintest of lights was already visible in the mouth of the basin; as it grew steadily nearer, the low purr of an engine became audible. With Andreas carrying their bag they all climbed down towards the water, waiting in a vertical queue for the boat to draw up alongside. It was a simple skiff with a one-man crew – a wizened old man who nodded a greeting from his seat by the tiller.

He gently opened the throttle and turned the craft back towards the dock entrance, running parallel with the barely visible quayside wall. He had extinguished his faint light, Russell noticed. Now that he was carrying illicit cargo, hitting something probably seemed a much better bet than being noticed. Russell asked Andreas whether the Gestapo had patrol boats.

'They borrow the Navy's,' he whispered back. 'But only one after dark. Usually. It's better that we don't talk,' he added. 'It carries further than you think.'

The wall to the right disappeared as their basin merged with the next, the one where they'd seen the ship being unloaded on the previous evening. Peering through the gloom Russell thought he could make out two large ships, but no lights were showing, either aboard or on the adjoining quay.

The channel narrowed again as they neared the junction with the Oder, and the water grew choppier, rocking the small boat from side to side. As they turned into the river, the opposing current seemed strong enough to stop them, and Russell had a nightmare vision of being stuck in the same spot until morning. But suddenly, for no reason that he could see, the pressure eased and the skiff resumed its steady progress, albeit more slowly.

He knew from previous visits that the Oder was about a hundred and fifty metres wide, but only the near bank was visible, a long quayside at which several small ships were berthed. There were lights in some of them, and on the quay behind them, but Russell hoped and guessed that their boat would be impossible to see against the darkness of the opposite bank.

A lighted shape appeared ahead, running across his line of vision. It was a tram, he realised, crossing the river. The bridge took form as another smaller light glided across, and as they neared the central piers a match flared above them. It was a man lighting a cigarette, and he was looking down at them.

Gestapo, was Russell's first thought.

'It's downstream,' the man said, loud enough for them to hear.

'The patrol boat,' Andreas explained as they passed under the bridge.

Russell breathed a sigh of relief, and asked himself why the comrades hadn't been this well organised when the government of Germany was still up for grabs. The boatman kept to the centre of the stream, out of sight from either bank. There was a surprising amount of traffic along the western side – trams, lorries, even the occasional private car – but no silhouetted pedestrians. The Nikolai Kirche rose out of the gloom, and soon they were passing under the other bridge connecting central Stettin with its Lastadie suburb. Even though he felt wracked with tension, Russell could see something magical in this journey, as they moved unseen through the heart of a living city.

The railway bridge loomed ahead, and beyond that the dark shapes of islands in the river, another bridge, and the long roof of the station rising above the western bank. The boatman steered them into a narrow channel, cut the motor, and drifted the skiff up to a small landing stage. 'This is it,' Andreas said unnecessarily, using one hand to hold the boat against the wooden staging. 'The station is over there, and there are steps up to the bridge at the other end of the path.'

'Thank you,' Russell said, shaking his hand. He offered the boatman a nod of gratitude.

Effi reached over and gave Andreas a quick hug. 'We'll make that film,' she said.

'Good luck,' he told them.

'And you.'

Andreas pushed them off, and the boat put-putted off into the darkness.

The steps were easy to find, and the bridge devoid of traffic. As they walked across to the Stettin side, Russell could feel his muscles tightening. The station was bound to be watched. Were their papers and disguises good enough?

'We must act like ordinary travellers,' he said, as much to himself as to her. 'Look confident. Do what ordinary travellers do. No skulking in the shadows.'

'Yes, husband,' Effi said.

They walked across the Schwedter Ufer and into the station. The small concourse was quite crowded, mostly with soldiers and sailors in uniform, which was probably fortunate. Their train, according to the departure board, was on time.

'The buffet,' Russell said. As they walked across the concourse, he saw no sign of a checkpoint at the tunnel entrance which led to the platforms. There might, of course, be guards waiting at each flight of stairs.

They found a table. The smell of food was inviting, but the queue was long and there was not much more than half an hour until their train's departure. 'Shall we go up now or wait?' he asked her.

'Let's leave it till the last minute,' she said, getting up again. 'I have to spend some time in the ladies.'

'I'll be here.' He watched her walk away, marvelling once again at how well she aged her movement, then leant over to gather an abandoned newspaper from the adjoining table.

After using the toilet, Effi stopped to examine her face in the long mirror behind the washbasins. There hadn't really been enough make-up left to work with, and she seemed to be getting younger again.

A middle-aged woman two basins down was staring at her in the mirror. 'Aren't you Effi Koenen?' the woman asked with barely suppressed excitement.

'No, please,' Effi heard herself say. Looking round, she saw that the cubicles were all open. There was no one else to overhear.

'I'm sorry,' the woman said. 'It must be so difficult having complete strangers come up and talk to you. I won't bother you with questions,' she said, rummaging through her handbag. 'But please, could I have your autograph?' She offered a pleading smile and held out a pencil and some sort of notebook.

It wasn't the look of someone who'd recognised a fugitive. Effi scribbled her name down and handed it back, praying that no one else would come in. 'Please don't tell anyone else that you've seen me,' she said.

'Of course not, and thank you. Thank you so much.' The woman hurried out, no doubt intent on sharing her secret with whatever companions she had.

Effi went back into a cubicle, shut the door and sat down. What was she going to say to John? He was so infuriatingly good at arguing – and this was one argument she had to win.

In the buffet Russell was finding it impossible to concentrate on the newspaper – the events in Russia, Africa and the rest of the wider world had lost their power to engage him. He was like a rat in a maze, he thought: all that mattered was the next turn.

Effi sat down, leaned her head towards him and took one of his hands. 'I'm not coming with you,' she said.

He looked at her blankly. 'What?'

'John, I was just recognised. A fan. A fan who wanted my autograph – she obviously hadn't seen our pictures in the papers. After she was gone I looked in the mirror, and I could recognise myself. The make-up's all gone, and I can't keep a scarf over my face for two days – even if I did there'll be inspections, there are bound to be. We would never get to Riga, but you can and you must.'

Her logic seemed inescapable, but logic had never been something he had associated with her, and it wasn't what he wanted to hear. 'No,' he said desperately. 'We're going together. We'll get there.'

'No, we won't. I'm going back to Berlin. We'll both have a better chance of survival on our own. You must see that.'

'No, I don't. How would you survive in Berlin?'

'As Eva Vollmar. Or Mathilde Sasowski. I don't know, but I'll manage. I *know* Berlin. In the last resort I have a sister there, and friends. I may go back to being Effi Koenen in a week or so – what can they accuse me of? No one saw us in the docks. I can just say I ran away with you, not knowing what you had done, and when I found out, I abandoned you. You won't mind that, will you? You'll be out of the country by then.'

'Of course not, but they'll never believe you.'

'They may want to. A film star who denounces a foreign spy must be good propaganda.'

Russell wanted to argue with her, but after almost a decade together he knew when her mind was made up. Given a few days he might be able to change it, but his train was leaving in thirteen minutes. He felt paralysed by the suddenness of it all.

'John, you know that I love you? And that I'll wait for you?'

'But how...'

'You must catch the train. Please.'

She was right and he knew it. If someone recognised her on the train they would both be trapped, caught, dragged back to Berlin for trial and execution. And someone probably would. They *would* both have a better chance if they went their separate ways – he would be more anonymous; she would be able to distance herself from his crimes.

But would she ever forgive him for abandoning her?

'I have never loved anyone the way I love you,' he said truthfully.

'I know that,' she replied, squeezing his hand and releasing it. Now go, she silently pleaded. Before she lost her nerve.

He got to his feet, and she followed suit. They held each other tightly, shared a long and tender kiss.

'The next time we meet, make sure you've shaved,' she chided.

'I will.' He picked up the bag and hesitated as he realised it also contained her stuff.

'Take it,' she said. 'You'll need the papers. I've got all I need in Berlin.'

He kissed her again, turned, and automatically wove his way through the tables, only remembering to age his stride when he was halfway across the concourse. There was still no one at the tunnel entrance, but there were checkers at the bottom of the stairs leading to his platform – one bored-looking Gestapo officer in a leather coat and a younger assistant in uniform. Russell moved slowly towards them, trying to 'walk old' in the way she had taught him.

The leather coat barely glanced at him, and let his subordinate check the papers. The young man took one look at the picture, one at his face, and handed them back.

He reached the top of the steps as the train was pulling in. It was long and crowded, but many of the passengers would be Stettin-bound. He waited patiently as they streamed off, and finally climbed aboard. There were vacant seats in the several compartments, but he knew better than to trust himself in company. Placing his bag on an empty rack, he moved back into the corridor and stood staring out at the empty platforms, a sense of utter desolation coalescing in his soul.

Separate hells

The day's last train to Berlin was scheduled to depart in just over an hour. Fearful of being recognised, Effi left it until the last few minutes to purchase her ticket, but no one on the concourse or in the queue came rushing up to demand another autograph, and the man behind the booking office window didn't even raise his eyes to look at her.

Perhaps the woman in the mirror had only recognised her because at that particular moment her face had been so unguarded.

Had she over-reacted? No, she decided. Not that it mattered any more.

The Berlin train was full but not overcrowded. She walked the length of it, and found the badly-lit compartment she was looking for. There was only one seat left, but that was in a corner, and would allow her to turn her face from her fellow passengers. A soldier's pack sat on the seat opposite her, and its owner was still leaning out of the corridor window, gazing into his sweetheart's eyes. When the young man finally took his seat, his eyes still seemed far away.

She knew how he felt. Would she ever see John again? And if so, in how many years' time?

She closed her eyes, and realised she had a fight on her hands to hold back the tears. An actress who could cry to order should be able to manage the opposite, she told herself. She could do it. She had to do it.

The need slowly receded and as the train rattled across the Pomeranian countryside she feigned sleep and told herself to concentrate on the next few minutes and hours. She left her ticket on her lap, and silently thanked the soldier for urging the inspector not to wake her. It seemed more than possible that she was going to reach Berlin.

But what then? The most important thing was not to get caught until John was safely out of the country. But how long would that take? A week? Ten days? If she was caught before then and forced to talk, she would say he had taken the train to Danzig, in the hope of finding a ship there. She would never mention Riga.

The train pulled into Stettin Station a few minutes after midnight. There were no leather coats waiting at the end of the platform, or at the entrance to the U-Bahn. The underground train was full of home-going Friday night revellers, all beer breath and sweat, and she relished the rush of clear cold air that hit her as she emerged onto Müllerstrasse. After walking briskly through the blacked-out streets to Prinz-Eugen-Strasse, she opened the doors to the darkened building and flat with the keys they'd almost left behind.

After checking that the blackout curtains were still in place, she turned on a single light and stood there for a moment, gazing at the once-abandoned apartment. It had been less than a week.

She walked into the other room, lay down on the cold bed, and wept.

On the Danzig train, the first inspection of papers and tickets took place at one of the old Polish border crossings. It was past midnight, and most of Russell's fellow passengers were asleep. Being woken made many of them irritable, which made the inspectors even more officious. Russell anxiously waited his turn, heart beating at faster than the usual rate, hands distinctly clammy. He explored the false moustache with his fingers, but couldn't really tell if it was still on straight.

The gun, he suddenly realised, was still in his bag. It was no good to him now – the reverse, in fact, if the men in uniforms started searching luggage. But there was no time to get rid of it.

They arrived at his compartment, two bleary-eyed men in old border police uniforms. One man looked at Russell's papers, then briefly at him, before handing the papers back and passing on to his neighbour. He closed his eyes in gratitude, and only opened them again when both inspectors had moved on.

As the sense of relief faded, the feeling of emptiness returned. He kept reminding himself that it was all for the best, that now Effi had a chance of escaping complicity in his crimes – but it didn't help. He knew he had to make his peace with their separation, had to keep himself focused on what he had to do. There was nothing he could do for her, except get himself out of Germany.

He eventually fell asleep, only to wake up terrified that he had smudged his facial make-up on the upholstery. But none of his fellow passengers were giving him strange looks, and a glance in the toilet mirror was enough to show him that Effi's artistry remained intact. It would soon have to come off, though. Look on the bright side, he told himself – after the last few days he was probably no longer in need of artificial ageing.

It was light outside, and they were running close to the Baltic coast, the wide grey sea sliding almost seamlessly into a wide grey sky. Russell recognised the station at Zoppot as they rattled through, and twenty minutes later the train was pulling to a final halt in re-Germanised Danzig. He hurried off the train, but needn't have bothered – the connecting service for Dirschau and points further east was not leaving for another six hours. Unwilling to risk that amount of time in the station, he crossed the street to the Reichshof Hotel, where he had stayed on his last visit. He was almost at the desk when he realised how stupid he was being, but the receptionist proved unfamiliar. He asked to be woken at twelve-thirty, and walked up to his second-floor room.

Feeling safer with the door locked behind him, he lay down on the bed and tried to take stock of his situation. It stank, was as far as he got.

He was exhausted, but still found it hard to sleep. He felt as if his eyes had just closed when a hand rapped on the door and a child's voice told him it was time to get up. He had a thorough wash for the first time in days, paid for the room, and walked back to the station in search of food. He hadn't felt hungry for a long time, and still didn't, but the weakness in his legs could no longer be ignored.

The train was delayed for another hour, and he had plenty of time to eat what proved a dreadful meal. The station buffet was crowded, with many uniforms visible, but there was no police presence, and no sign of leather coats. Danzig might now be a part of the German Reich, but it seemed a long way from Berlin.

After washing his meal down with a better-than-expected bottle of beer, he stopped at the kiosk for a newspaper. Handing over the pfennigs, he noticed a month-old film magazine which Effi had brought home several weeks before, and which he knew contained a wonderful picture of her. He bought it, walked out onto the platform, and found the relevant page. 'Effi Koenen, star of *Homecoming*', smiled out at him.

He gazed at her for several moments before turning to the newspaper. The German front line in the East was in the process of being 'rationalised', and the Army had a new commander-in-chief. Hitler had sacked Field-Marshal Brauchitsch and taken the job for himself. But, according to the official communiqué, nothing had really changed: since all the successes of the last few years had 'originated entirely from the spiritual initiative and the genius-like strategy of the Führer himself,' he had, 'in practice, always been leading the German Army.'

In the apartment on Prinz-Eugen-Strasse, she woke with a start, wondering for a moment where she was. Then memory kicked in, and she lay there in the darkness for a while, before angrily forcing herself up and into the bathroom. A slight tug of the blackout curtain revealed another grey day.

What was she going to do?

Stay in, she supposed. But not in darkness, not for days on end. That really would drive her mad.

She went into the kitchen, put on the kettle, and did an inventory of the food that they'd left behind. There was enough to last her a week, she thought. Maybe ten days. By then, John should be out of the country.

She would have to keep as quiet as she could, and pray that no one realised she was there. As long as she didn't use any lights, no one would notice that the blackout curtains were half open. If the air raid warning sounded, she would simply ignore it – there was no way she could risk going to the shelter in her unmade-up state.

Once the food was gone, she would need to find some way of getting more. But she could worry about that when the time came.

After reaching Dirschau late in the afternoon, Russell endured another long and anxious wait. The Berlin-Königsberg express finally arrived around nine. Two inspections and three hours later it reached the old capital of East Prussia, where falling snow was visible in the bright arc lights illuminating the yard. Leaving the train, he could see buildings with lighted windows. There really was a world beyond the blackout.

Riga, it transpired, was still two trains and a day away. The first, which wouldn't be leaving until eight the following morning, would get him to Tilsit, where, according to his old history master, Napoleon and Czar Alexander had met on a floating raft in the River Niemen. The second, a local stopping service, would carry him across the former republics of Lithuania and Latvia, which Hitler and Stalin had doomed between them.

So where to spend the night? Appalling weather conditions further to the east had wreaked havoc on what timetables there were, and filled the station platforms with enough soldiers and civilians to hide the odd fugitive. It seemed safer to stay where he was than wander the unknown streets of Königsberg, so he found himself a gap in the rows of sprawled-out travellers, and laid himself down on the hard platform with his bag for a pillow. He even managed a few hours' sleep.

When the cold woke him for the last time, light was seeping through the station's glass roof. He went in search of food, and found the buffet well stocked with rolls and coffee. Quality was clearly not an issue, because both were awful.

Back on the platform advertised for the Tilsit service, he saw a train of boxcars slowly approaching the station from the north. As he watched the locomotive steam by, his nose was suddenly assaulted by the stench of human waste. There was a hint of movement in the small openings high on the wagon-sides, and yellow-brown liquid was oozing out from under several doors. The train was leaking urine and excrement.

'Russian prisoners,' a voice said beside him. It was a German army captain. There was disapproval in his tone, and in the slight shake of his head, but he said no more. The train cleared the station, but the smell hung in the air, as if reluctant to disperse.

The officer disappeared up the platform, leaving Russell with no expectation of seeing him again; but half an hour later, just as his train was leaving, the man walked into his otherwise empty compartment. He seemed eager to talk, and Russell, after inventing some relatives as his reason for visiting Riga, was happy to let him do so. The captain had been involved in the Russian campaign since its inception, and was on his way back to the front after a week of compassionate leave.

How were things going, Russell asked him, in as a neutral a tone as possible.

Things were difficult, his companion admitted. Really difficult. But the men had been magnificent. People back home had no idea what it was like, but then how could they?

And the Russians? Russell asked.

'They're not like the French,' was the officer's answer.

Russell tried, ever so gently, to draw out his companion on the future course of the war, but all he got in response were pious expressions of hope. Once the winter was over, then things would become clearer. Once the winter was over, changes would have to be made. Once the winter was over, they would do what had to be done.

The possibility of defeat was there in the man's eyes, in his voice and his evident agitation, but it couldn't be admitted. Not yet.

The officer ended the discussion by saying he needed some sleep, leaving Russell to stare out at the snow-dusted East Prussian fields. Riga, he suddenly remembered, was icebound for at least part of the winter. Surely they hadn't sent him several hundred kilometres in search of a non-existent ship?

When the train reached Tilsit in mid-afternoon he discovered that there was only one daily connection to the old Latvian capital, and it left at seven in the morning. He would have to endure another night on a station platform.

There were worse places to spend one. Stuck on a far-off rim of Hitler's bloated Reich, Tilsit and its station seemed sleepy enough for any fugitive. There was only one limp swastika spoiling the sky, and the uniforms on display all belonged to the Reichsbahn. The only evidence of war was the traffic passing through – supply trains moving in both directions, a hospital train and rakes of empty flatcars travelling west, a troop train full of anxious faces heading for the front.

One particular transport caught Russell's attention. A long line of box cars drawn by an old and wheezing locomotive arrived just before dawn, and spent the next two hours stabled in a siding across from the station. SS guards strode up and down beside it, but a prolonged burst of banging was the only sound that reached across the tracks. Someone hammering on the inside of a door, Russell guessed. When the train clanked into motion, the fist fell silent.

His own much smaller train headed out in the same direction an hour or so later, and was soon rumbling over a long bridge above the Niemen. Another twenty minutes and it reached the frontier of the Reich, where the passengers underwent a surprisingly cursory inspection before travelling on into the newly-established *Reichkommissariat Ostland*. That afternoon, officials manning a checkpoint at the defunct border between Lithuania and Latvia proved considerably more zealous. Russell spent several fraught minutes in the queue, before realising that only the locals were being subjected to the sort of scrutiny that always accompanied one of Hitler's live appearances; Germans like Werner Sasowski were being waved through with a friendly smile. It was like being a white man in Africa.

The train re-started, and was soon threading its way through a large and seemingly uninhabited forest. It finally emerged on the outskirts of Riga. There was snow on the ground here, but only a couple of inches, and the sky was partly clear. As the train slowed on its approach to the station, Russell became aware of suitcases left beyond the adjoining tracks, some neatly stacked, some simply lying in the fallen snow. There were hundreds of them. A thousand, he guessed, remembering Ströhm's report of the SS prescription for an ideal transport.

Riga Station was the emptiest he had seen on his three-day journey. There was one group of Germans in civilian clothes sharing a joke on the concourse, but most of the other faces had Slavic features, and safely neutral expressions to go with them. The old man who gave Russell directions did so willingly enough, but with a noticeable lack of friendliness. Latvia had been invaded twice in the last two years, and its citizens were probably still having trouble deciding which of the bastards offered them less.

Satekles Street was only a five-minute walk away. No.16 was the Continental Hotel, a three-storey building sandwiched between another, seedier-looking hotel and a seemingly abandoned garage. A heavy front door let him into a large vestibule, where a wide staircase curved upwards over a reception area containing a large oak table, an antique filing cabinet, and the obligatory row of hooks for keys. A grizzled-looking old man looked up from his half-completed crossword with evident irritation.

Russell asked for Felix.

The man got slowly to his feet, visibly wincing at the pain in his knees. 'Wait through there,' he said, gesturing towards a door.

Pushing through, Russell found himself in a smart but empty café-bar. He took a corner seat and settled down to wait. Several minutes passed, and he began wondering whether someone in Stettin had been tortured into mentioning Riga. Who would be next through the door – the comrades or the Gestapo? Possible salvation or certain damnation? All he could do was wait and see.

The door eventually swung open to admit a broad-shouldered Slav with thinning brown hair and a broken-toothed smile. 'My name is Felix,' he said in German.

'I have a message from Stettin,' Russell told him.

'Oh yes? I was told there would be two of you.'

'My friend had to go back to Berlin,' Russell said. 'It's a long story.'

Felix took a deep breath, shrugged, and beckoned Russell to follow him. After collecting a key from the rack, he led the way up a flight of stairs and down a long corridor to the room at the end. A bed, a water basin stand and a door-less wardrobe took up most of the space. The single window overlooked the rear yard of the garage, where several vehicles had been left to rust.

'You'll be staying here,' Felix said. 'Now, let me see your papers.'

Russell handed them over for inspection.

'Not bad,' Felix decided after going through them. 'But you need something better, an identity that goes with an official job of some sort. That shouldn't be too difficult, but leave it to me. In the meantime, don't go out. I'll have meals sent up. Nothing fancy of course, but enough to keep you from starving. We're already on the lookout for a suitable ship.'

'Ships are still moving in and out of the harbour then?'

'Yes. But not for much longer. Winter has come early this year.'

When he was gone Russell lay down on the lumpy mattress, fingers entwined behind his head. 'The end of the line,' he murmured to himself. One way or the other, it would soon be over.

By Tuesday evening Effi felt like kicking the walls. After four days alone in the flat she thought she knew what a common prison was like. She couldn't risk listening to the radio, and there were only so many times she could do one jigsaw or read week-old newspapers. If she dozed off during the day she would spend long stretches of the night praying for sleep. Whatever she did, there was far too much time for thinking.

She decided she would make herself a pack of cards, and was still searching for suitable materials when the air raid warning sounded.

It was the first time this had happened since her return, and she felt a momentary pang of fear. She remembered all the times she'd complained about having to go to the shelter, all the times she had tried to persuade John that they shouldn't bother. He had always insisted, as she'd known he would, and on those few occasions when he hadn't been there she'd always gone down on her own. No matter how long the odds were on one's own house being hit, it still seemed foolish to tempt fate.

Well, she had to tempt it now. She could hardly turn up at the shelter looking twenty years younger than she had on her last visit. She would have to just sit there in the armchair, and let John's fellow countrymen do their worst.

Or not. Barely a minute had gone by when there was an urgent knock on the door. 'Frau Vollmar,' a male voice said loudly. It was the block warden.

Did he know she was there? How could he?

There was another knock. She rose to her feet almost involuntarily, and stood there, silently urging him to go away.

She heard the key jiggling in the lock.

The bedroom, she thought. She stepped quickly through the open door, relieved that she was wearing only socks on her feet, and realised that there was only one place to hide. Feeling more than a little ridiculous, she let herself down onto her back and squeezed herself under the bed.

She could hear footfalls in the adjoining room, and see flickers of light dancing across the carpet by the half-open door. He was using a torch, she realised. She thanked God she hadn't closed the blackout curtains, which would have allowed him to turn on the lights.

Had she left any obvious proof of her presence? Would he feel the warmth of the chair she'd been sitting in? Surely he couldn't stay much longer – it must be almost ten minutes since the sirens sounded.

He pushed the bedroom door open, and the moving beam of his flashlight seemed all around her.

Not under the bed, she silently pleaded.

He walked back out. A few seconds later she heard him walk into the kitchen. Was the kettle still warm from her last cup of tea?

More footsteps, then silence. Was he by the door? She heard the click as he opened it, and the twist of the key as he re-locked it from outside. She lay there, eyes closed, heart still thumping in her chest, suppressing an absurd desire to laugh.

There was no point in moving, she told herself. The bed might cushion her against a falling ceiling.

This theory was left untested – if any bombs fell that night, they fell a long way from Prinz-Eugen-Strasse. When the all-clear sounded she crawled out from her hiding-place and sat on the bed, wondering if he would come back that evening.

He might. Better to bolt the door, she decided, and went to do so. If he tried to use his key again, he would know that she was there, but she could always make up some excuse for not opening the door at this time of night. Tomorrow would be another matter. And the day after that. He was bound to return sooner or later, and bound to discover that she was back. And once he had, then a face-to-face meeting became almost inevitable.

There was nothing else for it – she had to get more make-up. Tomorrow was Christmas Eve, and the theatrical suppliers would probably close for several days. She couldn't afford to wait.

That same evening, Russell was lying on his bed when Felix arrived with new papers. The old ones were still valid, but now complemented by others attesting to his position as a high-ranking bureaucrat in Goering's organisation for the economic exploitation of the East, the *Wirtschaftsführungsstab Ost.* 'You'll only have to use these if the Gestapo raid the hotel, and as far as we know, there's no reason why they should. If they do, you should tell them that you're in Riga to organise supplies for the planned concentration camp at Kaiserwald – ordering the timber for the barracks, the wire for the perimeter, that sort of thing. But you fell ill on the train, and you're recuperating here. Hence the meals in your room, and the fact that you don't go out. That's what the other guests have been told, by the way. Those that asked, that is. Once the word gets round that you work for Goering, everyone will give you a wide berth. People are very nervous at the moment.'

'I heard gunfire last night,' Russell said, as he examined the documents.

'From the ghetto,' Felix explained. 'They've crammed all the Jews into a few hundred square metres, and already killed thousands of them, but they're still not satisfied. Some of the bastards go in at night, as if they're out on a hunting party. Anyone who gets in their way, they just shoot them.'

'Have any trains full of Jews come from the Reich?'

'Three, I think. One shipment was just taken out to Rumbula and shot. The others were led to the ghetto and given the houses of those locals who were shot earlier. There doesn't seem any rhyme or reason to it.'

'What's Rumbula?'

'The Rumbula Forest. It's about five kilometres from the city. Near enough for a forced march, and nice sandy soil for digging. They must have shot over twenty thousand in the last few weeks. One child who escaped said that the earth was still moving from all the people who'd been buried alive.'

Russell shook his head, closed his eyes and gripped the bridge of his nose between thumb and forefinger. 'Is there any resistance?' he asked eventually.

'From the Jews? No. They have nothing to fight with. And we're not in much better shape. Our organisation is still intact, and we're strong in the docks, but we have no weapons, and no allies to speak of.' Felix managed a rueful smile. 'When the NKVD left in June they killed almost everyone that they'd locked up over the previous year. That helped us, of course, because many of those people could have betrayed us to the Nazis. But it also caused a rift – to put it mildly – between us and the nationalists. There won't be a united front here for a very long time.'

'I see.'

'I used to be a docker,' Felix volunteered. 'But once you pass fifty the work gets difficult, particularly in winter. And my parents left me this hotel.'

'Whose ships are still coming to Riga?' Russell asked.

'The Swedes are the only neutrals who can get here.'

'What do they bring? What's left to trade?'

'Lots of things. Coming in, it's mostly luxury items. If you walked the streets you might think the rich had fled, but they haven't. They're just hunkered down in their mansions, waiting the war out, and they still want their nice soap, their proper coffee, their good cigars. They're not going to get them from Germany, are they?'

'I suppose not.'

'Going out, it's mostly processed foods.'

Remembering Jens's account of chronic shortages, Russell found that surprising. But only for a moment – the Germans needed something to exchange for all that iron ore and all those ball bearings.

After Felix was gone, Russell's mind kept returning to the mental picture of a shifting forest floor, and the last terrifying moments of those who were doing the shifting. His horror grew no less, but there was some compensation in the sheer power of the image, and the way it might be used to arouse the conscience of the outside world. He got out his paper and pencil and began writing it out, hammering another journalistic nail in what he fervently hoped would be the Nazis' coffin. If he ever reached Sweden, he wanted the story ready for printing.

Work also took his mind off other things, like a son betrayed and a love left behind.

Russell had used the one in Potsdam Station, but Effi's recent experience with station toilets was hardly encouraging, so she chose the Wertheim's on Leipziger Strasse for her transformation. She knew exactly where the ladies' room was, and the department store was only a few minutes' walk from the theatrical suppliers she intended to visit. Her one big fear was a chance encounter with her shopping-mad sister, but Effi could hardly imagine Zarah spending Christmas Eve afternoon with anyone but Lothar.

A week ago that thought would have reduced her to tears. So she must be getting stronger.

First she had to get to Wertheim's. She would have to leave Prinz-Eugen-Strasse in daylight, without make-up, and with every chance of running into someone on the stairs. It was crazy, but there was no way round it, and she would just have to do what she could. A little dust and household grime to give a wrinkled look around the eyes, a piece of sticking plaster across her upper lip to disguise the shape of her mouth. A hat pulled down to her eyes, a scarf pulled up across the lower lip, a pair of reading glasses. It was a pity it wasn't snowing, but it was cold enough to justify a lot of covering up.

The journey went well. She met no one on the stairs, no one on the street or in the U-Bahn to Leipziger Strasse. The walk to Wertheim's took only a few minutes, the long climb to the secluded toilets on the top floor rather longer – the lifts were all out of order. Ensconced in a cubicle, she unpacked the *Reichfrauenschaft* uniform. The blue-black jacket and skirt went on over the correct white blouse that she was already wearing, and she placed the matching fedora on her rigorously pulled-back hair at a slightly jaunty angle. She wondered about the sticking plaster, and finally decided that it detracted from the uniform's authority.

She was now a member of the National Socialist Women's Organisation National Leadership. Hardly someone to be trifled with.

Walking to the theatrical suppliers, it suddenly occurred to her that it might have been bombed, or closed down for some other reason. Had she gone to all this trouble, put herself at all this risk, for nothing?

There were lights in the shop window. She was just ten metres away from the door when an actress she knew almost pranced out onto the pavement and turned towards her. The woman gave Effi a single glance, and quickly averted her eyes from the stern expression and its accompanying uniform.

Effi let herself into the shop. There were two women behind the counter, both around forty. They looked like the keenest of filmgoers, but she didn't recognise them from her previous visits. One disappeared into a back room as the other offered a cautious smile of greeting. The uniform was earning its keep.

'I have a list of powders and creams,' Effi began, handing the sheet of paper over. 'There's quite a lot, I'm afraid. It hasn't been officially announced yet, but the Berlin *Bund Deutscher Mädel* are putting on a special production of *Tristan und Isolde* in the new year. It's possible that the Führer will attend. If his military duties permit, of course.'

'Of course,' the woman echoed. She began filling the order, plucking boxes and tubes from various drawers and cabinets.

Effi stared at the photographs covering a large part of the wall behind the counter, each one signed by the star in question. After the war she'd come back with her own.

The woman was checking the items through. 'I think that's everything,' the woman said, completing her check. She looked up at Effi and her face seemed to change.

Here it comes, Effi thought.

'Have you ever met the Führer?' the woman asked.

'Only once,' Effi admitted. 'He was charm itself.'

Fifteen minutes later she was back in the Wertheim's cubicle. After changing back into her normal clothes, she sat on the toilet seat and applied some of the new make-up with the aid of her compact mirror. Satisfied, she let herself out and headed for the U-Bahn, remembering just in time to age her walk. The train was crowded and smelly, but one young soldier insisted on giving her his seat, and when she finally closed the apartment door behind her she felt a quiet surge of triumph.

On Christmas evening, Felix came to tell Russell that a Swedish ship was due in port in less than forty-eight hours. Two days later, the small patch of sky outside his window was beginning to darken when the hotel owner entered with a thin young man named Rainis.

When Russell saw the bicycle, he realised that he'd been half-expecting another ride in the back of a van. 'I haven't been on one of these for twenty years,' he muttered, mostly to himself. With his bag tied on the back, he climbed gingerly into the saddle. A quick shake of Felix's hand, and he was off, wobbling down the street in Rainis' wake.

The two-kilometre journey to the docks took them around the eastern edge of the city centre, and Russell was left with an impression of towers and spires faintly silhouetted against a rapidly darkening sky. There was virtually no traffic, and a Mercedes 260 parked by the side of the road turned out to be empty. By the time they reached the docks all natural light had disappeared, but Riga, unlike Stettin, was still making full use of the artificial variety. Open warehouse doors were squares of bright yellow light, the cranes beyond them lit from below.

There were other cyclists about, and several lorries parked with their lights on. Rainis led Russell away from the lights, the two of them bumping across cobblestone setts and between buildings to reach a dark section of the quayside. Further down the basin a freighter was tied up, the name *Norma* emblazoned on its stern. The sea air was freezing cold.

'That's your boat,' Rainis whispered.

Russell could see at least two uniforms near the bottom of the gangplank.

'That's all they guard,' the young Latvian said, reading his mind. 'You'll be using the port side.'

Leaning the bicycles against a convenient wall, they walked on down the quayside, keeping close to the buildings until the *Norma* was several hundred metres behind them. After one long look back and a check of his watch, Rainis struck out across the wide quay, reaching the edge at the point where a flight of concrete steps led down to the water, and a tethered rowing boat lay gently bobbing in the tide. The young Latvian sitting in the bow looked anxious, but managed a smile of welcome as Russell clambered aboard. He quickly engaged the oars. Rainis, it seemed, was not coming.

Russell waved his thanks, wedged the bag between his knees, and suddenly remembered that he'd left the gun under his pillow back at the hotel. One for the Resistance.

His oarsman was taking the long way round, rowing out beyond the reach of the quayside lights until the *Norma* provided its own shadow. This should have been Stettin, Russell thought, with Effi there beside him.

There were no signs of activity on the seaward side of the freighter, which boded well. The apparent lack of a ladder, or any other means of getting himself aboard, was less auspicious; but the oarsman, seeing his confusion, first used two hands to mime a climbing motion, then one to indicate something dropping from the sky. A few moments later the rope ladder landed a few feet away from them, and a short whistle sounded above.

With one hand on the rope and one holding his bag, Russell struggled up the side of the ship, conscious of every scuff and bang which accompanied his laborious progress. He was almost at the top when a strong hand reached down to help him over the railing. As he regained his feet, a grinning young man put a finger to his lips, then pointed off to the right.

Russell nodded his understanding, and followed the man. Judging by the noise, the rear hold was still being loaded, but work had finished on the yellow-lit foredeck, with only the hatches to fasten. Emerging from the shadow of the superstructure, the Swede settled into a crouching walk reminiscent of Groucho Marx, and Russell duly followed him to the edge of the open hold. The Swede pointed his finger once more, this time at an iron ladder leading down. Russell nodded, and swung himself onto the top rung.

The man whispered one word – 'Midnight' – and disappeared from view.

Russell climbed down into the darkened hold, stopping when one foot encountered something solid and allowing his eyes time to adjust. A room full of dark rectangles suggested several layers of packing cases, a theory soon confirmed by touch. He worked himself into a corner, where he hoped he could not be seen by someone looking in. Once the hatches were down he would climb back on top of the cases to lessen the risk of being crushed.

How long, he wondered, would the voyage take? He should have asked Rainis.

An hour or so later the hatches were fastened, and the darkness became complete. Even an overcast, blacked-out Berlin had offered more in the way of visibility.

Another anxious hour followed, before the sudden rumbling of the ship's engines had him almost trembling with relief. A few more minutes and they were underway. Russell felt the change as they left the docks for the river, and wondered if he would feel another as they left the river for the bay.

He was lying across two crates, eyes closed, when he became aware of a slight shift in the light. A faint square had appeared in the ceiling above him, a square that was swiftly filled by movement. Someone was descending into the hold.

Whoever it was reached the bottom and switched on a torch. Russell shielded his eyes against the blinding light.

'Sorry,' a voice said, first in Swedish and then in English. 'But safe now. You come out. I take you to captain. You understand?'

'I do,' Russell said.

'I say I find you. Stowaway, yes. Captain a good man. But I lose job if he know I help you. I am Olle,' he said, extending a hand.

The captain's English was even better. He listened to Russell's fictional account of how he had stowed aboard with a slightly amused expression, and warned him that he would be handed over to the appropriate authorities when they reached Stockholm. They would be out in the open Baltic all the next day, he added, and Russell could make himself useful by joining the standing watch. An extra set of eyes might just save them all from a Russian torpedo. 'Now you can take him for some food,' he told Olle. 'He looks like he needs it.'

The galley chef had long since gone to his bunk, but Olle found some meatballs and potatoes to warm up. They tasted better than anything Russell had eaten since the summer. Neutrality obviously had its advantages.

A deep and dreamless sleep was interrupted by the call of duty, and a short hot breakfast was followed by two long shifts scanning the cold, rolling and almost empty Baltic. The only ships he saw were far away – German destroyers most likely, heading across the freighter's stern towards the Gulf of Leningrad.

That evening he played cards with several of the crew. No one asked him any questions, and the war was only mentioned in passing. All the talk was of girlfriends and wives, food and football, the sexiest bars in Helsinki.

He thought about that the following morning, as the lights of a country at peace brightened on the Swedish shoreline. He might be safe, but his escape had cost more than he could ever repay. Hans and Margarete Otting, the two comrades in the Kaiser Bar – they would be in concentration camps by now, if they hadn't already been executed. Ströhm might have evaded the Gestapo swoops in Berlin, but Russell doubted whether Ernst or Andreas would long survive the unravelling of the network in Stettin.

He had left the war behind, but those who had helped him, and those whom he loved, were all still trapped in its writhing coils.

The British came on New Year's Eve, and Frau Eva Vollmar spent three hours in the shelter with her neighbours. The block warden ticked off her name on his list, but said nothing of his visit to her apartment.

The first morning of 1942 was cold but sunny, and Effi decided she had to get out. The walk to Humboldthain Park took about half an hour, and she sat on a bench watching the birds, wishing she had brought them some breadcrumbs. Another huge flak tower was under construction on the northern edge of the park, the air full of the sounds of hammering, but even that failed to dampen her spirits.

She wasn't sure what had brought on her optimistic mood – perhaps there were only a certain number of days which the heart could spend immured in fear and loss. That and the fact that two other truths had become evident since her trip to the theatrical suppliers. For one thing, she was unlikely to starve in the near future; there were still items of food that one could buy without ration tickets, which she could add to her dwindling supplies. The second realisation – that women over forty were essentially invisible – was depressing in itself, but highly fortuitous in her current circumstances. The chances of anyone recognising her were slim.

Making herself up for years on end was a daunting prospect, but far from impossible. And things were bound to change. Once the hue and cry had died down – perhaps in a couple of months – she would find a way of contacting Zarah, who would gladly hand over every ration ticket in her possession, and help in any other way that was humanly possible. If that seemed too dangerous, she might come up with some variation on Ali Blumenthal's bombed-out office ploy to find herself a new identity, and the ration entitlement that went with it.

Sitting there on the park bench, watching the sun rise into the Berlin sky, she could imagine the producer's introduction to the script. A woman on the run. Alone and frightened and far from home. But determined to see her lover again, and resourceful enough to survive against all the odds.

It was a difficult part to play, and she meant to play it well.